MW01139815

THE CRUEL STARS

THE
CRUEL STARS

(ARK ROYAL, BOOK IX)

CHRISTOPHER G. NUTTALL

ISBN 13: 9781979807180
ISBN: 1979807183

http://www.chrishanger.net
http://chrishanger.wordpress.com/
http://www.facebook.com/ChristopherGNuttall

Cover by Justin Adams
http://www.variastudios.com/

All Comments Welcome!

AUTHOR'S NOTE

The Cruel Stars is set in the same era as *Ark Royal* - the First Interstellar War - and runs within the same timeframe. However, you do not have to have read *Ark Royal* to follow *The Cruel Stars*.

CGN

PROLOGUE

From: Commodore James Scorpio, Planning Cell Alpha Black
To: Admiral Sir Thomas Hanover, First Space Lord

Sir.

At the risk of sounding somewhat peevish, it must be noted that the sudden appearance of a new threat - an unexpected *alien* threat - is a tactical and strategic nightmare. Our contingency planning - and long-term construction schedules - were based around a limited war with another human power, rather than a conflict with an alien power of unknown origin, motives and technological base. The data from Vera Cruz, such as it is, tells us little about our opponents. It behooves us, therefore, to prepare for a long war.

This will not be easy. Assuming we cut as many corners as possible - and accept the risk of outright catastrophe - it will still take us six months to complete the fleet carriers under construction and another twelve to fourteen months to construct any *new* fleet carriers from scratch. (Frankly, the risk of serious system failure at the worst possible time cannot be discounted.) We are therefore faced with the prospect of a 'come as you are' war, with the danger - as in 2025 - that our forces and military stockpiles will be insufficient to the task at hand. Fifteen fleet carriers - sixteen, if we count *Ark Royal* - are a staggering force, yet we know nothing about our enemy. It is quite possible that they have enough fleet carriers at their disposal to outmatch all of humanity's put together.

While we can look to our allies - and the rest of the spacefaring powers - to assist in filling some of the holes in our order of battle, they will have similar problems of their own. Most notably, they will be reluctant to put their fleet carriers in unnecessary jeopardy as, like us, fleet carriers represent a massive proportion of their military budgets. Even if the various national governments devote a considerably greater percentage of their GNP to their militaries, it will still take time to bring new ship-yards online, train new personnel, and start churning out new carriers. Our most optimistic projections indicate that we will simply be unable to increase the pace of construction for at least two years. Realistically speaking, that may be *too* optimistic.

Therefore, I propose that we activate the escort carrier contingency plans at once.

I concede that this will cause us problems. Removing even a relatively small number of *Workhorse*-class bulk freighters from the shipping lanes will have knock-on effects, most notably disrupting our logistics during our frantic rush to establish forward lines of defence around New Russia. We simply don't have enough freighters at the best of times, despite nearly fifty years of trying to build up our interstellar shipping capability. (Construction of new freighters *is* something we can push forward, fortunately.) At the same time, we simply don't have enough starfighter launching platforms to fight a full-scale war. Losing a single fleet carrier, sir, means losing the personnel as well as the ship itself. The loss of a single carrier would severely dent our ability to meet our commitments to both Britain *and* the united defence force. From a purely cold-blooded point of view, sir, the destruction of a dozen *Workhorses* would not impede our ability to make war.

From a technical point of view, the conversion is only a matter of removing the hold facilities and replacing them with starfighter support and maintenance facilities. Given that normal safety procedures are sus-pended, the first escort carrier could be ready for deployment within a week of going into the yard. However, crewing does represent a prob-lem. While a significant number of freighter captains and crews are Royal Naval Reserve personnel, others are not and may be resistant to serving on the front lines. (If nothing else, the question of nationality comes into play; freighter crews, particularly belters, are notorious for not asking too many questions about a prospective crewer's past.) And our manpower resources are already stretched to the limit.

With that in mind, sir, I have the following suggestion…

CHAPTER ONE

No one, Captain Abigail Harrison had often reflected, would consider HMMS *Archibald Haddock's* bridge to be remotely photogenic. It was a cramped mess, with five consoles and chairs jammed so close together that a crewman couldn't wave a hand without striking one of his fellow crewers. Even the command chair was little more than a slightly elevated console, giving the merchant vessel's commanding officer a prominence that many military and survey officers would insist she didn't deserve. But it did have its advantages. She could not only keep a very close eye on her crew, but cut them out of the command network at once if she felt it necessary.

Which might well be necessary, she thought, as she eyed Midshipwoman Podkayne Harrison's back. *Poddy hasn't handled a proper jump since we left Britannia.*

She cleared her throat, loudly. "Poddy?"

"I'm working on it, Captain," Poddy said. She knew better than to call Abigail anything other than *Captain* when they were both on duty. "I've almost finished."

"Check and recheck everything," Abigail ordered, reminding herself to remain calm and composed. Military ships might want to go through the tramline at speed, but there was no need for *Haddock* to hurry. Her daughter had plenty of time to complete her calculations before making the jump. "One mistake here and you'll be in trouble."

"So will the rest of us," Lieutenant Anson Harrison put in.

1

"I'm relying on you to check your sister's work," Abigail said. Her eldest son could be relied upon to point out any flaws, not least because he didn't want to compete with his sister for postings on the *next* cruise. "And I'll be checking it myself too."

She saw Poddy stiffen and winced, inwardly. It didn't feel *right* to put such pressure on her daughter, even though Poddy *had* grown up amongst the asteroids, where the slightest mistake could spell utter disaster. But there was no choice. Poddy couldn't be given her spacer badge until she calculated at least three jumps in succession, each one as smooth as possible. Abigail certainly couldn't afford to develop a reputation for overlooking weaknesses in her children. Nepotism was hardly unknown amongst the RockRats and interstellar shipping communities, where family ties were stronger than anything else, but promoting an incompetent was a good way to lose everything. Poddy would have to start again - from the beginning - if she failed her last jump.

I went through it too, Abigail reminded herself. *Poddy can do it.*

She watched her daughter's fingers darting over the console. Poddy was slight, with long brown hair and a pale face that owed more to her father than her mother. It was hard to believe, sometimes, that they were actually related. Abigail's black hair, tanned skin and oval eyes - to say nothing of her heavyset body - spoke of a more exotic origin than the asteroid belt. But then, Poddy *had* had the latest set of genetic modifications spliced into her DNA before she'd been born. She wouldn't suffer from overeating unless she *really* overdid it.

Poddy's console chimed. "Done, Captain," she said. "It's ready."

"Anson, check it," Abigail ordered. She tapped her own console, bringing up Poddy's calculations on her screen. "You'll be rewarded for any mistakes you find."

Poddy tensed, slightly. Abigail felt a flicker of guilt and reminded herself, sharply, that it was for Poddy's own good. Better she had her mistakes pointed out by her family rather than some unrelated captain, who wouldn't hesitate to lock her in her cabin and throw her off the ship at the next port if he felt she was dangerously unreliable. Besides, their lives *were* at stake. A minor mistake in calculating the jump along the tramline might just destroy the entire ship.

Or risk getting our licence pulled, Abigail thought. Her lips twitched. *A fate worse than a fate worse than death.*

"It appears to be fine," Anson said, grudgingly. He turned to look at Abigail, his white teeth flashing against his dark skin. "Captain, I believe we can make the jump."

Abigail nodded, slowly. There wasn't anything wrong with the calculations, as far as she could tell. She'd checked everything with savage intensity, just to be sure. And that meant...

She leaned back in her chair. "Make the jump," she ordered. "Now!"

A low whine echoed through the ship as the Puller Drive powered up. Abigail braced herself, feeling her ears starting to hurt. *Something* was wrong with the drive field, although no one - not even her engineer - had been able to find the cause. Perhaps a handful of components were simply worn down, ahead of time. She'd replace the whole installation, if she could afford it. But she simply didn't have the money to even *begin* to replace it.

And there isn't much hope of getting a loan, she thought, as the whining sound rose to a crescendo. *Not unless we really hit it big...*

Haddock shook, violently. The displays blanked, just for a second. Abigail gritted her teeth, allowing herself a moment of relief as the displays started to come back online. A civilian would have assumed that Poddy had messed up her calculations, but Abigail knew better. It was a typical jump. She'd heard that the latest versions of the Puller Drive could take a ship through the tramlines without so much as spilling the captain's coffee, but she didn't believe it. Besides, even if it *was* true, there was no way she'd be able to afford a newer drive either.

"Jump complete, Captain," Anson reported. "We have arrived in the Sol System."

"Made it," Poddy crowed.

Abigail allowed herself an indulgent smile. "So you did," she said, trying to sound proud. "We'll go out for dinner once we reach Ceres - and you can choose where we go."

Anson looked up. "All of us?"

"Yes, all of us," Abigail said, firmly. Anson probably wanted to visit the brothel. She didn't blame him for that - God knew it had been a long time since *she'd* had anyone in *her* bed - but family came first. They'd be at Ceres for at least a week. "Poddy, send a standard message to the shipping coordinator. Inform them that we have returned."

"Aye, Captain," Poddy said.

"Anson, set course for Ceres," Abigail added. "No need to hurry."

"Aye, Captain," Anson said.

Abigail smiled as she pulled up the jump records and checked them against Poddy's calculations. The young girl had done a good job. The calculations matched the records perfectly. Not that Abigail had expected anything else - a *serious* mishap would probably have ended poorly - but it was still important to *prove* that Poddy had earned the right to style herself a navigator. The guilds would check the records themselves, if Poddy decided to leave *Haddock*. Abigail made a mental note to ensure that the records were copied over as soon as they arrived on Ceres. *One* of her adult children was probably going to seek a transfer soon, no matter what Abigail did. There was only limited room for advancement on *Haddock*.

And Anson wants to captain his own ship, Abigail thought. Her eldest son was twenty, more than old enough to strike out on his own. *He'll probably be looking for postings when we reach Ceres.*

Poddy's console bleeped. "Captain, I am receiving a priority message from the Merchant Shipping Guild," she said. "It's tagged as *urgent*."

Abigail frowned. The message *couldn't* have been sent from Ceres. It would take hours for the message she'd sent to reach the asteroid, let alone for any reply to be sent back. The light-speed delay would see to that. And yet…she keyed her console, bringing up the message. The header insisted that it had been sent from a monitoring station much closer to the designated emergence point. She felt a flicker of concern as she ran the message through the computers. The emergency codes all checked out.

ALERT. ALERT. STUFT EMERGENCY. YOU ARE ORDERED TO PROCEED IMMEDIATELY TO RNRB TALLYMAN. ACKNOWLEDGE, THEN RADIO SILENCE. MESSAGE REPEATS. ALERT…

"What?"

Anson glanced at Poddy's console. "A STUFT Emergency?"

"Ships Taken Up From Trade," Abigail translated, absently. "They expect us to head straight for Tallyman."

She sucked in her breath, thinking hard. She was, technically, a Royal Navy Reservist. It was the price she'd paid for the loan that had allowed her to purchase her ship. But she'd never expected to be actually called upon to serve. She'd never seen any of the authorisation codes attached to the message, outside a handful of update messages. Her ship had certainly never been summoned at short notice. They hadn't even been dragged into any *drills*.

"They're out of their minds," Anson said. "Mum…do you know what will happen if we don't meet the deadline…"

Abigail nodded, grimly. Interstellar shipping was never as predictable as travel on Earth - no one would risk setting their clocks by a starship's arrival - but they *were* expected to arrive at Ceres within a certain time-frame. Being late would cost them badly, particularly if the penalty clauses loaded into their contract went into effect. And besides, their cargo was perishable. They might wind up being sued if they failed to deliver it on time.

The Navy is supposed to indemnify us, she thought. *But we might lose everything by the time the bureaucrats actually get around to paying out.*

She shook her head. "Anson, set course for Tallyman," she ordered. "Poddy…"

"*Mum*," Anson protested. "If we don't get there…"

"I *know*," Abigail snapped. She made a mental note to chew him out later. Other captains wouldn't be quite so forgiving of outbursts on the bridge. "But what would you have us do?"

She watched Anson trying to think of a solution and coming up with nothing. There wasn't one, as far as Abigail could tell. *Haddock* could reverse course and go…go where? The Royal Navy would eventually realise that the freighter wasn't going to show up at Tallyman and file charges, at which point the ship and her crew would grow too hot to handle. Even the independent asteroid settlements would refuse to have anything to do with them, if they were lucky. They'd be far more likely to be arrested and be shipped straight to the nearest penal world. And the thought of being locked out of space was terrifying.

"…Fuck," Anson said.

"Don't worry," Poddy said. "I'm sure this will be nothing."

"Hah," Anson muttered. His fingers touched his console. "Course laid in, Captain. We should be there in seven hours."

"Very good," Abigail said. "Poddy, send an acknowledgement and then go silent. No one is to send a message without my direct authorisation."

"Understood," Poddy said.

Abigail rose. "Take the bridge, Anson," she ordered. "I'll be in my cabin, catching up with my sleep."

"I'll wake you if anything happens," Anson assured her.

"See that you do," Abigail said.

She stepped through the hatch and walked down to her cabin. It was a tiny compartment, barely large enough for a bed, a small desk and a private washroom, the only real luxury afforded to the freighter's commanding officer. Abigail had heard that military officers had *real* cabins, but there was no way anyone could fit anything bigger into *Haddock*. The freighter was huge, yet the crew spaces were small. She loved her ship, but she'd be glad to move into a hotel for a few days when they completed their voyage. A proper bath alone would work wonders. She was ruefully aware that she - and the rest of her crew - stank.

A good thing no one notices the smell after the first few hours, she thought, as she climbed into bed. *But they'll probably force us to go through decontamination when we reach Tallyman.*

Sleep didn't come easy. Indeed, by the time Anson paged her, she didn't feel as though she'd slept at all. She sat upright and keyed her terminal, linking to the external sensors. RNRB Tallyman was a fairly standard asteroid base - one designed for mining and zero-g construction work rather than habitation - but it was surrounded by a dozen *Workhorse*-class freighters and a pair of naval destroyers. Abigail shivered as she checked the freighter ID codes, recognising a couple of names. Whatever was going on was *serious*. The Royal Navy wouldn't yank so many freighters off the shipping lanes without a *very* good excuse.

"They want you to shuttle over to the base," Anson said, over the intercom. "Now, apparently. The shuttle is already on its way."

"Joy," Abigail muttered. "Open the lower hatch for them. Just let me slip into something a little less comfortable and I'll be down."

She stripped off her shipsuit, sponged herself down and rapidly donned a fresh outfit. It wasn't a dress uniform, but it would have to do. She literally had nothing else to wear. The stuffed shirts who ran the navy might be outraged if they saw her, but it didn't matter. They should *know* they hadn't called her after she'd arrived at Ceres. She'd have hired something more suitable if they'd arranged a meeting on the asteroid. God knew she didn't meet potential clients in smelly shipsuits.

Pinning her hair back into place, she hurried down to the hatch, checking the telltales before she opened it. The shuttle was fairly standard, the interior surprisingly luxurious for a military craft. A Royal Marine checked her fingerprints and DNA code, then directed her to a comfortable seat. Abigail wondered, helplessly, if she was in trouble. And yet, she *knew* it was absurd. The Royal Navy wouldn't have bothered to summon her to Tallyman if it wanted to arrest her. Ceres had an internal police force that would have happily taken Abigail and her crew into custody until matters were sorted out.

She forced herself to relax as the shuttle undocked and headed back to the asteroid. The pilot kept up a steady stream of chatter, speaking to his controller...Abigail had to fight to keep the contempt off her face. Didn't the navy trust its pilots? The endless checklists bred sloth and apathy, not efficiency. God knew *she* trusted Anson to handle her ship in her absence...*she* wouldn't insult his intelligence by forcing him to run through a checklist for something as simple as a docking manoeuvre. Maybe the pilot was new. But in that case, he shouldn't be flying the shuttle...

A low *clunk* echoed through the craft as it docked with the asteroid. Abigail rolled her eyes in annoyance - *Anson* wouldn't have banged a shuttle against the airlock - and then rose as the hatch opened. There was gravity inside, surprisingly. She'd half-expected the entire complex to be in zero-g. But then, the military could afford far more powerful and selective gravity generators than any civilian freighter crew. No doubt half their crew was composed of groundpounders. *She* could move easily from gravity to zero-g and back again, but groundpounders could not. Half of them couldn't even fly to orbit without throwing up.

Sad, she thought, as she stepped through the hatch. *Who'd want to live on the ground?*

A young man wearing a midshipman's uniform met her on the far side. "Captain Harrison?"

"That's me," Abigail said. She resisted the urge to point out that her identity had already been checked. The midshipman looked so young that she was tempted to check if he was still in nappies. *Poddy* looked older - and more responsible - and Poddy was *fifteen*! "What can I do for you?"

"Please, come with me," the midshipman said. His voice was very quiet. He turned, motioning for her to follow him. "There's a briefing in the…ah…briefing room."

"And where else would we hold a briefing?" Abigail asked, rhetorically. "Lead on, young man."

The back of the young man's neck went red, Abigail noted. She smiled to herself, then followed him through a series of drab - and unmarked - corridors. There was no personality to the complex at all, no decorations…there weren't even any paintings or drawings produced by the local children. But then, there were probably no children on the base. The RNRB complex might just have been reactivated at very short notice. She mulled it over as she followed him into the briefing room, where four other merchant skippers were waiting for her.

"Abigail," Captain Philip Chester said. He was a colossal man, with a beard that reached down to his chest. His shipsuit was carefully tailored to show off his muscles. "It's good to see you again."

"You too," Abigail said, warmly. They'd shared a bed a few times, back when they'd been younger. It hadn't meant much to either of them, she knew, but it had been fun. "What's an ugly bastard like you doing in a place like this?"

"Waiting for you, it would seem," Chester said. He waved a hand around the room. "We were all summoned here…"

"I'm sorry about the delay," a new voice said. A young man strode into the room, closing the hatch behind him. "We were hoping to get started earlier, but something came up."

"That's quite all right," Captain Dawes said, sarcastically. "We're just sitting here, twiddling our thumbs."

"Good," the naval officer said, as he motioned for Abigail to take a seat. He didn't seem to have any sense of irony. "My name is Sidney Jameson, *Commodore* Jameson. I'm sorry that you were all summoned here at short notice. Please rest assured that we wouldn't have called you if the situation wasn't truly urgent."

"I'd prefer to rest assured that you were going to compensate us for our losses," Captain Dawes told him.

"We will," Jameson said. He took a breath. "We are at war."

Abigail felt ice trickling down her spine. "At war? With whom?"

Jameson *looked* at her. "Aliens."

CHAPTER
TWO

One day in Colchester, Commander Alan Campbell had long since come to believe, was just like any other. He would be awoken at seven in the morning, fed something that might *just* have passed for a decent breakfast, then put through a routine of physical exercise, academic study and basic counselling. Alan wasn't sure why the Royal Navy bothered with the latter - as a member of D Company, he would be dishonourably discharged as soon as his sentence was up - and frankly he rather hated it. The military counsellors regarded him as a pimple on the Royal Navy's bum and the civilian counsellors found him incomprehensible. But then, he *was* in jail. He simply *couldn't* decline counselling if the jail's commanding officer thought he deserved it.

It's a punishment, he thought, when he bothered to think about it at all. *Making me talk to some bushy-haired, bright-eyed, over-educated idiot is cruel and unusual punishment.*

He deserved it, he supposed. He'd killed his wife, after all. And even though he tried to tell himself that the bitch had deserved it, he knew better. He'd ensured that his daughters would grow up without either a mother or a father, as well as ruining his career and the rest of his life. He knew better than to think there was any future for him, outside Colchester. A criminal record generally meant the end of any employment prospects, even if he could cope outside the military prison. The unstructured world outside the stone walls might defeat him even if he *did* manage to find a job and rebuild his life.

It was hard, so hard, to find the motivation to swing his legs over the side and stand. There was nothing to do, save for pacing the cramped cell and waiting for the redcaps to take him to class. Colchester was hardly as unpleasant as some of the other high-security prisons, if the horror stories he'd heard were accurate, but it was *boring*. The redcaps weren't openly sadistic, yet they were very careful. They didn't even let him have *books* in his cell. If he hadn't been used to military life, he suspected he would have gone mad by now. But if he'd been a civilian, he would never have been sent to Colchester.

And if I'd been a civilian, my wife would never have been alone, he thought, morbidly. *And she would never have cheated on me...*

He forced the memories back down as he heard the sound of approaching footsteps. *That* was odd. The redcaps were anal about sticking to their schedule, no matter what the inmates thought. Perhaps something had happened to one of the other prisoners. A young man who'd been sent down for a year had tried to hang himself in his cell a few months ago, somewhat to Alan's surprise. *He* certainly hadn't been able to figure out how the poor bastard had managed it. It wasn't as if there were hooks on the ceiling. The cells were as bare as a crewman's cabin on a frigate.

The footsteps stopped by his cell. Something banged against the bars. "Campbell," a voice growled. "On your feet."

Alan looked up, surprised. Perhaps he'd lost track of time...no, it was 0930. He wasn't due to be marched out of his cell for another thirty minutes. There was certainly no *reason* for them to come early, as far as he knew. Did they think he'd done something wrong? It was hard to imagine what he could do, in Colchester. The inmates were so carefully supervised that resistance was completely futile.

He stood, slowly. Two men stood on the other side of the bars, wearing the black uniforms and red caps of the Royal Military Police. They were seemingly unarmed, but he knew better than to believe that was true. Besides, the redcaps were used to wrestling drunken squaddies and hunting down the occasional rogue SF operator. Neither of them would have any difficulty flattening Alan, if he tried to put up a fight. And all it would get him would be a week or two in a smaller cell.

"You have a visitor," the lead redcap said. He wore no nametag, none of them did. The redcaps were completely interchangeable. "Hands."

Alan sighed and turned around, crossing his hands behind his back. The redcap snapped on the cuffs, then fixed shackles around Alan's ankles. It was pointless, Alan had always thought, but it was procedure. And yet...he froze, just for a second, as the redcap's words sank in. A visitor? Who'd come to Colchester to visit *him*? His parents were dead, while his daughters were too young to visit the prison. And their guardians probably wouldn't *let* them visit in any case. Alan's parents-in-law had never really liked him, even *before* he'd murdered their daughter. They'd probably helped convince the poor bitch to cheat on him...

You killed her, he reminded himself, sharply. *What exactly do you deserve?*

He banished the thought as the redcaps opened the cell, one of them staying on the far side of the bars while the other entered. Alan rolled his eyes as the man searched him quickly - it wasn't as if there was anything in the cell Alan could smuggle out - and then inched his way out of the cell. It wasn't easy to walk in shackles, despite five years of practice. And they weren't even necessary to keep him under control.

I suppose they don't know that, he thought, bitterly. *I might turn violent at any moment.*

The redcaps escorted him down the corridor, passing a handful of other long-term cells. No one else was moving about, as far as Alan could tell. Most of the other prisoners appeared to be trying to catch up on their sleep. He had no idea who most of them were, let alone what they'd done to get themselves thrown into the military prison. The prisoners simply weren't encouraged to socialise, even amongst themselves. And even when they did talk, they rarely talked about their former lives. No one wanted to think about the world outside the jail.

They passed through a pair of doors that could have passed for starship airlocks - so heavily armoured that he was sure they'd survive a direct nuclear strike - and walked down a wider corridor. Another prisoner was coming in the other direction, a middle-aged woman wearing cuffs, shackles and an orange jumpsuit that obscured most of her figure. Alan stared anyway, he couldn't help himself. It had been years since he'd seen a woman. It was unusual for a woman to be sent to Colchester, certainly into the long-term detention section. He couldn't help wondering what the woman had done to merit it.

At least she'll be safer here than in a civilian jail, he thought, as the woman and her guards walked past. He'd heard horror stories about female prisons too. *The redcaps won't treat her as a whore.*

They stopped outside another door and waited, patiently. The door hissed open slowly, revealing a barren room. There were two chairs facing each other, both fixed to the floor, but nothing else. One wall was dominated by a mirror, almost certainly a one-way mirror. Alan stared at his reflection, wondering who was on the far side. They certainly wouldn't be impressed by what they saw, he knew. Five years in Colchester had taken their toll. His blond hair was shaggy, his unshaven face utterly unkempt... he was lucky, he supposed, that it wasn't worse. But it could have been better too.

And Judith used to say I was handsome, he thought, with a trace of the old bitterness. *That didn't stop her opening her legs for the fucking neighbour.*

The redcaps marched him over to the nearest chair, pushed him down and cuffed him to the legs. Alan could barely move. He glowered at the military policemen, who ignored him as they checked the cuffs and then withdrew from the chamber. Alan scowled. He might be alone, but he wasn't fool enough to believe that he wasn't under observation. The entire prison was monitored 24/7. There were probably pickups embedded in the ceiling.

Another door opened. Alan looked up...and stared. A blonde woman stepped into the cell, wearing a baggy green jumpsuit that marked her as a visitor. There was something severe about her face, but Alan found it hard to care. Scrubbed clean of make-up, she was still the prettiest woman he'd seen in five years. He told himself, sharply, not to think about it. His visitor probably didn't consider him attractive. Whatever she was here for had nothing whatsoever to do with sex.

And it has to be important, if she came in person, Alan thought. Everyone who visited Colchester was strip-searched before they were allowed to enter the prison. It was why there were so few visitors. *What does she want?*

The woman sat down, resting her hands on her knees. "Commander Alan Campbell?"

"Yeah," Alan said. It would have been amusing if the redcaps had brought her the wrong person, but it was unlike them to make mistakes. "And you?"

"Commander Liana Mountebank, Naval Legal Services," Liana said. She had a firm voice, almost completely devoid of emotion. It was still the sweetest sound Alan had heard for years. "I have a proposition for you."

Alan bit down on a number of droll remarks and forced himself to think. The Royal Navy's lawyers were drawn from senior ranks, but it was difficult for them to reconcile a law degree with a full-time military career. Chances were that Liana had been pushed into a naval career, then urged to take a law degree instead of serving on a starship...he felt a flicker of contempt, mingled with droll amusement. At least she'd had the sense to realise that she was better off in a support role.

"I see," he said, finally. Somehow, he doubted it was *that* kind of proposition. "What do you want?"

Liana studied him for a long moment. "You were born in Glasgow," she said. "You attended Park Bank Primary School, then Robert Burns Secondary School. In your second year, you were expelled from Robert Burns after an...incident...and transferred to Kenilworth Borstal, where you spent the remainder of your schooling. You attempted to join the Royal Navy at sixteen, but were told to wait two more years; you reapplied at eighteen and were accepted, after aptitude testing, into the starfighter training program."

"I *know* all this," Alan said, sharply.

Liana ignored him. "You spent a year in the training program, after which you were assigned to Nelson Base's defence squadrons for two years. During that time, you met and married Judith Foster, who encouraged you to apply for mustang status when you started to age out of starfighter service. You switched to command track, eventually rising to the point of Commander Air Group on HMS *Formidable*. Your family grew too, with the birth of Jeanette and Alice. You appeared to have a bright future ahead of you.

"And then you murdered your wife."

"I know what I did," Alan snapped.

"You came home early to discover your wife in bed with John Slater, a neighbour," Liana said, remorselessly. "You pitched Slater through the window, inflicting serious injuries, then proceeded to beat your wife to death. The police were called and you were arrested, charged with murder, and eventually sentenced to ten years in Colchester. So far, you have served five of those years."

She paused. "Why didn't you just file for divorce?"

Alan glared at her. "Do we *have* to talk about it?"

"Yes."

Alan paused, trying to control his temper. He *could* have sought a divorce, on grounds of adultery. The law would have been on his side, too. He would have won custody of his daughters, while Judith would have been left with nothing but the stigma of cheating on a serving military officer. The days when she could have walked away with two-thirds of his paycheck were long gone. But...

"I was angry," he said. "I..."

He tried to put it into words, but failed. He'd thought they'd had a partnership, that he could trust her not to betray him...he'd come home early because he'd thought his wife would *welcome* him. And then he'd caught her in bed with another man...he didn't care, in the end, *why* she'd betrayed him. All that mattered was that she *had* betrayed him. He'd been so angry that he hadn't quite realised what he was doing until it was too late.

"The headshrinkers are fairly confident that you are unlikely to reoffend," Liana said, when he'd finished. "You would not have been kept here if they'd felt otherwise."

Alan nodded, curtly. A life sentence would have seen him transferred to the work camps in Antarctica, if he simply wasn't dumped on a penal colony or marched to the hangman's office and unceremoniously hanged. Ten years in Colchester had been remarkably merciful, under the circumstances. But it was still a harsh punishment.

And you deserve it, he reminded himself.

"We have an offer for you," Liana said. "There is a war on. The Royal Navy has a significant shortage of trained manpower. If you..."

Alan stared. "A war?"

"A war," Liana repeated. "You'll get a full briefing later, if you accept our offer. Right now, all you need to know is that the navy is desperate for manpower. If you are willing to return to service and serve for the duration of the conflict, we will cancel the rest of your sentence and scrub your record clean."

"You can't be *that* desperate for manpower," Alan said, carefully. Hope warred with fear in his breast. "There's no shortage of recruits."

"Which gives you some idea of just how serious the situation is," Liana said. She leaned forward, meeting his eyes. "You *won't* be going back to *Formidable*. You'll have another assignment. I won't lie to you and tell you it'll be a walk in the park, because it won't be anything of the sort. If you refuse to take on the post you're offered, you will be returned to your cell and left to rot."

Alan swallowed, hard. Hope…he'd had *no* hope, only two short hours ago. And yet…

He thought, fast. The Royal Navy had never had a shortage of personnel. It had been able to pick and choose recruits from a vast pool of applicants. Hell, even crewmen who completed their short-term contracts and transferred to the merchant navy could be recalled to the colours if necessary. For there to be a manpower shortage, the demands on the navy's personnel had to be vast. It would take time to expand the training program to turn weedy young groundpounders into qualified personnel…

Time they may not have, Alan thought. He'd seen some of the projections. Modern wars were supposed to be short and sharp, brief exchanges of fire to establish positions before the diplomats got involved and sorted out the mess. *If the demand for manpower is so intense…*

He sighed, inwardly. Liana was right. He *wouldn't* be going back to *Formidable*. The best he could hope for was…was what? Something dangerous, no doubt. He was *sure* that he - and everyone else in Colchester - was considered expendable. Perhaps they wanted to put him back in a starfighter cockpit. It wasn't impossible, but it was unlikely. Starfighter combat was a young man's game. The Admiralty would have to be *really* desperate before they put him in a cockpit again.

"You'll scrub my record," he said, slowly. "What does that *mean*?"

Liana shrugged. "Assuming you survive the war, you'll be discharged from the navy and allowed to make your own way in life…as if you hadn't killed your wife. You'll have at least a *chance* to build something for yourself, perhaps on an asteroid settlement. Should you do anything criminal in the future, of course, the record will be de-scrubbed and you will spend the rest of your life in prison. Does *that* answer your question?"

Alan nodded, slowly. There was no point in pretending to think about it. The prospect of being killed was bad, but staying in Colchester was worse. He silently damned Liana for bringing him hope…he could have endured the prison, perhaps, if there hadn't been any chance of early release. But now…

"I accept," he said.

His thoughts ran in circles. Going back to space…it was worth any danger. The chance to sit down and eat a good meal, even navy rations… he'd have to see if he could find a brothel. Or an enthusiastic amateur. A Royal Navy uniform drew attention from every woman in the room. And yet…he felt a stab of bitter guilt. He'd never slept with anyone, after marrying Judith. The thought of going to a brothel felt like betrayal…

Sure, his thoughts mocked him. *And what was killing her, exactly?*

"Very good," Liana said. She rose. "The military police will arrange your transfer, along with anyone else who accepts the opportunity, to a base where you will receive a fuller briefing and your assignments. I *suggest* you don't waste this opportunity. You will not receive another one."

"I know," Alan said. It was an unwritten law that anyone who declined a promotion would simply never be given another one. "Where are we going?"

"Classified, for the moment," Liana said. There was a hint of irritation in her voice. "Like I said, you'll get a briefing when you arrive."

She turned and walked out of the chamber. Alan was too distracted to follow her with his eyes. A war, a chance to return to the uniform…Liana was right. It could not be wasted. And yet…

His blood ran cold as the implications dawned on him. *If they're so desperate for manpower that they're willing to recruit violent criminals*, he thought, *what the hell are we facing?*

CHAPTER

THREE

"Aliens," Abigail repeated.

"Nonsense," Dawes said. "This is a joke. Some depraved sick arsehole in the Admiralty has dreamt up an exercise and…"

"I'll show you the sensor records in a moment," Jameson said, coolly. It was clear, just from his tone, that he'd had the same conversation before. "Suffice it to say that, four weeks ago, the Vera Cruz colony was attacked by alien forces. Several other outposts in that sector have gone quiet. I'm sure I don't have to explain to you what *that* means."

Abigail nodded, slowly. Four weeks…the aliens might already be halfway to Earth. The situation was serious, if it wasn't some insane drill. She didn't blame Dawes for being sceptical. A hundred years of extra-solar expansion and colonisation had turned up no forms of life more intelligent than a dog. Humanity was alone in the universe.

We were alone in the universe, she thought. It couldn't be a drill. No matter the reasoning, no matter the compensation, a drill would have serious long-term effects on the relationship between merchant spacers and the navy. Dawes wasn't *wrong* to worry about his cargo, even if everyone was compensated appropriately. *But right now cargo is the least of our worries.*

Chester snorted. "I've heard nothing about this," he said. "The news channels were silent."

"There's a total news blackout, for the moment," Jameson said. "We don't expect that to last indefinitely, of course, but it gives us a chance to get organised before the public starts to panic."

"True," Abigail said. In her experience, groundpounders were a pan-icky lot. They knew nothing about science or technology or how it could be used to make life *better*. "Let's cut to the chase, Commodore. Why did you summon us here?"

"All five of you are Royal Navy Reservists," Jameson said, bluntly. "And, perhaps more importantly at the moment, the Royal Navy financed the loans you used to purchase your ships. You signed an agreement, when you accepted the loan, that your vessels would be placed at our disposal if a war emergency situation was declared. It *has* been declared and yes, your ships are being requisitioned."

Dawes choked. "And my *cargo*?"

"We'll try to have it forwarded to its final destination," Jameson said, curtly. "But right now, it is the least of our concerns."

Abigail exchanged glances with Chester, thinking fast. Legally, they didn't seem to have a leg to stand on, if they wanted to resist. They *had* signed the papers, after all. And even if they wanted to resist anyway, it wouldn't get them very far. The Royal Marines could board a freighter and arrest the crew if they wished. She felt a stab of pain, deep in her gut. The ship was *hers*. She didn't want to lose her. And yet, she might have no choice.

"We captain freighters, not warships," Chester said. "Do you want us to haul military supplies?"

"No," Jameson said. "We want to convert your ships into escort carriers."

Abigail stared. "Are you *joking*?"

"No," Jameson said. He tapped the terminal, activating a holographic display. A giant image of a *Workhorse*-class freighter appeared in front of them. "The original specifications for the *Workhorse* included options to convert the freighters into escort carriers if necessary. As you can see" - the diagram opened up to reveal the starship's interior - "we'd strip out the main holds and replace them with modular components, everything from living quarters for a much larger crew to starfighter launching racks. The life support system is already over-engineered, but we'd expand it anyway..."

"Clever," Dawes said, grudgingly.

"Thank you," Jameson said. He nodded to the diagram. "We can't replace the drives without committing ourselves to a much longer refit, but we will be replacing the computer cores and supplying additional spare parts. We'll also be fitting close-in point defence weapons to the hull, along with their support systems. It will not be the most elegant design, but it will work."

I suppose that would appeal to someone who grew up in an asteroid community, Abigail thought, reluctantly. She'd been taught to value function over form since she'd been old enough to play with her first construction kit. Looking good took a second place to being practical and reliable. *And the ship is designed to take the modifications without a serious refit.*

Chester cleared his throat. "I assume you expect us to captain these ships?"

"Correct," Jameson said. "Unless you wish to surrender your command, in which case you will be transferred elsewhere."

"Transferred," Dawes repeated.

Jameson's voice hardened. "You are a Royal Navy Reservist, Captain Dawes. The price for the loan we gave you, ten years ago, was your ship and your service, should we have need of it. Your commission has been reactivated - activated, I suppose - and you are called upon to serve your country. And, I might add, the entire human race. This is not a human foe. We are facing aliens who probably can't tell the difference between a RockRat and a groundpounder. We all look alike to them."

Abigail couldn't help it. She smiled.

"If you refuse to honour your obligations," Jameson added, "your ship will be confiscated and you will be dispatched to prison. I *assure* you that your joint citizenship will *not* save you. Your government - both governments - are aware of the scale of the threat. You could easily be painted as a traitor to the entire human race."

He paused, just for a moment. "I understand that this isn't easy for any of you," he said, his eyes sweeping the room. "Suffice it to say that every major government - including the Belt Federation - is in agreement that we have to prepare for war. There should be no reason to be concerned about divided loyalties. If you feel otherwise...well, there are some reasonably comfortable places where you can be interned for the duration."

"Thanks," Chester said, dryly.

"And, assuming we survive, we *will* pay for your ships to be returned to their original state and do everything in our power to ensure that your reputations don't suffer," Jameson told them. "I believe that most people in the Belt will recognise that you had no choice."

"Hah," Dawes said.

Abigail shrugged. The Belters were remorselessly practical. Better to prepare for the worst and hope for the best than vice versa. It *would* be awkward if the war fizzled out after the diplomats started talking, but no one would blame her and her crew. And besides, the Royal Navy could offer a number of incentives to get *Haddock* back on the shipping lanes. A naval contract didn't offer much money, but it *was* fairly stable.

She cleared her throat. "What about our crews?"

"The ones who happen to be in the Naval Reserve will have their contracts reactivated at the same times as yourselves," Jameson said. "We will expect them to continue serving with you, unless their services are required elsewhere. The others may leave your ships, if they wish; they can transfer to other freighters or simply return to their homes for the duration of the conflict."

Abigail made a face. The Belters would not be impressed by any of her crew who left the ship, not when they were being called upon to serve. She'd have to find a way to dismiss anyone who didn't *want* to serve, something that wouldn't be easy without blackening their reputations in other ways. The Belters didn't indulge in tasteless displays of patriotism, unlike so many groundpounder nations, but they understood duty and responsibility...and cared little for those who shirked when the call came.

"So, you expect us to take our ships into combat," Dawes said. "How?"

"We expect you to escort convoys," Jameson said. "Right now, we have no other plan for your deployment. If that changes - *when* that changes - we'll let you know."

"I have two crewmen from China," Captain Hawke said. "What about them?"

"They can stay or go, as they wish," Jameson said. "The Chinese are preparing for war too."

"I see," Hawke said.

Chester leaned forward. "I have another question," he said. "Are you planning to assign military personnel to our ships? In which case, who's in charge?"

"You will be in command of your ships," Jameson said, reassuringly. "There *will* be a military officer serving as your XO, but you *will* be in command."

Abigail wasn't so sure. She understood ship handling, but she'd never served on a carrier or commanded starfighters. It probably *wasn't* anything like flying shuttles. And if there were enough military personnel on the ship, the XO could take over at any moment...she shook her head, telling herself that she was being paranoid. She *was* a reservist, as little as she might like to remember it.

Dawes frowned. "What's the catch?"

Jameson looked back at him. "The catch?"

"You're being very reasonable," Dawes said. "*Something* must be wrong."

"Good point," Hawke agreed.

"We *do* need to get you and your ships ready for deployment as fast as possible," Jameson pointed out. He sighed. "But yeah, there is a problem."

He took a long breath. "We are *very* short of manpower right now," he said. "Our pool of trained officers and crewmen - even reservists - simply isn't big enough to meet all our requirements. We can - and we will - offer battlefield commissions to civilian crewers, on the understanding that their ranks won't last past the end of the war, but even that isn't enough to fill every billet that *needs* filling. Even dropping some of the training requirements isn't going to be enough."

Abigail made a face. She'd heard enough about the Royal Navy's training to know it was far from perfect, but random cuts weren't going to make matters better. She'd met too many senior officers to have any confidence that they were going to make *effective* cuts. They'd probably cut half the zero-g training, but keep Saluting 101. A sloppy salute might be indicative of a sloppy mind - or so she'd heard - yet she couldn't help regarding airlock training and weapons handling as far more important.

"Go on," Chester said.

"We're going to be drawing prisoners from various holding centres, if they have the right qualifications," Jameson said. "I…"

Abigail felt a hot flash of anger. "Out of the question," she said. "Do you think I'll allow a convicted criminal on my ship?"

Dawes nodded in agreement. "Did your planners watch *The Dirty Dozen* before coming up with this concept?"

Jameson rubbed his forehead. "Let me finish," he said. "First, we will *not* be making these offers to men we feel are likely to reoffend. No serial killers, no paedophiles…the handful that escaped being sentenced to death will not be released from prison until they die. The people we *have* selected are not people who pose a permanent danger."

"You can't be sure of that," Dawes muttered.

"The reoffending rate is actually quite low," Jameson pointed out. "In any case, like I said, we are desperate for manpower."

"Desperate enough to overlook…what?" Abigail asked. "Murder? Arson? Or jaywalking?"

"You'll be given their files, assuming that they're assigned to your ship," Jameson said, bluntly. "I shouldn't have to warn you that such files are highly classified. You are *not* to share details with anyone, unless you are prepared to explain yourself to a court-martial board."

"It seems you expect us to take a risk," Chester observed.

"If it was entirely up to me," Jameson said, "there wouldn't be any war. And there would be no need to turn your ships into escort carriers. And there would be no need to look at *every* possible source of manpower. But it isn't up to me."

He looked from face to face. "You took our money so you could buy and operate your freighters. Right now, we're calling in the loan. You are under military authority and that means following orders. If you are unable or unwilling to accept the current state of affairs, you can leave - now - and we'll give your ships to someone else. We know this isn't easy and we wouldn't be considering it if the situation wasn't desperate.

"We don't believe that any of the prospective candidates pose a serious risk. If that changes, our approach will change too."

"So put up and shut up," Chester said.

"Or fuck off," Dawes added.

Abigail scowled, inwardly. She was aware, all too aware, that people made mistakes. She'd grown up in a society where people were publicly whipped for minor errors and completely ostracised for major mistakes. It had always struck her as severe, until she'd come to understand just how much depended on people *not* making mistakes. The lives of everyone on an asteroid *depended* on a complete lack of mistakes.

But people don't go to groundpounder jail for minor mistakes, she thought. Groundpounders were rather more forgiving than RockRats. *Whatever they did had to be serious.*

She closed her eyes for a long moment. There was no point in trying to argue, not when she *had* signed the contract. And there was no way she was abandoning her ship and crew. She *loved* the old freighter more than she loved her husbands and wives…

And if any of the criminals step out of line, she told herself firmly, *there will be an unfortunate accident.*

She nodded to herself. Groundpounders and RockRats might disagree on what constituted a dangerous and irredeemable criminal, but they both agreed that certain kinds of people could never be let free. The simple fact that the criminals *hadn't* been executed suggested that the judge and jury had believed there was no reasonable possibility of reoffending. And yet…no one would blame her if she executed a criminal who misbehaved on her ship. It was technically within her authority, even as a civilian. She was damned if she was allowing anyone a second or third chance.

Jameson cleared his throat. "Are there any other points you wish to raise?"

Abigail nodded. "How long do you expect the conversions to take?"

"Roughly two weeks," Jameson said. "The modular components have already been transported here, along with additional dockyard workers. We've already done one conversion, so most of the kinks in the system should be worked out by now. There's no guarantee, of course, that we *will* meet our deadline. We're planning on the assumption that the schedule will slip at some point."

"How reassuring," Chester said.

"True," Abigail said. Refitting a giant freighter wouldn't be easy, even if they didn't run into any major problems. Two weeks might be ludicrously optimistic. "At least we can't be blamed for any delays."

"Or strikes in the dockyard," Dawes added.

"There *is* a war on," Jameson said. "All strikes have been suspended for the duration."

You mean, anyone who strikes will be arrested, Abigail thought. Industrial action was rare in space - there were more jobs than there were trained workers - but it had been known to happen. And yet, if a state of emergency had been declared, any strikers would be arrested...and then what? Put back to work? *We couldn't arrest everyone without shooting ourselves in the foot.*

"I'll make sure you have copies of all the files," Jameson said. "I should add, again, that all of these files are classified. You are *not* to share them with anyone. Indeed, we are under complete radio silence. You are not to contact anyone without sending the message through the censors here."

"Because you don't want to tell the little people that Armageddon is approaching," Dawes muttered.

"We don't want a panic," Jameson said. "The news will be released soon, I believe, once the first wave of preparations has been completed. That should convince the public that we know what we're doing."

Abigail snorted. "How can that possibly be true? We've encountered *aliens*. Even if the war comes to an end tomorrow, *nothing* is ever going to be the same. We're just pretending that everything is normal because we don't know what will change when we admit that everything is no *longer* normal!"

"That's somewhat above my pay grade," Jameson said. He shrugged. "Yeah, I admit there are philosophical implications here. Contact with an alien race, us no longer being alone...yes, there is much to consider. But right now, our *real* concern is that the aliens are not remotely friendly. They attacked us, not the other way around. Preparing for war is more important than trying to make contact with them."

"Maybe they're too alien to understand us," Hawke mused. "We humans have problems talking to each other when we come from different cultures. The gulf between us and the aliens must be far wider than the gulf between spacers and groundpounders."

Abigail nodded. There were things - spacer things - that no ground-pounder would ever understand. They might claim to understand intellectually, but emotionally? They simply didn't understand. It was impossible to discuss such matters because the groundpounders refused to accept them.

"Or maybe they're just nasty bastards," Dawes said. "How many historical *humans* can claim to be nasty bastards? Genghis Khan? Napoleon? Hitler? Bin Laden? Sir Charles Hanover? Chairman Shan? It's not like they *needed* excuses to be bastards."

"There are people who will find humanity even in Hitler," Hawke said.

"Which goes to prove that a great many people are idiots," Dawes said. "What excuse do our new enemies have for being nasty bastards?"

"I dare say we'll find out," Jameson said. He smiled, humourlessly. "If any of you want to leave your ships now, say so. If not...we'll start the refitting as soon as possible."

Abigail sighed. "I don't think any of us want to leave our ships."

And if any of the criminals act up, she added mentally, *I'll put him out the airlock first and worry about coming up with a story later.*

CHAPTER

FOUR

"All right, everyone out," a voice barked. "Move it!"

Alan jerked awake. He'd tried to stay awake, when they'd been marched out of their cells and into the bus, but the vehicle's steady motion had lulled him into sleep. It hadn't helped that the windows had been tinted, making it impossible for him to see outside. He thought they'd been driving for around three hours, but it was impossible to be sure. They could be anywhere in England by now.

He staggered to his feet, joining the others as they stumbled towards the door and piled out onto the tarmac. They were on a military base, all right; there was no mistaking the bland buildings, the ugly signs on the walls and the guards, standing by the fence. It *looked* as though the base had been hastily reactivated, he decided as he looked around. The fence didn't look very secure, he thought. Normally, a military base would look like a garrison in a hostile city.

Which isn't really a good thing, he thought. *But too many bases were attacked during the Troubles.*

"Proceed into the first building," a redcap barked, as pre-packed overnight bags were handed out. Unusually for a redcap, he wore rank insignia. A colonel, apparently. "Take one of the shower cubicles and wash thoroughly, then dress and make your way down to the mess. Do not delay."

Alan shrugged as he walked into the building and found a private shower room. It was tiny, no larger than a washroom on a starship, but it was *private*. He undressed, turned on the water and stepped under the flow. It felt heavenly. He ran his fingers through his hair, wishing he'd had a chance to have it cut properly, then rubbed shaving gel on his cheeks to remove the stubble. The water washed the bristles away without hesitation. He wanted to linger - a long shower seemed the height of luxury after prison - but he knew better than to delay too long. Turning off the water, he dried himself and changed into his new uniform. It had no rank insignia, nothing to suggest his assignment or status, but it was still far superior to prison jumpsuits.

He stepped outside and stopped in front of a mirror. The blue uniform looked good on his pale skin, matching his blue eyes. He looked like a new recruit, save for his unkempt hair and obvious age. The dark lines around his eyes *proved* he was in his thirties, at the very least. Alan studied himself, then sighed. Colchester had probably made him look at least ten years older. It would be a long time before he managed to get himself back in shape.

You have a reason to stay in shape now, he told himself, firmly. There would be an exercise room on the base, somewhere. He'd have to go regularly, at least until he received his assignment. *You need to be fit for what's coming.*

He made his way down the stairs and into the underground mess. It looked as if it had been designed for over five hundred soldiers, not forty men and three women. Everyone was a little spread out, eying each other - and the guards - with some concern. Alan shrugged as he walked over to the counter, where the cook splashed sausages, potatoes and beans on a military-issue plate. The food might be disgusting, by civilian standards, but it was better than Colchester's. And it looked as though there was plenty of it.

Sitting down, he allowed his eyes to roam the room as he ate. He recognised a handful of the men from Colchester, but the remainder were strangers to him. The women were complete unknowns…had they come from Colchester too? Or had they been brought from another prison? It was hardly unknown for female convicts to be transferred to a civilian prison, after sentence had been passed. Maybe someone had decided to spare them Colchester. If so, they'd done the women no favours. Colchester was harsh, but there were worse places to be.

"There are books and other entertainments in the next room," a red-cap boomed, pointing towards a far door. "When your name is called, walk into the interview room and sit down."

Alan rolled his eyes as he finished his second helping, then walked into the next room. It was a small library, complete with row upon row of paper books and a handful of computer terminals. A quick check told him that the computers weren't linked to the datanet, unsurprisingly. It didn't look as though they were linked to MILNET either. He supposed *that* wasn't a surprise. The base looked old enough to predate the Troubles. Maybe it had been an internment centre rather than a *real* base.

A young man winked at him. "There are pretty-looking chicks in there," he stage-whispered, mischievously. "You want to ask one of them to fuck?"

Alan shook his head, curtly. They were being watched. The chains might have been loosened - they hadn't been cuffed and shackled for the journey - but he would be surprised if every last inch of the base wasn't under constant observation. And besides, the redcaps were a constant presence. Any misbehaviour would just get him shipped back to Colchester to serve the rest of his sentence.

He pulled a book from the shelf - the latest in a series he vaguely recalled reading before he'd been sentenced to spend ten years behind bars - and sat down to read. The author had started well - he'd captured the life of a space marine quite accurately - but he'd clearly gone downhill over the last five years. *This* book was nothing more than a hodgepodge of plotlines that didn't quite blend together and sex scenes that would probably result in physical injury if someone tried them in real life. By the time his name was called and he walked into the interview room, it was something of a relief.

"Commander Campbell," a young man said. "Thank you for coming."

Alan sat down, studying the younger man closely. He wore a plain blue uniform, without any rank insignia or nametag. Intelligence, perhaps? In Alan's experience, REMFs tended to wear the fanciest uniforms they could get away with, at least in public. They hated it when anyone questioned their right to wear the uniform, or when someone addressed them by the wrong rank. Or maybe he was a naval reservist who hadn't been allowed to return to his former rank. There was no way to know.

"You're welcome," Alan said, finally. He reminded himself, sharply, to behave. This young man could probably wreck his sole hope of getting out of jail with a word in the right - or wrong - set of ears. "What can I do for you?"

"I have a file for you," the young man said. He passed Alan a paper file. "Read it."

Alan frowned, then opened the file. The first page was a summary; short, informative and completely unbelievable. Aliens? There was no such thing as aliens. Everyone *knew* there was no such thing as aliens. Every stray signal that humanity had detected, every vague sensor contact...all of them had, eventually, been proven to have a natural explanation, one stripped of all wonder and terror. Aliens didn't exist...

...And yet, no one would recruit convicted criminals from Colchester unless they were desperate.

She mentioned a manpower shortage, Alan thought, weakly. His mouth was suddenly very dry. *The nation is gearing up for war.*

He looked up. "This is real?"

"Yes," the young man said, flatly. "Keep reading."

Alan read through the next few pages, torn between disbelief and outright shock. Aliens...hostile aliens. It couldn't be happening, could it? And yet, it was. He had no doubt that aliens *would* choose to wage war on humanity, if they thought they could win. The galaxy might not be big enough for *two* intelligent races. Perhaps the aliens thought they had exhausted their tramlines and now they were moving into the human sphere. Or...he shrugged. It didn't really matter. All that mattered was that there was a war on.

"There isn't anything here about their technology," he mused, slowly. "Was something redacted from the report?"

"Very little is *known* about their technology," the young man said. His voice was very calm, but there was an undercurrent of concern, perhaps even fear. "We know they must be capable of using the tramlines, as they're clearly not native to Vera Cruz, and they apparently do have something akin to our drive system, but beyond that? We know nothing."

And it must cost you to say that, Alan thought. Intelligence officers, in his experience, liked to pretend to be omniscient. It was a rare officer who realised, let alone admitted, the limits of his knowledge. And yet... he frowned. *If we know nothing about their technology, we have no way of knowing how our weapons and defences stack up against theirs.*

He flipped through the report, trying to get the high points. The first contact - the first *reported* contact - had been nearly a month ago. He concentrated, trying to recall the starcharts he'd seen before being imprisoned. The aliens might well be a great deal closer to Earth by now. Or they might be feeling their way along the tramlines, as unaware of the interior disposition of human space as humanity was unaware of *theirs*. Unless they'd captured a database from Vera Cruz. The civilians might not have thought to destroy their libraries before they were overwhelmed.

They might know everything, or nothing, or somewhere in-between, he thought. *And the only thing we really know about them is that they're hostile.*

"I see," he said, finally. Aliens. He could cope with aliens. "What - exactly - do you want from me?"

"We are currently putting together crews for escort carriers," the young man said. "You are qualified to serve in a role that is a cross between CAG and XO. If you choose to accept it, you will be shipped out in the next couple of days to your new home. If you refuse..."

He left the rest of the sentence unspoken. But Alan could guess. It was possible - even probable - that the Royal Navy would have another role for him. And yet...the navy might also think that he'd had his chance and blown it. He could be put back on the bus and sent straight back to Colchester. There was no way to be sure.

An escort carrier, he told himself. *It wouldn't be that bad, surely.*

"Very well," he said. "I accept."

The young man nodded, curtly. "Very good," he said. He tapped his wristcom. "Officer Bennett, please join us."

Alan's eyes narrowed in suspicion. *Officer*? That was odd...a redcap rank? Or an intelligence officer? No, intelligence wankers normally used naval ranks in the hopes civilians wouldn't pay too much attention to them. If half the stories Alan had heard were true, intelligence officers spent a fair percentage of their time pretending to do nothing more important than ordering paperclips and stapling documents. An officer would be...

The door opened. Alan turned, just in time to see a grim-faced man step into the room. He was short, but surprisingly muscular, his dark hair topping a face that had clearly taken one too many beatings over the past few years. Alan met his dark eyes, fighting the urge to recoil. The sense of violence - of *threat* - was almost overwhelming. He wanted to step back, yet he knew that showing weakness would be the worst possible thing he could do.

"Thank you," Bennett said, curtly. He had a London accent, one that spoke of growing up in the East End. "Campbell. Come with me."

Alan rose and followed Bennett through the door, down a corridor and through a guarded gate into a small conference room. Bennett moved with absolute confidence, the kind of movement that suggested he *knew* no one would dare block his way. Alan watched his back, silently evaluating. Bennett would have grown up honing his talent for violence on the streets, then trained to use it in the service of his country. Whatever else could be said about Bennett, he was clearly a very dangerous man.

"You make me sick," Bennett said, closing and locking the door. "You killed your wife."

He moved forward with lightning speed. Before Alan could react, he was pinned against the wall. Resistance was futile. Bennett was pure muscle, stronger than anyone Alan had ever faced...even on the streets of Glasgow. And he was clearly *very* well trained, utterly disciplined...

"I'm your supervisor," Bennett said, after a moment. His voice grew louder. "Your job is to serve your country. *My* job is to make damn sure you behave yourself. Fuck around onboard ship and I'll fucking toss your fucking arse out of the fucking airlock. You will not get another fucking chance to do *anything*. Get me?"

Alan gritted his teeth. "Yeah."

"If it was up to me, you'd fucking *rot* in Colchester," Bennett snarled. "The thought of hurting my wife - of *killing* my wife - God! You make me sick!"

He leaned closer, so close that Alan could smell...*something*...on his breath. "As far as everyone else is concerned, I'm your assistant, your batman, your gofer, your security adviser...whatever you want me to be. But don't ever forget that my *real* job is to keep an eye on you. I will not let you do anything stupid. Get me?"

"Yes," Alan said. "I'm not going to fuck it up."

"Really," Bennett said, doubtfully. "Do you know how many men fuck up their second chance?"

He let go of Alan and stepped back. "They say you and the other fuckers are necessary," he said, walking around the table and picking up a paper file. "And they say you won't re-offend. But personally I have my doubts. You're not some idiot who had a wee bit too much to drink and ended up mooning the Sergeant Major. You brutally beat a woman to death and seriously injured a grown man."

Alan straightened his collar. "She cheated on me."

Bennett glared. "I'm not here to listen to your excuses," he said. His accent grew stronger, harsher. "My dad beat my mother until I was old enough to stop him. Not little smacks either, proper blows that left her bruised and bloodied and broken. That bastard would beat her senseless for even *looking* at another man. What makes you think I'll take *any* of your excuses seriously?"

He shoved the file towards Alan. "Read this," he growled. "Once you're done, I'll take you to your room. You may no longer be a *formal* prisoner, but you are *not* to leave your room without permission unless the base is on fire. Do *not* attempt to speak to anyone, apart from myself. Got it?"

"I thought I was getting a pardon," Alan said.

"You're getting your record scrubbed, *after* the war ends," Bennett said. "You are not - yet - forgiven. And as far as I am concerned, you will *never* be forgiven."

"You're very kind," Alan murmured.

Bennett eyed him narrowly, then sat down. "Read the file," he ordered. "And then I'll take you to your room."

Alan nodded, curtly. He supposed he shouldn't have been too surprised at being supervised, although there was no reasonable prospect of escape. Even if he got past Bennett and over the fence, the prisoner's implant in his arm would lead the redcaps straight to him. He'd be arrested, dragged back to Colchester and thrown into a cell. And then they'd throw away the key.

Unless they decide to hang me instead, Alan thought. *If there really is a war on, they might not want to waste time and effort supervising the prisoners.*

He opened the file and read through it, carefully. Someone had done good work. Alan was no engineer, but he knew enough to be confident that the original designer was right and the *Workhorse*-class freighters *could* be converted into escort carriers. A set of supplementary notes detailed what had happened during the first conversion, with short outlines of small problems and suggestions for avoiding them in future. None of the issues were particularly bad, with the exception of a small problem with the fusion plant. The engineers had solved *that* problem by adding a second plant and a number of military-grade power cells. Expensive, admittedly, but workable.

Not enough to keep the ship going indefinitely, but enough to keep us alive long enough to fix the damage, Alan thought, although he had few illusions. A single direct hit would probably be enough to put the escort carrier out of commission - and a nuclear strike would vaporise the vessel. Damage control was going to be an absolute nightmare. *We're not going to be in the line of battle, I hope.*

He studied the designs, carefully. The *Workhorses* did have plenty of interior space, although they were small compared to a full-scale fleet carrier. There certainly *should* be room for an entire crew, although they were going to be cramped. It couldn't be helped. Besides, anyone who served in the navy would be used to cramped quarters, poor food and a complete lack of privacy.

Just like being in jail, Alan thought, wryly. *Except the food isn't much better.*

Bennett cleared his throat. "Well?"

"It looks workable," Alan said. "I'd have to see the carrier itself, of course, but…"

"I'm sure that the First Space Lord is just *dying* to hear your opinion," Bennett said, cutting Alan off. His voice dripped sarcasm. He rose, holding out his hand for the file. "Shall we go?"

Alan shrugged. It wasn't as if he had a choice.

"Sure," he said. "Why not?"

CHAPTER

FIVE

"You have *got* to be joking," Chief Rating Steven Phelps said.

"I'm afraid not, Steven," Abigail said. She didn't blame him for being unconvinced. *She* wasn't quite convinced herself. "This is not a joke."

She took a long breath as her eyes swept the forward hold. It was the largest space on the ship, now the other holds were crammed with cargo; the only space large enough for her to gather the entire crew. Fifteen men and women…tiny, compared to a military crew, but very close-knit. The thought of breaking up the core of her crew *hurt*, even though she knew that some of the younger crewmen were already planning to jump ship. She couldn't really blame them, either. There were few opportunities for advancement on *Haddock*.

"I've been given copies of the briefing notes, which you can review at leisure, but the important details - right now - are as follows." Abigail paused, allowing them a moment to process her words. "Aliens have arrived - and attacked. Our ship has been requisitioned for conversion into a makeshift carrier, with us expected to serve as the crew. Any of you who *aren't* reservists and *don't* want to stay on the ship can leave now, if you wish. Changing your mind later will get you into trouble."

"I don't know anything about serving in the military," Fatima Roberson said. The cook leaned forward, one hand playing with a long strand of dark hair. "Is there anyone here who *does*?"

"I was in the Royal Navy before transferring out," Vassilios Drakopoulos said. The Chief Engineer looked grim. "It is *very* different to the merchant service, I'm afraid. But given that we'll be running the ship, I don't think *our* experience will be quite as bad."

Abigail gave him a sharp look. "Are you staying?"

"You'd only get into trouble without me," Drakopoulos said, deadpan. "Besides, I suspect I'll be called back to the colours whatever happens, if the situation is as bad as they appear to believe. Pulling freighters out of the shipping lanes isn't something they'd do unless they felt the situation was desperate."

"But the situation can't be *that* bad," Anson said. "The news broadcasts aren't talking about aliens, are they?"

"Not yet," Abigail confirmed. "That will change."

"And that means the contacts haven't been *that* significant," Anson added. "For all we know, this is a border squabble."

"Or the start of a full-scale invasion," Drakopoulos said, quietly. "Or even a probe intended to gauge our response before the main fleet is dispatched."

"And First Contact was a month ago," Poddy put in. "A lot can happen in a month."

Abigail tapped her foot on the hard metal deck. "The situation isn't up for debate," she said, firmly. "We - I - signed a contract, so I am now obliged to offer my ship and my services to the Royal Navy. I won't say I'm happy about this because I'm not, but we don't have a choice."

She made a show of looking at her watch. "The preliminary refit crews are meant to be boarding at oh-nine-hundred tomorrow. If you don't want to stay with the ship, let me know before then and I'll arrange for your transfer to Tallyman. I expect you'll go into lockdown unless you have skills the Royal Navy desperately needs, at least until the news breaks and there's no longer any need to keep it under wraps. Everyone else…make sure you get as much sleep as you can. I imagine tomorrow is going to be a very busy day."

"No doubt," Phelps said. "We're going to have to empty the holds before we start pulling out the modules and replacing them."

Farris Ashburn cleared his throat. "We have a signed and sealed contract to deliver our cargo to Ceres," he said. "If we don't get it there by the end of the week, Captain, they'll invoke the penalty clauses."

"If we're lucky, the cargo pallets will be delivered to Ceres by the navy," Abigail said. She rather doubted they'd be that lucky. The Royal Navy wouldn't *intend* to screw her and her crew, but her cargo would be far down the priority list. "And, if we're *unlucky*, the Royal Navy has agreed to compensate us for the loss."

"Assuming there's an Earth left afterwards," Drakopoulos said. "Or a Royal Navy."

Abigail shot him a warning look. "The navy has sent us the refit specs," she said. "Study them now, then inform me if there are any problems we need to account for before the refit begins. You'll be supervising the process from start to finish."

"Will do," Drakopoulos said.

Ashburn snorted. "Do you trust the navy?"

"I expect that compensation will be paid, eventually," Abigail said. She understood his problem, but there was no point in going on and on about it. "And as we don't have any choice in the matter, all we can do is put our faith in them."

She looked around the compartment. "Anson, Poddy, stay with me," she ordered. "Everyone else, let me know if you want to leave the ship."

Anson waited until everyone else had left the compartment, then swung around to face Abigail. "Mum...Poddy can't stay."

"I'm staying," Poddy said, sharply. "Mum..."

"She's far too young to see combat," Anson said. "The youngest crewman in the Royal Navy will be at least eighteen..."

"We are born into danger," Poddy quoted. "We only leave it when we die."

"She's a child," Anson said. "Mum, Poddy should be removed..."

"I will not," Poddy snapped. "Mum..."

Abigail rubbed her forehead. There were times when she thought that allowing her children to serve under her command was a bad idea, even if it *did* give her a chance to make sure they had the proper skills before they served under a captain who would be less tolerant of mistakes. If nothing else, Anson and Poddy could make emotional demands on her, something the rest of the crew couldn't do. And yet, she understood Anson's concern.

She sighed, inwardly. On one hand, Anson was right. Poddy was young, far too young to see combat. Every motherly instinct in Abigail's mind demanded that she send her daughter away, even if it meant souring their relationship. Poddy would hate her, but at least Poddy would be *alive* to hate her. But on the other hand, her upbringing in an asteroid settlement had taught her that danger couldn't be avoided. Poddy couldn't be wrapped in cotton wool and preserved, let alone protected against every conceivable threat. Abigail had met too many spoilt brats from Earth, girls and boys who'd grown up in a sheltered environment, to want to smother her daughter. There were some things Poddy could only learn from experience.

Which doesn't make taking her into danger any easier, Abigail acknowledged. *And she really is too young to serve on a naval vessel.*

"You haven't even lived alone," Anson was saying. "You don't know the universe like I do..."

"You elderly man," Poddy mocked. "Let me fetch your slippers, then you can have a nice sit down by the fire while I make you a cup of hot milk."

"Shut up, the pair of you," Abigail snapped. It was good, she supposed, that Anson cared about his sister. And it was also good that Poddy was confident enough to push back when she felt her brother was being overprotective. But it gave her a headache. "Anson, Poddy, pay attention."

She waited for them to fall silent, considering her next words carefully. "First, *neither* of you have any obligation to stay with the ship," she said. "You're not reservists and your shipping contracts don't include military service. I won't complain if either or both of you want to jump ship now. That said..."

Anson opened his mouth. Abigail spoke over him.

"That said, we will be flying into danger...probably. We don't know *anything* about the aliens, beyond the mere fact of their existence and apparent hostility. There has always been a certain level of danger, of *risk*, but this will be worse. And there will be strangers on the ship. Some of them will not be *quite* so tolerant of your behaviour."

Anson and Poddy exchanged glances. Anson spoke first. "What's *wrong* with our behaviour?"

"You're arguing with me now, for one," Abigail said, dryly. She was happy to discuss her decisions with her children - as long as they had privacy - but a naval officer wouldn't feel quite the same way. "And I could point to quite a few others."

She looked from one to the other. "Like it or not, you are *both* members of my crew," she added. "And I won't toss you off the ship if you don't want to go. However" - she held up a hand to keep them from interrupting - "there *will* be risks, some necessary and some…rather less necessary. If you want to leave the ship, I won't hold it against you. *Either* of you."

"Poddy is a child," Anson protested.

"I'm *fifteen*," Poddy countered. "I'll be *sixteen* in four months…"

Abigail sighed. Poddy's physical age didn't matter, as far as the RockRats and the Belter Community were concerned. What mattered was her mental maturity *and* her ability to actually *do* her job. Abigail herself had shipped out when she was *twelve*, serving under her paternal uncle. The old man had kept a sharp eye on her, but he'd also let her make a number of mistakes that had become learning experiences. It hadn't been until she became a mother herself that she'd truly understood just how much her uncle had done for her.

But Poddy isn't old enough to go to the Naval Academy, Abigail reminded herself. *The groundpounders won't understand.*

She pushed the thought aside. "Poddy has the skills and qualifications to serve on this ship, if she wishes," she said, flatly. "I do understand your concerns, but…it has to be her choice."

Anson scowled darkly, but he knew better than to argue with his mother once her mind was made up. He understood the chain of command…and that his mother wouldn't tolerate open insubordination. Abigail didn't expect him to be happy with it, just as he hadn't been happy with some of her other decisions. But she did expect him to obey - or leave the ship, if he couldn't obey. It wasn't as if he'd be leaving under a cloud.

"I'm staying," Poddy said.

"Me too," Anson said. He smiled, suddenly. "Will we have to salute you?"

"Probably," Abigail said. "And you'll have to be reasonably respectful to the military officers."

"Perhaps we'll get Stellar Star," Anson said. "Or…"

"Stellar Star doesn't exist," Poddy said, in a long-suffering tone. "And nor do those green-skinned babes from that movie you wouldn't let me watch…"

Anson coloured. "Man Jack doesn't exist either," he snapped. "That didn't stop you from covering your cabin with pictures of him!"

"Quiet," Abigail said. "Go back to your cabins and get some sleep. I'll see you both in the morning."

"I'm on watch," Anson said. He yawned, suddenly. "Aren't I?"

"I'll take the first watch," Abigail said. Anson *should* have been sleeping for the last few hours, just so he'd be refreshed for his watch. But she'd slept instead. "Steven or Carl can take the second."

"Unless they decide to jump ship," Anson said. "Mum…not everyone is going to be happy, serving under the military."

"I suppose not," Abigail said. Two of her crewers had ties to various belter independence movements. It wasn't the sort of thing that would impress the military, if they cared enough to vet the freighter's crew. But even if they did, it was unlikely they'd turn up anything incriminating. "And, like I keep saying, we don't have a choice."

She dismissed them, then walked slowly back to the bridge. Her ship felt odd, even though nothing had changed. Yet, she reminded herself. Tomorrow, they'd remove the cargo pallets and then start refitting the vessel. And then she'd be commander of a light carrier instead of a freighter.

And I'll have a target painted on my arse, she thought, as she stepped onto the bridge. *It isn't as if they're going to tear out the drive and replace it with something that can actually turn on a dime.*

Carl Rogers looked up, then nodded to the status board. Everything was green. Abigail dismissed him with a nod, picking up her datapad as he left the compartment. There were a handful of messages waiting in her inbox, including a pair of agitated demands from her client for an updated ETA. She cursed under her breath as she read the second message, knowing she couldn't reply. Her name was going to be mud in shipping circles, if the Royal Navy refused to allow her to explain what had actually happened. By the time the truth came out, her client would have slandered her to the entire community.

And he'll be convinced he's doing the right thing, Abigail told herself, crossly. The Belt practically *ran* on reputation. No one would care if someone uploaded nude photographs or videos of her to the datanet, but breaking a contract...? She'd be shunned and abhorred by all right-thinking Belters. *And the hell of it is that he'll have a point.*

She considered her options for a long moment, then dismissed it. There was no point in worrying about something outside her control. Either the news broke before the client could start smearing her or it didn't. If the former, she could explain; if the latter, she could put forward a convincing case to regain her reputation. It would just be tricky to avoid hammering an understandably-outraged client in the court of public opinion.

The hatch opened. Farris Ashburn stepped onto the bridge.

"It's late," Abigail said. "You should be sleeping."

"I wanted to tell you in person," Ashburn said. He looked ashamed. "I'm jumping ship."

Abigail looked him up and down. He had a carryall slung over one shoulder, suggesting he'd taken the time to pack before coming to the bridge. She didn't really blame him for that, not when she knew there were captains who'd frogmarch a deserter to the airlock and kick him off the ship. *Abigail* wouldn't do that, not unless she was firing a crewman, but Ashburn had no way of knowing it. He hadn't served with her for very long.

"I'm sorry you feel that way," she said. "May I ask why?"

"I'm not remotely comfortable serving under the military," Ashburn said. "And I would prefer not to discuss it further."

Abigail nodded, slowly. Privacy was practically a holy concept in the belt. Too many of the original settlers had fled an Earth that had grown less and less private until the government, corporations and even ordinary civilians could find out almost *anything* about *anyone* just by exploring the datanet. And besides, too many Belters shared cramped quarters. What little fragments of privacy they had were jealously guarded. Whatever Ashburn's reasons, she had no right to pry into them. He was leaving her crew, after all.

"You'll be going into lockdown," she pointed out. She'd told them that, hadn't she? Yes, she had. And she wouldn't let Ashburn change his mind, not now. A man who had declared his intention to leave could no longer be considered reliable. "And after that…"

She lifted her datapad and brought up Ashburn's file. It was simple enough, merely recording his time on four separate freighters. None of his commanding officers had had *much* to say about him, although they'd vouched for his competency. Abigail had thought that that wasn't actually a *bad* thing. The crewers who were remembered were either extremely good or so unspeakably bad that they posthumously won the Darwin Award.

"I don't have any complaints about you," she said. She *could* have bitched about him jumping ship, but it wouldn't be particularly fair. He'd been given the opportunity to leave and he'd taken it. It wasn't as if he'd deserted at short notice. "I'll give you a reference, but" - she waved a hand at the bulkhead - "it may be a while before anyone sees it. Or hears from me, if they want to check."

"I understand," Ashburn said. "I think I'll head further out, anyway. They say there's good work in the Terra Nova System."

"As long as you don't mind the risk of being blown up," Abigail pointed out. The civil war on Terra Nova was heating up, again. She'd once transported a load of emigrants from Terra Nova who'd wanted to go somewhere - anywhere - else. "But I suppose the asteroids will be reasonably safe."

"I hope so," Ashburn said. "And thank you."

Abigail shrugged. "It's no trouble," she said. She nodded to the hatch. Technically, she should have walked him to the airlock, but she wasn't feeling gracious. "Watch yourself out there."

She watched him go, feeling torn. She knew better than to have a crewman who didn't want to be there, but - at the same time - she felt as though he'd deserted her. And yet, she knew she was being unfair. Farris Ashburn hadn't signed up for naval service, any more than he'd signed up to spend his whole life working under her.

And he probably won't be the only one, either, she thought. Two of her crewers were reservists, not counting herself, but the others had no obligation to stay with the ship. *How many others are going to want to leave?*

She shook her head in annoyance. There was no point in worrying about it, not now. The die was cast. In truth, it had been cast the moment the aliens had shown themselves.

"Too many other things to worry about," she muttered. "Starting with the criminals in my new crew."

CHAPTER
SIX

It was typical of the Royal Navy, Alan had often considered, that 'hurry up and wait' was practically its unofficial motto. After racing him and a number of other convicts from Colchester to the isolated - and apparently unnamed - military base, the Royal Navy hadn't shown any particular urgency about shipping him to his new post. It took five days for a shuttle flight to orbit to be arranged, then another for Alan, Bennett and Alan's new assistant to be transferred to an intersystem high-boost shuttle for the flight to Tallyman. The only advantage, as far as he could tell, was that it gave him time to read the files and think about the future.

He looked over at Bennett, sleeping in an acceleration couch, and sighed. The big man was a consummate actor, among other things. When they were in company, Bennett was polite and respectful and everything Alan might want from a junior officer; when they were alone, Bennett allowed his dislike and distrust to shine through. Alan had been tempted to make remarks about daddy issues, but it had seemed pointless. He was stuck with Bennett until the war was over or, more likely, they were both blown out of space.

It could be worse, he told himself, firmly. *I could be back at Colchester.*

Lieutenant Madison Hudson cleared her throat. "Do you want another mug of tea?"

"No, thank you," Alan said. Tea was the one thing that *wasn't* in short supply, even on a tiny intersystem shuttle. The Royal Navy practically *ran* on tea. "But feel free to get one for yourself, if you want it."

He watched his new assistant as she rose and headed for the dispenser. Lieutenant Madison Hudson - she'd told him that she preferred to be called Maddy - was young and beautiful, with curly red hair, bright green eyes and a body that reminded him, once again, that it had been too long since he'd lain with anyone. And yet, she was young enough to make him feel slightly guilty about looking. The way she practically bowed and scraped in front of Bennett and himself suggested she hadn't had a very good time in her prison. God knew where she'd been, but it probably hadn't been Colchester.

Which isn't too surprising, he thought. *A young woman probably wouldn't be sentenced to Colchester unless there was something very significant about her crimes.*

He sighed, inwardly. Maddy's career had been fairly normal for a logistics support officer - a stint in starfighter command, a desk job on Nelson Base, an assignment as personal assistant to a senior officer - until she'd been caught embezzling money from the navy's funds. It had been quite clever, according to the report. Maddy's superior had come very close to taking the fall, as he'd signed a number of financial documents without bothering to read them very closely. Indeed, it had been sheer luck that the scheme had been uncovered before Maddy had quietly left the navy, taking her ill-gotten gains with her. Maddy had been sentenced to five years in prison, three years ago. Alan was mildly surprised she'd agreed to serve in exchange for a formal pardon. She had far less time on her sentence

Her prison must have been bad, Alan told himself. A young and pretty woman behind bars would be victimised by her fellow inmates, even if the guards were too professional to take advantage of her themselves. *And she doesn't look as though she can defend herself.*

He leaned back in his chair, silently counting down the minutes to arrival. Maddy had the skills he needed, at least on paper. Once the remainder of the crew arrived - the starfighter pilots and their support staff - they could get to work. He'd have to make sure that everyone drilled as hard as possible, no matter the situation. The pilots assigned to an escort carrier would not be the cream of the crop. Chances were that most of them would not have had their contracts renewed when they finally expired.

And some of them probably have disciplinary problems, he thought, morbidly. *I'll have to knock them all into shape.*

The shuttle shivered, slightly. "Attention," the pilot's voice said. "We will be docking in twenty minutes. Please gather your luggage and prepare to disembark."

Alan rolled his eyes. It wasn't as if they were on a monorail, with only a few minutes to jump off before the doors slid closed and the train resumed its journey. He wasn't sure how long the shuttle would be docked to the converted freighter, but it would be more than long enough for them to collect all of their belongings and depart in a calm and reasonable manner. Besides, they only had one carryall each. It wasn't as if naval personnel were allowed to take more than the basics when they travelled to their latest assignments.

Bennett opened his eyes. "Twenty minutes, he said?"

"Yeah," Alan agreed, shortly. He stood and removed his carryall from the overhead compartment. "Do you have everything you need?"

"Yes, sir," Bennett said. "Maddy?"

"I have everything," Maddy said, quietly.

Another shudder ran through the shuttle as it slowed. Alan walked to the nearest porthole and peered out into interplanetary space. A freighter - a giant *Workhorse*-class freighter - was floating nearby, illuminated by powerful spotlights. Dozens of dockyard workers, some in spacesuits and others in worker bees, were swarming over the hull, slowly manoeuvring prefabricated pieces of material into place. When assembled, the entire lower half of the ship would be converted into everything a couple of starfighter squadrons needed to operate for quite some time. *Archibald Haddock* wouldn't have anything like the flexibility of a fleet carrier, he told himself, but she would suffice. He felt his heart starting to pound as they drew closer. Two weeks ago, he'd *known* he'd never serve on a starship again. Now...

The freighter was ugly, he noted. She looked like a brick, with only a handful of sensor blisters breaking the monotony of the hull. *Ark Royal*, for all her crudity, was far more elegant than *Haddock*. And yet, there was something about her that called to him. Perhaps it was just the realisation that she represented his last chance. If he screwed up now, during a war, he'd be lucky if he was *just* pitched out the airlock.

Then I better hadn't screw up, he told himself, firmly.

He turned away from the porthole as the shuttle docked and followed Maddy down to the opening hatch. It was hard not to stare at her rear, despite the loose-fitting naval overalls she wore. She was perfect...he shook his head, angrily. He couldn't allow himself to become distracted, not now. Besides, he had a sneaking suspicion that Maddy's looks had helped her convince Admiral Givens not to read the paperwork too closely. Alan had *met* Admiral Givens, seven years ago. He'd never struck Alan as particularly competent. It was a surprise that he hadn't been unceremoniously transferred to *Ark Royal* years ago.

He probably had friends in high places, Alan thought. *That's why he was allowed to retire after Maddy nearly framed him for grand larceny.*

There was, technically, a formal protocol to be followed when boarding a starship for the first time. Alan had decided not to bother, when he'd heard about the assignment. He wasn't the commanding officer, let alone an admiral. And besides, a freighter crew couldn't be expected to present arms...if they had the *room* to present arms. *Haddock* didn't have a flight deck - yet - and even when she did, it wouldn't be designed for formal receptions. He allowed Maddy to step through the hatch, then followed her. The smell struck him as soon as he was through the hatch.

He wrinkled his nose, despite himself. The air smelled of too many people in too close proximity, mingled with a faint hint of ionisation and burning. It could have been worse, he reminded himself sharply. Crewmen on long-distance voyages often lost their sense of smell after a few weeks - or, at least, they grew accustomed to the pong. He looked around, pushing the matter out of his mind. A painting of a bearded man in an old-style naval uniform had been drawn on the nearest bulkhead. The man looked to be on the verge of exploding with rage.

"Our namesake," a quiet voice said. "Captain Haddock himself."

Alan turned. A middle-aged woman was standing by the bulkhead, wearing a form-fitting shipsuit that looked to have seen better days. He studied her for a long moment, noting the dark hair, almond eyes and heavyset body...her mother or grandmother, he decided, had probably been one of the mail order brides from the security zones. They'd preferred the uncertainties of married life in space to life in the zones. Alan didn't really blame the poor women. The security zones were constantly torn apart by civil and religious conflict and women, as always, got the worst of it. A spacer's bride would have a better life than someone trapped in the zones. Women were treated with respect in space.

The woman looked back at him, her eyes cold and dispassionate. "Welcome onboard," she said. "I'm Captain Harrison, *Abigail* Harrison. I'll show you to your quarters so you can drop off your bags, then I'll give you a tour of the ship. Or what parts of it you can access at the moment, anyway."

"That would be very interesting," Alan said. He winced, inwardly. It was clear that Captain Harrison knew *something* about them. What had she been told? If she knew that Alan had been in Colchester, what did she think he'd *done*? "Thank you for your time."

Abigail eyed him for a long moment. "Follow me," she grunted. "And *don't* stick your hand into any of the open panels."

Alan looked around with interest as they walked up the corridor. Abigail hadn't been joking about the open panels. A dozen wall and ceiling panels had been removed, exposing the ship's power distribution network. Alan frowned as he realised that half the visible components were no longer original, perhaps not even from British factories. Belters were supposed to be good at getting Russian and Chinese components to mesh with their British counterparts, but he couldn't help being concerned. The original components had been significantly over-engineered. He had no way to know if their replacements lived up to the same standards.

We'd better hope, he told himself. *And check everything, twice. Better to have a blow-out here than in deep space.*

The corridors were decorated with all kinds of paintings and pictures, some clearly drawn by children while others owed their existence to more talented artists. Alan felt a stab of envy, mingled with grim amusement and regret. *Haddock* was a home as much as she was a ship, a home that was being turned into a fortress. His training told him he should order the decorations taken down, common sense insisted he should keep his mouth shut. The civilian crew wouldn't be happy if they were told to embrace military culture. If they'd wanted to follow orders without question, they would have joined the military.

They stopped outside a pair of hatches. "You and Lieutenant Bennett will be sharing this compartment," Abigail informed them, as the closest hatch hissed open. "Lieutenant Hudson has this cabin to herself, for the moment. She'll be paired up with another woman when we have a suitable candidate."

"Thank you," Maddy said, quietly.

Abigail nodded, then indicated the open hatch. "Two bunks, a wardrobe and a private washroom. Water is limited at the moment, so showers are restricted to five minutes each. Hopefully, we'll get the recyclers back online in the next few days and then we can take longer showers. There's a small terminal in the bulkhead, but I suggest you use your datapad for anything private. I can't guarantee computer security."

Bennett cleared his throat. "I presume we're still in lockdown?"

"More or less," Abigail said. "Any messages you send will be routed through the asteroid's signal buffer, so don't write anything you don't want the censors to see. We're too far from any other settlement for real-time communications, for better or worse. I haven't been told what will happen if you *do* try to break the information embargo, but I don't think it will be pleasant."

She stepped inside and opened the wardrobe. "I want all three of you in shipsuits at all times," she added. Her voice turned faintly sarcastic. "Wear your overalls over them, if you wish, but make sure your masks are easily accessible. You can't breathe outside the hull, as I'm sure you're aware. We don't *want* to suddenly have a hull breach, but the way they're buzzing around outside..."

"I thought the hull was armoured," Maddy said.

"Technically, it is," Abigail said. "But if there's an accident with a cutting torch, well..."

She shrugged. "The engineers swear blind that we'll be ready for departure in eight days," she said. Her lips quirked, as if she was making a joke. "It was ten days, two days ago. I suggest you spend the time familiarising yourselves with the ship, but stay out of their way. I don't want any accidents. My insurance won't stand it."

"Understood, Captain," Alan said. Perhaps it would be better to stay in the cabin. A datapad full of eBooks or videos would be better company than Bennett. And having a datapad would make up for the cramped compartment. There was no way Bennett and himself could dress simultaneously. "Is there anything else we ought to know?"

"Two things," Abigail said. She stepped back outside the cabin, meeting his eyes. "First, most of my crew are civilian volunteers. They might be being paid hazard rates, but they're not naval personnel in anything... even in name. Do *not* treat them as slaves. You'll find they're good at their jobs, but they're not so good at discipline."

"I have never treated *anyone* like a slave," Alan said.

"Goody," Abigail said. "Second, then. The files weren't too clear on what you actually *did* to earn yourselves a jail sentence. I have been assured that none of you pose a serious risk to my crew, but I have been given no way to judge that for myself. I have *not* shared what little I know about your pasts with my crew, just to ensure they don't allow it to affect their work - and, frankly, I'm not sure that was wise."

She kept her eyes firmly fixed on his. "I will not tolerate anything that smacks of criminal behaviour," she warned him. "From any of you - starfighter pilots as well as support crews. And if I get a single *hint* that you're going back to your old ways, you will be pitched out of the airlock. Do I make myself clear?"

"Yes," Alan said, flatly.

It was hard, so hard, not to shake his head in disbelief. He was meant to work with this woman? He didn't really blame Abigail for being concerned, not when she didn't know what he'd actually done, but it would sour their relationship completely. Perhaps he should tell her the truth. Or Maddy should tell Abigail about *her* crimes. The RockRats would enjoy the story of an over-promoted aristocratic pig being taken for a ride by someone he'd considered nothing more than arm candy. They might even side with Maddy when they found out the truth.

"Get into your shipsuits," Abigail ordered. "I'll be back in twenty minutes."

"A woman after my own heart," Bennett said, once they were inside the tiny cabin. "I like her."

Alan snorted. "She thinks you're a criminal too."

Bennett laughed. "I have ID I can show her, if necessary," he said. "You do realise she's married?"

"No," Alan said.

"Four husbands, five wives," Bennett said. "Group-marriages are not uncommon in the belt, as you know. Four of them stay in their warren, looking after the younger children, while the remaining adults go out to bring home the bacon. The older children are already moving into adulthood. Captain Harrison has two children, both serving on this ship."

Alan shrugged as he stripped off his tunic and reached for the ship-suit. It was a naval design, as ugly and uncomfortable as he remembered. Wearing it was like wearing a second skin, but he knew he'd be glad of it if there *was* a hull breach. It wouldn't provide *quite* as much protection as a normal spacesuit, yet it might just make the difference between life or death.

As long as you're close to a shelter or emergency supplies, he thought, remembering his instructor's warnings. The man had put the cadets through hell, but they'd known it was necessary. *If you're too far from either, take advantage of the last few seconds to bend over and kiss your arse goodbye.*

"Tiny shower too," Bennett said. "No room to bend over if you drop the soap."

"How fortunate," Alan said, crossly. He was getting tired of Bennett constantly poking and prodding to see what would draw a reaction. "And these beds were obviously not designed for your enormous bulk."

Bennett leered, cheerfully. "I suppose I might *just* break the upper bunk and land on your head," he said. "That *would* solve one problem rather nicely, wouldn't it?"

"Get bent," Alan said. He refused to consider the possibility. Military bunks might be small, but they were designed to take far heavier weights... weren't they? This was a civilian ship...he pushed the thought aside before it could depress him too much. "I'll be outside."

"Don't go wandering off," Bennett told him. "The Captain will not be pleased."

Alan nodded and stepped through the hatch. Maddy was waiting for him, wearing her overalls over the shipsuit. It did nothing, this time, to hide the shape of her body. Alan looked away, cursing himself. He'd just have to keep himself under control.

You can always take matters in hand, later, he told himself. *You should be used to being watched by now.*

CHAPTER SEVEN

Abigail hadn't been sure *what* to expect from the convicted criminals. The belt shunned minor criminals, to the point where they either took their own lives or shipped out somewhere no one had ever heard their name, while major criminals were simply executed and their bodies fed into the recycler. It was rare for a belter criminal to ever earn forgiveness for his crimes, if only because anything the belt considered a crime was *serious*. It *had* to involve someone getting hurt or a very good *chance* of someone getting hurt.

She allowed her gaze to flicker across them as they waited. The red-headed woman looked innocent, but Abigail had been a daughter and then a mother. She wasn't fooled by an act designed to make people overlook the actress. Men could be such fools, at times. A woman who looked weak and helpless would spark either protective or predatory instincts, rather than warning the men to watch their backs. An entire ring of thugs had been busted a year or two ago, on Ceres, for using young women as Judas Goats. They'd picked up wealthy men and lured them into their apartments, where they'd been robbed and drugged by the male thieves. The redhead might not be physically dangerous, but that meant nothing. Abigail would keep an eye on her anyway.

The two men were odder. Lieutenant Bennett was rough and crude - Abigail had no trouble recognising a very dangerous man - but there was something about him that made her feel safe. *That* puzzled her, more than she cared to admit. She'd had worse vibes - far worse vibes - from men who hadn't looked anything like as dangerous. But then, the belt rarely had time for politeness. It was considered better to say what you meant and deal with the consequences rather than hide behind half-truths and passive-aggressive verbal conflict.

And Commander Campbell was...odder. Clearly an educated man, but...weighed down by guilt. Guilt for what, exactly? Abigail cursed, again, whoever it was who'd refused to forward the uncensored files to Tallyman. She wanted - she *needed* - to know what he'd done. There was something about Campbell - she supposed she'd better get used to thinking of him as *Alan*, if he was to be her XO - that bothered her. He didn't have the same...*presence*...as Bennett, yet there was a sense of violence below the surface. What the hell had he done?

Better find a way to ask him, she told herself. *And hope to hell he tells the truth.*

"As you can see, the entire upper section has been converted into a maze of living quarters, control centres and a couple of training suites," she said, as she led them through the corridors. They weren't seeing the ship at her best, but it couldn't be helped. "There are two sections set aside for the pilots, with twelve bunks in each one. I assume that will be suitable?"

"It won't be any worse than the quarters on a fleet carrier," Alan said. His voice held a faint accent that reminded Abigail of one of her distant relatives. "Do you have an exercise compartment?"

"And a gaming room," Abigail said. "One of my kids is very fond of *Sonic the Hedgehog* - he downloaded copies of everything from the classical versions to the fifth or sixth VR reboot. You're welcome to play the games, if you have time."

"Maybe after I've brushed up on starfighter flying," Alan said. He sounded oddly amused by her words. "Is there enough space for the support crews?"

"Aye," Abigail said. They stopped outside one of the sleeping quarters. Abigail opened the hatch, allowing them to look inside. "We're sleeping six to a compartment here - again, it's not ideal, but it's the best we can do."

"I've been in worse places," Alan said.

"Try sleeping in a foxhole sometime, sir," Bennett told him. "It's uncomfortable as *fuck*."

Abigail glanced at him, puzzled. *Lieutenant* Bennett was outranked by Commander Campbell, but…Bennett didn't *act* like a naval officer. His file had been curiously sparse, too sparse. She wondered, suddenly, if he'd been in the army instead. Or maybe he'd been in a deniable unit and very little had actually been committed to the datafiles. There was no way to know, short of trying to talk him into revealing his past. And she had a feeling that Bennett, for all of his crudeness, actually kept himself under very tight control.

"There are two showers at the rear of each compartment," Abigail said, dismissing the mystery. She could think about it later. "By the time the crew arrive, the water restrictions should have been lifted. If not…" - she shrugged - "…they'll just have to get used to it."

She led them out the hatch and down the corridor. "There's no such thing as a secondary bridge on a freighter, so we put the CIC in here," she explained, as she opened another hatch. "It's very makeshift, but it should do."

"I hope so," Alan said.

Abigail tried to see it through his eyes. A pair of consoles and chairs, a holographic projector…she'd seen footage of life onboard a fleet carrier. *Their* Combat Information Centres were immense, with enough space for a couple of dozen staffers. *Haddock* barely had room for two or three people, unless they were very good friends. She glanced at Maddy, trailing behind the men. Was she close to either of them? Or was this their first meeting? It was impossible to be sure.

"We built as much redundancy as we could into the network," she told them. "But this ship is still very fragile. A direct hit will be enough to put us out of the battle."

"Blow us into atoms, you mean," Alan said. He sat down in one of the chairs and looked around. "Have you tested the systems?"

"We did the basics," Abigail said. "But actual drills and live-fire exercises…? No."

"Something to do then, as soon as we're ready," Alan said. "The sooner we figure out the problems, the sooner we can fix them."

"Yes, sir," Maddy said.

Abigail kept her thoughts to herself as they walked through the rest of the upper decks, pausing briefly to introduce the newcomers to her crew.

Sickbay was a joke, compared to a military facility; there was no trained doctor, merely an autodoc. Abigail and several of her crew had some medical training, but not enough to cope with more than a handful of basic injuries. The life support units were over-engineered, yet they were still going to be pushed to the limit. And Engineering was in complete disarray.

"We think we've worked out most of the kinks," she said, as they headed back to the CIC. "But we have no way to be sure."

"We'll find out when we go to work," Alan assured her. "How many spare parts are we carrying?"

"Not as many as I'd like," Abigail admitted. "We're on the list for whatever's available, but…"

She gritted her teeth in frustration. On one hand, the Royal Navy had given her a blank cheque; on the other, there just weren't enough supplies to go around. The peacetime navy simply hadn't built up the stockpiles it would need to fight a major war. She hoped *some* barmy bureaucrat was going to be penalised for *that* particular balls-up. It would take time, perhaps too much time, to kick-start production to meet wartime requirements. Until then, the Royal Navy was going to be facing all kinds of shortfalls.

"Maybe we can requisition a couple of extra starfighters," Alan said. "We could turn them into hangar queens if necessary."

"And you could fly one yourself, sir," Bennett offered. "We might need you out there."

"I haven't flown a starfighter for years," Alan pointed out. "I'm not even sure what model starfighters we'll be getting."

"Better to be out there shooting back," Bennett said. "Maddy can handle starfighter operations if necessary."

Abigail cleared her throat. "I trust you to handle such matters yourself," she said, as they walked into the cramped CIC. "You have authorisation to use the shipboard datanet, but be careful. Make sure you clear anything you want to upload with the engineers first."

Bennett gave her an odd look. "Is the system *that* fragile, Captain?"

"Right now, yeah," Abigail said. "They tore out one of our two datacores and replaced it with an updated version, then spent a day rewriting the programming to convince the newer datacore to talk to the *older* datacore. I've been assured that the command and control system remains intact - and isolated - but I'm not actually sure. Given time, the AIs will bridge the gap permanently..."

She sighed. AI had never *quite* lived up to its promise, unless one believed that the AIs actually *were* intelligent and chose to hide it. Talking to an AI was like talking to a child who never actually learnt from experience, let alone grew up. Learning systems never seemed to make the jump into genuine intelligence. The military was reluctant to allow AIs anywhere near its vessels, pointing out the dangers involved. She was tempted, for once, to think that the military might have a point.

"Again, we'll work on it," Alan said. He looked down at the darkened console. "If you don't mind, we'll start at once."

Abigail's lips twitched. She couldn't complain about his work ethic, she supposed, even though he'd only arrived a couple of hours ago. But she would have urged them to have a nap, if she'd thought they'd take the advice. She had no idea if they'd slept on the shuttle or not, but it couldn't have been very comfortable.

"It is fifteen-hundred-hours now," she said, glancing at her wristcom. "I...*request*...the pleasure of your company at nineteen-hundred-hours for dinner."

She watched them, closely. Bennett showed no visible reaction, but both Alan and Maddy looked uncomfortable. What did *that* mean? No one on the ship, apart from her, knew they'd been in jail. Were they reluctant to meet the rest of the crew? Or were they feeling a little overwhelmed? Abigail could move between crowded asteroids and empty ships without a qualm, but she had a feeling jail would be a little different.

"It will be our pleasure," Alan said, finally. "We thank you."

Abigail nodded, then spun on her heel and walked out the hatch. It hissed closed behind her, cutting off the sound. She would have liked to listen to whatever was said, after she left, but she knew it was impossible. Instead, she checked her wristcom's inbox as she headed down the corridor. Their client was somewhat bemused by how the cargo pallets had arrived at Ceres, but he was relieved to receive them anyway.

It won't be long before the truth gets out, Abigail thought. The news corporations might be closely supervised on Earth, but it was a great deal harder to keep spacers from talking to one another and sharing notes. And there was no shortage of hackers ready to spread news - and rumours - through the datanet. *And then...who knows what will happen?*

She stopped outside the shuttle hatch and keyed the switch. It opened, revealing the interior of a military-grade shuttlecraft. Abigail guessed that whoever had designed the craft had either been a Royal Marine or a Belter, as the design was ruthlessly practical instead of comfortable. Anson was seated in the cockpit, his fingers dancing over the keyboard. He seemed to be having fun.

Abigail cleared her throat. "What do you make of it?"

Anson looked up and smiled. "Awesome," he said. "This baby is light-years ahead of our old piece of junk."

"It isn't as if we ever had to make planetfall," Abigail pointed out, dryly. Trying to land *Haddock* on a planetary surface would be an expensive form of suicide. "How many times did we actually *use* the shuttle?"

"Twice, at Wayland," Anson reminded her. "But those were meant to be once-offs."

He tapped the control stick. "I can put this baby down in a storm," he said. The confidence in his voice sounded unshakable. "And then land her on a dime..."

"Be very careful," Abigail warned. "You've never flown through a *real* storm, have you?"

Anson nodded, but he looked unabashed. Abigail sighed, inwardly. *She'd* handled a couple of rough landings, but otherwise she'd stayed in space when she hadn't let someone else do the flying. It was hard for a Belter to understand just how rough a planetary atmosphere could be, if one didn't take very good care. She honestly couldn't understand why immigration to outer space wasn't much higher. Unlimited space, unlimited resources, unlimited wealth...and no weather. Why would anyone choose to live on a planetary surface when they could live in space?

"I've been downloading training simulations," Anson said, after a moment. "The shuttle isn't *that* different from the standard designs. I should be able to fly it without problems. And we have everything from military-grade emergency beacons to military grade emergency kits. They even gave us some suspension drugs..."

"Very good," Abigail said. She walked into the cockpit - there was no bulkhead between the cockpit and the passenger compartment, something that puzzled her - and sat in the co-pilot's seat. "What else do you have to tell me?"

"I got a data packet from George," Anson said. "Apparently, rumours are getting out. And a number of people have noticed that we never arrived on Ceres, but our cargo *did*. We're not the only ones, it seems. There's some quite accurate speculation running around the datanet."

His face darkened. "And Cindy has apparently started dating Peppy."

"I'm sorry to hear that," Abigail said. She was torn between relief and profound sympathy for her son. Cindy was strikingly pretty, but Abigail had never considered her suitable marriage material. Too self-centred, at least by Belter standards. And probably not inclined to join a group-marriage where everyone either worked to support the family or took care of the children. "There are plenty more fish in the sea."

"*You* were married at twenty," Anson pointed out. "Dad was…what? Twenty-five?"

"Boys do tend to get married a little later than girls," Abigail pointed out. She allowed herself a smile. "I did have to have children, you know."

"I don't want to know," Anson said, quickly.

Abigail laughed, then sobered. It wasn't uncommon for children - even *grown* children - to deny the idea that their parents might have been sexual beings. Abigail knew *her* parents must have had sex at least five times - she had four siblings - but she didn't want to think about it. No doubt her parents had reproduced by using an exowomb…although they would still have had to get the eggs and sperm from *somewhere*.

She dismissed the thought in amused irritation. "Cindy's just playing the field before she settles down and gets married," she said. Personally, she doubted Cindy would *ever* settle down, but there was no way to be sure. God knew *Abigail* had done some pretty silly things in her day. "When you get back from our next cruise, you'll be a war hero."

"They won't be able to say I was a coward," Anson agreed. "But…serving on an escort carrier isn't really that heroic."

"That's what the Japanese believed, back in the Second World War," Abigail said. The briefing notes had been *very* detailed when it came to historical examples. "They didn't put any real *effort* into protecting their freighters when they sailed to and from the Japanese Home Islands. And so the American submarines sank pretty much all of the freighters..."

She shrugged. "Meanwhile, the British and Americans *protected* their freighters. Ships ran in convoys, escorted by warships. And so the shipping got through and the good guys won the war."

Except in Eastern Europe, she added, silently. She'd looked up some of the context too, just to try and determine if she was being snowballed. *One set of very bad guys was defeated by another set of slightly less bad guys.*

She snorted at the thought. The Second World War was over two hundred years in the past, a simpler time in many ways. She had very little in common with the women of that era, although she imagined she had a great deal in common with the freighter captains. And yet, it had laid the seeds for the *next* set of global conflicts, as well as the technology that had allowed humanity to finally escape its homeworld.

"I'm glad to hear we're doing something useful," Anson said. He didn't sound particularly convinced. "But it's hardly heroic."

"It's still a vital contribution," Abigail said. She would have expected the belters to understand, even if the groundpounders did not. "Could they keep those fleet carriers flying if they didn't get regular deliveries of supplies from home? Or new crewmen and pilots for those immense ships? Or...they need freighters, Anson. We're as much a part of the war effort as any warship."

She leaned forward, resting a hand on his arm. "Look, here's a suggestion. Spend some time in the starfighter training simulators. They won't be in use 24/7, so you should be able to find a time when you can have a go. See if you can pick up enough to request a transfer to the starfighter training centre. And if you can, you can put in the request when we return to Sol."

Anson looked doubtful. "Would they take me?"

"You're an experienced spacer," Abigail pointed out. *Her* children knew how to think - and operate - in three dimensions. How many groundpounders could say the same? "You have much less to unlearn."

She rose. "But wait until we get back from our first voyage," she added. "You don't want to give the navy the impression you want to desert."

"No," Anson agreed. "That *would* be awkward."

CHAPTER EIGHT

"You know," Alan muttered to Bennett, "the Royal Navy has set new records for efficiency."

"The prospect of hanging does tend to concentrate a few minds, sir," Bennett agreed, as the starfighter pilots filed into the briefing room. "Unfortunately, as a very great man put it, the prospect of hanging tends to concentrate the mind on the fact that it is about to be hanged."

Alan shot him a sidelong look. "You read *Making Money*?"

"*Going Postal*," Bennett corrected. "And yes, I read it."

Alan shook his head in wry amusement, then turned his attention back to the compartment. It was a ramshackle affair, one that would have shocked any fleet carrier commander. Thirty chairs, a single table, a simple projector...it was a far cry from the high-tech surroundings he'd been used to on *Formidable*. But it would have to do. He leaned against the bulkhead and watched, grimly, as the starfighter pilots filed into the compartment. Twenty-four men and women, eighteen to twenty-four, wearing basic blues. Perhaps it was his imagination, but there was a sloppiness about them that galled him. *He'd* never been so sloppy when *he'd* been a starfighter pilot.

But you did your own share of stupid things, his thoughts reminded him. *You're not in a position to bitch and moan about pilots who merely got drunk in the wardroom and rendered themselves unfit for duty.*

He pushed the thought away as his eyes swept the room. A handful of names and faces were familiar to him from the files - Wing Commander

Mike Whitehead and Wing Commander Marc Savage, in particular - but others were complete unknowns. They'd all have disciplinary records, though. Drunkenness, fighting in bars…in one case, even being caught in bed with a senior officer. *She* was damn lucky not to have been immediately discharged, according to the files. Her paramour had been tossed into the brig and unceremoniously booted out of the navy when their starship had returned home.

And now he'll probably be summoned back to the colours, Alan thought, sourly. *Along with everyone else who didn't go too far.*

The room settled down, quickly. Alan allowed his eyes to wander over the small crowd, wondering which of them would cause trouble. There was usually one troublemaker per squadron…hell, he'd *been* the troublemaker as a younger man. The pilot who wore a uniform that looked two sizes too big for him? Or the pilot who wore a uniform that was too tight around her chest to pass muster on a *regular* carrier? Or the one who'd been caught in a drug den when he'd gone on leave? It wasn't illegal for a civilian, but it was a court-martial offence for a military officer. Alan made a mental note to keep an eye on him. Abigail might swear blind that her crewmen were clean, but in Alan's experience there was always some smuggling going on. *And* someone would have set up an illicit still by now.

Alan cleared his throat. "Welcome onboard," he said, shortly. "I am Commander Alan Campbell, the senior military officer on *Archibald Haddock*."

He paused. Did they *know* him? It was possible they'd heard the story. He'd been told it had been extensively reported in the national news, five years ago. But then, some of the pilots would have been in secondary school at the time. They probably didn't remember his name.

All they'd have to do is look me up on the datanet, he thought, sourly. He had no idea how many people were called Alan Campbell, but it was unlikely that many of them had served in the Royal Navy. *And who knows what they'd think if they knew the truth?*

"I won't waste your time with pleasant speeches," he added. "You were assigned to this vessel because you're screw-ups. You have disciplinary records longer than my arm."

"Longer than my *dick*," Flight Lieutenant Shawn Greene catcalled. "It's *big*."

"How lucky for you," Alan said, as pleasantly as he could. "And if you interrupt me again, I'll cut it off."

A low ripple of amusement ran around the compartment. Alan ignored it.

"I don't think any of you would have gotten through your review hearing, if you lasted long enough to face one," he told them. "And you know what? I don't care. You've all heard the news. We are at war - and standards have been lowered, sharply, to ensure that the navy's manpower requirements are met. If you do well, on *Haddock*, your records will be scrubbed clean. Fuck up and there's a very good chance you won't live long enough to be dishonourably discharged.

"I don't care what you did before you reported to me. I don't care about the warnings your former commanders wrote into your files. I don't give a damn what you did when you went on leave. All I care about is getting this ship up and out into the fight. Do well and we'll get along fine. Do poorly and you'll find me the worst nightmare you'll ever have to face. There won't be a second warning."

He paused, giving his words a moment to sink in. The Royal Navy had always tolerated a certain degree of immature behaviour from its starfighter pilots, knowing that the odds of any of them surviving a combat mission were terrifyingly low. Alan looked back on his past record and cringed, inwardly. He couldn't blame his pilots for their stupidity when he'd been just as stupid himself. And yet, an escort carrier simply didn't have the space to tolerate foolishness. He was damned if he was putting up with it.

"This is war," he said. "We're going to be spending much of our time drilling. When you're not drilling, you'll be in your bunks. Don't expect any downtime for the next few weeks. By the time we actually see combat, I want us to be ready for it.

"There will be no alcohol, no drugs, no immersive VR sims…nothing that could impair your performance. I don't have the manpower to tolerate any of you taking the day off because you have a hangover. Do *not* defy me on this unless you want to be tossed out the nearest airlock. This is war. You will receive absolutely no sympathy whatsoever if you run to the nearest admiral and start bitching about not being able to drink. I'll be inspecting your quarters later. I *suggest* that you ship any bottles of rotgut you might have brought with you back home before I find them. They'll be poured into the shitter if I do."

He sighed, inwardly. There *would* be a bottle or two, of course. *Someone* would have obtained a cheap bottle of shipboard rotgut, or splashed out half a month's wages on Scotch or Vulcan Ale. He wouldn't make any friends, either, when he confiscated the alcohol. But it couldn't be helped. He simply didn't have the manpower to cover up a hangover, even if he'd *wanted* to. Hard questions would be asked about why one of his pilots wasn't flying.

And someone will take a look at our statistics, he thought, sourly. The Admiralty had been demanding regular reports as the refit progressed, apparently so they could decide if they should start the next set of conversions. *There's always some jumped-up beancounter eager to prove he isn't a complete waste of space.*

"Two other points to go over, then," he told them. "First, the captain and most of the crew are civilians, rather than military. Don't expect them to salute when they meet you or to honour the finer points of military etiquette. That said, their ranks are to be *treated* as military ranks for the duration of the conflict and you are to show them proper respect. The captain may not be a military officer, but she's been working in space longer than any of you have been alive. Do *not* dismiss them as useless."

He kept his face impassive. Some of the pilots would understand, he was sure, but others wouldn't. They'd absorbed a general contempt for civilians - for those who couldn't or wouldn't put their lives on the line - during basic training. And he had no idea how many of them were mature enough to understand that a merchant spacer would have more experience than themselves. Starfighter pilots were used to thinking of themselves as the best. They wouldn't *want* to take orders from a civilian.

"Second, most of the crewers come from the asteroid belt, where things are different," he added. "They have a different culture, so don't assume that you can treat them like crewmen on a fleet carrier. This ship is too small for you to have a brief affair and then end it without repercussions. In particular, two of the crewmen are very young. Be careful who you try to lure into bed. It would probably be better to stay celibate while you're on this ship."

"Ouch," Greene said.

Alan shrugged. It wasn't technically illegal for starfighter pilots to chase crewmen on fleet carriers, where the pilot and the crewman were in different chains of command. And no one under eighteen would serve on a fleet carrier. It was a different story on a belter ship. He had no idea how Abigail would react to a starfighter pilot trying to seduce her daughter and he didn't want to find out. Starfighter pilots were alarmingly good at letting their dicks get them in trouble.

"There will be shore leave, at some point," Alan assured them, dryly. Sin City wasn't *that* far away. "And I'm sure *some* of you brought wank material with you."

He paused as a faint titter ran around the compartment. "I expect you all to act like adults, even if half of you *are* overgrown children. This is war. We don't have *time* to deal with minor problems. I expect complete professionalism when you're on duty - which will be most of the time. And I do *not* expect anything that happens off-duty to affect your performance. If it does, I'll make damn sure you'll regret it.

"Wing Commanders, remain behind. Everyone else, report to the starfighter launch tubes at fourteen-hundred-hours. I'll be inspecting your quarters before then, so you should have *just* enough time to get rid of anything illicit before I see it. Any questions?"

Greene stuck up a hand. "What is the price of sliced ham, per portion?"

"*Relevant* questions," Alan clarified. He supposed he should have seen that coming. The joke was older than interplanetary spaceflight. "No? Dismissed!"

He watched as the pilots rose and headed through the hatch. Some of them were standing upright, walking like men who knew who and what they were; others looked as if they could barely be bothered walking in a straight line. They wouldn't have long to shape up either, not when the ship was due to depart in four days. Ideally, Alan would have busted the worst of the troublemakers out of the squadrons - perhaps sending them to other starships so they'd have a chance to shape up - but that wasn't an option. The starfighter pilots he'd been sent had been on their last chance, before the war began. None of them would have been allowed to remain in the navy if the navy hadn't been so desperate for trained manpower.

At least they weren't in jail, he reminded himself, dryly.

"Take a seat," he ordered the Wing Commanders. He glanced back at Bennett, then shrugged. "Do you have any concerns you want to raise?"

"Hundreds," Wing Commander Mike Whitehead said. "I assume it would be pointless?"

Alan had to smile, sourly. "If you want to kick half of the pilots off the ship, then yes," he said. Whitehead had a bit of a reputation as a worry-wart, an odd trait in a squadron commander. He even *looked* like a weak-chinned milksop, the kind of person who'd never be allowed to serve on a recruiting poster. But then, it had taken him time to climb the ladder. His stats simply weren't very good. "Do you have any others?"

"They're a fine group of men," Wing Commander Marc Savage said. "They might be rowdy, sir, but they'll do their damned jobs."

"Glad to hear it," Alan said. Savage was competent - *that* wasn't in doubt - but his disciplinary record was poor. He'd gone up and down the ranks as many times as a whore's knickers. If his stats hadn't been so good he would probably have been discharged long ago. "That said, I wasn't kidding about no drink or drugs. Make sure your pilots understand it."

"They're only human," Savage pointed out. "A man who won't drink won't fight."

Alan looked back at him, evenly. Savage had a certain rough charisma, the kind of man who'd be *happy* in a fight and sullenly resentful out of it. Maybe not the sort of guy the navy would want to put on a recruitment poster either, but someone the navy would find useful as long as his violent streak was pointed in the right direction. They tended to cause problems on shore leave because they were bored.

"And a drunkard on deck risks the lives of his fellow crewmen," he said. "I expect you to make it clear that there will consequences for anything of the sort."

"Better shut down the still," Whitehead said. "*Someone* will be making rotgut, sir."

"I know," Alan said. "And when we catch them, they'll wish they'd never been born."

"They're civilians, sir," Savage said. "I don't think we can take them round the back and give them a beasting."

Alan shrugged. Abigail had assured him that her crewers wouldn't start brewing alcohol for themselves. That left the military personnel. He'd already read the support staff the Riot Act, but Whitehead was probably right. *Someone* would start fermenting alcohol for themselves pretty soon. It was an old tradition, one that senior officers normally chose to ignore as long as it didn't impair performance. But *Haddock's* crew wasn't large enough to compensate for a crewman who'd managed to impair his performance.

"We'll see," he said. "Any other concerns?"

"I dare say some will manifest when we start drilling in earnest," Whitehead said. Beside him, Savage nodded in agreement. "They know what they're doing, but they also have problems."

"And there's a war on," Savage said. He sounded oddly cheerful. "The prospect of getting out there, of getting stuck into the enemy...it'll put fire in their bellies."

Alan shrugged. There had been disputes between America and China - and scrabbles over a handful of newly-discovered systems and tramlines - but the Great Powers had worked hard to avoid a general war. The Royal Navy's starfighter pilots hadn't seen action, real action, outside a handful of exercises and simulated drills. Now...now there actually *was* a war to fight. They'd soon find out just how effective their drills had actually *been*.

"We shall see," he said. He glanced at his wristcom, then rose. "We'll go check the quarters now, I think."

"But dawdle along the way," Savage said.

Alan shot him a sidelong glance. "I hope you haven't brought anything I'd have to throw out," he said. "You are meant to set a good example."

Bennett followed them as they walked out of the room, his presence a silent reminder that Alan was under constant supervision. Alan tried to forget him as they made their way down the corridor and into the first set of quarters, where six pilots were waiting for them. Bags were resting on bunks, already open. A sealed box, marked for transfer to Tallyman, rested on the floor. Alan nodded in approval, then turned a blind eye. Hopefully, the pilots wouldn't be foolish enough not to actually send the box off the ship. He couldn't turn a blind eye to *that*.

The pilots didn't *have* much, not when space was so tight. Alan inspected their bags anyway, noting the uniformity. The navy had issued them with everything from basic uniforms and overalls to underwear and medical supplies. Alan made a mental note to check that everyone's medical records were up to date - *Haddock* didn't have a proper sickbay, with a doctor who'd force the crew to undergo regular checks - as he moved from bag to bag. The pilots had definitely done a good job of removing anything illicit.

Unless they didn't have anything illicit in the first place, he thought. *But that's about as likely as me passing SAS Selection.*

"Very good," he said, when he'd finished. The only item that had been remotely out of place was a pair of lacy panties, owned by Greene. Alan had been careful not to ask. He was pretty sure he didn't want to know. "And now you can all relax until we start the first set of exercises."

Bennett nudged him as they left the compartment. "Men and women sleeping together?"

"They're not men and women," Whitehead said. "They're starfighter pilots."

Savage put on a mock-falsetto. "Wing Commander, is it alright to sleep with a fellow pilot? Why yes, yes it is…except you young pilots don't want to *sleep*."

"No, they don't," Alan said. He wasn't too concerned. Mixed wardrooms were a fact of naval life. And besides, it was against regulations for starfighter pilots to sleep together…at least when their fellows might catch them. Anyone who wanted to have an illicit affair would be better off waiting until they could go on shore leave. "It should be fine."

Bennett didn't look impressed. "And when it isn't?"

"Then we deal with it," Alan said. The army did *not* have mixed barracks. It was actually quite rare for women to serve in the combat arms. "They're grown men and women."

"They're starfighter pilots," Whitehead said.

"They'll be fine once we actually start drilling," Savage said. "And we'll start doing *that* in an hour."

CHAPTER
NINE

"Our orders seem to keep changing," Abigail said. She sat in her cabin, reclining on the bed while Alan sat on the single chair. "Yesterday, we were going to Picard; today, we're going to New Russia."

"The diplomats are trying to smooth out the politics, now the entire world knows what's happening," Alan said. He took a sip of his tea. "The Great Powers have never had to work together before."

Abigail nodded. The news had leaked three days ago - followed rapidly by a formal announcement - and, so far, the groundpounders had confirmed every negative stereotype the belters held about them. Riots in the streets, panic-buying...anyone would think that a moon-sized starship had suddenly materialised in the night sky. The more thoughtful commenters had pointed out that the aliens were still dozens of light years away, but the effect had been undermined by a couple of smartasses on the datanet pointing out what the time delay actually *meant*. It was quite possible that the aliens were closer than they knew.

Not that the belt is doing much better, she conceded, ruefully. Entire *settlements* had gone dark, trying to hide from prowling alien starships. *We thought we might have to fight the groundpounders one day. Instead, we're allied with them against a far greater foe.*

"We're due to depart in two days," she said. "Or has our departure date been put back again?"

"I'm planning on the assumption that we will be leaving on schedule," Alan said. "We might be delayed, again, but..."

He shrugged. Abigail wondered how he could be so calm. On one hand, she was accustomed to schedule slips; on the other, *these* delays were caused by some idiot groundpounder who apparently thought he could move starships around like pieces on a chessboard. It was maddening to realise that her authority had been expanded in some ways, but circumscribed in others. *And* that she had to answer to a bureaucracy. She'd had to write more reports, over the last couple of weeks, than she'd had to write in the last ten *years* of her captaincy. It was frustrating as hell to know that *some* requests would be met without question, but others would require detailed requests before some timeserver stamped APPROVED on them.

She met his eyes. "How *do* you handle it?"

"The delays?" Alan considered her question for a long moment. "They're part of military life, really. You get used to them."

"It isn't very efficient," Abigail pointed out, dryly. "I'd be in deep shit if *I* was that inefficient."

"We're not *quite* at the bottom of the supply chain, but we're *almost* there," Alan said. "I'm not sure if we're above or below *Ark Royal*. They'll be more concerned with getting the fleet carriers and their escorts ready for action than us."

"Ouch," Abigail said. She leaned forward. "And the politics? Was there any update?"

"Nothing, really," Alan said. "On one hand, we're all one big happy family; on the other, that family is scrabbling like…a scrabbling family. We're supposed to be allies with the other spacefaring powers, but no one has managed to sort out a chain of command yet. Which is awkward, as we'll be heading to New Russia unless someone changes our orders yet again."

Abigail nodded, slowly. The naval beancounters didn't seem to believe that *she* deserved detailed updates, but she was an old hand at reading between the lines. New Russia was the largest human colony between Vera Cruz and Earth, the logical place for the Multinational Fleet to assemble. The aliens would have to punch their way through New Russia if they wanted to drive on Earth…assuming, of course, that they knew anything about the human sphere's astrography. There was no way to be sure what they knew - or didn't know. All the reports agreed that they *could* have captured navigation charts on Vera Cruz, but no one knew if they *had*.

And some talking head was screaming about information security on the datanet, she thought, remembering the updates her family had forwarded to her. *They'll make life harder for everyone else, now they're locking the stable doors after the horse has bolted.*

She leaned back on the bed and picked up her mug. It was empty.

"What do you think will happen?" She asked, as she started to search for something else to drink. "I mean…who'll be in command?"

"I think they won't care that much about a lowly escort carrier," Alan said, thoughtfully. "A fleet carrier? Sure, they'd care about a fleet carrier. But us? I don't know."

"A fleet *has* to have an unquestioned chain of command," Abigail said. Her fingers found the bottle she was searching for and pulled it out. "Pass over your mug. I think you need something a little stronger."

Alan looked doubtful. "I made my pilots send their alcohol back to the asteroid," he said. "I really shouldn't be drinking…"

"You're off-duty," Abigail reminded him. "Please. I insist."

She kept her face impassive as he wrestled with his conscience. She'd looked him up in the shipboard records, but found nothing. Whatever Alan had done hadn't been considered important enough to add to the onboard encyclopaedia. She was reluctant to try to ask through the datanet, if only because all messages and search requests still went through the censors on the asteroid. *Someone* might object to her trying to find out what her XO had actually done to get himself thrown in jail.

And I need to know before we leave, she told herself. Normally, she would have respected someone's privacy, but matters were far from normal. *Even if it does mean trying to get him drunk enough to loosen his tongue.*

Alan surrendered and held out his mug. Abigail splashed a generous helping into his mug, then filled her own. Her alcohol tolerance was pretty high - she'd had all kinds of minor improvements spliced into her genome - but she reminded herself to be careful anyway. She was too old to go to a bar, get extremely drunk and wake up the following morning in a stranger's bed. Her parents hadn't been particularly sympathetic when she'd been nursing hangovers either.

"Cheers," Alan said. He took a swig - and choked. "What the hell is this stuff? Paint stripper?"

"Genuine Firewater, from Ceres," Abigail said. "I was told that naval types could hold their beer."

"This isn't beer," Alan said. "This is…this is…"

He took another swig. "I suppose it grows on you."

"It does," Abigail agreed. "You just have to drink enough of it."

She took a sip herself, wincing slightly as it burned her throat. No one bought Firewater for the taste. Back when she'd been young, it had been considered the height of manliness to drink a whole bottle without pausing to take a breath. In hindsight, they'd all been very lucky not to die of alcohol poisoning. Or be shunned for putting everyone else in danger. Belters didn't care if someone drank themselves silly every night, but they'd take immediate steps if the drunkard tried to pilot a shuttlecraft while drunk.

We were silly bastards and bitches back then, she thought, ruefully. *Out on leave, away from our parents and commanders…we wanted fun and we didn't care about the price.*

She watched Alan drink, torn between amusement and a peculiar kind of guilt. Alan had been cooling his heels in jail, not sunning himself on a beach. The Firewater was probably the first alcohol he'd had for five years, perhaps longer. And he was gulping it down as though it truly *was* water. It wouldn't be long before he was completely blotto.

He isn't going to thank me for this, she told herself. *The hangover alone will feel like an elephant stamping on his skull.*

She told herself, firmly, that it was necessary. She *needed* to know what he'd done. And yet…she kicked herself, mentally. She was the commanding officer of a starship, not some random stranger. Duty came before anything else, even morality. If she was prepared to pass judgment on a member of her crew, she was sure as hell prepared to get someone drunk so she could get some answers. And yet…

"I think you've had enough," she said, as she filled his mug again. "I drank too much when I was a young woman."

"So did I," Alan said, woozily. "I smuggled two bottles of beer into the dorm when I was in school. The headmaster found out, too late. We'd already drunk the beer."

"Oh dear," Abigail said. She felt her lips thinning in disapproval. How old had Alan been when he'd smuggled beer into his school? Groundpounders kept children in school until they were sixteen, at least. *They* didn't seem to understand the value of a practical education. Or the importance of allowing a child to grow up in a house filled with love. "I hope you didn't do it when you were older."

"I feel like a heel," Alan said. His voice steadied, just for a second. "I tell my pilots not to pull the dumb shit *I* pulled when I was a pilot. Do you have any idea how much dumb shit I pulled when I was a pilot?"

"I pulled a lot of dumb shit when I was a crewwoman," Abigail said. She wanted to encourage him to talk. "I was lucky my uncle didn't just throw me out of the airlock. If I hadn't been family…"

"Family," Alan said. "You can't trust family, you know."

Abigail frowned. "They're all I can trust," she said. "Who *else* would I trust?"

"That's what I thought," Alan said. He swallowed the rest of his drink, then coughed so violently that she thought he was going to throw up. "Family. Who can you trust, but family? And then the bitch cheated on me."

"The bitch?"

"My wife," Alan said. He put the mug down. "She *cheated* on me."

Abigail studied him for a long moment. She'd heard of the *concept* of adultery, but it wasn't something the belt took particularly seriously. Group-marriages were the norm, after all. She wouldn't fault her husbands or wives if they wanted to have a fling outside the group, or if they wanted to bring in someone new. It wasn't as if she could be with her partners 24/7…

"There I was, working my butt off to ensure a stable income for her and the kids, while she was fucking the neighbour! That arsehole was a friend, I thought. Who knew he was bonking my wife? I didn't know…"

The words came tumbling out. "I thought she loved me. I thought she supported my career. And then I walk in on her being fucked by the fucker…by that fucker Slater. And…and I killed her."

Abigail recoiled in shock. She knew that *some* group-marriages had broken down spectacularly, normally because some of the partners were too immature to make the relationship work, but she'd never heard of one that ended in murder. It was horrific! The mere thought was disgusting. She'd had disagreements with her partners - everyone had - but she would never kill them. The worst that could happen was an acrimonious division of the family's wealth and permanent separation.

They put a murderer on my ship, she thought, numbly. *And not just any murderer either.*

She would have been happier, she thought, if Alan had murdered a random stranger. Or perhaps not...she could see the navy's logic, even if she didn't like it. Alan had killed once, under conditions that were unlikely to reoccur. But to her, Alan had committed an unspeakable betrayal. He'd turned against his own family.

And his wife's adultery does not justify her death, Abigail thought. *Their kids grew up without either of their parents.*

Perhaps it was different for groundpounders, her mind suggested. Groundpounders were immature children, lacking the maturity and common sense of the asteroid belt. Alan might have every right to think that *he*, not his wife, had been betrayed. But it still wasn't anything like enough to excuse murder. The groundpounders had clearly agreed. Alan *had* been in jail, after all. He'd been looking at another five years in custody before his eventual release.

She listened as the drunken words came bubbling out, feeling sick. She'd wanted to know, hadn't she? And now she *did* know. What had the other convicts done? Did she want to know, now?

And he wouldn't have had anything alcoholic for years, she reminded herself, sharply. *I probably gave him far too much to drink.*

She dug into her emergency kit and found a sober-up. "Here," she said. She jabbed a finger at the washroom hatch. "You can use this in there."

Alan eyed her for a long moment, then took the tab and rose, stumbling as he walked into the bathroom. Abigail allowed herself a sigh of relief, even though she knew she'd probably have to clean up the mess afterwards. Thankfully, Alan didn't seem to be so far gone that he'd need help to use the injector tab, then keep his head pointed in the right direction as he threw up. Abigail would have felt sorry for him - she'd used enough sober-ups to know she'd prefer a hangover - if she hadn't known what he'd done. He'd murdered his wife...

You still have to work with him, she thought. *And now...*

She sighed. She'd needed to know. But now she'd have to pay the price for her curiosity.

———

Alan felt his legs tremble as he forced himself back to his feet. His mouth tasted awful, worse than the time the matron had washed his mouth out with soap for swearing at a particularly unpleasant teacher. The old crone had been a horror, the kind of person who should never be allowed authority over *anyone*. He'd been privately delighted when she'd died, a year after he'd left the school. The Old Boys Club had joked that the only reason anyone had attended her funeral had been to make sure she was actually dead...

He turned on the water and washed his mouth thoroughly, spitting out the water into the toilet. He'd drunk...something...and he'd gotten drunk. Abigail had gotten him drunk and then...and then what? His mind wasn't quite clear. The sober-up had chased all the alcohol out of his system, at the cost of making him feel thoroughly unwell. A wave of guilt and self-recrimination overwhelmed him. He'd told the pilots, time and time again, that they were not to even *think* about touching alcohol. And now he'd managed to get drunk.

"Fuck," he said. His mouth still tasted awful. Firewater? Someone had probably relabelled a bottle of bleach or hull cleanser or...something. His thoughts were still tangled. What the hell had he been doing? "Fuck it!"

He turned and stumbled back into the tiny cabin. Abigail was sitting on the bed, fully dressed. He supposed that was a relief, at least. There would be no embarrassed breakfasts or embarrassed screaming, not like he'd endured as a young pilot. He'd thought his hard drinking days were over after he'd been promoted out of his cockpit. A CAG might outrank his subordinates, but he wasn't allowed anything like as much leeway. It didn't seem fair, somehow.

"You murdered your wife," Abigail said, flatly.

Alan stared back at her, too woozy to be angry. The sober-up might have spared him a hangover - and the embarrassment of being revealed as a hypocrite - but it hadn't made him feel better. Of course not. *That* would have been too easy. A moment later, the underlying meaning of her words dawned on him. She knew what he'd done. And *that* meant he'd told her...

He took a breath. The air tasted awful too. "I know what I did."

"Really," Abigail said. "You left your children without their parents..."

"I know what I did," Alan repeated, sharply. His head started to throb the moment he raised his voice. "I have had plenty of time to regret it."

"All the regret in the world will not bring her back," Abigail said. "If you'd lived in the belt, you would have been executed for your crime..."

A dozen answers ran through Alan's head. He said nothing.

"Fuck it," Abigail said. She jerked a hand at the hatch. "Get out."

Alan looked down at his shirt - now stained - and then did as he was told. Abigail hated him now...so what? He'd always known their working relationship would be a little strained. They would just have to be professional about it. He stepped outside and leaned against the bulkhead, silently grateful that it was shipboard night. One very definite advantage of serving on an escort carrier was that there were times when most of the crew were sleeping. A fleet carrier operated 24/7.

That'll have to change, he told himself. *We can't afford to be caught with our pants down.*

He sighed. There was no way to hide the fact he'd fucked up. Allowing himself to get drunk had been foolish. And he hadn't realised the danger until it had been too late. He was a lightweight now. One sniff of the barmaid's apron and his mouth had run away with him.

It was a little more than a sniff, he thought. *I drank...*

He groaned. Not being sure of how much he'd actually drunk was *not* a good sign.

Shaking his head, he stumbled down the corridor. He needed something to eat before he went back to his bunk. A sandwich, perhaps. Or even a ration bar. He wasn't fussy.

And pray that Bennett never finds out about this, he thought, crossly. *That would really put the cat amongst the pigeons.*

CHAPTER
TEN

"They look as though they're drunk," Poddy said. She jabbed a finger at the newly-installed display. "Mum?"

Abigail gave her a sharp look, then cursed herself under her breath. Poddy didn't know...of course she didn't know. She'd simply looked at what passed for a starfighter formation and made a caustic remark. Abigail made a silent promise to do something to make it up to Poddy, later. The poor girl didn't deserve a fright.

I got someone drunk because I wanted to know what he was hiding, she reminded herself, crossly. *And what does that make me?*

"It's deliberate," Anson said. If he'd picked up on the sudden tension, he said nothing. "They don't fly in predictable formations because they'd make themselves easy targets."

Abigail nodded, slowly. There was no such thing as an orderly formation in space, not outside the handful of military displays. Better to keep a wide gap between expensive starships than risk a collision. Not that accidental collisions were *that* common, she had to admit. The odds of accidentally ramming another starship were only marginally higher than the odds of flying through an asteroid field and hitting one of the asteroids. She'd always laughed when she'd seen groundpounder depictions of the asteroid belt. The asteroids had been so tightly clustered together that a starfighter could barely fit through the gaps.

Instead of being so far apart that you could fly every starship in the human sphere through the gap and still have room to spare, she thought, wryly. *Anyone who hits an asteroid is either blind or trying to scam the insurance company.*

"It still *looks* bad," Poddy said. She glanced at her mother. "I'd be in trouble if I flew like that."

"You're not trying to dodge incoming fire," Abigail pointed out. "And if you tried to fly *Archie* like a starfighter, you'd probably rip the ship apart."

She broke off as Poddy's console chimed. "What's that?"

"An important message from the Admiralty," Poddy said. "It's being automatically forwarded to the XO."

"Oh, goody," Abigail said. She keyed her console, bringing up the latest set of readiness reports. "I..."

Her console bleeped. "What now?"

"Captain, we have finally received our official orders," Alan said. His voice was very steady, very calm. If she hadn't *known* he'd been drunk last night, thanks to her, she would never have believed it. "Please could you join me down here to discuss them?"

"As you wish," Abigail said. She rose. "Anson, you have the bridge."

The CIC was as cramped as always, with Alan, his three subordinates and his shadow seated in uncomfortably small chairs. Maddy made her way out of the compartment as Abigail entered, leaving her alone with the men. Abigail didn't really blame her. The compartment was uncomfortably small with four big men, let alone Maddy and Abigail herself. She had never been claustrophobic, but part of her just wanted to insist they took the discussion somewhere else.

Alan tapped a key. A holographic starchart appeared in front of them.

"The Multinational Fleet - eight fleet carriers, which will join four more at New Russia - is already departing the system now that the last-minute preparations have been completed," he said. "That will give them an overall strength of twelve carriers, two of which are ours. The Russians will hold overall command, apparently, as they have committed six fleet carriers to the formation. I don't think I need to remind you that this will leave them with only three carriers in home waters."

"New Russia is also their world," Abigail pointed out, tersely.

"Correct," Alan said. "Regardless, the Great Powers have decided that humanity will be making its stand at New Russia. Updated reports suggest that alien probes have moved into a number of systems on the far side of New Russia" - he nodded to the display, indicating the red icons - "and an attack on the system itself must be imminent. Of course, it might already have taken place. All our reports are at least a week out of date."

He tapped the display, again. "The MNF will proceed at its best possible speed to New Russia, which will mean abandoning the fleet train. Accordingly, our task - and that of five other escort carriers - is to shepherd the fleet train to New Russia. Once we arrive, we will either be assigned to protect the system's installations or escort a convoy on the return trip to Earth."

Abigail did the calculations in her head. "We'd need at least three weeks to get there," she mused, as she studied the starchart. "More like four, really."

"We've been ordered to proceed at our best possible speed too." Alan looked downcast for a moment. "Unfortunately, that will be the speed of the slowest ship in the convoy."

"Ouch," Abigail said. "And if we get attacked?"

"We have orders to defend ourselves, if fired upon," Alan said. "If we detect their ships, we have orders to attempt to make contact. An updated first contact packet has already been uploaded to the database. Ideally, we should be able to talk to them, which will hopefully end the war."

Abigail shook her head in mild disbelief. She'd been briefed on first contact protocols when she'd assumed command, although most of the belter crews had believed they were just a waste of time and energy. There was no such thing as aliens - and even if aliens *did* exist, what were the odds of an interstellar freighter making first contact? Now, such precautions were starting to look prophetic.

"There's no reason to assume that they'll agree to open communications," Savage said. "So far, all they've done is point their weapons at us and open fire."

"Pointing your weapon at someone *is* a form of communication," Bennett pointed out. "And so is opening fire."

"I don't think anyone in the Admiralty believes that we can convince the aliens to back off," Alan said. "I'd say that someone in the Houses of

Parliament pushed for us to *try* to make peaceful contact, even if the aliens show no apparent interest in it."

"So we are being put at risk because some political oxygen thief wants to feel good about himself," Abigail growled. The belt, at least, demanded a certain level of competence from its leaders. "Are we allowed to fire first?"

"If we believe we're under threat," Alan said. He shot her an unreadable look. "That will be your call, Captain."

"Thank you," Abigail said, sourly. "When do they want us to depart?"

"Yesterday," Savage said.

"The fleet train is moving to the RV point now," Alan said. He didn't look pleased, just for a second. "We'll link up with them in a couple of hours, then depart when Commodore Banks says so."

"Joy," Abigail said. She'd never liked flying in convoy. It hadn't been necessary very often, save for a handful of drills. Space pirates were the stuff of pulp fiction and bad movies that were no more realistic than the muscles and chests displayed by the actors. But then, aliens had been the stuff of bad fiction only a few weeks ago. "Do you know Commodore Banks?"

"He's CO of HMAS *Melbourne*," Alan said. "Australian, not British. Other than that…I've never met the man. He'll have a good record if they put him in charge of an oversized light cruiser, but" - he shrugged - "read the files. I dare say they'll be more informative."

"As long as he isn't one of those officers who think us merchants are all smuggling something," Abigail said. "That might be bad."

"It might," Alan agreed. "Remind your crew to make sure they update their wills before we depart. The odds are not on our side."

Abigail nodded, tightly. "Is there anything else?"

"I'll be recalling the starfighters shortly," Alan said. "We'll continue drills as we plod our merry way to New Russia."

"Very good," Abigail said.

She turned and left the compartment, keying her wristcom as she made her way back to the bridge. It was a relief to finally have orders, she thought, even though they were going to be away from their homes for at least two months. She'd hoped she could swing a trip to Ceres, but the

Royal Navy hadn't been interested in ensuring her crewers got some shore leave somewhere away from their ship. VR had its limitations, after all. No matter how detailed it was, there was no way to forget that the user was on a cramped starship.

"We'll be departing in two hours," she said, as she entered the bridge. "If any of you want to record a final message, do it now."

She leaned back in her chair and watched as word spread rapidly through the ship. If nothing else, the constant series of orders - and replacement orders - had ensured that her ship was ready to depart at a moment's notice. The starfighters were already returning to the ship, landing - one by one - in the hangar bay. She grimaced as she silently calculated just how long it would take to recover all twenty-four fighters. Doing *that* while taking fire - or waiting to cross a tramline - would be a nightmare. They might have to abandon some of their pilots just to save the ship.

Unless we have them latch onto the hull, she thought. It was theoretically possible. *But that would be dangerous too.*

Her console bleeped. "I've not gotten the final set of supplies from the station," Vassilios Drakopoulos said, grimly. "Should we be pressing them?"

"Yeah," Abigail said. In theory, they could operate without so many spare parts, but in practice...a single failure might doom the entire ship. She had no illusions about how highly the Royal Navy valued her ship - they wouldn't have given her a murderer for an XO if they considered her anything other than expendable - but *she* liked to think that her crew were worth a little more. "Send me the request. I'll forward it to them."

Someone had definitely lit a fire under the beancounters, she thought, as the two hours ticked steadily away. She'd expected a fight, but instead the transfer was authorised within seconds. A team of dockyard workers even moved the pallet to *Haddock*, rather than waste time scrabbling over who'd have the honour of doing the work. The spare parts were neatly stowed away, just as the timer reached zero. It was time to go.

"Anson, set course for the RV point," she ordered, as soon as she'd checked with Alan. "And take us out."

"Aye, Captain," Anson said.

Abigail felt her heart starting to pound in her chest as a low quiver ran through the ship. She kept a wary eye on the status displays, trying to reassure herself that everything was going to be fine. The dockyard workers had done a good job convincing equipment from several different eras to work together, but she was too experienced a spacer to believe that it would work perfectly. A tiny error in the programming nodes might cause the entire system to crash, no matter how many precautions had been worked into the system. Hell, too many precautions might bring the system down by themselves. And if that happened while they were a long way from help, they might be in real trouble.

There's no might about it, she thought, as they slipped away from the asteroid. *We will be in trouble.*

She keyed her console, bringing up the long-range sensor display. The military-grade sensors were good, good enough that she was seriously tempted to try to keep them after their military service was over. Hundreds of starships, intersystem spacecraft and shuttles were clearly visible on the sensors, making their way backwards and forwards across the Sol System. Tiny icons followed them, warning of time delays and potentially inaccurate projections. Abigail felt a flicker of contempt, mingled with amusement. Belters didn't need computers to tell them about the damned time delay!

"We'll be at our destination in three hours," Anson said. "Unless you want to redline the drive…"

"Bad idea," Abigail said, flatly. They'd been assured that the compensators could handle the acceleration, but one failure and everyone onboard would be smashed against the nearest bulkhead. There were plenty of redundancies worked into the system, yet it wasn't something she was inclined to test. "Keep us moving safely, please."

She leaned back in her chair and forced herself to relax. It wasn't easy. They were moving at a speed most groundpounders would have found unimaginable, yet they were crawling along compared to a warship - or a starfighter. HMAS *Melbourne* could give *Haddock* a few hours start and *still* overhaul her before she reached safety. It was hard to believe the aliens couldn't catch them either, which meant…

We'll be a magnet for trouble, she thought. *And as long as we soak up missiles aimed at the bigger ships, the Admiralty won't care.*

"Captain," Drakopoulos said. His face appeared in front of her. "The drives appear to be living up to their promises."

"Very good," Abigail said. She sat upright, crossly. "And the power cores?"

"They appear to be working at an acceptable level," Drakopoulos said. He didn't sound particularly pleased. "But you know my concerns."

Abigail nodded, curtly. A rule of thumb - a very *basic* rule of thumb - was never to rely on anything the crew couldn't fix if it broke. Fixing a fusion core onboard ship was a nightmare, but being stranded in interstellar space would be worse. But the latest generation of fusion cores were designed to be impossible to repair, at least without specialised - and extremely expensive - tools. Drakopoulos had objected, strongly, to having them installed on the starship. If the navy hadn't had her by the short hairs, Abigail would have objected too.

"We can rely on batteries long enough to get us back to safety," she said. *That* wouldn't be pleasant - everything would have to be cut back to the bare minimum - but it was the only way to stay alive. "Make sure the power cells remain charged."

"Aye, Captain," Drakopoulos said.

His face vanished. Abigail sighed and reached for her datapad, bringing up the raw data. The newer systems all appeared to be operating according to projections, something that worried her more than she cared to admit. *Nothing* was perfect, not even military-grade starship components. Experience told her that *something* was going to fail, sooner rather than later. And when it did, it would fail at the worst possible time.

Maybe we'll stress-test them later, she thought. *That might tell us something useful.*

The display changed as *Haddock* approached the convoy. It *was* an impressive sight, even though the cynical part of Abigail's mind insisted that another word for convoy was *target*. Forty freighters, five other escort carriers and a trio of warships...perhaps they were enough to beat off an alien attack, perhaps not. She couldn't help wondering if sneaking the freighters through individually would be a better idea. Hiding the freighters in the interstellar void would make them immensely difficult to detect.

"We're being hailed," Poddy said. "On screen?"

"Yes, please," Abigail said.

She straightened, reluctantly, when a middle-aged man in military uniform materialised in front of her. His uniform was similar to the Royal Navy's, but different enough to make it clear that it wasn't the *same* navy. His brown hair was barely visible under a peaked cap...

"Captain Harrison," the man said. He had an odd accent, one she couldn't place. "I am Commodore Banks, Leo Banks. Thank you for joining us."

"You're most welcome," Abigail said. "Where do you want us?"

"My staff will send you the details," Banks informed her. "I just wished to welcome you personally."

They exchanged a few more pieces of small-talk before Banks withdrew, closing the connection. Abigail wasn't sure if she should be flattered or concerned that Banks had called her personally. It wasn't as if they had any real connection, after all. But then, she wasn't a naval officer by career. Banks might have thought it would be better to be polite to her rather than risk causing offense.

Which makes him more or less unique, she thought, wryly. *Every other military officer I've met has been rather full of himself.*

"Captain," Poddy said. She glanced back, indicating her console. "I've received our orders."

Abigail stood and peered over Poddy's shoulder. *Haddock* had been assigned to a position at the rear of the formation, covering the other *Workhorses*. She wondered, absently, if someone thought they were meant to be a Q-Ship, then dismissed the thought. *Haddock* could no longer pass for a harmless freighter. The starfighter launching tube was a direct giveaway.

And the weapons and sensor blisters on our hull, she told herself. Even from a distance, *Haddock* no longer looked harmless. *And our power signature is different too.*

"Take us into formation," she ordered, shortly. Thankfully, they weren't expected to follow a *perfect* formation. Banks had a working brain, if nothing else. Freighters - and converted carriers - were hardly designed to turn on a dime. "And then inform the XO of our updated orders."

"I can take them in person," Anson said. "He told me I could use the simulators while the pilots were outside the ship."

Abigail frowned. She didn't *want* Anson and Alan to become friendly. And yet, she had no way to stop it without revealing far too much. Hopefully, a few hours in the simulators would convince Anson that he didn't want to be a starfighter pilot. It wasn't as if he was flying a worker bee or orbital shuttle. A starfighter would be far less forgiving of mistakes.

And if he does want to join after all, she told herself, *he can go to the training centre instead of learning here.*

"Sure," she said. "But wait until we're in position."

CHAPTER
ELEVEN

It was impossible to tell, with the naked eye, that the convoy had entered the Terra Nova System. The stars were still unblinking, glaring down at the tiny humans who had dared to enter their domain. There was no visible difference between one system and the next, not as far as anyone could tell. Alan felt as though he was completely alone in infinite space.

He peered out of the starfighter's cockpit, futilely looking for the other fighters - and the convoy. It was useless, of course. A starship - even a fleet carrier - was little more than a speck of dust on an interplanetary scale. He wouldn't see the ships with the naked eye until he was far too close for comfort. Even knife-range starfighter combat was fought with instruments rather than anything else. He wouldn't even see the enemy starfighter that killed him, if it got into firing range...

Assuming they have starfighters, he thought. He'd read all the speculations - but, in the end, they were *just* speculations. The aliens might have starfighters or they might have gone down a whole different route. Battleships instead of starfighters, perhaps. Or something so alien that humanity had never thought of it. *There are too many unknowns in this business...*

His intercom crackled. "Sir, ready for some fun?"

Greene, Alan thought. The younger man had been a minor problem over the last few days, but thankfully he seemed to be shaping up as the convoy moved away from Earth. *That* was a relief. Alan would have hated to lock Greene in his cabin until they returned home. *If he wasn't such a good flyer, he would have been discharged long ago.*

"Ready," he said. He leaned forward, resting his hands on the controls. It had been so long since he'd flown a real starfighter, but it was like riding a bicycle. Once you got the hang of it - and took a number of tumbles - you never quite forgot. Thankfully, he'd had a few days in the simulators before taking a *real* starfighter out into space. "Switching to practice mode...*now.*"

A red light appeared on his display, a warning that he'd be firing harmless laser pulses rather than flechette rounds. He checked and double-checked, just to make absolutely sure. There had been enough vague sensor contacts over the last week to make him reluctant to send his pilots out without the ability to shoot back at whatever they encountered, even though he wasn't inclined to believe that the aliens had already reached Terra Nova. But there was no way to be entirely sure. If half the unexplained sensor contacts were real, the aliens had already infested the human sphere.

And they could have crawled through the tramlines long before reaching Vera Cruz, he thought, as he kicked up the drive. *They might have been watching us for a long time.*

Ice ran down his spine. Interplanetary space was vast, easily large enough to hide an entire *fleet* of alien scouts as long as they were careful. The aliens *could* have sneaked a fleet of battleships through the tramlines and attacked Earth, right at the start. They would have caught the human race completely by surprise. But they hadn't...what did *that* mean? Had they attacked Vera Cruz without realising that they were dealing with a spacefaring race...?

"Let's go, sir," Greene said. "Attack Pattern Omega?"

"Herring Squadron, form up on me," Alan ordered. "And *go!*"

He felt his lips curve into a smile as the starfighters picked up speed, falling into a formation that looked like organised chaos. A civilian would see it as nothing more than randomised flying, but it was far more than *that*. Computers handled most point defence weapons, these days, and computers were very good at picking out patterns. A starfighter that flew on a predictable trajectory was dead, the moment it strayed into range. The formation might look bad, but it would keep its pilots alive. It wasn't as though they were putting on a show for the King's birthday.

And they'd be keeping us out of sight if they did, he reminded himself. *The Red Arrows would be putting on* that *show*.

The enemy starfighters moved away from the convoy, spreading out to intercept the incoming starfighters. Alan switched his weapons to automatic, trusting the computers to take shots at targets of opportunity while he concentrated on flying. New alerts popped up in his display as the enemy starfighters converged, opening fire with savage intensity. They had good *reason* to try to break up his formation, he knew. They could kill his entire squadron and still lose, if they lost their carrier too. Starfighter life support wouldn't last anything like long enough for the starfighters to reach Terra Nova.

And in a real battle we might be in the midst of some unexplored star system, he thought. An enemy starfighter snapped past him, evading his shot with practiced ease. *There might be nowhere to go.*

"Stay focused on the objective," he ordered, curtly. The pilots were getting drawn into dogfights, trying to win their spurs rather than complete their attack runs. "Don't let them lure you away."

He winced as the death toll started to mount. Starfighters were *fragile*. A single hit was almost always enough to destroy them, although there *were* vague tales of pilots who ejected *just* in time and survived long enough to be picked up. Alan had practiced bailouts, when he'd been in training, but his instructors had warned that the odds of survival were very low indeed. There was no point in forcing his pilots to bail out in the middle of a practice mission...

"Got him," Greene carolled. "Bart owes me a drink tonight!"

"Yes," Alan said. He checked the exercise results as the two sides grew apart, the brief engagement over in a matter of moments. The timer insisted they'd been skirmishing for ten minutes, but Alan didn't believe it. "And they also managed to protect their carrier."

He shook his head in annoyance. The pilots were all hotshots - they wouldn't have been allowed to graduate if they weren't hotshots - but they weren't a team. Not yet. Too many of them had tried to rack up their kills, rather than take out the actual target. They'd need to do more exercises, he told himself. Mike Whitehead would have to force them to keep their eyes on the prize.

And Greene and his fellows don't make that easy, Alan reflected. *They're more interested in personal glory than anything else.*

"Form up on me," he ordered, curtly. "We'll reset the exercise. Kipper can have a go at attacking the carrier instead."

"Thank you, sir," Wing Commander Marc Savage said. "We look forward to getting those drinks back."

Alan snorted to himself. There were *no* drinks on the ship - nothing alcoholic, at least. If someone *had* set up a still - and it was practically a tradition - it was *very* well hidden. His warnings and bloodcurdling threats had apparently been taken to heart...he cursed under his breath as he zoomed back into position. For all his harsh words and promises of dire retribution, he'd still managed to get drunk with Abigail. There were words for commanding officers who didn't practice what they preached. None of them were pleasant.

He opened his sensors, checking the entire convoy. Commodore Banks had been surprisingly understanding, under the circumstances. All of the escort carriers were practicing hard, although it would be a while before they were ready for actual war games. Alan hoped that time would come soon. Practicing attack runs on *Haddock* was growing tedious, even for him. The chance to engage someone *new,* someone unpredictable, couldn't be missed.

It isn't as if we're going to be engaging the enemy carriers ourselves, he thought. *They'll keep us on milk runs until the end of the war.*

The part of him that had been a hotshot pilot - still was, in many ways - thought that was dreadfully unfair. No one became a starfighter pilot without a thirst for glory, without the urge to paint the hull with as many enemy silhouettes as possible. The certain knowledge that they'd never see real combat - not unless they were *very* unlucky - burned at him. He and his squadrons would never have a chance for real glory...

He shook his head in annoyance. *Haddock* wasn't designed for fleet operations. Her only role in the line of battle was to provide a single flight deck...if she didn't soak up a handful of missiles instead. Alan shrugged, dispassionately. *Haddock* couldn't pass for a fleet carrier...and if she did, somehow, it wouldn't last. The enemy would throw everything, up to and including the kitchen sink, at a ship that couldn't hope to survive. *Haddock* would be vaporised by the missiles and that would be the end.

And every other pilot in the fleet has a better record than you, his thoughts mocked him, sardonically. *They didn't kill their wives…*

"All right," he said, as they fell into formation. "Let's go."

He tensed as Kipper Squadron roared down on their position. Like it or not, they *were* confined to escort duties for the foreseeable future…and they had to practice, just to make sure they were ready for a *real* attack. And yet, half of his pilots were still too intent on personal glory. Greene allowed himself to be pulled out of formation, just long enough for two enemy starfighters to sneak past him and fall into an attack run. If they'd been carrying torpedoes, Alan noted, they would have had a *very* good chance at taking out the carrier.

A real fleet carrier might soak up the hits, Alan thought, making a mental note to berate Greene later. *But an escort carrier doesn't have a chance.*

He keyed his console. "Well, gentlemen," he said. "Our ride home appears to be nothing more than a cloud of expanding dust. We're all dead."

"Sucks to be you, I guess," Flight Lieutenant Patsy Govan said. "And now we're going to run…"

"Coward," Greene said.

"As you were," Alan said, before the banter could turn into a real argument. "Herring Squadron will be buying the drinks, when we actually go on leave."

"Blast," Greene said. "Hey, sir. Is there any prospect of shore leave on New Russia?"

"I have no idea," Alan said, curtly. He rather doubted it. The escort carrier crews wouldn't be on the top of the list for shore leave, if there *was* a list. It was far more likely that they'd simply be turned around and ordered to escort another convoy home. "Return to the barn, ladies and gentlemen. We'll go over the engagement this evening."

He turned the starfighter slowly, wishing he could remain outside the ship. It hadn't been easy to put himself on the flight roster, not when Bennett had clearly been suspicious of his motivations. But then, he *had*

had a good reason to go flying. He needed to understand what his pilots could - and couldn't - do before it was too late. It had been too long since he'd flown a starfighter for himself.

But at least I remembered how to fly, he told himself. *And I can go out again, later.*

He peered forward, straining his eyes as a faint flicker of light slowly became the escort carrier. He'd never really understood why the designers had given the starfighters cockpits - there was no way he could land on the carrier without using his instruments - but he had to admit there was something reassuring about being able to see his mothership with the naked eye. Space was his home - he hadn't realised how much he'd miss it until he'd been thrown into jail - but it was also utterly lethal. The vacuum would kill him, if he popped open the cockpit. A single mistake could get them all killed.

Maybe I'll take one last flight, after the war, he thought. *And simply never come back.*

His threat receiver lit up, red icons flashing over the display. Alan reacted instinctively, yanking the starfighter to one side as...*something*...flashed past him. Newer alerts blinked up, warning him that the carrier had opened fire...opened fire on *him*. He heard someone yelping in shock over the command network, curses echoing through his ears as the starfighters scattered. They were all far too close to the suddenly-hostile carrier for comfort.

"Cease fire," he snapped. He threw the starfighter into a series of evasive manoeuvres as another round of pellets shot past him. Those were *real* projectiles! Was someone trying to kill him? Bennett? Or Abigail? Or...none of them made *sense*. Bennett wouldn't have any trouble killing Alan and convincing everyone else that it had been an unfortunate incident, if he wished. "I say again, cease fire!"

The threat receiver blanked, so sharply he thought it had gone on the blink. He stared at it for a long moment, then looked up at the carrier. Or where the carrier should be...what the hell should they do? Fly to one of the other carriers? Or...

"Sir, I've disengaged the point defence system," Mike Whitehead said. The acting CAG sounded shaken. Blue-on-blue incidents were rare, but they did happen. "You should be safe to return to the ship."

"Make sure you isolate the entire system," Alan ordered, stiffly. "I want to know *exactly* what happened."

He felt his heart begin to race as he guided the starfighter back towards the carrier. He'd expect an enemy carrier to fire on him, of course, but a *friendly* ship? Even if it was just a glitch, it boded ill for the future. And what if it *wasn't* a glitch? What if it had been attempted murder? Alan *thought* his pilots and support crews didn't know what he'd done, but it wasn't *impossible* that one of them had found out. They could have sent a query back home if they'd had any reason to suspect that he was more than just another starfighter pilot who hadn't made the transition to command track.

And someone on Earth could dig up the news records, he thought, numbly. He wasn't the only person who happened to be called Alan Campbell, but it was quite possible that he was the only starfighter pilot of that name. *They'd know who I was and what I'd done.*

He tensed as the carrier grew larger and larger until it dominated the viewport, grimly aware that he might be picked off at point-blank range, but nothing happened. His starfighter landed neatly on the deck, automatically moving forward and through a pair of airlocks into the next chamber. Alan opened the cockpit as soon as the starfighter had come to a halt, jumping down to the flight deck rather than wait for the ground crew to bring him the ladder.

Damn it, he thought, as he felt his body start to shake. He hadn't shook so badly since his first flight, years ago. *What happened?*

He made his way to the hatch and stepped through, trying to keep from showing any sign of tension or fear. He'd thought he'd understood combat, but this…an accident would be bad enough, but at least it would be an accident. It was not *knowing* that tore at him. Jail hadn't been too bad, all things considered. Colchester was better-run than some of the civilian hellholes. Civilian wardens had a reputation for everything from beating prisoners to sexually abusing them, but the redcaps had been strictly professional. None of *them* had tried to kill him.

His wristcom bleeped. "Sir, the remainder of the pilots are landing," Whitehead said. "Their timing isn't good."

"Call a general meeting for nineteen-hundred-hours," Alan said. He fought to control the shakes. He'd been in danger before, but this…he pushed the thought aside, sharply. "Inform the pilots that there is to be *no* chatter until the meeting. They can go get some food or something, but there is to be *no* discussion until a full investigation is held."

"Yes, sir."

Alan ran his hand through his hair. It felt sweaty. He'd enjoyed being outside the ship, right up until the moment *Haddock* had tried to kill him. It was a grim reminder that *nothing* could be fully trusted, not even a piece of equipment that had been checked and rechecked time and time again. Just for a moment, he thought he understood the neo-villagers he'd seen in the countryside. They'd tried to go back to an era of thatched cottages and small fields that had never really existed, save in story and song. And while he'd thought they were silly at the time, he understood them now. *Their* lives were not dependent on technology.

And yet, they'd be dead if an alien fleet materialised in their skies, he reminded himself, sourly. Unarmed primitives wouldn't stand a chance against modern firepower. *Or even if they caught something dangerous.*

He forced himself to stand up straight. He'd go for a shower, perhaps grab a ration bar or two. By then, Abigail and Bennett would probably have completed a preliminary investigation. And then...he shook his head. A glitch would be bad...worse, perhaps, than a deliberate attempt at murder. The prospect of losing control over the ship was terrifying. What would go next? Life support? There was no shortage of horror stories about starships that had slowly poisoned their own crews when the life support systems had glitched. He'd thought the stories existed to remind crews not to take anything for granted, but now...now he wasn't so sure. A single flaw in the air mix might kill the entire crew.

And if we can't rely on the ship, he mused, *what can we rely on?*

CHAPTER
TWELVE

"I want a full explanation," Abigail said. Her eyes swept the compartment. "What the *fuck* happened?"

She looked from face to face. Alan was pale. He'd clearly had a nasty shock, even though he was trying to hide it. Beside him, Maddy looked worried. She wasn't guilty, Abigail was sure, but her motherly instincts told her that Maddy expected to be blamed for whatever had gone wrong. The two squadron commanders - and Bennett - appeared grim. They - and a handful of their subordinates - had been tearing apart the point defence system, trying to find out what had gone wrong.

Maddy cleared her throat. "As far as I can tell, there was a glitch in the point defence sensor node," she said. "The system…ah…the system managed to confuse two files and the logic subroutines failed and…"

Abigail gave her a sharp look. "And *what*?"

"The computers believed two things to be true at once," Maddy said. "On one hand, it believed that we might be under attack at any moment; on the other, it knew we were carrying out training exercises. I…ah…I *think* what happened…I think the system basically classed our starfighters as the enemy, tripping the automatic point defence system as the starfighters moved into engagement range."

Whitehead frowned. "So the computers thought we were carrying out a live-fire exercise?"

"No, sir," Maddy said. "The point defence system is programmed to engage - automatically - any targets that come within torpedo range.

When we go to battlestations, the human element is completely locked out of the loop. There just isn't *time* to ask for orders. When our starfighters approached, it defaulted to emergency protocols, classed *everything* as a potential enemy, and opened fire. It simply didn't have time to reassess the situation."

She took a breath. "The full report will be a little more complex," she added. "But I think I've parsed out the basics."

"So it was a glitch," Abigail said. "And not an attempt at" - she allowed her voice to harden -"outright murder."

Maddy paled. "I'm not a trained investigator, Captain," she said. "All I can say is what I *believe* to have happened."

"Right," Abigail said. The Belt Federation accepted that accidents happened. She didn't think the Royal Navy would be quite so sanguine. "Can you ensure it doesn't happen again?"

"I think a couple of command nodes would need to be rewritten," Maddy said. She bit her lip. "That's a task for a proper WebHead, not me. It would be better, I think, to take the system offline while we're carrying out exercises."

Abigail nodded, sourly. Maddy deserved one point, at least, for being smart enough to admit her limitations. Trying to reprogram a computer core was incredibly difficult. Abigail had never been comfortable with a system she couldn't control perfectly, let alone repair. There were too many horror stories about hacker anarchists, dating all the way back to the Age of Unrest. Hanging a few hundred of the bastards hadn't stopped others from trying to break into sealed computer networks. Abigail could lose control of her ship and never know it.

"If we take the system offline," Whitehead said, "how long will it take to get it back online?"

"Five minutes," Maddy said.

"Which would be too long, if one of those sensor contacts happens to be *real*," Whitehead said. "Are there no other options?"

Maddy hesitated. "We can alter our programming to some extent," she said. "If I fiddle a little, I can draw a line between exercises and reality. But realistically I can't go too far without risking a total collapse."

"I see," Abigail said.

She scowled in disapproval. There had been too many vague sensor contacts since the convoy had left Earth, some of which had been close enough to force Commodore Banks to alter course. None of the contacts had opened fire, at least, but everyone was jumpy. There was no way to know if the contacts were alien starships or simple sensor glitches. Logic suggested the latter, yet no one *knew*.

"Alan," she said. "What do you think?"

Alan started, as if he hadn't expected her to ask him *anything*. "We cannot stop exercises," he said, slowly. "I think we'll have to coordinate with the rest of the convoy, ensuring that we can take down our point defence network long enough to carry out the exercises in peace."

"We could simply tell the computers not to do it again," Savage pointed out.

"Yes, we can stop *this* problem from repeating itself," Alan said. "But what about the *next* problem? What will happen next?"

We don't know, Abigail thought. *And if we knew, we could stop it.*

She shrugged. "We'll take down the network when we start the next set of exercises," she said. It was a risk, but she saw no alternative. "Alan, make sure that Commodore Banks knows what we intend to do."

"Aye, Captain."

"Good," Abigail said. "And now we have that matter under control" - she ignored Whitehead's snort with the ease of long practice - "what do the exercises tell us?"

"That we have a great deal of work to do," Alan said. "We lost the carrier, twice."

"Ouch," Abigail said.

She listened to the discussion that followed, noting where the navy and the belt seemed to agree and where they differed. Some of their points were good ones - the quest for glory versus the need to actually win the engagement - and others seemed flawed. She couldn't help thinking that navy pilots were far too much like overgrown children, rather than responsible adults. But then, she'd seen the projected loss rates...such a bloodless term for the deaths of hundreds of starfighter pilots. Very few Belters would be comfortable with flying such craft, knowing the odds of long-term survival to be poor.

"I'll leave you to handle it," she said, rising. "And inform me when you intend to launch the next set of exercises."

"Aye, Captain."

She walked out of the compartment and down the long corridor to engineering. The ship felt different now, in so many ways. *Haddock* had never been so *crowded* before, even though her crew was tiny. But then, the living spaces had been tiny too. It wasn't really her ship any longer, she felt. The freighter she'd loved had been replaced by a mobile community she didn't quite know how to handle. She found it difficult to understand how fleet carrier commanders coped. *Their* crews numbered in the thousands.

Vassilios Drakopoulos looked up as she entered the compartment. "Captain."

"Vass," Abigail said. "A word?"

Drakopoulos nodded and motioned for her to step into his cabin. It also doubled as his office, insofar as he had one. He didn't spend much time in it, Abigail knew. When he wasn't sleeping, he was in engineering. There was always something to fix on the ship or journals to read. His cramped cabin was really nothing more than a place to sleep.

"The navy thinks the system glitched," she said, shortly. "Do you agree?"

"I think so," Drakopoulos said. "Basically, the system got confused..."

He started to lurch into an explanation. Abigail held up a hand, cutting him off. He would have taken part in Maddy's investigation and, if he'd had doubts, he would have taken them to her long ago. She didn't need to hear more technobabble.

"That's not the issue at the moment," she said. "Will it happen again?"

"I don't know," Drakopoulos admitted. "Captain, we've spliced together quite a few systems that were never *designed* to work together. And we didn't have time to stress-test any but the most important systems. I can point to a dozen places that *could* glitch, Captain, yet I don't know which ones *will* glitch."

"And there's nothing we can do about it," Abigail said.

She cursed under her breath. It was sheer luck that no one had been killed - *this* time. The next time might be a great deal worse. And then... she shook her head in dismay. The Belt might understand that accidents happened, but this...the Royal Navy would want answers. And then it would probably try to turn her into a scapegoat...

"At least it wasn't deliberate," she muttered.

"I don't think so, Captain," Drakopoulos agreed. "There would be no way to *know* who'd be targeted."

Abigail made a face. Perhaps Alan's wife had had a friend who was now serving on *Haddock*, a friend who might want to avenge her death. Or...she shook her head in annoyance. That was the stuff of bad detective novels or late-night movies that required only that the viewer sat and watched. No, logic dictated that the glitch had been nothing more than a glitch. The real problem was that it might happen again and - next time - someone might die.

"Fuck," she said. "See what you can do to minimise the risks."

"I'd *like* to tear out all the older systems and replace them," Drakopoulos said. He lifted his bushy eyebrows. "Is that likely to happen?"

Abigail made a rude sound. "What do you think?"

She looked down at the hard metal deck. The Royal Navy was unlikely to authorise a refit that would take *Haddock* out of service for at least six months. It would be cheaper to build a modern freighter from scratch - or a purpose-built escort carrier, come to think of it. And there was no way *she* could afford to purchase top-of-the-line gear without the navy's contribution. They'd just wind up more in debt than ever before.

Drakopoulos cleared his throat. "I'll see about stress-testing some of the less important systems," he said. "But you know what could happen if it really *doesn't* live up to specifications."

Abigail nodded, curtly. If the stress-test was *too* good, or the equipment *too* frail, the whole system would collapse. And then the navy would demand explanations for that too...

"Do the best you can," she ordered. She rose, careful not to bang her head on the metal ceiling. "I'll be on the bridge."

"In summary, we will be conducting more exercises over the next two weeks," Alan concluded, after a long discussion of the exercise. The starfighter pilots looked back at him with varying degrees of interest. "By the time we arrive at New Russia, I want to have us working together as a team."

He paused. "Any questions?"

"But what about our *scores*?" Greene leaned forward, sharply. "We have to rack up the kills…"

Alan bit down on several nasty responses. "Bugger the scores," he said, finally. He waved a hand at the nearest bulkhead. "This ship is our *home*. Blasting a hundred alien starfighters into dust will *not* save our asses if this ship is *also* blown into dust. Our job is not racking up the kills, but protecting the ship. Let me know if you have a problem with that and I'll beach you."

Greene, thankfully, had the wisdom to keep his mouth shut. Alan sighed, inwardly. It hadn't dawned on them, yet, that they could win the battle and still lose the war. Or at least their lives. Starfighter pilots rarely saw anything of the bigger picture, but *he* had to keep it in mind at all times. Perhaps it would be better, he told himself, if he didn't take a starfighter into combat again.

But I'm not going to stop, he thought, wryly. *I can't stay cooped inside forever. I'll go mad.*

"Report to your bunk beds and get some sleep," Alan finished. "We'll be going back outside tomorrow morning."

He sat back and watched as the starfighter pilots filed out of the room. Some of them were cheerfully discussing the prospects for shore leave on New Russia, others were more subdued as they thought about just how badly things could have gone. Death was a constant threat, but dying because of friendly fire - when they were trying to land on the carrier, of all things - would be particularly galling. Hopefully, the incident would concentrate a few minds. They were at war.

Bennett cleared his throat. "An unusually blunt assessment, from you."

"Thank you," Alan said, suspiciously. He'd been ruthless, tearing apart everything that had happened and highlighting every mistake. He rather suspected he'd sounded more like a flying instructor than a CAG. *His* first CAG had never talked to him as though he was a naughty schoolboy. And yet, praise from Bennett was rare. "Do you have any thoughts?"

"The one point you missed," Bennett said. He smiled, but it didn't touch his eyes. "A point I suspect you didn't want to acknowledge."

Alan eyed him for a long moment. For once, Bennett *didn't* sound like he was having a go at Alan. Instead, he sounded almost thoughtful. Perhaps it was an act…no, Bennett had no *reason* to act. They were alone. He could spend the next hour insulting Alan and no one would ever know.

"There's a lot of points I don't want to acknowledge," he said, finally. "Which one do you have in mind?"

"You're still alive," Bennett said.

Alan blinked. "Is that a bad thing?"

Bennett shrugged. "The point defence railguns fired at you from practically point-blank range," he said. "Maybe not knife-range, but still…they should have scored a direct hit. It wasn't as though you were corkscrewing your way towards the ship. You should have been hit."

"I jerked out of the way," Alan protested.

"I checked the records," Bennett told him. "You *should* have been hit. At that range, you shouldn't have been able to evade the pellets."

"How *terrible*," Alan said, dryly.

"Quite," Bennett agreed. "What happens when a *real* target makes a *real* attack run?"

Alan scowled. He didn't want to admit it, but Bennett had a point. Perhaps the railguns *hadn't* been zeroed properly. And *that* meant…

"We need to check the whole system, again," he said. They'd been very busy in the last few days before leaving Earth. *Something* had clearly been overlooked. The real question was how much *else* had been overlooked. "And probably do a few more test firings."

He made a face. Target drones cost over a million pounds apiece, which was why the navy had been reluctant to assign any to *Haddock*. She was an escort carrier, the beancounters had said. She'd never see *real* combat. It was more important to get the drones out to the fleet carriers, where they'd make a *really* important contribution. Simulated firing exercises weren't bad - mucking about with live ammo was always risky - but they were useless if the weapons weren't zeroed properly. Perhaps, in hindsight, the whole incident had been a blessing in disguise.

"*Melbourne* might have a few drones we can borrow," he said, although it was unlikely. "If not, we can probably rig up a few makeshift targets and dump them out there for target practice. And then try and get the weapon calibrated properly."

"Good thinking," Bennett said. "Perhaps there is something to be said for letting you out of jail after all."

"And now you're back to being an arsehole," Alan said, crossly. It had been foolish of him to think, even for a moment, that he could have any actual camaraderie with Bennett. They were from very different worlds. "Do you have any other points you want to make?"

"Stay in the CIC and let the squadron commanders handle their jobs," Bennett said. "You don't want to give them the impression that they can be pushed aside at any moment, do you?"

Alan sighed. If he *could* convince Whitehead or Savage to take his place...he shook his head. Bennett would never let him get away with it. Besides, neither of them were qualified to serve as CAG for very long. They could probably handle the job if Alan died, at least until a replacement was assigned to the ship, but there would be problems. Some of them would probably haunt the ship for years.

Not least because someone who does the job will resent being pushed aside by a newcomer, Alan thought. He'd seen once-good crews collapse when someone's morale had been accidentally destroyed. *Or because it will be a long time before anyone appoints a replacement for me.*

Bennett cleared his throat. Alan realised he hadn't actually answered the question.

"I suppose not," he said. "But you *do* realise I might have to go out there...?"

"You might," Bennett agreed. "And if you do, you do. But until then..."

He made a show of checking his watch. "You'd better get some sleep. Morning will come far too soon."

Alan cocked his head. "You're not coming?"

"I have a report to write," Bennett said. "And a couple of letters to my family."

"Just remember they'll be going through the censors," Alan reminded him. "Poor Jock didn't get *that* memo."

Bennett smiled. Alan smiled too, although it wasn't really *that* funny. Flight Lieutenant Jock Hazelton's v-mail to his girlfriend had been shockingly explicit, including footage of him performing sex acts in the shower. Thankfully, no one else in the squadron knew what he'd done. They'd either laugh at him or be horrified, depending on their mood. The censors, for better or worse, had forwarded the v-mail to Alan. He'd had to chew Hazelton out for sending it. In truth, he wasn't sure which one of them had been more embarrassed.

"My siblings won't want *that* sort of letter," Bennett assured him. "I just have to avoid committing outright lies to paper."

"True," Alan agreed. *That* could be embarrassing, if they were the wrong *kind* of lies. There was nothing particularly *shameful* about serving on a fleet carrier, but Bennett was very obviously not a naval officer. "We don't want them to think you're a Walt."

Bennett pointed at the hatch. "Out."

Laughing, Alan did as he was told.

CHAPTER
THiRTEEN

"Transit complete, Captain," Anson said. "Welcome to New Russia."

Abigail nodded, curtly, as the display began to fill up with green, blue and yellow lights. The convoy, slowly slipping back into formation as the ships transited one by one; military starships, holding position near the planet; interplanetary spacecraft, fewer than she'd expected, moving between New Russia and the daughter colonies scattered all over the system. New Russia was nowhere near as industrialised or as densely populated as Earth, but it was still impressive. The system had only been inhabited for ninety years.

"Poddy, inform the CIC that we have arrived," she ordered. "Anson, take us out with the rest of the convoy."

She leaned back in her chair, silently grateful that the mission was nearly over. There hadn't been any more...*incidents*...but they'd kept picking up vague sensor contacts that could have been *anything*. Commodore Banks had launched starfighters after some of the contacts - more solid than most, apparently - yet they'd found nothing. Abigail was torn between assuming the contacts were stray flickers of energy - space wasn't *actually* silent, no matter what the groundpounders claimed - and a feeling that something awful was about to happen.

But nothing I can put my fingers on, she thought crossly. *And nothing I can take to Commodore Banks.*

A low shudder ran through the ship. "We're moving now, Captain," Anson said. "Apparently, we're going straight to New Russia."

Poddy glanced back at her. "Shore leave?"

"Don't count on it," Abigail growled. She wasn't sure she would allow Poddy to go down to the surface, assuming it was an option. New Russia was hardly the Exclusion Zone, on Earth, but she'd heard stories. Russia was hardly the friendliest place for foreigners and *New* Russia, she suspected, would be even worse. "It isn't as if we've been on this ship for a year and a day."

Poddy looked disappointed. "But Mum..."

"Your mother is not in charge here," Abigail said, sharply. And wasn't *that* a bitter pill to swallow? She was absolute mistress of her ship, as long as she did what she was told. But then, there had always been limits to her power. Taking the ship on a deliberately unprofitable voyage would have cost her everything. "You will get what you get and be happy with it."

She felt a flicker of guilt at the way Poddy's face crumpled. Snapping at her daughter...she hadn't done that, not much. Poddy had made mistakes, of course, but she hadn't done any of them deliberately. Abigail could hardly have punished her daughter for mistakes she'd made herself, when *she'd* been a young girl. And Poddy had learnt from her mistakes. She'd certainly never made the same mistake twice.

"We don't know where we'll be going next," she said, lowering her voice. "If we spend a week or two in orbit, we might *just* be able to arrange something."

"You could spend a few hours in VR," Anson suggested. "Put on a headset and block out the world."

"It isn't real," Poddy said. "Is it?"

Abigail shrugged. She'd never really cared for VR entertainment. The games were fun, sometimes, but they gave her headaches when reality warred with fantasy. And the VR movies were even worse. There was no way to give up completely and slip into the story, doing things that she knew she could never do. Her brain just refused to surrender its grip on reality.

"It would be a distraction," she said, curtly. "You could *also* spend a few hours studying for your next exam. *That* would be a kick in the backside, would it not?"

She leaned back in her chair, watching the holographic display. The system was so *sharp* that she wanted to keep it, after the war was over. Perhaps they could work something out with the military. Or...she shrugged, watching the fleet carriers as they held position near the planet. Like all Belters, she was suspicious of the Great Powers and their massive warships, but she had to admit she was glad they'd been built now. The universe was nowhere near as peaceful as she'd thought.

They look impressive, she thought, ruefully. The smallest fleet carrier was two kilometres long, bristling with weapons and surrounded by a swarm of starfighters. *Haddock* was hardly *small*, but she'd vanish without trace in the immensity of their hulls. *And if they're as powerful as they look, perhaps the aliens will think twice before engaging us.*

"ETA roughly one hour, forty minutes," Anson said. "A couple of ships are lagging."

"I suppose that speaks well of Banks," Abigail said. She'd known military officers who appeared to believe that their engineers routinely over-estimated how long it would take to complete repairs. "Better to slow the convoy than risk leaving ships behind."

"It isn't as if anyone actually *was* following us," Anson said. "And, if they were, surely they would have ambushed us somewhere short of New Russia."

Abigail shrugged. She was no military officer, but she understood the realities of spaceflight far better than any pampered desk-flyer on Earth. They'd crossed a star system that was empty, save for a handful of aster-oids and a lone comet. The perfect place for an ambush, she'd thought at the time. But realistically, if the aliens were careful, they *could* ambush the convoy in the New Russia System. They'd just have to complete the slaughter before the warships could race to the rescue.

"We shall see," she said. The sense of looming disaster refused to fade, no matter how much she bombarded it with cold logic. Her eyes kept straying to Tramline Four, leading towards Vera Cruz. Who knew *what* was lurking on the far side? There would be scouts watching the other tramlines, wouldn't there? "Until then, concentrate on your duties."

And I shall do the same, she told herself.

The minutes ticked away, one by one. She was agonisingly aware of each and every passing second. *Haddock's* speed had never been a problem before - Abigail had *known* her ship was slow, compared to some - but now she just wanted to overload the drives and *rush* to New Russia. And yet, it would be pointless. There was no way she could boost their speed enough to matter. All it would do, if she tried, would get her in trouble with the navy. They wouldn't thank her for embarrassing them in front of countless foreign eyes.

Twelve fleet carriers, she thought, numbly. *And only two of them are ours.*

It was an odd thought. She was British - she held a Royal Navy Reserve commission, for God's sake - and yet, she'd never considered herself *truly* British. She'd been part of the Belt since birth, heir to a civilisation that lacked the hang-ups and foibles of those who remained resolutely trapped in the gravity well. She liked to think she was part of something better. Hell, she *was* part of something better. She'd seen enough of Earth to know she didn't want to live there. A person who shot his mouth off at the wrong time could easily wind up in jail - or worse.

And yet, looking at the carriers, she felt an odd flicker of pride. She thought...

Anson's console chimed. "Captain, I'm picking up an all-ships alert," he snapped. His voice was suddenly hard. "Hostile starships have been detected!"

Abigail sat upright. "Order all hands to battlestations," she ordered. She keyed her console, opening a channel to the CIC. "Alan, we've picked up an alert."

"Understood," Alan said. He sounded calm, thankfully. "We're rushing to launch stations now."

Abigail nodded. She wasn't sure if Alan was *truly* calm or if he was just faking it, but she was glad he sounded calm anyway. *She* sure as hell didn't *feel* calm. The alert had been passed from ship to ship, but no red icons had appeared on the display. A drill? An all-ships drill? It was possible, yet...she shook her head. Commodore Banks wasn't the sort of asshole who'd hold a surprise drill just before they reached safe harbour.

"Where are they?" Poddy barely glanced up from her console. "Where *are* they?"

"Lost in space," Anson said. "Or just out of sensor range."

Abigail nodded, curtly. Unless the aliens had some kind of drive technology that no one had ever heard of - in which case the war was probably already lost - it would take them some time to reach New Russia. There was certainly no hope of outrunning whatever warning message had been sent, not when the message was racing into the system at the speed of light. The fastest starship ever clocked had barely been able to make a *third* of the speed of light...

And only then by overloading the drive fields until the nodes started to melt, she thought, grimly. *A modern starship might be able to do better, but...*

She pushed the thought aside as she studied the empty display. The fleet carriers were launching hundreds of starfighters, tiny icons blurring together as her sensors struggled to isolate individual craft. Beyond them, the planet's orbital defences were launching their own starfighters and shuttles. It couldn't be a drill then, she thought as she watched the escort craft move into position. No one would waste so much time and effort on a drill...

Her thoughts seemed to freeze, just for a second, as red icons flared into existence. They were close to the fleet carriers, too close. Her mind yammered in horror as it tried to grasp what had just happened. That should have been impossible. The aliens were *far* too close to the fleet carriers...that should have been impossible. Had they somehow used New Russia's gravity field as a makeshift tramline? It *was* theoretically possible, but...she felt ice running down her spine. If it *was* possible, the aliens might have a very real advantage over the defenders.

"But where did they come *from*?" Poddy's voice was plaintive. "Mum... they didn't come through the tramlines!"

"They must have done," Anson said.

Abigail wasn't so sure. The aliens were in the wrong place for a least-time transit from Tramline Four. Or for *any* tramline, as far as she could tell. It was quite possible they'd sneaked into the system and altered course long before they'd been detected, but...it was odd. Either they were utterly confident in their superiority or…or what? Did they have a way of jumping through star systems without using the tramlines? Nearly two centuries of dedicated research hadn't been able to create a working FTL drive that *didn't* use the tramlines, but there were theories…

"Orders from the flag," Poddy said. "We're to alter course, away from the combat zone."

"Very good," Abigail said. "Anson, see to it."

"We should be helping them," Anson muttered.

"We're not going to be able to do *much*," Abigail pointed out. "And the military won't want us underfoot."

She sucked in her breath as she studied the alien fleet. It was hard to make out many details - the aliens seemed to be using some kind of stealth field to confuse her sensors - but it was clear that they'd brought at least eight fleet carriers to New Russia. Or at least they were the right *size* to be fleet carriers. She wondered, absently, just how many starfighters each of them could deploy. If the aliens had cut down on weapons and armour, they might have been able to cram extra starfighters into their hulls. Or…she shook her head. There was no way to know.

"The fleet is attempting to signal the aliens," Poddy said. "No response."

"Like they're going to say anything *now*," Anson muttered.

"Concentrate on your job," Abigail ordered.

She studied the alien formation for a long moment. The aliens were moving towards New Russia, forcing the MNF to block their advance, yet…yet there was something *sloppy* about it. The aliens were both immensely capable - they had to be, if they'd managed to get so close without being detected - and immensely stupid. She didn't like it. Some of the sneakiest people she'd met had been very good at pretending to be idiots, at least until they got what they wanted. What did the *aliens* want?

"They're not replying," Poddy said.

Abigail nodded, slowly. The aliens were practically standing still, on an interplanetary scale…it made no sense. Why not drive on New Russia? Why give the MNF all the time it could possibly need to launch starfighters and prepare for combat? Why…?

Her console bleeped. "The Commodore is deploying drones," Alan said. "We're going to go on a little detour."

"Good thinking," Abigail said, slowly. *Haddock* and the rest of the escorts couldn't add much to the firepower already facing the aliens. And yet…something kept nagging at the back of her mind. The aliens were being obliging. Suspiciously obliging. "What are they doing?"

"I don't know," Alan said. More green and blue icons winked into existence. Smaller ships, coming to join the defence. "But we can't let them dominate the rest of the system unchallenged."

He sounded as perturbed as herself. Abigail was torn between finding that reassuring and scary. She would have preferred to be told she was being silly. She wouldn't have *liked* it - there were too many military officers who looked down their noses at merchant spacers - but it would have set her mind at rest. Instead, Alan seemed to be having doubts himself. What were the aliens doing?

"We have the advantage, don't we?" She keyed her console, bringing up the fleet list. There was no way to be sure, but it looked as though the MNF outmassed its opponent by quite a considerable margin. "We have enough firepower to make them regret sticking their noses into our space."

"Perhaps," Alan said.

"I've seen platoons of Royal Marines pitched against hordes of rampaging fanatics," a new voice said. Bennett. He sounded as though he was recalling a pleasant memory. "They have numbers, but we have superior weapons. We mow them down in their hundreds, then dump the bodies into ditches. If it looks like we're going to be overrun, we call in helicopters and long-range artillery - even orbital strikes. The bastards don't stand a chance."

Abigail felt a shiver of disquiet. She'd known there were endless skirmishes on Earth, but…she shuddered. Better to tap the endless resources of space, and leave those who wanted to stay in the mud to their fate. Her mother might have been a mail order bride - a whore, some less enlightened people had called her until Abigail had taught them better - but at least she'd had the sense to leave. Life in Britain was hard enough. She dreaded to think what life in the Exclusion Zone must be like, particularly for women. Hard times were always hardest on the women.

But she took Bennett's point. The wooden navies of the Napoleonic Era might have looked impressive - she'd watched a few historical dramas - but they wouldn't have lasted long against an ironclad ship. And then the battleships had given way to aircraft carriers, which in turn had fallen to cruise missiles and orbital kinetic strikes. The aliens might just have a technological advantage that would tip the balance of power permanently in their favour.

But they could have driven straight on Earth, she thought. *We had enough time to move entire* fleets *to New Russia while they dawdled. They should have reached the system within a fortnight of Vera Cruz, before we knew that alien life was more than a myth...*

Her blood turned to ice. *Unless we did what they wanted us to do.*

The display shifted, rapidly. Clouds of starfighters lanced away from the MNF, heading straight for the alien fleet. Starfighters leading the way, followed by torpedo-bombers...she winced, remembering some of the combat simulations they'd run. A full-sized fleet carrier wouldn't stand a chance if so many starfighters and bombers roared down on her. *Haddock* would be *vaporised* by a force a tenth of the size. It looked an irresistible force...

"Something is wrong," she said.

"I know," Alan agreed. His voice was tightly controlled. "But what else *can* they do?"

Abigail swallowed. The MNF *couldn't* just sit there and do nothing, could it? There was no way the *Russians* would want to surrender the rest of their system, no matter how the other nations felt about it. And besides, no one would *want* to leave the MNF pinned against New Russia while the aliens made mischief elsewhere. And yet...

"They're not launching starfighters," she breathed. It was the strangest, most *alien,* thing of all. "Where are their *starfighters?*"

"Perhaps they don't *have* starfighters," Anson suggested. "Or perhaps..."

New red icons flared into existence on the display. Abigail heard Alan's stunned curse through the intercom as he struggled to process what they were seeing. The aliens *did* have starfighters, starfighters that had somehow managed to appear between the MNF and *its* starfighters... starfighters that were roaring straight towards the fleet carriers. Abigail watched, in horror, as the human starfighter formation came apart, the pilots seemingly unsure what to do. Should they continue the offensive against the enemy carriers or turn back to reinforce the CSP?

"Shit," Anson said.

Abigail stared in horror. The alien starfighters were descending on the human carriers, firing...Abigail wasn't sure *what* they were firing. Superhot flashes of energy? Plasma pulses? Human plasma cannons had never managed to do more than fire a handful of shots before overloading and exploding, if they lasted long enough to do that. But the alien weapons were firing constantly, burning deep into their target's hull...

And HMS *Formidable* vanished from the display with a sudden, *terrible*, finality.

CHAPTER
FOURTEEN

For a long moment, Alan refused to believe his eyes.

HMS *Formidable* was an *Illustrious*-class fleet carrier. Two kilometres long, carrying four entire wings of starfighters and a crew of over a thousand…he'd served on her, once upon a time. She couldn't be *gone*. But her icon was gone, replaced by an expanding cloud of debris and hundreds of alien starfighters seeking new targets. She was just…*gone*.

He stared, trying to understand what it meant. Captain Napier - if his former CO was still in command - was dead. Commander Higgins was dead. Wing Commanders Arden and Smith were dead. Everyone he'd known on the ship - if they'd still been *on* the ship - was dead, unless they'd had a chance to get to the lifepods. But there was no hint that any lifepods had made it off the giant carrier before she died…

Bennett poked him, hard. "Snap out of it!"

Alan glared at him. Bennett didn't understand. A fleet carrier had been torn apart in less than a minute. And that meant…he shuddered as a Russian carrier staggered under a hail of plasma bolts, exploding into debris bare seconds after the attack began. The alien starfighters didn't *seem* to be that much faster than their human counterparts, but they definitely seemed to be more manoeuvrable. And they *all* packed one hell of a punch. The plasma cannons tipped the odds squarely in their favour.

He forced himself to watch as a third carrier died, then shuddered as the human starfighters tried to press their offensive against the alien ships. But the aliens had mounted plasma weapons on their starships too, putting out hundreds of thousands of plasma bursts every second. Their firing didn't seem to be very accurate, but it didn't need to be. All they had to do was break up the human formations and prevent the torpedo bombers from closing on their targets. Hundreds of starfighters died before someone - whoever had assumed command - ordered a retreat. And yet, it wouldn't be enough. Two more human carriers had died while he was watching the starfighters.

"Signal from the flag," Maddy said. She sounded badly shaken. She'd served long enough to understand the implications. "We're to alter course towards Tramline Two and run silent."

Run silent, Alan thought, sarcastically. *As if we have a hope of remaining hidden.*

He gritted his teeth as the disastrous battle unfolded in front of him. The MNF seemed to have fallen apart, pilots flying with whatever wingmen they could find rather than staying in their national formations. British pilots flew beside Russians, Americans flew beside Chinese...and it didn't seem to matter. The aliens fought with a cold, lethal precision, concentrating on the remaining fleet carriers and warships. Their plasma weapons really *had* tipped the scale, the analytical part of his mind noted. They didn't *have* to keep some of their starfighters in reserve, did they? They certainly didn't need a CSP.

Another icon - USS *Obama* - vanished from the display. Four more warships followed her into destruction: three frigates and a cruiser. The MNF command network, such as it was, appeared to have gone down completely. The flagship was gone, as were the two secondary command ships. No one might be sure who *should* be in command, let alone who *was* in command. The loss of the datanet meant certain destruction if they didn't manage to withdraw in time.

Which isn't going to happen, he thought, numbly. *The carriers can't get out of the killing zone.*

He was beyond shock now, his thoughts sluggish as he watched the display. Part of him felt as though he was watching a training simulation, with the enemy forces drawn from a science-fantasy rather than real life. And yet, it was real. He forced himself to think, assessing the situation as best as he could. The alien starfighters definitely didn't appear to be any faster than their human counterparts, but they could still catch a retreating fleet carrier. Only three carriers were left now, drawing fire from hundreds of alien craft. Alan sourly admired the alien discipline as they closed on their targets. *Their* pilots didn't seem to be wasting time shooting down other starfighters.

A low quiver ran through *Haddock*. Alan glanced at the display, half-convinced that the aliens were already coming after them. But instead, the escort carrier was slowly turning away, retreating with the rest of the convoy. Commodore Banks was doing the right thing, Alan knew, and yet it felt as though they were abandoning their comrades. He felt a flicker of surprise as he realised just how much the navy meant to him, despite everything. He'd been raised to believe that the navy never abandoned its own. But there was no choice. The escort carriers couldn't *hope* to stand off a single alien carrier.

And the freighters don't have any stealth systems, Alan thought. *We'd have to go doggo and deactivate the drives completely if we wanted to hide.*

He shook his head, grimly. The aliens had had plenty of time to get a solid lock on the convoy. There was no way the freighters could hide, not if the aliens came after them. The aliens might not know *precisely* where they were, but they'd certainly have no trouble calculating which volume of space to search. A freighter - even forty freighters - was still tiny on an interplanetary scale, yet they couldn't hide forever. A single emission would be more than enough to lead the aliens right to them.

Perhaps we should scatter, he thought. Commodore Banks had probably made the right call in heading for Tramline Two instead of Tramline One, but they were still going to be far too close to the aliens for hours. *That might give some of the freighters a chance to escape.*

And doom any that get caught, his own thoughts answered. *We'd have a better chance to fight if we stay together.*

"They won," Maddy said. "Sir..."

Alan looked back at the display. The last human fleet carrier was nothing more than an expanding cloud of debris, while the remainder of the human starfighters were either falling back on New Russia or launching suicide attacks into the teeth of enemy firepower. They hadn't done anything *wrong*, as far as he could tell. The MNF had followed doctrine to the letter. But traditional doctrine had been written for a very different weapons mix, one where starfighters launched long-range strikes while fleet carriers tried to stay out of the line of battle...they'd never anticipated being so heavily outgunned. He silently cursed the aliens under his breath. In hindsight, it was clear that they'd waited *deliberately*, holding their cards in reserve until humanity had assembled a force to challenge them. And *then* they'd pounced.

Maddy stared at him, her eyes wide with horror. "Sir..."

Alan wondered, suddenly, just who *she'd* seen die. Maddy might have known some of the dead too...come to think of it, she might have better reason to believe that some of her former friends were dead. Alan could hope, at least, that none of the crewmen he'd known on *Formidable* had still been on the ship. It wasn't as if most starfighter pilots - and starship officers - stayed with a single ship for their entire career. If he recalled correctly, the average officer served on at least four ships...

"Bring up the sensor records," he ordered, harshly. He couldn't afford to have Maddy go to pieces, not now. "See if you can find something we can use."

Maddy gulped. "Aye, sir."

Alan nodded, then keyed his console. The aliens were concentrating on New Russia - their starfighters were already heading towards the planet, without bothering to recharge and rearm - but it wouldn't be long before they started hunting the convoy. *New Russia* wasn't going anywhere, after all. He'd read a handful of vague articles about moving entire planets, but they'd never been anything more than theoretical studies. Dyson Spheres were more practical and it would be a very long time before humanity could construct a shell around a star. There was certainly no sign that the aliens possessed the technology to do anything of the sort.

Bennett cleared his throat. "Did we get *any* of them?"

Alan shrugged. Post-battle analysis would tell them, he supposed. But then, the only thing they could *count* on were long-range sensor records. If *Melbourne* had drawn data from the in-system network, it hadn't been shared with *Haddock*. The time delay alone would make it problematic. A hundred alien starfighters might have been killed and no one would know. It was certainly clear that no alien capital ships had been destroyed. He didn't think any of them had been so much as *scratched*.

"We'll find out," he said. On the display, the alien starfighters were tearing into New Russia's defence grid. The orbital defences had had *some* time to get over the shock and prepare, he noted. But it didn't look like it was going to be enough. The orbital network wasn't designed to cope with alien starfighters. "I wish…"

He looked at the timer and swore out loud. Ten minutes. Barely even that, really. Ten minutes…twelve fleet carriers had died in less than twelve minutes. It had been the single most one-sided engagement in the Royal Navy's long history, worse even than the loss of *Queen Elizabeth* during the Second Falklands War. He couldn't even begin to calculate how many people had been killed. The two British carriers alone would have had over three thousand souls onboard, if one included the Royal Marines and Royal Engineers. Unless they'd been offloaded before the engagement…

"Shit," he said, quietly. The Russian defence grid had been brushed aside. "What happens now?"

Bennett was watching the displays as the alien starships entered orbit, systematically dropping KEWs on anything that might be dangerous. They didn't have much to fear, Alan knew. Ground-based beam weapons didn't pose much of a threat to starships, while missiles would be easily tracked and intercepted as they boosted out of the atmosphere. New Russia was naked and helpless now, the forces on the ground utterly unable to keep the aliens from landing wherever they wanted. Alan had watched as the Royal Navy had pummelled a warlord-run state from orbit years ago, teaching the local barbarians not to mess with British citizens. The boot was on the other foot now. It would be very difficult for the Russians to muster any serious resistance to the alien invaders.

"It depends," Bennett said, turning away from the displays. "What do the aliens *want*?"

Alan shrugged. He'd read all the speculations, or at least the ones the Royal Navy had considered creditable enough to forward to its officers, but none of them were based on anything beyond science-fantasy and wild imaginations. Certainly, it was hard to take some of the suggestions seriously. The aliens might want to keep humanity from posing a long-term threat, but it was hard to believe that they actually wanted to *eat* humans. Or cross-breed with human women, for that matter. But human history showed a wide range of possible motives as well as outcomes. It was quite possible that the aliens believed they had a *right* to humanity's planets. And convincing them otherwise might be difficult.

"If they're unsure about the outcome, they'll probably leave the civilians alone," Bennett commented. "They wouldn't want to give us any excuse to retaliate against *their* civilians, if they lose the war. But that assumes they think like us."

"Yeah," Alan said.

He shivered. He'd studied the Age of Unrest. Tin-pot dictatorships and religious fanatics had often moved helpless civilians into danger zones, daring their enemies to slaughter innocents. It had worked once, when the war had been genteel. Years of increasingly bitter conflict and hatred had hardened attitudes and dehumanised enemy civilians. Surrounding a power station or military installation with human shields just meant a lot of dead civilians, none of whom had had a choice. By then, the war had been seen as total. It was a minor miracle that large swathes of the planet hadn't been depopulated.

And aliens might not even need to invent justifications for mass slaughter, he thought. *If invasion and settlement is their goal, they might want to wipe New Russia clean of human life before landing their own colonists.*

"It'll be nasty," Bennett added. "Even for trained soldiers, it's not always possible to tell if something is a weapon or not. People can be shot just for pointing a fake gun at a soldier on guard. And aliens would be even less able to tell the difference between a friendly gesture and a threat."

Alan nodded, curtly. The aliens seemed to be entering orbit...it didn't *look* as though they were landing troops, but there was no way to tell. It was quite possible that they'd been holding the occupation force on the far side of Tramline Four, just in case the battle went the other way. There was certainly no need to *hurry*. New Russia *definitely* wasn't going anywhere.

He tried to imagine what it would be like, when the aliens landed. Interstellar invasion had always been seen as difficult, if not outright impossible. Dominating a planet's high orbitals was easy, assuming one managed to capture them, but landing enough troops to occupy an entire planet? Alan didn't know how many Russians had military training, let alone weapons in private hands, yet he found it hard to believe there were none. Besides, the Russian soldiers had probably left their bases before the KEWs started raining down. They'd be hidden now, waiting for a chance to strike.

A memory flashed into his mind - and refused to fade. Years ago, he'd watched a movie with Judith. She'd been pregnant with Jeanette at the time, if he recalled correctly. They'd gone to a cinema and watched a chick-flick about a pair of lovers during the Troubles, lovers who'd been separated during the mass round-ups. He'd found it hard to be sorry for either of the characters - he was still surprised that the film had been made, let alone distributed - but now…now he thought he understood how they'd felt. Their country had been transformed, overnight, into a hostile environment. And they'd been torn apart by a war neither of them had chosen.

But we didn't choose this war either, he told himself. *None of us did.*

He keyed his console. "Herring Squadron is to remain on alert status," he ordered, shortly. "Kipper Squadron is to return to the ready room."

Not that we need to worry, he thought. *Kipper's pilots will have more than enough time to get into their craft before Herring has finished vacating the launch tubes.*

He forced himself to pull up the raw sensor data as the minutes slowly turned into hours and the convoy crawled away from New Russia. The analysts would check everything, of course, but he didn't have time to wait for the official reports. Gleaning something from the raw data might make the difference between life and death. Besides, there weren't many analysts attached to the convoy, if any. *Melbourne* wasn't large enough to have an analysis section of her own.

"I think we did kill a handful of their starfighters," Maddy said, slowly. "But it's hard to be sure."

Alan looked up. "I hope you're right," he said. "What have you found?"

Maddy held out a datapad. Alan took it. He couldn't help noticing that there were dark circles around Maddy's eyes. She was young, but they'd been awake for hours before entering the system. He was tempted to order her to go back to her cabin. God knew she wasn't the only one who needed a rest. But he might need her…

"A handful of sensor contacts vanished," Maddy told him, as he scanned the pad. "There is at least a possibility that most of them were picked off by our starfighters."

Alan frowned. "But there's no way to be sure," he said. He looked at the display. The gulf between the convoy and New Russia was growing wider by the second, but he had no illusions about just how easily the aliens could catch them if they wanted. "You can't prove it."

"No," Maddy said. "But my analysis is sound."

"It's also what you want to believe," Alan said. He tried not to see the crushed expression on her face. "We have to be careful that we don't make the mistake of seeing what we want to see."

He studied the rest of the analysis carefully. The aliens didn't seem to use their stealth systems very often, which was odd. On one hand, firing plasma cannons in all directions was the very opposite of stealthy; on the other hand, the aliens could definitely get into firing position before dropping their stealth and opening fire. Their starships had certainly managed to get very close to the planet before they'd been detected. Did the stealth system consume a great deal of power? It was possible, he supposed. Attempts to produce a cloaking device had failed, as far as he knew. And yet, *someone* might have made a workable version over the last few years. He wouldn't have been told about it, even if he hadn't been in jail.

I was never assigned to a top secret research base, he thought. *I wouldn't have had a 'need to know' until the device entered the mainstream.*

"It's a good piece of work," he said, softly. Maddy deserved some encouragement…she'd spotted a few things he'd missed. He felt a rush of affection and he reminded himself, again, that she was his subordinate. "And I hope you're right."

The klaxons began to howl. Red icons flickered into life on the display.

"Shit," he said. "They've found us!"

CHAPTER
FIFTEEN

Abigail had been reprimanded - once - for dozing off while she'd been on duty, when she'd been a young girl on her first cruise. Her uncle had been very scathing about it, pointing out that the entire crew relied on the watch officer to keep her eyes open at all times. She'd never made that mistake again as she'd climbed the ranks to captaincy. In hindsight, she'd even wondered if her uncle had been deliberately watching for her to make the mistake. It was something she'd needed to learn before she rose too high.

Now, she felt tired as the convoy crept towards Tramline Two, tired and worn. She'd sent half her crew to their bunks, once it became clear they weren't in immediate danger, but she hadn't left the bridge herself. How *could* she? She was responsible for her ship and crew, even if she *was* playing at being a naval officer. But the stimulant she'd taken, when she'd realised just how long it was going to be before they finally jumped out of the system, was starting to wear off. And when it wore off completely, she knew all too well, she was going to crash hard. It was almost a relief when the aliens finally showed up.

She jerked upright, adrenaline coursing through her system. Red icons were sparkling to life on the display, followed by convoy-wide alerts. Commodore Banks had ordered the convoy to maintain radio silence, but there was no point in being quiet now. The aliens had found them. There could be no mistake. Even as she watched, the enemy starfighters altered course to intercept the convoy.

They didn't have a solid lock on us, she thought. The aliens *had* been caught by surprise, if she was reading their trajectories correctly. They'd probably thought the convoy was somewhere else and only caught a sniff of the *real* location by accident. *And now they're moving into attack position.*

"Call Anson back to the bridge," she ordered, curtly. He *was* the best helmsman on the ship, although she wouldn't tell him that for fear of boosting his ego. And besides, as much as she might want to let him sleep through the engagement, she knew he'd never forgive her if they survived. "And then ready the weapons."

"Aye, Captain," Poddy said. She sounded nervous. "Point defence weapons are coming online now."

Abigail frowned, eying the back of Poddy's head. Her daughter *did* sound nervous. If she panicked under fire…Abigail keyed her console, silently readying herself to take over Poddy's duties if necessary. She hated to even *think* of the possibility, but she knew it had to be acknowledged. *She'd* been seventeen when *she'd* faced her first real emergency.

Her console bleeped. "Captain," Alan said. "I request permission to launch starfighters."

"Granted," Abigail said, curtly. It was a meaningless formality, now that Commodore Banks had ordered the convoy to go to battle stations. There was certainly nothing to be gained from keeping the starfighters in the launch tubes. The aliens had destroyed twelve fleet carriers in less than ten minutes and she was all too aware that *Haddock* was flimsy by comparison. "Are you going to fly yourself?"

There was a brief hesitation. "Both of my Wing Commanders will be out," Alan said, reluctantly. "I have to stay inside."

Abigail felt her lips twitch in cold amusement. There were people on Earth who'd send Alan white feathers for refusing to put his life at risk, although anyone with half a brain would realise that Alan *was* at risk. *Haddock* wouldn't stand a chance if those plasma weapons started burning into her hull. Alan would have a better shot at survival if he was outside the ship. She snorted at the thought. Stupid groundpounders didn't realise that maintenance and logistics could be just as important as fighting.

The aliens clearly understand, she thought, as Anson entered the bridge and sat down. *That's why they came after us.*

She pushed the thought aside. "Understood," she said. She didn't have to worry about keeping derision out of her tone. Spacers understood the realities, even if groundpounders didn't. "Tell your pilots I said good luck."

"The flag is ordering us to pick up speed," Poddy said. "We're going to make a run for the tramline."

"As long as we stay in formation, we should be fine," Anson said. "But if we get strung out…"

"I know the dangers," Abigail said. "And so does the Commodore."

She turned her attention to the display and watched, grimly, as the starfighters were ejected into space. It was slow, too slow. The aliens didn't seem interested in giving them the time to get the starfighters out, either. Any purpose-built escort carrier would have to include more launch tubes, she noted absently. She promised herself that she'd bring the concept to the attention of the Belt Federation, if she made it home. Building fleet carriers was beyond them, but escorts might just be possible…

Particularly as we're at war, she thought. *There won't be any objection from the Great Powers if we start cannoning up.*

"Enemy craft will enter presumed engagement range in two minutes," Poddy said. She sounded calmer now, thankfully. "Twenty-two minutes to the tramline."

Anson snorted. "How long did it take them to tear apart twelve *fleet* carriers?"

"That will do," Abigail snapped, although she'd been thinking the same thing herself. "Do they have any capital ships within detection range?"

"Not as far as I can tell," Poddy said. "But that means nothing."

Abigail nodded, grimly. Commodore Banks had launched a shell of recon drones and long-range probes, but all they were picking up were enemy starfighters. And yet, those starfighters *had* to have a mothership *somewhere* close by…unless, she supposed, they had far more endurance than their human counterparts. It was vaguely possible. There was no way to guess what other surprises the aliens might have up their sleeves.

They might not even wear sleeves, the irreverent part of her mind pointed out.

She studied the sensor readings as the final seconds ticked away. The alien starfighters appeared to be slightly *larger* than humanity's, although they also seemed to be more manoeuvrable. It was difficult to be certain, but it looked as though the point defence sensors would have no difficulty telling the two sides apart. The aliens weren't using their stealth systems either, which meant...what? She had no difficulty in believing the system was a power hog, but she couldn't help feeling as though that was too good to be true.

"The aliens are engaging the first squadrons now," Poddy said. A handful of icons vanished from the display. "I..."

Abigail heard a note of pain in Poddy's voice and winced. She'd told Poddy not to spend too much time with the starfighter pilots, but Poddy hadn't been able to avoid getting to know some of them. A couple of her friends might be dead now. At least they'd taken out a pair of aliens too. It was clear that some of the wilder speculations - force fields, at least - were not grounded in reality.

Which is lucky for us, she told herself, as the alien starfighters broke through the defenders and roared down on the convoy. *They already have too many advantages.*

"They're coming right at us," Poddy said. Her voice rose, sharply. "The CSP is moving to intercept."

"Open fire the moment they enter the kill-zone," Abigail ordered. She doubted the CSP could stop the aliens, not before they engaged *Haddock*. The point defence would have to shoot first and ask questions later. Thankfully, the starfighter pilots understood the danger of straying into the kill-zone themselves. *This* time, there would be no incidents. "We'll give them a beating."

She tensed as the aliens swept into engagement range, blowing through the CSP with a grim determination she could only admire. The point defence opened fire a second later, blasting two of the alien starfighters into dust. Abigail felt her heart leap, an instant before one of the alien craft opened fire. Alarms sounded as plasma bolts plunged into her ship.

"Direct hit, lower holds," Poddy said. The alarms went quiet, so abruptly that silence fell like a hammer. "I think they took out one of the launch tubes."

And all the starfighters are already out, Abigail thought. The aliens presumably didn't know it, but switching out the damaged launch tube and replacing it wouldn't take more than a few hours. If, of course, they made it back home. *We won't be so lucky next time.*

"Seal off that section," she ordered. "We'll try to make repairs once we're through the tramline."

The remaining alien craft broke and fled. Abigail frowned, trying to figure out what they were doing. Another pass would have destroyed her ship...hell, all they'd have to do was shoot out the drives if they wanted to render her dead in space. The freighter might survive that sort of treatment, but she'd be good for nothing more than scrap afterwards. And then she saw the aliens regrouping, altering course towards...

"They're targeting *Melbourne*," Poddy breathed.

Anson didn't look up from his console as the aliens began their attack run. "We have to do something!"

Abigail shook her head. There was nothing they could do. The convoy's CSP was already moving to intercept, but she doubted they could keep the aliens from breaking through and falling on the cruiser. Their tactics *did* make sense, she supposed, as the aliens started tearing *Melbourne* apart. It took longer - much longer - to produce a warship than a freighter. A clear shot at a cruiser was not to be missed. And killing the convoy CO was just the icing on the cake.

"She's gone," Poddy said.

"Keep us on our current course," Abigail ordered. The aliens were already regrouping. Of *course* they were. There were other warships, real as well as makeshift, to be killed. "Once we're over the tramline, we can go silent again."

She studied the empty display. She *knew* the aliens had to have a mothership out there somewhere, a mothership that could presumably cross the tramlines too. The pursuit would not be long delayed, if it was delayed at all. And yet...she glared at the barren reaches of interplanetary space. Neither her sensors nor the recon drones could pick up much of anything.

They'll have to pick up their starfighters first, she told herself. She knew *that* wouldn't slow the aliens down much, if at all. A fleet carrier could recover all of her starfighters with terrifying speed. *And then…and then they'll come right after us.*

"Captain Hyatt has assumed command," Poddy reported. "He's ordering us to keep going."

"Very good," Abigail said, dryly. The aliens were moving back into attack formation now, isolating their targets one by one. "It isn't as if we have anywhere else to go."

———

Alan felt sweat trickling down his back as he tried to make sense out of the chaos. The alien attack patterns made sense, yet they *didn't* make sense. They'd attacked *Haddock* and two other escort carriers briefly, then moved to attack the *genuine* warships instead of the freighters or escort carriers. Perhaps they were more interested in wiping out the remainder of the MNF than anything else.

"Herring Nine is gone, sir," Maddy said. "There's no sign she ejected."

"Understood," Alan said.

He felt a pang of bitter regret. Herring Nine - Flight Lieutenant Sofia Augusta. A fun-loving young woman who'd been transferred when she'd been caught having an affair with one of her wingmates. She'd been good enough, barely, not to be discharged on the spot. And now she was dead. He told himself, firmly, that he'd mourn later. Right now, he had to concentrate on the engagement.

The aliens pushed the offensive hard, systematically wiping out the remaining warships one by one. It cost them, but it didn't cost them *enough*. Trading a handful of starfighters for a single frigate was a winning equation, even if it *was* hard on the starfighter pilots. Alan had no idea what sort of intelligence was directing the aliens, but he thought he understood its logic. The aliens were quite happy to spend starfighters to kill capital ships.

We'd do it too, he thought, as HMCS *Seaford* exploded into fire. Captain Hyatt was dead, bare minutes after assuming command. *But they're using our own logic against us.*

"They're swinging around to target us," Maddy reported. "Two more squadrons are closing in on the other escorts…"

"Let the point defence handle them," Alan ordered. There was no point in trying to micromanage, not now. His subordinates knew what to do. "Is there still no sign of their starships?"

"No, sir," Maddy said.

Alan forced himself to think, carefully. The aliens clearly *hadn't* known precisely where the convoy was, forcing them to send out recon squadrons to locate the human ships before whistling up something stronger to destroy them. But they'd definitely found their targets now, which meant…either there was a fleet carrier somewhere nearby or the aliens were operating right on the edge of their endurance.

Or we might simply have underestimated their endurance, he thought, sourly. *The aliens might be able to endure much longer flights - and fights.*

The ship shuddered. "Direct hit, port armour," Maddy said. "I…"

She broke off. "*Red Wedding* is gone," she added sharply, as another icon vanished from the display. "They just blew right through her."

Alan winced. An escort carrier and her crew, just gone. It was nothing compared to the sheer number of lives already lost, but…he told himself, again, that they'd mourn later, once they were safe. They were nearing the tramline. If no enemy capital ships showed up, at least some of the freighters would be safe.

"Point defence network has been updated," Maddy told him. "I think we've got a better chance at hitting the bastards now."

"Yeah," Alan said. On the display, a freighter died in fire. The bastards hadn't even *tried* to disable the ship. "But they're still hitting us."

He cursed the aliens under his breath. A human starfighter would have to be very lucky to inflict serious damage on a fleet carrier with flechette guns, but the aliens didn't seem to have that limitation. They certainly didn't have to fly back to their carriers to reload after launching their torpedoes…they didn't *have* torpedoes. They didn't *need* them.

"Make sure you make every shot count," he ordered, although he knew it was impossible to save their pellets. The aliens had another advantage there, as much as he hated to admit it. Sooner or later, *Haddock* would shoot herself dry. And then she'd be utterly defenceless against even a single alien starfighter. "And make sure the CSP knows too."

"They know, sir," Maddy said. "They know."

———————

"They just caught us a glancing blow," Poddy reported. "Minor damage, but the hull is breached…"

"*Minor* damage," Abigail repeated, sardonically. *Haddock* was designed to seal off any compartments that were suddenly exposed to vacuum, but with her ship taking a pounding it was hard to be sure the safety precautions would actually take effect. Losing her entire ship to a single hull breach would be embarrassing, although right now it was actually the least of her worries. "Time to tramline?"

"Five minutes," Anson said. "As long as the drive holds out, we'll make it."

Abigail winced. *City of Truro*, a *Workhorse*-class freighter that might have been earmarked for later conversion into an escort carrier, had suffered a major drive failure and fallen out of formation. She'd hoped - and hated herself for hoping - that destroying a disabled ship would keep the aliens from taking out *more* ships. But the aliens had swept past the wounded vessel, no doubt marking her down for later attention. Abigail didn't know the vessel's commander, but she was sure he didn't deserve to be stuck in an occupied system. The aliens would have no trouble picking him up, afterwards, and dumping the crew into a POW camp.

If they bother to set up POW camps, Abigail thought. The Great Powers rarely bothered to take prisoners, these days. She'd heard the horror stories. The Geneva Conventions had fallen by the wayside long ago. *They might just exterminate the ship and crew.*

"They're coming back at us," Poddy reported. "The CSP is badly weakened."

"Keep us going," Abigail ordered. "And prepare to recover fighters."

The aliens attacked viciously, as if they sensed there wouldn't be another chance. Abigail watched two more ships die, a third losing power and falling out of formation. And then the first freighters reached the tramline and vanished…

"Start recovering starfighters," she ordered. "I…"

"Negative," Alan said, over the intercom. "Have them land on the hull!"

Abigail winced. *She* should have thought of that. They didn't have *time* to recover the starfighters, not on this side of the tramline. The aliens were pushing them hard. Once they realised the starfighters were being recovered, they'd do everything in their power to disrupt the process. And she'd have to decide between leaving people behind or risking the rest of her crew.

"Do it," she ordered. "And jump us out the moment we have everyone onboard."

She keyed the console, looking back at New Russia. There was no sign of the aliens, not at this distance, but she knew they were there. They'd sweep the system, destroying facilities and occupying asteroid settlements…if they didn't simply destroy them. Maybe the aliens were too advanced to need asteroid mining stations. Or maybe…

An instant later, the display blanked. Her stomach heaved.

"Jump completed, Captain," Anson reported. He sounded woozy. Jumping at speed felt like being punched in the gut. "We're clear."

For the moment, Abigail thought. *But what happens when they come after us?*

CHAPTER
SIXTEEN

There was nothing particularly interesting about the Kiev System. A Russian survey ship had visited the system over a century ago, but a brief survey hadn't turned up anything worthy of later attention. There was nothing in the system, save for a single gas giant and an asteroid cluster that might - once upon a time - have been a planet. The Russians had formally claimed the system, but - apart from using the tramlines - they hadn't actually *done* very much with it. There was no point in expending resources on settling Kiev when New Russia was just one tramline away. The only installation in the system was a refuelling station orbiting the gas giant.

"We appear to be clear, sir," Maddy said.

Alan nodded, tiredly. Assuming an alien fleet carrier *had* been lurking out of sensor range, assuming...he shook his head. There were too many assumptions, too many things he simply didn't know for sure. Right now, *Haddock* and her remaining comrades were in no state for a battle. If the aliens came after them, they were dead.

"Get the fighters inside," he ordered. He glanced at the latest update and winced. Only fifteen pilots had survived the brief, but brutal engagement. Nine of his pilots were dead, blown to dust...so many others were also dead that their deaths might have passed unnoticed. "And tell the pilots to go straight to bed."

He glanced at Bennett. "Who's in command now?"

"Good question," Bennett said. He studied the display for a long moment. "Is there any senior military officer left alive?"

Alan gritted his teeth. The warships were gone, leaving four escort carriers and thirty freighters...none of which were in any state for a fight. He honestly wasn't sure *who* was in command now. Technically, it should be the captain with the longest time in grade, but the belters might have different ideas. Perhaps Abigail would assume command. He wondered, absently, if he should encourage her to do it. But, right now, there was a more important problem.

He keyed his console. "We need to run silent, the moment we have all the starfighters onboard," he said. "Make sure *everyone* knows that a single leak could kill us."

"I'll see to it," Abigail said. She sounded as tired as he felt. "And I'll check our remaining supplies, see what can be shared."

"Good thinking," Alan said. He should have thought of that, but it had slipped his mind. They didn't have time to swap spare parts and ammunition around now - not unless they wanted to remain close to the tramline, which would just get them killed when the aliens finally crossed - but they'd have to do it later. "See if anyone has a recon probe too. We might need it."

He closed the connection and sat back in his chair. "Maddy, go get some rest," he ordered, once the starfighters were all back onboard. "I'll call you if you're needed."

Maddy didn't argue. That, more than anything else, proved that she was reaching the limits of her endurance. Instead, she stood and walked through the hatch. Alan resisted the urge to watch her go. Instead, he turned his attention to the display as the convoy slowly started to move. If his calculations were correct, they should have a reasonable chance of remaining hidden if they managed to get well away from the tramline. A dogleg course would add *days* to their journey home, but there was no choice. The aliens would expect them to take a least-time course to the next tramline.

Unless they're planning to drive on Earth instead, Alan thought. *Should we be trying to warn them?*

He stared down at his hands. Doctrine insisted that all fleet deployments should be quietly monitored by picket ships, a precaution that everyone had ridiculed when he'd been on the command track. It didn't look so stupid now. Surely, *someone* would have watched the battle, then hurried back to Earth. He tapped the console, bringing up the starchart and running through the calculations. Assuming they didn't encounter the aliens for a second and final time - another assumption he knew better than to take for granted - it would take at least five weeks to get back home. The aliens would have plenty of time to stomp Earth flat by the time the convoy arrived.

And there's no way to speed it up, he told himself. None of the freighters were particularly fast. He could shave a day or two off, if he tried, but not much more. The only way to *really* cut it down was to go back to New Russia, which ran the risk of being intercepted. *We can't warn them to prepare for hell.*

He looked at Bennett. "There would have been a picket ship, right?"

"Perhaps," Bennett said. He didn't look tired, the bastard. Alan was starting to wonder if he was actually the product of a top secret genetic enhancement project. Or maybe he just had some really neat modifications spliced into his DNA. "But we don't know."

"No," Alan agreed. "We don't."

He rose. "Get some sleep yourself," he ordered, as the convoy kept moving away from the tramline. They *should* be safe now, as long as they were careful. At the very least, they'd have some warning before the aliens jumped them. "I'll get some sleep too."

"Make sure someone is keeping an eye on the sensors," Bennett advised. "And *don't* take anything to go to sleep."

Alan nodded, tartly. Somehow, he doubted he needed it.

He walked through the corridors, trying to ignore the faint smell of ozone in the air…and Bennett's constant presence, behind him. He'd been more than a little resentful, at first, when he'd been sentenced to prison, even though he knew - on some level - that he deserved it. God knew he'd murdered his wife, throwing away both his career and his freedom in a single moment of naked violence. And yet…he'd never resented the *navy*.

It had been his home, his tribe. The navy might have rejected him, but he'd never returned the favour. He was a navy man…

He shuddered, helplessly. Twelve fleet carriers, the strongest ships humanity had produced, had been blown away in less than ten minutes. Compared to them, the other warships barely merited being mentioned in dispatches. He couldn't think of anything that could be done to safeguard the remainder of the navy from alien weapons. Bolting heavy armour to the hulls, perhaps? It might work, if the crews worked fast. Perhaps the aliens simply hadn't understood just how well their weapons would work on human hulls. They sure as hell knew now.

And they'll punch right at Earth, while we're still trying to adapt, he thought. *And that will be the end of the war.*

The hatch hissed opened. He didn't bother with a shower. He just took off his shoes and climbed into the bunk. His thoughts haunted him as he closed his eyes. What would they find, when they got home? A destroyed navy and a world swept clean of life? Or…or what?

And yet, we have to go home, he told himself. *We can't go elsewhere.*

He was tired. But it was a long time before he could sleep.

———

"Those weapons were *hot*, Captain," Drakopoulos said. The Chief Engineer looked as tired as Abigail felt. "They burned right through the hull. We're damn lucky they didn't hit anything explosive or we wouldn't be here right now."

"That's probably what killed the carriers," Abigail said. She'd managed to snatch a few quick hours of sleep, but her body was loudly insisting that she hadn't slept at all. "Did you find the bodies?"

"We pulled the remains of Rating Akuna out of the lower bay," Drakopoulos said. "Rating Wayland remains unaccounted for."

"May the stars protect him," Abigail said. "He deserved better, didn't he?"

She shivered as a thought struck her. Wayland had been wearing his shipsuit. If he'd been swept into space when the lower bay decompressed, which seemed the most likely scenario, he might have survived long enough to know his body would be lost forever. She'd study the records, of course, in the hopes of finding his body one day, but she knew success was unlikely.

"He deserved much better," Drakopoulos agreed. "And so did the others."

He held up a datapad. "I've been in touch with the other engineers," he told her. "We do have a list of spare parts we need to swap, so...I'd like to start transfer flights as soon as possible. Once we have the parts onboard, we can start work at once."

"Once we're well away from the aliens," Abigail said. She glanced at her wristcom, silently calculating the vectors. They should be safe now, but there were too many question marks surrounding the aliens for her to be sure of anything. For all she knew, they were being tracked right now. "Can we survive without the spare parts?"

"Probably," Drakopoulos said. "But we did lose a handful of computer nodes. Fortunately, the remainder of the system compensated."

He paused. "I can have the lower bay repressurised in an hour," he added. "It's the only place big enough to gather the entire crew."

"Good thinking," Abigail said. Belter custom demanded that the dead be honoured as soon as possible. And that went for the starfighter pilots too. They deserved to be honoured, even if they weren't Belters. Their deaths might just have saved the ship. "We'll hold the funeral in two hours."

"But no wake?" Drakopoulos said. "I could put together a still."

"No," Abigail said, flatly. She felt a pang of bitter guilt, which she ruthlessly pushed aside. Getting her CAG drunk might not be illegal, but it had been stupid. "We are *not* getting drunk in the middle of a warzone."

She nodded to him, then started to walk through the ship. The damage was fairly minor, in the grand scheme of things, but it shook her more than she cared to admit. She knew, intellectually, that the ship was far from invulnerable, yet it was still a shock to see damage to the hull. The grim knowledge that they'd been very lucky not to be ripped apart by alien fire didn't help. Thankfully, the aliens hadn't known *precisely* where to place their shots. Taking out the bridge would have been utterly disastrous.

It could have been worse, she told herself. *But it could have been better too.*

Alan led the way into the lower hull and stepped to one side, allowing his surviving starfighter pilots and support crew to find places amidst the civilians. Someone had been busy. After patching the hull, the engineers had stuck a handful of pictures to the wall, each one representing a crewman who'd died in the brief, savage engagement. He wasn't sure how he felt about the starfighter pilots being included, although…

Stop that, he told himself, sharply. *They're trying to honour all the dead.*

Abigail stepped up to the front of the room and turned to face the crowd. Alan watched her as the chamber fell quiet, then glanced behind him. Everyone was in the chamber, save for a skeleton crew. He couldn't keep himself from hoping that the hull patches would hold, at least long enough for the service to be finished. If the hull broke open again, everyone in the chamber would be dead if they didn't manage to get their shipsuits on in time. And even if they did, survival would be challenging. Alan doubted many would make it.

It isn't going to happen, he told himself. *Relax.*

"Death is a part of life," Abigail said. Her voice was very clear. "We who live beside the vacuum know this for a fact. Death stalks us every day, waiting for the moment when our lives come to an end. And we accept this to be true, because death cannot be evaded permanently. We do not fear death, for death is a part of life. Instead, we strive to accomplish something with our lives before our time runs out, something that our families and friends will remember when we are gone.

"Today, we gather to honour our comrades who died so that we may live. Seventeen people on this ship were killed in the battle, all members of our crew. Their deaths will not be forgotten. We will remember them as long as life itself endures."

She paused. "It is customary for the captain to speak briefly about each of the dead, but time is not on our side," she added. "And so I will speak of two and Wing Commander Marc Savage will speak of a third. We ask your forgiveness - and that of the dead - for cutting the service short. The others will be remembered when we return home."

If we return home, Alan thought. The system was quiet, as far as their sensors could determine, but that meant nothing. The alien stealth systems were too good. It was quite possible that the aliens were already closing in. *We may never see Earth again.*

"Rating Akuna Yu was young, yet she had an inborn engineering talent that only needed a little direction to flourish into light. I saw something in her, when she applied to join the crew, that could become something great. And so I allowed her to join. In the two years she was with us, she was beloved by everyone, credited for squeezing a *little* more power out of the drives. She will be sorely missed.

"Rating Wayland was older, yet he was young at heart. He told me, once, that he never intended to rise in the ranks. He merely wanted to see the universe and serving on a freighter seemed a good way to do it. Perhaps he was right, too. In his time as a spacer, he saw more planets and star systems than anyone else, even me. I often wondered why he didn't apply for survey work instead of freighters, but he never answered. Perhaps he was happy where he was. He made us happy too.

"His body has not been recovered. We cannot take his ashes home, nor can we launch him into space. And yet, I pledge he will not be forgotten. *None* of them will be forgotten."

No, Alan promised himself. *None of them will be forgotten.*

She looked at Savage, who stepped forward. "I wish there was time to speak of everyone," he said. "Fifteen starfighter pilots died, seven of them under my command. But I can only speak of one, Flight Lieutenant Sofia Augusta."

He took a long breath. "Sofia was a wild young woman, at heart. She was a thrill-seeker, willing to do anything for a dare. She confided in me, once, that she'd come very close to being expelled from her school after a streaking prank resulted in great embarrassment for her teachers.

Thankfully, she was introduced to starfighters, where being willing to risk everything is considered an advantage."

Alan winced. *That* hurt, more than he cared to admit.

"There was nothing *bad* about her," Savage said. "She was not malicious. She wanted to live life to the fullest, not torment others. She could laugh at herself, rather than laugh at others. I liked her. We all liked her. And while she did deserve a severe reprimand for her conduct on her last posting, she didn't deserve to die. I like to think that she's laughing at us - and herself - from beyond the stars.

"I wish I'd known her for longer. I wish I'd known the others for longer. But what I know of her will be remembered."

It will, Alan promised himself. He wished he'd known Sofia Augusta better too. *And so will all of the others who died in the battle.*

Abigail looked at him. "Alan? Would you like to say a few words?"

No, Alan thought. *But there are some things that have to be said.*

"I promised you that I wouldn't bullshit you, when we first met," he said. He'd said that to the starfighter pilots, but he thought the rest of the crew would understand. "We have just watched helplessly as thousands of people, some of them our friends and family, were blown away by our new foe. It won't be long before they resume their advance on Earth. And if they take Earth - or even devastate the system - the war will be over.

"This is a war for survival, a war waged against a race that seems to think the galaxy isn't big enough for both of us. This is not a little border skirmish or a struggle with religious fanatics, not even a war between Great Powers! This is going to be worse than any war humanity has ever fought. The loss of twelve entire fleet carriers may be only the beginning. It will get worse. Our very existence as a species is under threat!

"I wish I had some comfort to offer. I wish I could promise you victory. But all I can say is that we *will* continue to fight, we *will* do everything in our power to hold the line until we can teach these bastards that humanity will *never* give up. We will fight. We will win. And we will make them pay for what they've done!

"Remember the dead. And avenge them!"

He stepped back. Abigail spoke a few brief words - Alan barely heard them - and then dismissed the crew. Alan started to follow them, tiredly. He wanted more sleep - he thought they *all* wanted more sleep - but there was no time. They *had* to get the ships repaired before the aliens showed up. They *had* to.

And if they catch up with us after the repairs, he thought numbly, *they'll kill us anyway.*

Abigail caught his arm. "A word with you," she said. "Now."

CHAPTER
SEVENTEEN

Abigail's cabin hadn't changed, Alan noted, as he followed her into her private compartment. Of *course* it hadn't changed. It was still cramped, despite being the largest cabin on the ship. A datapad sat on the table, blinking for attention. The hatch hissed closed as Abigail pointed him to the chair, her movements less graceful now they were alone. He couldn't help wondering what was bothering her.

"Sit," Abigail ordered, when he made no move to sit down. She softened her tone, just slightly. "Please?"

Alan sat and watched, with growing alarm, as she pulled a box out of a compartment and opened it to reveal a bottle of dark red liquid. The bottle was unmarked, something that would not have passed muster on Earth. There was no list of ingredients or warnings about alcohol content, let alone snide notes about drunkards still being responsible for anything they did while under the influence. He'd always found them infuriating as a young man, although he supposed the warnings did make a certain kind of sense. A man who drank and then did something stupid would not be able to use drunkenness as an excuse when he was hauled up before the magistrate.

"There are glasses in the compartment under your butt," Abigail said. She sounded angry, although her anger wasn't directed at him. "Take out a couple, would you?"

Alan hesitated, torn between doing as he was told and walking out. Abigail had given him alcohol before and the results had not been good.

And he was supposed to set an example for the other pilots. God knew they'd think less of him if they found him wandering the ship in a drunken state, tunelessly singing the nine verses of *Merlin the Happy Pig*. But, at the same time, part of him wanted to drown his sorrows. He'd watched twelve fleet carriers die in less than ten minutes. The war had taken a very nasty turn.

He reached under the chair, opened the compartment and produced two shot glasses. Abigail sniffed when she saw them - there were bigger glasses too - but took them without comment, pouring a splash of wine into each glass. Alan frowned as she passed him a glass, lifting hers to her lips. The smell was strong enough to bother him. He couldn't help wondering if the two-pint rule should be replaced by the one-shot rule.

"Absent friends," Abigail said. She looked down at the liquid for a long moment. "Cheers."

She drank. Alan drank too, carefully. The wine tasted strong, as if it had been left to ferment for too long. He wondered, as he put the empty glass down on the table, just how much alcohol he'd drunk. Shipboard rot-gut was normally not made with scientific precision. It could be anything from mildly-fermented grape juice to something so strong that a sniff of the liquid would make his head spin. No one had actually been *poisoned* by rotgut, as far as he knew, but that didn't mean the wine wasn't strong. His superiors on *Formidable* would not have been amused if he'd turned up for duty drunk out of his mind.

He shuddered as it hit him, again. *Formidable* was gone. The carrier had seemed invincible, utterly untouchable by modern weapons. But the aliens had changed the rules and *Formidable* had died and...

Abigail held up the bottle. "Another?"

Alan shook his head. "No, thank you," he said. "We have to keep a clear head."

"It's a little late for that," Abigail said. She put the bottle back in the box and returned it to the compartment. "She was a pretty young girl, you know?"

"Akuna?"

"Yeah," Abigail said. "She could have gone far, if she'd lived. The belt doesn't care about tangled family trees, does it? All that matters is competence and ability and…she had those, in spades. I knew she wouldn't stay with us forever, but I didn't care. I liked her more than I should."

She looked at him, sharply. "Does it ever get easier?"

Alan shook his head. "No," he said. Men and women had died under his command. They'd died in training accidents, not wartime, but it didn't make it any easier. He knew accidents happened, he knew the board of inquiry had determined that the accidents hadn't been his fault, yet he kept thinking that there was something he could have done. "The pain dulls, but it never goes away."

"She wasn't military," Abigail said. She sounded as though she hadn't heard a word he'd said. "I should have kicked her off the ship, when we were told that we were going to become an escort carrier. God knows it wouldn't have been held against her. She could have gone back to the belt and become a research scientist or something…not stayed with us and flown into danger. I could have saved her life."

"You didn't know," Alan said, quietly.

He sighed, inwardly. He'd been told not to get too attached to his pilots, but that was impossible. When he'd been a starfighter pilot himself, he'd shared in the camaraderie; when he'd been CAG, he still hadn't been able to distance himself from the younger men and women. Hell, it was *worse* on *Haddock*. He'd had twenty-four pilots under his command, not three hundred. He'd gotten to know them better than he should.

"I should have known," Abigail said. "She was barely three years older than Poddy. I shouldn't have let her come with us."

And the ship's crew is too small for Abigail to detach herself from her subordinates, Alan thought. *Akuna might not have been her biological daughter, but Abigail thought of her as a child.*

"She made her choice," Alan said, unsure what to say. "It was what she wanted."

"She didn't know *what* she wanted," Abigail snapped. "Is it so easy for you to dismiss her death?"

"No," Alan said. He honestly didn't know what to say. "But she knew the risks."

Abigail snorted. "We all know the common risks," she said, bitterly. "A war is a little different, isn't it?"

"Yeah," Alan said. "It is."

He looked down at the metal deck, trying to think of something he could say. But nothing came to mind. He'd known - he'd always known - that everyone who joined the Royal Navy was a volunteer. The navy didn't take conscripts. Even the *army* didn't take conscripts, although that might change in a hurry. The last conscriptions had been nearly a century ago, but the legislation remained on the books. He had no doubt the government would reintroduce conscription as soon as it dawned on the politicians that the navy might not be able to keep the aliens from landing on Earth.

And we might not be able to resist, if they did, he thought. He wished, suddenly, for another drink. *As long as they control the high orbitals, we'd have no hope of driving them off our world.*

He shuddered. He knew enough about counter-insurgency tactics to understand that the aliens would have little trouble defending their positions. If, of course, they didn't simply exterminate the human race. Wiping out every population centre was the work of an afternoon, if they wanted Earth for themselves. Or they could drop a genetically-engineered virus, once they'd captured the high orbitals. That particular demon had nearly escaped the bottle before the Great Powers had managed to slam the lid into place and weld it shut. And it had been *humans* who'd created the first tailored virus...

How can we blame the aliens for being inhuman, he thought, *when man is so inhuman to man?*

"People have died before," Abigail said. "I killed...I killed a man who thought I'd be an easy target. He dragged me into a cabin, I drew my gun and shot him. I didn't feel anything as I watched him die. It didn't really shock me."

She looked at her empty glass. "He deserved it. I carried...I had a gun. Didn't he think I knew how to use it? And my uncle died because he made a careless, but understandable mistake. I mourned him, yet...his death was understandable. He pushed the life support too far, you see. It caught up with him eventually. But Akuna died in the middle of an incomprehensible war. Why does it bother me so much?"

"She did nothing to deserve it," Alan said, quietly.

"No, she didn't," Abigail said. She looked up at him, sharply. "Did your *wife* do anything to deserve it?"

Alan felt a hot flash of anger, mingled with bitterness. The pain had dulled, in time. Colchester had helped, if only by forcing him to keep a steady routine. And yet, he was torn between self-justification and the grim knowledge that he'd deserved far worse. He'd been very lucky not to be marched into the execution chamber and hanged. If Judith hadn't been cheating on him...

But if Judith hadn't been cheating on me, he thought, *I would never have killed her.*

"I don't know," he said, finally. His feelings were awash. "I don't know *what* she deserved."

Alan studied his hands for a long moment, unwilling to meet her gaze. "I thought she loved me," he said. "I thought...we were building a family. I was sending her enough money to ensure that we'd have a comfortable life, once I retired. I wouldn't have any problems finding a job afterwards, if I wished. Military vets get preference almost everywhere. Five more years..."

He swore as it dawned on him. If she hadn't cheated on him - if he hadn't caught her - he would have retired before the war. He'd never really expected to command his own starship, not when there were more potential captains with better connections than there were commands. He might have had a shot at XO - or wound up spending the last two years flying a desk - but command would have been beyond him. And he wouldn't have waited around, either. He'd always intended to retire when his daughters started secondary school. God knew they'd need a father in their lives *then*.

And now they don't have anyone, but their grandparents, he thought. Hot tears prickled at the corner of his eyes. *Who'll keep a sharp eye on them then?*

"You killed her," Abigail said. Her voice was very hard. "You made the *choice* to kill her."

Alan sighed. He didn't *know*. Everything was a blur from the moment he'd walked into the house until the police arrested him. Flashes of memory, images of Judith screaming and...and...he shook his head. He didn't *want* to remember. Even thinking about losing control so badly scared him. He'd loved her. And yet…

"I know what I did," Alan said. The first *clear* memory was being interrogated by the police, his hands cuffed to the table as they fired questions at him. There had been blood on his hands…Judith's blood. "And yet I don't know what choice I made."

He gritted his teeth. A woman who cheated on her husband could expect nothing, after the divorce. And that went double for a wife who cheated on a military husband. She might get custody of the children, but even *that* came with a steep price. Hell, she'd be lucky not to be charged with demoralising the troops. Who'd want to go to war - and accept a long separation from his wife and children - if he thought there was a chance his wife would cheat on him?

No one, he thought. *The day of the 'Dear John' letter is long gone.*

It wasn't fair, he told himself. Judith could have gotten a divorce at any moment, if she'd been willing to pay the price. No one would have forced her to stay in the marriage if she'd been unhappy. They could have sat down like adults and discussed custody and visitation rights in a calm and reasonable manner. He'd loved her, but he would have let her go if she'd wanted to go. Instead…she'd had her fling. And he'd killed her…

"Everyone makes choices," Abigail said. "They just have to learn to deal with the consequences."

Alan felt his temper flare. "You could have handed the ship over to some other captain," he said, tartly. The days when the Royal Navy had more captains than ships were long gone too, but the navy wouldn't have had any problems digging up a CO for an escort carrier if necessary. "You didn't have to stay in command."

"This is *my* ship," Abigail snapped back. "I am in command. Not some…numbnut from Earth who doesn't understand how to handle a freighter crew. We're not *soldiers*, you know."

"But you're still going into a warzone," Alan pointed out. "You *knew* the ship might be attacked."

"I knew that," Abigail said. "But that doesn't make it any easier."

She glared at him. "Did you kill your wife because you were used to losing people?"

Alan clenched his fists. "No," he said. "I…"

"Did you not care about the dead?" Abigail pressed. "Or…a young woman is dead!"

"I know," Alan shouted. He fought to control his growing anger. "I *know* she's dead. And her death is a tragedy and nothing I can do will bring her back and…I can't bring her back."

He sagged, unclenching his fists. "It won't get any easier," he said. "You'll just get better at handling it."

Or you can hand the ship over to someone else, he added, silently. *If the navy lets you go…*

"Hah," Abigail said. She laughed, humourlessly. "We're a ship of the damned, aren't we?"

"No," Alan said.

"You murdered your wife," Abigail said. "And, for some strange reason, you were allowed to live until they found a use for you. What *shitty* people you groundpounders are, to be sure."

She laughed, again. "What did your ugly friend do?"

Alan gaped at her, then started to laugh himself. Bennett? She thought *Bennett* was a convict too? His laugh turned into hysterical giggles as he realised that they'd never actually *told* her that Bennett was his *watchdog*. God only knew what she'd been thinking. A serious criminal would have been executed - or at least exiled - but that still left plenty of room for all sorts of misbehaviour. For all she knew, Bennett had murdered his wife too.

"He didn't do anything," Alan said. It was hard, so hard, to keep from breaking into another fit of giggles. "He's there to make sure I don't do anything!"

"Oh," Abigail said. She looked at him, then chuckled. "*That* must be annoying."

"You have no idea," Alan said. He didn't really blame the Royal Navy for wanting to keep an eye on him. But Bennett's constant presence was more than a little irritating, even if they *had* managed to form a working relationship. "He does have his uses."

"I'm glad to hear it," Abigail said. "But…"

She looked down, grimly. "But…all those ships were destroyed. What happens now?"

"I don't know," Alan said. He felt numb. If the aliens could wipe out twelve fleet carriers so casually, what was to keep them from smashing the rest of the Royal Navy? And every *other* navy? The war might be over by the end of the month. "I just...don't know."

"And we won't know until we get back home," Abigail said. She shifted until they were facing each other, their legs almost touching. "All we can do is pray."

She leaned forward. Alan wasn't sure, afterwards, which of them actually kissed the other first. He was surprised at himself, surprised at her too. Their lips met, pressing together in a manner that had nothing to do with love and affection, but an urge to do something - anything - to remind them that they were still human. He drew back, just for a second, as his heart started to pound. Her eyes were hard, yet desperate. And then she kissed him again.

His body took over, his hands pulling her upright and scrabbling with her shipsuit. It had been too long, far too long, since he'd been with a woman. He couldn't keep himself from reaching up to stroke her breasts, feeling her hard nipples under his fingers. Her hands roamed his body too, unbuckling his suit and pushing his trousers down. She pushed him against the bulkhead, kissing him time and time again as he entered her...

It crossed his mind, as he started to move inside her, that it was a mistake. They shouldn't be having sex, not when they were meant to work together. But it had been so long...he heard her gasping, deep in her throat, as he fucked her harder and harder. She moved too, her hands gripping his buttocks and encouraging him to move faster. He wasn't sure which of them was in charge. Perhaps they were just being driven by their hormones, by the need to forget - just for a while - the death and destruction.

He came, hard. His legs buckled. And yet...part of him felt as though he'd betrayed his wife. God knew he'd had sexual partners before getting married, but God *also* knew he'd never had anyone else since the day he'd sworn himself to her. His fellow pilots had teased him for not taking advantage of shore leave, yet...he'd thought the marriage meant something. And there had been no women after Judith's death...

I'm sorry, he thought, although he wasn't sure if he *was* sorry. Judith *had* cheated on him, after all. And she hadn't even had the decency to tell him. *I...*

And then he met Abigail's eyes and *knew* they'd made a terrible mistake.

CHAPTER
EIGHTEEN

Fuck, Abigail thought.

She was dazed, her mind unable to form a coherent thought as he slid out of her. And yet…she knew, with a sickening certainty, what she'd done. She'd had sex with Alan. She wanted to blame it on the wine, but she knew all too well that she hadn't drunk anything like enough to impair her judgment *that* much. And he hadn't forced her either. She'd made a very poor decision, based on the urge to do something - anything - that distracted her from the deaths.

Fuck, she thought, again.

Abigail pulled back, staring at him. He was half-dressed, his cock hanging out of his trousers…she would have laughed, if the situation wasn't so serious. He'd fucked her so hard that…she fought down the urge to giggle helplessly. He'd made love like a man who'd just got out of prison. But that was exactly what he *had* done. Her eyes trailed over his body, unsure where to look. He was more muscular than she'd expected, for a groundpounder who'd been trapped in a cell for five years. It had been a long time for her too.

Abigail bit her lip, forcing herself to concentrate. She was an adult, old enough to have grown children of her own. And she was part of a group-marriage that understood that - sometimes - a partner would want to go elsewhere for sex. None of her husbands and wives would blame her for having sex, although they might have quite a bit to say about the person she'd had sex *with*. Alan had murdered his wife. That alone would be enough to make him a pariah in the belt, if he wasn't executed on the spot. No one would blame his wife's family for killing him if the law refused to do the job.

She looked down at herself. Her shipsuit trousers were around her ankles, crumpled on the deck; her shirt was open, revealing her breasts. She was too much a Belter to be embarrassed by casual nudity, too old a player to feel vulnerable. Hell, Alan was at least five years younger than her, perhaps more. His file hadn't been clear on that either. Would he have a fit when he realised she was in her late forties? Or would he care, after spending so long in jail?

"Fuck," she said, out loud.

It had been quick, but good. She hadn't felt *quite* so much determination to lose herself in raw sensation since she'd become a married woman. And yet, she knew it would lead to complications. Belters wouldn't object to a quick tryst, but groundpounders took matters much more seriously. Alan was a physical adult - he had children, for crying out loud - but she knew he might not be emotionally mature. A man who could kill his wife in a fit of rage certainly wasn't *that* mature.

It might be different for him, of course, Abigail reflected. *He pledged himself to a single woman.*

"Fuck," Alan echoed.

Abigail sighed and reached for her trousers, pulling them up as quickly as she could. She'd have to shower, of course…she wondered, inanely, what she was supposed to do. She kicked herself, mentally. There weren't many options on the ship, if she'd wanted to find a partner for the night, but she could have just used a VR tape. Or even…she sighed. Alan had killed his wife. It wasn't something she was inclined to forgive. She buttoned up her shirt, resisting the urge to watch as Alan fixed his clothes. It felt better, somehow, to be covered. And yet, it was not a pleasant sensation.

"Abigail," Alan said. "I…"

Abigail did not want to have that talk, not now. "Get out," she said. He needed a shower too, but…she wanted to be alone. She'd done something stupid. "Now."

Alan opened his mouth, then turned and opened the hatch. Abigail allowed herself a sigh of relief as he stepped through, the hatch hissing closed behind him. If they were lucky, no one would see him before he'd managed to shower and change. No one would say anything, out loud, but there would be whispered rumours. God alone knew where they'd lead.

Fuck, she thought, once again.

She checked the status display, then started to undo the shipsuit. Her breasts were covered with faint marks, testament to their brief passion. She touched one of the bruises lightly and shook her head. Given how hard she'd squeezed his buttocks, she was fairly sure he was bruised too. His skin was lighter. It was quite possible someone would see the marks and jump to all sorts of conclusions. She wondered, with a flicker of grim amusement, just what they'd say.

The two glasses stood on the table, mocking her. She eyed them for a long moment, then picked the glasses up and carried them into the wash-room. She couldn't blame the alcohol, any more than she could blame Alan himself. And yet, she *wanted* to blame him. All of a sudden, she thought she understood how he felt. If he blamed his wife for cheating on him - if he considered that sufficient reason to kill her - he could avoid the guilt. The delusion kept him from having to face what he'd done.

He was inside me, she thought, as she turned on the shower and stepped into the water. *And I felt...what?*

She snorted in annoyance. The hell of it was that she *had* enjoyed herself. It had been brief, but intense. She was certainly old enough to make her own decisions. And most of her crew were mature enough to understand that she had desires too. Anson and Poddy were the only ones who would be horrified at the thought of their aged mother having sex...

Reaching for a sponge, she scrubbed herself down. It was hardly the first time she'd had a one-night stand, although she'd always been fairly sure she wouldn't have to see her partner again afterwards. But now...she wasn't sure how she felt. Alan had done things she couldn't forgive. And yet, she'd been so desperate for human touch that she'd kissed him.

You are responsible for what you do, she reminded herself, sharply. Her parents and uncles had said the same thing, when she'd been younger. *And you have to deal with the consequences.*

She turned off the water and stepped out of the shower. She'd get dressed, then go to the bridge. They hadn't seen any sign of the enemy, but that didn't mean that the convoy was *safe*. She was all too aware that the aliens wouldn't need to strain their drives if they wanted to catch up with the fleeing freighters, assuming the aliens had a rough idea where to start looking. The convoy didn't even have a nominated CO to take command, if the aliens *did* show themselves. A military CO would probably have assumed overall command by now.

Perhaps we take our independence a little too far, she thought, as she pulled on her underwear and reached for a fresh shipsuit. *There's a war on now.*

Tying her hair back, she studied herself in the mirror. She looked tired, but there was no visible sign she'd had sex. That was something, at least. No one would judge her for having a one-night stand when they were docked at an asteroid station, but they were in the middle of a warzone. *Someone* would probably insist she was neglecting her sworn duty. Perhaps she was. Her lips twitched into a humourless smile. If the aliens had shown up when they were fucking…

Don't delude yourself, she told herself, sharply. One of the reasons she let herself go - one she wouldn't acknowledge outside the privacy of her head - was the grim awareness that they could die at any time. *If the aliens show up, we're dead.*

She took one last look in the mirror, then strode out of the cabin. She had work to do. And if Alan couldn't be professional about it…?

Fuck him, she thought. *And not literally, this time.*

———

Alan felt…he wasn't sure *how* he felt.

He forced himself to walk down the corridor, praying with a fervour he hadn't felt in years that no one noticed him until he was safely in the cabin. He hadn't prayed like that since the time his best friend had brought illicit cigarettes into school, even though he'd known the headmaster was on the warpath. Being caught would mean real trouble…he might even have been expelled, although it hadn't been his idea. Alan's father wouldn't have taken *that* lightly. God knew he'd been furious when Alan really *had* been transferred to a borstal…

The hatch opened as soon as he keyed the switch. Bennett was lying on his bed, reading a datapad. Alan cringed, inwardly. Some men would slap him on the back and congratulate him for scoring, but he doubted *Bennett* would do anything of the sort. He was Alan's watchdog, not his friend or comrade. And Alan was ruefully aware that the truth was written all over his face. He probably *smelled* of sex...

He pushed that thought out of his head as hard as he could, then headed straight into the shower. Bennett didn't say a word, although Alan could *feel* Bennett's gaze burning into his back. The younger man was a soldier, after all. He was no stranger to finding female companionship for the night, then walking away in the morning. If half the stories about squaddies on leave were true, they made starfighter pilots look positively genteel.

All those stories about prison weren't true either, he reminded himself, as he stripped off his shipsuit. *Colchester wasn't bad...*

Alan turned on the water, scrubbing himself down as quickly as he could. Water might not be rationed any longer, but he was still meant to set a good example. Besides, if the aliens jumped them, he'd have to run to his starfighter. There was no point manning the CIC when an extra starfighter might make the difference between survival and death. He sighed, shaking his head in dismay. There was a good chance that an extra starfighter would only mean one more craft blasted out of space during the battle.

Shit, he thought.

He wasn't entirely sure what had happened. No, he knew what had happened, but he didn't know why. He wasn't even sure which of them had made the first move. God knew *that* hadn't happened before, even when he'd lost his virginity. It was funny to remember, now, the handful of times he'd managed to sneak out of the borstal with the other lads and go drinking and skirt-chasing in the nearest town. In hindsight, he wondered if they'd been winked at by the teachers. God knew the police could have rounded them up if they'd caused real trouble. He had no idea what would have happened then - teenage delinquents were normally sent to the borstals - but he doubted it would have been pleasant. Perhaps they would have been treated as adults and marched off to jail.

Good thing we weren't officially caught, he told himself. *I might never have had a chance to go to the stars.*

He groaned as he dragged his thoughts back to the present. His mind was a whirlwind of complicated emotions, blurring together so rapidly that he couldn't get a grip on them. He wanted to go back to her cabin and have sex with her again, he wanted to run as far from her as he could, he wanted...he wasn't sure *what* he wanted. He'd been faithful to Judith while they'd been married, then involuntarily celibate during his incarceration. He cursed himself, savagely, for thinking with his smaller head. This was going to make his life harder...

Shutting off the water, he towelled himself down. He and Abigail had had a complicated relationship even *before* the battle. She'd gotten him drunk and tricked him into telling her the truth...he shook his head in amused disbelief. Abigail was *not* like any other woman he'd met, for sure. But then, if half the tales about the asteroid settlements were true, she was only a *little* eccentric. He reminded himself, sharply, not to take the stories too seriously. It wasn't as if the stories about prison had been accurate either.

That's because you watched too many chicks-in-prison movies when you were younger, he reprimanded himself. *And, like most pornographic shit, it bears as much resemblance to reality as a government white paper.*

He stepped out of the washroom, completely naked. Naval service - and then prison - had erased what little modesty he'd felt, once upon a time. God knew the borstal hadn't encouraged modesty either. Had there actually been a time, in his life, when he'd enjoyed true privacy? He couldn't think of one, after his transfer to the borstal. Privacy was a privilege, the headmaster had said, not a right. And it wasn't one extended to teenage boys who'd exhausted society's good will.

Bennett looked up. "I hope it wasn't Maddy."

Alan felt himself flush. "No," he said, stiffly. "It wasn't."

"Good," Bennett said. He sounded strikingly disinterested. "Are you going to tell me all about it or do I have to drag the truth out of you?"

Alan glared at him. "How old do you think I am?"

"Your file says you're forty-one," Bennett said. "Personally, I would have put you at ten or eleven."

"I'm too old to engage in locker-room talk," Alan said, curtly.

He felt a hot flush of shame as he remembered just what he'd said - and heard - in the changing rooms. They'd talked about girls, bragging of sexual exploits that were probably physically impossible - and, in any case, certainly hadn't happened. He'd told his friends that he'd lost his virginity a long time before he'd even kissed a girl. They probably hadn't believed him, but then…he hadn't believed them either. It had all been part and parcel of growing up.

"Glad to hear it," Bennett said. "I trust that you and the captain will be professional at all times?"

Alan jumped. How had he *known*?

He realised his mistake an instant later. Bennett hadn't known… although he might have guessed, the way Abigail had hauled Alan out of the hold. But it didn't matter. Bennett had probed lightly and Alan's reaction had told him everything he needed to know. The amused look on his face - a smirk that made Alan want to punch him - only confirmed it. Bennett knew.

"We can be professional," Alan said, crossly. "I don't think…"

"I had noticed," Bennett said. His voice was very dry. "That's a very strange woman, that one. And also one who isn't likely to let you get away with anything."

He sat upright, nearly cracking his head on the upper bunk. "I don't give much of a shit about what you do on your time off, as long as you do your duty," he added. "You can always be returned to your cell if you fuck up. But I *suggest* that you keep it completely professional while you're on duty. This isn't a naval crew…"

"If it was a naval crew," Alan pointed out, "I'd be in real trouble."

"Quite," Bennett agreed. "And so would she."

Alan nodded as he opened the compartment and retrieved a shipsuit. Regulations were clear - and backed up by a great deal of precedent. Senior officers were *not* allowed to have sexual relationships with their subordinates. The senior officer would be lucky if he - or she, in some cases - was allowed to retire, rather than being dishonourably discharged, while their junior would be on very thin ice. *Haddock* didn't have a naval crew, which was all that might save Abigail and himself if the truth ever came out. She hadn't had the regulations drilled into her from the moment she wore a cadet uniform.

"Be careful," Bennett said. "You're expendable."

"Right now, we're all expendable," Alan pointed out. He pulled the shipsuit over his head, then started to tighten the fastenings. "This whole *ship* is expendable. *You're* expendable."

"I know," Bennett said.

He didn't sound bothered, but Alan was sure he *must* be. Bennett was not a stupid man. He'd know just what the destruction of so many fleet carriers *meant*. Even if the Royal Navy managed to devise a counter to the alien weapons, they'd already taken heavy losses. And there was no way the other human nations could make up the shortfalls. They had problems of their own.

"Be careful," Bennett said. He smiled, suddenly. "You do realise that Anson has been courting Maddy?"

Alan blinked, surprised. "But you implied..."

He shook his head. "Should we be worried?"

"Perhaps we should be more worried about *him*," Bennett said. He shrugged. "You killed in a fit of rage, rage aimed at a very specific target. Maddy cold-bloodedly set out to defraud the navy of a great deal of money."

Alan sighed. It was hard to believe that the young woman he knew was a cold-blooded fraudster. Maddy looked so young that he was tempted to wonder if she had joined the navy at sixteen, rather than waiting until she was eighteen. It was rare, but it did happen. She made him feel protective, even though...

"Right now, it isn't a problem," he said. Maddy *was* old enough to make certain decisions for herself. She could handle the consequences too. Besides, there was nothing on *Haddock* worth stealing. "And we have a great many other things to worry about."

"Sure," Bennett agreed. He stood and walked towards the hatch. "Your relationship with the captain, for one."

And he laughed.

CHAPTER
NINETEEN

"Ready to jump, Captain," Anson said.

Abigail allowed herself a moment of relief, mingled with fear. Five weeks of making their way down the tramlines had left them jumping at every sensor contact, even after they'd entered a populated star system and exchanged notes with the defenders. Word was spreading, but...she still had no idea what was waiting for them on the far side. Earth might have been smashed flat by now. The only real consolation was that Earth - according to a freighter they'd encountered - hadn't been attacked a week ago.

Which doesn't mean the system wasn't attacked yesterday, she thought, grimly. *This tramline network attracts less attention than the others.*

"Jump," she ordered, quietly.

She glanced down at the display as it blanked, then rebooted. Cold logic told her that they were in no danger of being intercepted, but she didn't find it very reassuring. She would almost have welcomed another fight - or fuck - with Alan, if only to keep her from brooding on what they'd find when they got home. Her nerves kept insisting that the aliens were lurking on the far side, ready to blow them away within spitting distance of Earth.

"Transit complete, Captain," Anson said.

"Local space appears clear," Poddy said. "I'm picking up transmissions from Earth now."

Which may well be meaningless, Abigail thought. The makeshift analysts hadn't been able to figure out a way to defeat the alien stealth systems.

She hoped the boffins back home would do better or it would be a very short war. *But at least Earth wasn't attacked a few hours ago.*

"Send our IFF," she ordered, grimly. "And then take us back to Tallyman."

She leaned back in her chair as the convoy started to crawl towards the asteroid base. Sol looked more industrialised than ever, power signatures glowing all over the system. And yet, a number of familiar ports had gone dark. She hoped that was a good sign, perhaps one that suggested the inhabitants were trying to hide. If word had already reached Earth, the belters would either be hiding or planning their exodus. She knew her own people too well to expect them to gamble everything on a desperate last stand.

Alan's face appeared in the display. "Captain," he said. His voice was coolly professional, just as it had been for the last five weeks. "Long-range sensors suggest that the system has not been attacked."

"So it would seem," Abigail agreed, equally professionally. At least he wasn't sulking. She hated men who sulked. "It'll be a while before we get a response from Tallyman."

"They should have received word already," Alan said. "And they may be suspicious of our safe return."

Abigail nodded, slowly. The defenders *might* assume that her ship - and the remainder of the convoy - was nothing more than a Trojan Horse. She didn't think the aliens would need to bother, but groundpounders were rarely logical. It was hard to blame them, for once. Losing so many fleet carriers so quickly *had* to have shocked them. They might even have stopped running in circles, screaming and shouting...

Or maybe they'll be so panicky they'll fire on us, she thought. *That would be bad.*

"We won't go too close to the base until we get a reply," she said. They'd need hours to reach their destination, whatever happened. "And they'll probably insist on searching the ship."

"Probably," Alan agreed. "I'd better get on with writing the report. The navy will want to see it as soon as they know who we are."

Abigail resisted the urge to point out that he'd had five weeks to finish writing the report. He *had* written a very basic summary, which they'd forwarded to every starship, colony and orbital installation they'd encountered, but the navy's senior officers would probably want something a little more comprehensive. She'd read some of Alan's speculations and had been left wondering why he hadn't been snapped up by the analysis department long ago. He was good at figuring out ways to minimise the alien advantages.

At least on paper, she reminded herself. *It might not work so well in the real world.*

"Good luck," she said. She'd written a report of her own for the Belt Federation, although she wasn't sure if the Royal Navy would allow her to send it. Perhaps she should just fire it off before the navy had a chance to object. It was easier to beg forgiveness than permission, after all. "Let me know when you're ready."

She sat back in her chair and reached for her datapad. The final report was already complete, so she uploaded it to the message queue for later transmission. They'd send it directly to the belt as soon as they were within range. She reread the report, then skimmed through a couple of others. Her eyebrows lifted in surprise as she noted the author. For someone who looked like a thug, Bennett was a surprisingly decent writer.

"Captain," Poddy said. "We just picked up a message. They want us to head straight for Tallyman, where we will receive new orders."

"Understood," Abigail said. "Anson, maintain current course."

"Aye, Captain."

Abigail frowned as she glanced at the timer. *That* was quick. Tallyman had responded almost as soon as they'd received the first message. Unless it had been sent by a ship or installation closer to the tramline. She glanced at the header, but there was nothing to suggest who'd sent it. It wasn't really a problem, anyway. They certainly hadn't been ordered to maintain radio silence.

"See if you can pick up any news broadcasts," she ordered, after a moment. "And inform me if they know what happened at New Russia."

"Aye, Captain," Poddy said. She worked her console for a long moment. "I'm not picking up any news broadcasts, but…I'd expect more panic."

"True," Abigail agreed. More and more icons had flashed to life on the display, but it didn't *look* as though the system was panicking. She ran through the possibilities in her head, time and time again. *Someone* should have brought word of the defeat to Earth by now. A warship or scout could have reached the homeworld before the convoy had left Kiev. "There should be something..."

"Maddy says the government doesn't tell the people everything," Anson said. "They might not have told the public about the battle."

Abigail scowled. Maddy was pretty, but she was a groundpounder who'd been in jail...hardly the sort of girl she wanted her son to court. And yet, she knew her son - and men in general - well enough to know that opposing the match would only drive the young lovers deeper into each other's arms. Besides, she was in no position to complain too much. She'd done enough stupid things when she'd been his age to fill a book.

"Perhaps they didn't," she said. It didn't sound likely, but it was precisely the sort of thing a groundpounder government would do. The belt didn't know either, then. They'd have spread the story right across the system if they knew. "But that's their problem."

She brought up the next report and frowned. "Time to Tallyman?"

"Four hours at current rate," Anson said. "If we boost the drive, we leave the freighters behind."

"No, we'll stay with them," Abigail said. "There's no hurry, after all."

Unless they really don't know what happened, she thought, grimly. *But the odds of that are...what?*

She sighed. She didn't want to know.

———

Alan wasn't too surprised when, as *Haddock* approached Tallyman, they were greeted by the Royal Marines. Everyone on the ship was rounded up and held in the hold while the marines searched the ship from top to bottom, then tested everyone's DNA records before they relaxed. He didn't really blame them for being paranoid, even though he suspected that *someone* had watched too many movies about alien infiltrators. The search was an unsubtle indication that Earth *knew* what had happened at New Russia.

Someone got through, he thought, grimly. *And Earth is doing...what?*

"The ship will hold position here, for the moment," Captain Yates said, once the majority of the crew had been told to go back to their duties or cabins. The Royal Marine was burly enough to give Bennett a run for his money. "You and Officer Bennett will accompany us to the base."

"Understood," Alan said. He knew he wasn't being given a choice. "I'll just inform the Captain, then I'll be on my way."

He felt an odd pang of bitter regret as he keyed his wristcom, updating Abigail on his movements. Abigail had been coolly professional, so emotionally detached that he was tempted to wonder if it had all been a dream. They hadn't spoken in private since...since the night they'd fucked. He regretted that in some ways, even as he found it a relief in others. The sight of Anson and Maddy being together really didn't help. They seemed to have all the traits of young love.

Which might not survive the return to Earth, he thought, as he followed the Royal Marines onto their shuttle. *There are other girls and boys here now.*

Tallyman Base had grown over the last month, he noted. There were nine other freighters in the docking slips, in various stages of conversion. The makeshift escort carrier had clearly proved its value, he determined. He didn't want to think about any of the alternatives. A fleet carrier took nearly sixteen months to build, starting from scratch. He puzzled over just how many corners could be cut without risking the ship, then gave it up as a bad job. The navy's engineers would already be struggling to solve *that* problem.

But new fleet carriers would be sitting ducks, he thought, as the shuttle docked. *We really need something new.*

There was an air of desperation in the base as they were escorted through the corridors and into a small briefing compartment. Hundreds of men and women, most clearly reservists, were hurrying from place to place, their faces pale and wan. They knew, all right. The civilians might not know - yet - but the military knew. A month ago, humanity had been confident that the massed power of its space navies was hard to beat. Now…

We all got smashed, he told himself. *Us, the Americans, the Russians, the French…*

"Commander Campbell," a voice said. Two men were sitting at the table, wearing unmarked uniforms. Spooks, probably. He doubted they were his parole officers. "Take a seat."

Alan sat, bracing himself. Bennett stood behind him. Perhaps it *was* a parole meeting, after all. The beancounters wouldn't let a little thing like catastrophic defeat and the death of thousands of personnel get in their way, if they had procedures to follow. They hadn't bothered to tell him about any conditions that might be attached to his parole, but that didn't mean they didn't exist.

"We received word from New Russia, two weeks ago," the first man said. His nametag read TAGGER. "Your records have filled in some of the gaps, thankfully."

Alan nodded, concealing his relief. He'd feared that they would be the first to bring word from New Russia. Humanity would have lost more time while the aliens gathered their forces and drove on Earth. His worst nightmares, at least, had not come to pass.

"We also read your report with considerable interest," Tagger added. "Why do you believe the alien stealth systems are power hogs?"

"If they could use them all the time, they would," Alan pointed out. Firing plasma weapons while under stealth would defeat the whole object of the exercise, but if the aliens were careful that wouldn't matter. "Instead, they don't use them at all during engagements. I think the system has its limits."

"So the live feed from the MNF suggests," the second man said. He didn't have a visible nametag. "But it cut off rather sharply."

Tagger gave him an unreadable look, then turned his attention back to Alan. "How do you propose we proceed?"

Alan frowned. He wouldn't be the only one being asked, of course. The records from New Russia had already been forwarded to the boffins. But he was one of the battle's few survivors. There weren't many people in the Royal Navy who'd engaged the aliens and survived. His insights might be very useful indeed.

And they might also be a waste of time, he thought. If matters hadn't been so serious, he would have been amused at how they hung on his words. *I was also too close to the battle.*

"The lightly-armoured carriers are just oversized targets, sir," he said, bluntly. "The plasma bursts go right through their hulls, often setting off secondary explosions that rip the carriers apart. They really need heavier armour. Even a thin layer of something stronger might give them a better chance to survive."

A thought struck him. "*Ark Royal*," he added. The old carrier might move like a wallowing bull, but she was armoured so heavily that she might survive a close-range encounter with the aliens. "She's still in service, isn't she?"

Tagger's lips flickered into something that could - charitably - be called a smile. "Yes, she is," he said. "But that's above your pay grade."

Alan nodded, accepting the rebuke. "Yes, sir."

He paused, considering his next words. "We can also improve the internal armour on the carriers, although that might impede their operational tempo. And we could add additional point defence, maybe even outfit shuttles with close-in weapons to give the carriers some additional protection. But I don't think we can do *that* much more to give them a chance to survive, sir. The odds are not in their favour."

"The boffins *say* they can come up with something new," Tagger said. "But can they come up with something new in *time*?"

Alan winced. Half the battle was knowing that something was possible - and the aliens had certainly proved that plasma guns and stealth systems were possible. But actually developing such technologies could take months or years, after which they would have to be put into mass production. How long did they *have*? If the aliens realised the human navies couldn't stand up to them in open battle, they'd abandon the subtle approach and drive on Earth. The war would be lost along with humanity's homeworld.

"We may have to muddle through," he said. "But as long as they have such a decisive advantage, sir, the advantage rests in their hands."

"Very true," Tagger said.

He glanced at his companion, then nodded. "You have the thanks of a grateful nation, Commander. However, for the moment, you will have to go into lockdown until we decide how best to inform the public. There will be panic when the truth comes out."

"And a loss of confidence if the truth is kept secret for too long," Alan countered.

"That may be true," Tagger said, with a shrug. "But the decision was made well above my head. Putting that aside" - he met Alan's eyes - "how do the escort carriers stand up in combat?"

"We beat off an enemy probe, sir," Alan said. "But we were being worn down. I don't think we would have survived if we hadn't jumped through the tramline. And the lack of pursuit worries me. If they weren't heading straight to Earth, sir, that suggests that their starfighters were operating without a fleet carrier…"

"Which means that their operational range may be vastly greater than ours," Tagger said. "I see your point."

Alan couldn't help being impressed. Intelligence officers were supposed to be smart, to the point where they were too focused on their own brilliance to be effective, but Tagger had understood the implications of Alan's words. All of their comfortable projections about alien ranges - starfighters as well as starships - might be completely wrong. And if that was the case, the aliens might have far more flexibility than any of the Royal Navy's previous opponents.

He rubbed his forehead. "The only good news is that their starfighters were apparently unable to transit a tramline without a carrier," he said. "But that isn't a particular advantage."

"True," Tagger agreed.

"The escort carriers also have problems in launching and recovering starfighters," Alan added. He nodded to the terminal. "It's all in my report, sir. I've suggested a handful of modifications, including additional life support packs, but…really, we need a technological breakthrough and quickly. Time is not on our side."

"We know," Tagger said. "Your pilots were very sure they could win a one-on-one fight."

"Starfighter pilots think they can handle anything," Alan said. "I should know, sir. I was one of them. But in reality…we took punishing losses. We would have lost the entire convoy if we hadn't crossed the tramline. Next time, we'll know what we're up against. But unfortunately the aliens will know too."

And they won't be careful next time, he added, silently. *They know their strengths now.*

He yawned, suddenly. Being in lockdown was going to be a pain. He'd already rebuked a pair of pilots for talking about a trip to Sin City. It would be fun, but…he shook his head. They were going to be in lockdown. There would be no trips outside the hull for anyone.

"You'll be taken back to your ship," Tagger said. "Officer Bennett will be debriefed extensively before we send him back to you. Hopefully, we'll have new orders for *Haddock* within the week, but…right now, a great many senior officers are running around like chickens who've had their heads cut off. We don't know what to do."

Neither do we, Alan thought. *We need to knock the aliens off-balance long enough to recover our footing.*

"Your country thanks you," Tagger said. "And so do I."

"Thanks," Alan said. He rose. "But will we be remembered after we're gone?"

CHAPTER
TWENTY

Being in lockdown, Abigail had decided very quickly, was boring.

She supposed it was a good thing, in some ways. She hadn't been arrested for sending word of the battle to the Belt Federation, although she knew that could change in a hurry if the groundpounder governments demanded a scapegoat. The file had leaked very quickly, prompting a number of hurried disclosures from planet-side governments. Surprisingly, the belters had panicked more than the groundpounders. The belters knew that New Russia wasn't *that* far away.

And the aliens could be probing Terra Nova by now, she thought. The news was maddeningly out of date. *They've already occupied a handful of systems surrounding New Russia.*

She sat on her bridge and read the latest update. *Haddock* was being repaired as fast as possible and a new set of modifications were being included. New crewmen and starfighter pilots were already on the way. It looked as though they'd be going out again, unless the aliens attacked Earth first. The news spoke of planetary drafts and mass civil defence preparations, ready for when the aliens took the offensive. Abigail couldn't help feeling that, despite everything, the news was oddly optimistic. The planetary governments didn't want the population to feel as though defeat was inevitable.

And yet, there was an *edge* in the news - and the private messages - that suggested the human race was starting to understand it could lose the war. It wasn't something she could put her finger on - the official broadcasts spoke of high confidence and struggled to minimise the losses - but it was there. The universe had changed twice in quick succession, even though the vast majority of the groundpounder population hadn't managed to emotionally grasp what had happened. It was too distant from their experience for the news to have any significant impact. But to her, a spacer born and bred, there was no hiding from the truth.

She flicked the datapad to a new update and frowned. The planetary governments were still implying that the matter would be resolved quickly, although she didn't know who they thought were fooling. No one would miss the military vets - *all* of the military vets - being recalled to duty, let alone the draft and weapons training. Even if the war ended tomorrow with a negotiated peace, the long-term effects would be immense. She couldn't help thinking that the groundpounders were trying to pretend that everything was still normal, even though the universe had changed beyond repair. They probably didn't know what else to do.

Poddy's console chimed. "Captain, Commander Campbell has returned to the ship."

Another debriefing, Abigail thought. *Her* debriefings had been remarkably simple, but Alan seemed to be having a harder time. Perhaps the groundpounders were looking for someone to blame. It was the way they normally reacted to cold hard truth. *At least they let him return to the ship.*

"Ask him to meet me in my cabin," she said. "And then tell Anson I want him on the bridge."

Poddy snickered. "He won't like that, Mum."

Probably because he's sharing a cabin with Maddy now, Abigail thought. Her children - and the rest of the crew - had bitched and moaned about being in lockdown. *I wonder what we're interrupting.*

She dismissed the thought with a shrug. "He'll come, if he wants to keep his place," she said, instead. She normally didn't bother keeping a watch when they were in harbour, but there *was* a war on. The aliens could attack the Sol System at any moment. "And if he isn't here in five minutes, I will be pissed."

"Aye, Captain."

Abigail rose and checked the various consoles, making sure that there was nothing in interplanetary space that should concern her. And yet, she knew the apparent lack of alien ships could be an illusion. Sol was the most heavily populated and industrialised system in the human sphere - her sensors were picking up thousands of interplanetary ships and tiny colonies - but there was still plenty of space for an alien fleet to hide. There were scout ships heading out in all directions, she'd been told, yet she knew they might be worse than useless. The cold realities of interstellar flight insisted that the aliens would have no trouble getting a fleet to Earth without being detected, as long as they took basic precautions. And they might get very close to the planet before they were spotted.

Anson entered, buttoning up his shipsuit. He didn't look too annoyed, thankfully. Abigail would have torn him a new asshole if he'd dared complain. He was a bridge officer first and foremost, even in harbour. Taking the watch when the captain had to be elsewhere was part of his job. And if he didn't like it, he could go elsewhere. Anson might be her son, but there were limits. The freighter came first.

"Alert me if anything happens," she ordered, as she headed for the hatch. "I'll be back as soon as possible."

She strode through the hatch and walked down to her cabin. Alan was waiting outside, looking tired and wary. They'd been dancing around each other for weeks, ever since...she sighed, inwardly, as she opened her cabin. Getting him drunk had been a mistake and drinking herself had been worse. And sleeping with him...she'd needed the release, she knew, but still...

"No alcohol this time, please," Alan said.

Abigail nodded, curtly. "Of course. Would you like tea or coffee or chocolate...?"

"Tea would be lovely," Alan said. He sounded like he needed *coffee*. "It's been a long day."

"At least you were doing something," Abigail said, as she closed the hatch. "We've been bumming around in orbit, waiting for something to happen."

Alan smiled, although it didn't quite touch his eyes. "That sounds very restful. It's certainly better than going over the same things, time and time again."

Abigail keyed the dispenser to heat the water, then went looking for a pair of mugs. "Didn't they believe the reports?"

"They don't *want* to believe the reports," Alan said. He sat on the chair, resting his hands on his lap. "They're searching for good news and not finding it."

"I suppose there's only a limited supply of good news," Abigail said. She dropped a flavour capsule into the first mug, then filled it with water. The steaming liquid rapidly started to turn brown. "Twelve fleet carriers blown out of space...and the rest of the fleet just as vulnerable. I can see why they don't want to believe it."

She shrugged. Bad news didn't go away, just because someone didn't want to listen. She'd been taught, from the very first day she'd held a wrench, to understand that reality had to be accepted, whatever it was. It could be something as minor as her crush having no interest in her or something as major as the fuel tanks running dry, but it had to be accepted before she could come to terms with it. The groundpounders seemed to lack that attitude. She supposed it made sense. For all the horror stories she'd heard about Earth, it couldn't be denied that the environment was a great deal less hostile. On a planet, an air leak wouldn't mean a gruesome death.

But it's still stupid of them, she thought. *Those carriers and their crews are dead. They're never going to come back.*

She passed him his mug, then sipped her own. Flavour capsules didn't have *quite* the same taste as tea leaves, but she was in no place to complain. The flavour capsules would last indefinitely, unlike natural food. Natural food was often tastier, but storing it was often a pain in the bum. She had no idea how the interstellar liners handled it. Anyone rich enough to afford an interstellar cruise would throw a tantrum if they were told they had to eat nothing but ration bars.

Her lips quirked. *I suppose we might throw a tantrum too.*

"This tastes better than the wine," Alan said. "And it's less distracting."

"I'll let you in on a little secret," Abigail said. "If you bring a box of tea-bags - even very basic teabags - to an asteroid settlement, you can charge through the nose for it. Everyone drinks tea and coffee out here."

Alan smiled. "You don't grow tea leaves out here?"

"Most asteroid settlements prefer to grow food," Abigail said. Earth could afford to grow tea as well as food crops. Asteroid settlements rarely had the space to indulge themselves. Tea might be *considered* a vital necessity, but everyone knew that it was secondary to food people could actually *eat*. "It'll be a long time before the colonies start producing luxury goods for themselves."

"If they ever do," Alan said.

"True," Abigail said.

She met his eyes. "We need to talk."

His face reddened, just slightly. Abigail felt a hot flash of irritation, which she swiftly suppressed. He wasn't a belter. She really shouldn't hold him to the same standards. And yet, part of her was frustrated. He might have been born on Earth, but he was serving with a belter crew. It was high time he learnt to adapt.

"I am sorry," he said, finally. "The drink made it hard to think straight and…and it was a long time and…"

Abigail made a rude sound. "I'm not *complaining*," she said. She allowed herself to be deliberately crude, just to shock him. "I wanted to fuck. That it was you…"

"Oh," Alan said. He sounded confused. "I don't…"

"It doesn't matter," Abigail said, flatly. "We're both adults. And neither of us was drunk enough to be unable to give consent. And I *assume*" - her voice hardened - "that you tearing at my clothes was a way of giving consent. Unless you want to insist that I raped you…?"

Alan's face twisted. He looked as though he was torn between shouting in anger and giggling helplessly. She *hadn't* forced herself on him and he knew it. Perhaps it had been a bad decision, one born of a desperate desire to feel human again, but it had been one they'd made together. He could have walked out of her cabin if he hadn't wanted to fuck. She would have let him go.

"No," he said. There was a hard undercurrent of anger in his voice, mingled with…*something*. "I don't think you raped me."

"Glad to hear it," Abigail said. She'd done nothing wrong, by belter standards, but groundpounders had different attitudes. And the navy had countless rules and regulations governing sex. Clearly, the bureaucrats didn't trust their subordinates to be responsible adults. The belt took a simpler approach. "Can I be blunt?"

"I have never heard you trying to be anything but," Alan told her.

Abigail laughed, then leaned forward. "I wanted to feel human again, after everything," she said. "You were...convenient. And I imagine you felt the same way."

"Yeah," Alan said.

"I'm not going to demand you marry me," Abigail said. She'd watched historical VRs where sex always led to marriage, although she found them hard to believe. Was that *really* how groundpounders did things? "But what I want - what I *need* - is you working with me. Like it or not, there is a war on. Afterwards...you can do whatever the hell you please."

Alan studied her for a long moment. "Did it really mean so little to you?"

Abigail resisted - barely - the temptation to roll her eyes. "Did it actually mean anything to *you*?"

"I don't know," Alan said. "I...I haven't had sex for nearly five years. And now..."

"And now you feel like a teenage boy who thinks his first girlfriend is his one and only," Abigail said. God! She hoped *Anson* didn't feel that way about Maddy. "You're old enough to know better, aren't you? You're what? A hundred? A couple of hundred?"

"Old enough to know better," Alan said, tartly.

"Good," Abigail said. She pointed a finger at his chest. "It was good. I needed it and so did you. And if you want to do it again, I might say yes. But I can't have you avoiding me or being so painfully formal that everyone *knows* we did something. Understand?"

"Yes," Alan said. He paused. "You want to do it again?"

"Later," Abigail said. She glanced at her wristcom. "I shouldn't leave Anson on the bridge for *too* long."

Alan nodded. Abigail couldn't tell if he was disappointed or not. She reminded herself, once again, that belters and groundpounders were different. Perhaps she'd be considered too old on Earth, even though she was only forty-five. Or perhaps he'd invested more emotion in the sex than she'd realised. It was hard to understand, sometimes, how groundpounders actually managed to function in society. Their safe environment made them soft.

"I understand," Alan said. He took a sip of his tea. "Are *all* belters like you?"

Abigail took a moment to consider. "In what way?"

"In being so blunt," Alan said. "And in…"

He didn't seem to know how to finish the sentence. Abigail gave in - this time - to the temptation to roll her eyes. Groundpounders were so… *strange.*

"The belt is a blunt place," she said. "There can be no room for misunderstandings. We speak the same language in all respects…yes, we're blunt, because anything less could lead to tragedy. And we can't afford to pussy-foot around. Sex…no one cares who fucks who, or how they do it, as long as it's between consenting adults in private. No one back home will give a damn that we fucked. They *will* care if our relationship buggers up the mission."

Alan frowned. "Why?"

"Because we're adults," Abigail said. "And we're supposed to be responsible."

She frowned. "Do your daughters not work now?"

Alan blinked in surprise. "Jeanette is *twelve!*"

"Old enough to learn the basics," Abigail said. "I shipped out when I was fourteen."

She sighed. She'd watched a handful of dramas set on Earth, but she'd never really believed they were real. There were only so many shows about adults acting like oversized children one could take before deciding there was no intelligent life on the planet. She dreaded to think what her parents would have said, if she'd acted like a five-year-old when she'd been fifteen. She'd be lucky not to be unceremoniously disowned for irredeemable idiocy. Her uncle had always said that stupidity killed and she knew, from bitter experience, that he'd been right.

"Jeanette is too young to work," Alan said. "She won't even be able to take on an apprenticeship until she turns sixteen…and only then if she leaves school."

"And is she learning anything useful *at* school?" Abigail found it hard to comprehend how anyone could send their child to a groundpounder school. "What will she be when she finally grows up?"

"I don't know," Alan said. "I haven't heard from her in years. I..."

He shook his head, slowly. "I was in jail," he reminded her. "We lost touch."

Abigail winced. She wasn't sure if she should feel sorry for him or slap him. Hard. Family was family. And while Alan's daughters had every right to hate their father, they were still family. He shouldn't abandon his child.

It wouldn't happen in the belt, she thought, tartly. *None of this would happen in the belt.*

"Write to her," she said. "Write to *both* of them. Give them a chance to get back in touch with their father."

Alan looked at her as if she'd said something really stupid. "Do you think they want to get in touch with me? I killed their *mother!*"

"Give them the choice," Abigail urged. She found it hard to imagine how Jeanette and her sister felt about their father. But then, she couldn't imagine her father killing her mother either. "At the very least, they deserve a chance to hear your side of the story."

"I killed your mother in a fit of rage," Alan said, dryly. "I don't think they'll want to hear *that.*"

He laughed, humourlessly. "Do you know what would have happened if I'd filed for divorce?"

Abigail shrugged. She had no idea.

"She would have been hammered by the courts," Alan told her. "There are *laws* against adultery, if one partner is in the military. It was bad for morale, apparently, when a man's wife cheated on him while he was at the front. And socially? She would have been crucified. It wouldn't have been *hard* for her to wait until I got home, then ask for a separation. No one would have blamed her for that."

"Except you," Abigail said.

"But I was too angry to care," Alan said. He looked down at his hands, perhaps imagining them covered with blood. "And I killed her. And I..."

"And nothing," Abigail said. She met his eyes, daring him to say something. "You groundpounders and your warped ideas about sex."

She glanced at her wristcom, again. "Be an adult. Do your job. And while you're at it, record a message for your daughters. The next mission might kill you. Give them a fucking chance to get back in touch before it's too late."

"Thank you," Alan said, sourly.

"You're welcome," Abigail told him. She rose. "I'll see you for dinner. Until then, go write that letter. Or record a v-mail. Or *something*."

"If you wish," Alan said.

Abigail shrugged. "I'm not telling you this for *my* sake," she said, although she knew that wasn't entirely true. "I'm doing it so you'll be in a better state when we go back to war."

"How ruthlessly practical," Alan said.

"That's the belt in a nutshell," Abigail said, bluntly. It was the way she'd lived, right from the start. Her family wouldn't have accepted anything else. "Ruthlessly practical is how we *live*."

CHAPTER
TWENTY ONE

"We're being called to the station," Bennett said. "Grab your jacket and let's go."

Alan nodded in relief as he sat up. He'd spent the last two hours in his cabin, trying to write a letter to the girls. Abigail had been right, he acknowledged, but he had no idea what to say to them. The in-laws had probably poisoned their minds against him. Not, he supposed as he reached for his jacket, that they'd have to work very hard. There was no denying that the reason his daughters were growing up without a mother was that their father had *killed* their mother.

And they never liked me anyway, he reminded himself. *They thought I wasn't good enough for their daughter.*

He pulled on his jacket and followed Bennett down to the shuttle. Abigail met them there, looking disgustingly fresh for someone who'd been on the bridge for at least two hours, perhaps longer. Alan nodded to her - he didn't have time to sort out his feelings - as they stepped through the hatch and into the shuttle. The pilot undocked as soon as they were onboard, taking the shuttle directly to the asteroid base. Alan glanced at the scanner and saw five other converted freighters - and a pair of frigates - holding position near the station. The Royal Navy had clearly decided to do *something*.

The shuttle docked with a loud *clang*, the hatch hissing open a second later. A pair of Royal Marines met them, checking their IDs before hurrying them into the briefing room. Alan looked around, spotting a handful of military and civilian personal waiting for them. He couldn't help wondering what crimes the military personnel might have committed, if they'd been assigned to the escort carriers. There weren't many possibilities. Someone considered to be a permanent risk would never be let out of jail, if he hadn't simply been hanged. Society wasn't kind to serious criminals.

Perhaps they just fiddled their expenses, Alan thought, as he sat down next to Abigail. *Or some other harmless little prank like talking back to a senior officer.*

He looked up as a man strode into the room, the lights dimming as he took the podium. "Thank you for coming," he said, briskly. "For those of you who don't know me, I am Commodore Sidney Jameson, currently in command of Task Force Woodbine. You and your ships have been assigned to my command."

Woodbine, Alan thought, amused. The MOD assigned operational code names at random - unlike the Americans, who tried to be dramatic - but he felt the Admiralty might prefer something a little more *purposeful*. And yet, being dramatic had its disadvantages. *I suppose the Yanks always did tip off their enemies when the names became public.*

He studied Jameson for a long moment. The brown-haired officer looked young, suspiciously young, to be a commodore. Good genes or the Old Boys Network? Alan was inclined to think the latter. An older man would have given an impression of being more mature, even if his face appeared young. Jameson probably had friends in high places. The name was common enough not to suggest any aristocratic ties, but that meant nothing. There was no shortage of aristocrats who insisted on serving under false names.

"You'll receive a complete set of briefing notes once this meeting is over," Jameson informed them. "However, I will go over the basics to make sure we are all caterwauling off the same song-sheet."

And to prove you love to hear yourself talk, Alan thought, rudely. *Are you ever going to get to the point?*

"The Admiralty has conducted an extensive analysis of the records from New Russia," Jameson continued. "It is their conclusion that we are dangerously outmatched in space combat."

"No shit, Sherlock," someone muttered from the back.

Jameson showed no visible reaction. "The plasma weapons are just one part of the problem," he added. "Our analysis suggests that the aliens entered the New Russia system through a weak tramline, one of the gravitational lines we believed was too weak to allow starships to transit. We are not entirely *sure* of this, I should admit, but their attack force did *come* in on a vector that leads back to the weak tramline."

Alan glanced at Abigail, who looked as stunned as he felt. The analysts could be wrong, of course. He certainly *wanted* to believe they were wrong. There was no reason the aliens couldn't have jumped through any of the usable tramlines, then sneaked around the system until finally selecting their attack vector and moving in for the kill. And yet, the longer they delayed before the attack, the greater the chance of being spotted. Sheer practicality alone suggested that the analysts might be right.

And there's no sign the aliens think that *differently from us,* he told himself. *Technology aside, their tactics are entirely conventional.*

"If this is accurate, the situation is grave," Jameson warned. "I don't believe I have to explain the implications."

He tapped a switch, activating the holographic starchart. A network of tramlines appeared in front of them, a handful shaded in red. Alan felt a chill run down his spine as he picked out the tramlines that had been supposed to be inaccessible. If the aliens really could use them, they could outflank the defenders and thrust straight at Earth. Gasps echoed around the room as the audience worked it out for themselves. They were all experienced spacers, they knew the realities of spaceflight. The new tramlines would change the universe once again.

"We may be wrong about this," Jameson cautioned. "But there is enough evidence to back up the analysis."

Alan gritted his teeth. The nature of the tramlines made it impossible to fortify them. None of the Great Powers - or all of them working together - could hope to line a single tramline with orbital battlestations. The costs would be staggering, the requirements utterly incomprehensible...and even if they fortified one tramline to the point where any intrusion could be detected and destroyed, the others could still be used. That was one of the realities of interstellar spaceflight. They all understood how the tramlines shaped interstellar commerce - and war.

But if the aliens could use inaccessible tramlines, they could evade most of the outer colonies and make their way directly to Earth without fear of interception. That alone limited humanity. There was no way they could spare forces for the outer colonies if Earth itself might be attacked at any moment. But the deeper implications were worse. No one knew where the aliens were based, save for a rough idea of their general location. And yet, if the only link between human and alien space was an inaccessible tramline...

We might not be able to get at them, he thought.

Someone coughed for attention. "Do the boffins have any theories about *how* this could be done?"

"Not as yet," Jameson said. "I've been given to understand that research is underway, but beyond that...I know nothing."

He cleared his throat. "Precisely how we stack up against them on the *ground* is unknown, but unlikely to matter. As long as they control the high orbitals, they can smash resistance with ease. We believe that it is only a matter of time before the aliens mount an offensive against Earth itself. The defenders are scrambling to get ready for the attack - the boffins have identified a number of ways to minimise the alien advantages - but we need time. That's where *we* come in."

Of course, Alan thought. *The Admiralty wants us to go out and commit suicide to buy time.*

"Intelligence has been doing its level best to watch the aliens," Jameson informed them. "We do not - as yet - know anything about their physical form, let alone their language, internal politics and, most importantly of all, the reason they started the war. Infiltrating their society is obviously impossible as we know next to nothing about them. *However*, we have been tracking their movements as best as we can and we have uncovered something interesting. It may give us a chance to take the offensive and score a victory of our own."

He altered the starchart, zeroing in on a single system near New Russia. "Our analysis of their tramlines is not yet complete," he said. "However, we believe they're running supplies through this system. To us, the system is on the far end of a tramline chain and thus useless for anything other than a black colony; to them, the system is potentially a transit point. If our analysis is correct, they're using the system to support their offensive."

Alan frowned, stroking his chin as he studied the display. It made sense, he supposed, if one accepted that the aliens could ride previously-inaccessible tramlines. The unnamed system - no one had bothered to give it any more than a numerical designation - was only two jumps from New Russia, if one used the weaker tramlines. Coming to think of it, the alien attack force might well have come through the system itself. It was certainly on the right vector.

And it would allow them to outflank our scouts, he thought. *If, of course, they can use the weaker tramlines.*

"Our mission is to get into the system, then intercept and destroy any alien convoys that pass through the tramlines," Jameson said. "We believe that they will feel reasonably safe, as the system is of very limited use to us. Hitting their convoys will give them a nasty surprise and force them to reassess their tactics. It will also, hopefully, slow their preparations for an assault on Earth."

"Makes sense," Abigail muttered.

Alan nodded in agreement. Few civilians understood the logistics of interstellar spaceflight - and interstellar war - either. The alien fleet would require replenishing before it proceeded onwards, unless they'd brought their fleet train with them. But that would have been very dangerous, if the battle for New Russia had gone the other way. No, the aliens would need to run everything from freighters to troop transports through the tramline chain before they advanced towards Earth. The plan made sense.

"Ideally, we'll try to capture their freighters, rather than destroy them," Jameson added. "I don't think I need to tell you just how important it is to capture samples of alien technology for the boffins to study. But, if worse comes to worst, aim to destroy the ships instead of letting them go. We *must* buy time for Earth to prepare for the coming storm."

There was a long pause. "Are there any questions?"

Abigail leaned forward. "The quickest route to this system would take us within a jump of New Russia," she said. "Would we not be running the risk of encountering the aliens before we reached our destination?"

"Yes, we will," Jameson said. He nodded at the starchart. "Our last reports - which are about a week out of date - suggest that the aliens have occupied all the star systems within a jump of New Russia. So far, there's been no reports that they have landed on Clement or Oswego, but they smashed asteroid habitats in both the Oswego and Carissa systems. The remaining settlements in the systems have gone dark."

He took a long breath. "Yes, there is a very good chance that we will encounter the aliens prior to reaching our target. But there is very little we can do about that, save for sneaking around the edge of the systems rather than trying to get close to them."

"It will add several days to our journey, at best," Alan pointed out.

"I know," Jameson said. "And so does the Admiralty.

"Something - I haven't been told *what* - will also take place at roughly the same time, hopefully distracting the aliens. But the time delay alone may make it difficult for the aliens to realise that they're *meant* to be distracted. The timing is very far from precise, so we'll do everything in our power to avoid a confrontation until we reach our destination."

And if you're wrong, we die, Alan thought.

He looked at the starchart, trying to gather his thoughts. He'd been expendable as a starfighter pilot, but now…he shook his head. Losing the escort carriers wouldn't materially affect the balance of power, as far as anyone knew. The odds were already stacked against humanity. If they could distract the aliens, throw them back on their heels…it would be worth any price. He didn't like the thought of dying, but it would be worth it…

And it isn't like I have much of a future anyway, he thought. If he couldn't put together a letter to his daughters, why in the name of God Almighty should he be able to slip back into their lives? *Better I die amidst the stars then go home, even as a war hero. My past will haunt me wherever I go.*

Jameson was speaking. Alan dragged his attention back to the younger man.

"…New starfighter pilots and starfighters," Jameson said. "Ideally, you'll be ready to depart in two days."

Captain Chester leaned forward. "Am I to understand that my pilots will have no time to train together?"

...*Shit*, Alan thought. He hadn't heard everything Jameson had said, but he could guess the rest. *No time to get the newcomers integrated into the rest of the squadrons?*

"We don't have time for much of anything," Jameson said, sharply. "You'll have to rely on simulations."

Brilliant, Alan thought, sarcastically. Jameson seemed to understand the problem, but he wasn't doing anything to *fix* it. And yet...was there *anything* he could do? A week spent training might cost them their chance to do real damage. But then, not training might also cost them their chance to hurt the enemy. *We'll get our asses kicked if we don't train...*

"It isn't good enough," Captain Chester said. There was a dull murmur of agreement from the others. "Commodore, we need time..."

"We don't *have* the time." Jameson cut him off. "I understand the problem, Captain. In an ideal world, we'd have plenty of time to train until the pilots could fly their starfighters in their sleep. But we don't have the time. If we don't manage to cripple the enemy, even hurt them just a little, we will lose the war."

We may lose it anyway, Alan thought.

He shivered. It was a truism that Britain could not be defeated. Britain was a Great Power, capable of destroying any of the other Great Powers. A small war could be lost, perhaps, but a bigger one? The Great Powers knew better than to let one take place. But the aliens were an outside context problem, their mere existence changing the balance of power. A total defeat had been unthinkable, only a few short months ago. Now...it was possible.

And will they enslave the entire human race, he wondered, *or will they destroy us?*

"There will also be some modified scanners and remote sensor platforms," Jameson added, slowly. "We believe they *may* be effective against the alien stealth systems, but we don't know for sure. We'll be testing them in combat for the first time."

"Joy," Abigail muttered.

Alan nodded. In his experience, new technology - no matter how much it was hyped - always produced unexpected surprises when it was taken into the field. *He* would have preferred to test the new systems thoroughly before trying to use them in combat, but it looked as though they weren't going to have a choice. Besides, the systems probably couldn't be tested *outside* combat.

"We will depart in two days, once the remaining personnel have arrived," Jameson concluded. His gaze swept the room. "I am aware of the problems. This would not be an easy mission, even under better circumstances. But I don't think we have any choice. We need to buy time and, right now, we don't dare risk a major clash. Hitting their supply lines is our best bet."

He nodded, slowly. "Thank you for coming," he said. "Dismissed."

Abigail caught Alan's arm as they headed for the hatch. "Do you have time to get your people ready?"

"I hope so," Alan said. "Time is not going to be on our side."

He scowled, considering the problem. They knew enough about the aliens now to run some proper simulations, but *nothing* beat actual exercises. Perhaps they could hold a couple before they made their way into disputed territory. Jameson probably wouldn't object to that, as long as the squadron didn't slow down. It wouldn't be ideal, but it would be better than relying on simulations. Emergency drills *always* left out the emergency.

"I don't think we have a choice," he said. Abigail could leave, he supposed, although she might wind up being charged with desertion. He, on the other hand, would be going straight back to jail. "The commodore is right. If we can't buy time for Earth, we could lose the war."

"And the aliens don't seem inclined to take prisoners," Abigail agreed. "That bodes ill for the future."

Alan nodded. It was impossible to say how many lifepods had been launched before the MNF had been annihilated, let alone what the aliens had *done* with them. Perhaps, just perhaps, they'd been allowed to land on New Russia. Or, equally possible, they'd been blasted out of space... or left to float forever, utterly alone. The aliens might have watched from stealth, hoping the emergency beacons would lure a stray ship into range. But was there anyone left to listen for the beacons, let alone try to rescue the lifepods?

He shivered. He didn't know.

"We'd better get back to the ship," Abigail said. She patted his back. "It looks like we have a lot of work to do."

"Yeah," Alan said. He supposed she was trying to be reassuring. It wasn't working. "We have far too much work to do."

And a damned letter to write, he added, silently. *I can't procrastinate any longer.*

CHAPTER
TWENTY TWO

Alan tried - hard - to hide his wince as he strode into the briefing compartment, Bennett dogging his heels like an overgrown puppy. There were just too many new faces in the crowd, ranging from pilots so young he couldn't help feeling they should be in diapers to pilots so old he had grave doubts about their reflexes. Starfighter piloting was a young man's game. Old age and experience might beat youth and speed in the movies, but it was a different story in real life.

At least we got to keep a couple of pilots from the other ships, he thought. *But they took some of our experienced pilots in exchange.*

He felt a flash of *Déjà Vu* as the compartment quieted, slowly. He'd been here before, back when they'd been preparing for the convoy to New Russia. The faces were different, but the intent was the same. And yet... it was different, too. They'd known the universe had changed, but they hadn't believed it. They sure as hell believed it now.

"Welcome onboard," he said. He winced, again, as he surveyed the room. The newcomers were all too easy to spot. "I hope you all managed to claim your bunks and stow your bags without trouble. I *also* hope, for the newcomers, that your bunkmates warned you that this is a *dry* ship. No alcohol, no drugs...nothing that might distract you from the mission. I'll be checking your bags later, so if there's anything you don't want me to find I suggest you send it back to the station. There will be no further warnings."

There was a faint murmur of irritation. He ignored it.

"Those of you who weren't at New Russia should have had a chance to review the recordings," he continued. "If you haven't done so, do so now. You have to understand what we'll be up against when we reach our destination. The aliens are not gods, but they are powerful and they know how to use their advantages against us. I'm counting on you - all of you - to stand your ground when we encounter them for the second time. This war is a war for survival. We are all expendable in the defence of our homeworld and our people.

"I've heard some of the stories from the training centres, from snide jokes about grey hairs to suggestions that some of the recruits have to be taught how to go potty. Forget them, right now. You're here because you passed the basic proficiency tests - and because your country needs you. Your *planet* needs you. We need you to work as a team, not sharpen your claws on each other. If any of you, and I mean *any* of you, tries to break apart the team, for whatever reason, you'd better damn well hope the aliens kill you before I do."

He paused, just long enough to allow his words to sink in, then looked at Maddy. "The floor is yours."

"The ceiling is ours," Greene said, quickly.

Alan glared him into silence. "Maddy?"

Maddy took a breath. "Post-battle assessments of the alien starfighters suggested…"

Alan watched their faces as Maddy spoke, quietly noting who was listening and who was too self-obsessed to pay attention. They weren't - quite - the dregs of the service, but they weren't the Royal Navy's aces either. Too many of *them* had died at New Russia. The younger pilots had been rushed through the training program, while the older reservists had spent years out of a cockpit. Too many of them hadn't bothered to keep up with their training either. Alan had a feeling that there were going to be a few changes, once the war was over…if humanity survived. The entire reservist system was buckling under the strain of so many people having to rejoin the navy at short notice.

And the older ones will be a steadying influence, he told himself, firmly. *Perhaps they can keep the younger pilots in check.*

He didn't think the message was really sinking in, not amongst the younger pilots. They'd been taught to be hot dogs, to use their craft to best advantage, but the threat environment had changed sharply. They might have flown the trench run in the simulators - no one had ever had to launch a torpedo into an exhaust vent on a moon-sized starship in real life - yet they'd never experienced so much counterbattery fire. The aliens might be able to shoot torpedoes out of space, just by filling space with plasma bolts. They'd have pretty low odds of hitting anything with a single blast, but they fired so many that the odds tipped sharply in their favour.

And if they manage to improve their targeting, he thought grimly, *they might wipe out entire wings before they get into attack position.*

"You won't feel it in your bones, not yet," he said, when Maddy had finished. She'd kept herself strictly to the facts, but very few of the new-comers looked convinced. "You won't grasp the sheer power they possess. That's why we're going to be in the simulators, sparring with their craft until you *all* understand what we face. And this time" - he hardened his voice - "the aliens will not have any computer-given advantages. You will be facing them as they really are."

He sucked in his breath, wondering how many of them would actually *believe* him. Their trainers at the Luna Academy had always tipped the balance in favour of the enemy, giving them speeds and accuracy that were almost superhumanly good. The simulated enemy *always* scored hits when the computers deemed there was a greater than forty percent chance of hitting the target. It wasn't officially discussed, but everyone knew the simulations were tougher than reality. And when they asked, they always got the same answer. Hard training, easy mission; easy training, hard mission.

But the aliens were just too good to simulate, not without making them completely unbeatable. Humanity did have some advantages - the analysts had made that clear - but not enough to give them an edge. A Spitfire or a Hurricane starfighter enjoyed greater accuracy than their alien enemies, yet what did that matter when the aliens could fill space with lethal plasma bolts?

"I'll be checking your quarters in thirty minutes," he said, making a show of checking his wristcom. "After that, we'll be going straight into the simulators. If you haven't freshened up, make sure you do. There won't be another chance. Any questions?"

A pilot stuck up his hand. "Is it true we're getting long-range life-support packs?"

"Yes," Alan said, bluntly. He wasn't looking forward to using them, but the packs might come in handy. "And a few other surprises too."

He looked from face to face, then nodded to himself. "Dismissed."

The pilots rose and filed out of the room. He met Maddy's eyes and nodded to the hatch, silently ordering her to leave too. The hatch closed behind her, leaving him alone. He looked at the datapad, unsure if he wanted to see a new message or not. He'd written a letter to his daughters, the night after the briefing, but there had been no reply. It didn't bode well, he feared. Jeanette had never had any trouble responding instantly to her friends, even when she'd been seven years old. Perhaps she was just having problems deciding what to say.

Or perhaps the in-laws have told her not to reply, Alan thought. There were no rules barring him from visiting his family, but...he'd been in jail. And he didn't think he'd be allowed to leave the ship long enough to go to Earth, even if he wanted to. *God alone knows what the in-laws told them.*

His inbox wasn't empty, but none of the messages were particularly important. The beancounters seemed to believe he needed hundreds of generalised updates, very few of which had anything to do with him. And he'd signed up for a handful of news services, hoping to catch up on how politics and technology had evolved while he'd been in jail. There had been very little news in Colchester and he hadn't paid attention, not really. He didn't even know the name of the Prime Minister.

He opened the first message and read it quickly, trying to read between the lines. There would be censors in each of the news offices now, invoking DORA and making sure that the editors didn't print anything without prior approval. No matter what happened, most of the news was terribly bland. No actual untruths, as far as he could tell, but a great deal of misdirection. The government would probably get away with it, too. Sir Charles Hanover had believed the media to be nothing more than enemy combatants and he'd slapped all sorts of control laws on them. Hanover might be dead, but the laws lived on.

And yet, reading between the lines, there were hints of trouble, of people becoming aware of the truth. There was a sense that the ground was shifting, of the world changing in an unpredictable way…that nothing, perhaps, would ever be the same again. He remembered reading some memoirs from the world before the Troubles, memoirs written by people who had tried not to think about the way society was slowly tearing itself apart. They hadn't *wanted* to acknowledge it, he recalled. Acknowledging that their sacred cows were nothing of the sort would have broken them. The more honest ones, in hindsight, had recognised the truth. They'd been nothing more than useful idiots.

Alan shivered, despite himself. He'd once been caught in a blow-out, a hiss of escaping air all the warning he'd had before the gravity had failed and he'd plunged towards the hull breach. It had been a drill, an unannounced drill. There had been no real danger. And yet, just for a second, time had seemed to freeze while the awful truth had dawned on him. Now…it was no drill. Twelve fleet carriers were dead. The rest of the fleet might not be enough to stop the aliens.

You're being maudlin, he told himself, sharply. *Stop it.*

His wristcom bleeped. It was time to inspect the pilot quarters. And he hoped, as he rose and walked to the hatch, that they'd listened to him. He wanted to chew someone's ass, just to make it clear that they had to *listen*, but he didn't have time. There was too much else to do.

At least it will keep me busy, he thought. *I'll have no time to brood.*

———

"The fleet command network has been updated," Anson said. "You're apparently third in command of the fleet."

"Flotilla," Abigail corrected. "Calling seven ships a *fleet* is a little unbelievable."

Poddy coughed. "Do you get extra pay?"

"I don't think so," Anson said. "Just command, if Commodore Jameson and Captain Smith get blown away."

Abigail nodded, studying the display. Five escort carriers and two frigates held station near Tallyman, the latter playing host to Commodore Jameson and his staff. She had to give him credit for risking his ass as well as hers, particularly as the frigates would draw a great deal of enemy fire. The engineers had bolted extra armour to the hull, as well as additional close-in point defence weapons, but Abigail had her doubts. There was no way the frigates could carry the same weight of armour as *Ark Royal*.

And we can't either, she thought. *We're as defenceless as a newborn baby.*

She scowled. The extra plating might help, if the aliens strafed the ship, or it might not. She would be happier, she admitted privately, if she knew for sure. Her simulations suggested it *might* give them some extra survivability, but it depended on what assumptions were programmed into the computers. The only good news, as far as she could tell, was that the enemy plasma cannons were apparently short-range weapons. They didn't have to worry about being sniped from extreme range.

Anson coughed. "Mum?"

Abigail gave him a sharp look. "I think that we'll have more important things to worry about if I take command," she said, flatly. Losing both frigates would be bad, not least because the aliens could then concentrate on the escort carriers. The chances were the aliens now knew a great deal about what *Haddock* and her sisters could do. "Do we have an updated flight path yet?"

"No change," Anson told her. "I think he's planning to reconsider if we run into trouble."

"Smart move," Abigail agreed. She silently gave Jameson credit for that too. "We have no way to know how the situation might have changed in the last few days."

She checked the latest set of reports, silently grateful that the bean-counters - for once - had been silenced. Alan had told her that he no longer needed to file requests in triplicate to get what he wanted, as long as it could be found. *Haddock* had been resupplied with everything from medical gear to food, drink and even a handful of portable gaming machines. Abigail wasn't sure if there was a valid use for the machines or not, but she had to admit their presence was a good sign. And yet, it was worrying too. A great deal depended on their mission.

We have to buy time, she thought. *And if that costs us our lives…*

It wasn't something she'd thought about, before the war. She'd been a patriot, but a *belter* patriot. She'd feared, as had many others, that there would be a clash between the Great Powers and the Belter Federation; she'd known, if that day had come, that she would have to choose a side. And yet, interplanetary war had always seemed pointless. The belt had imposed change, even on Russian or Chinese facilities. They hadn't had a choice, not when their best personnel started to desert. The Great Powers might win the war, only to discover that they'd laid the seeds for the *next* war.

But now, the universe had changed. And the belt could not stand alone. She was a *human* patriot now, just as they all were. The ruthless pragmatism of the belt demanded it. But would everyone else feel the same way? Or was her sacrifice going to pass unremarked?

Poddy cleared her throat. "Signal from the flag, Mum," she said. "We're leaving at nineteen-hundred-hours precisely."

Abigail nodded. "Spread the word," she said. "And remind everyone that this is their last chance to write a will. They'll want to make sure everyone knows what they want to do with their ill-gotten gains."

She smiled at the thought, although it wasn't really funny. The Royal Navy had paid a major bonus for the combat recordings. Maybe not enough to repay the loan she'd taken out, years ago, but enough to put her in a very good position if she wanted to buy another ship. And even the junior crewers on *Haddock* had enough bonus money to give them an excellent chance of buying a ship of their own. Some of them would certainly want to do so, after the war. It wasn't something she wanted to discourage.

And Anson might be able to get a loan from the rest of the family, if he wants a ship himself, she thought. *It would take him years to repay it, but the terms would be good.*

Her heart sank as she realised it might not be so easy to buy a starship after the war. The civilian shipyards were already being repurposed to construct warships, rather than commercial ships. And even if the war ended, there would be a push to rebuild the space navies rather than the interstellar shipping fleets. Anson and Poddy might have the cash, but would they find anyone willing to sell?

Stop worrying about the future, she told herself, as she rose. *The future can take care of itself. The present is now.*

Leaving Anson in command, she walked her ship from bow to stern, inspecting each and every one of the refits and modifications. The engineers had done a good job, she considered, although the *Workhorse* freighters had been designed to be easy to repair or modify. Whoever had approved the design had shown a grasp of long-term thinking she'd assumed to be beyond most groundpounders. *Haddock* still wasn't a warship - she was too slow and bulky to be effective in a knife-range fight - but she did have some advantages of her own. Abigail just wished they had more armour.

She returned to the bridge as the drives started to power up, a low *thrumming* echoing through the hull. The last set of reports were on her display, waiting for her. *Haddock* was as ready as she was ever going to be. The engineers had already disembarked. Abigail felt a pang of regret, mingled with the grim awareness that extra engineers wouldn't help if they came under heavy attack. *Haddock* wouldn't survive if the aliens bore down on her with all their might. She didn't know any starship that *would*.

"The flag is signalling for us to take our place in formation," Poddy said.

"Anson, take us out," Abigail ordered. She braced herself as the drives grew louder. "And then follow the flag to the tramline."

"Aye, Captain."

Abigail felt her gut clench. She'd thought she'd understood there was a war on, but she hadn't until she'd actually seen the aliens. This was no genteel shoving match between Great Powers, or a punitive expedition against a rogue state. This was a war to the death, with no surrenders accepted. And humanity could lose...

She shook her head, slowly. She'd read all the speculations, all the suggestions that humanity had somehow mortally offended an alien foe or that the human form might be terrifyingly ugly to the aliens. But none of them meant anything, compared to the simple fact that the aliens had started the war. And now humanity had to fight or die.

And now we're on our way, again, she thought. *Who knows what we'll run into this time?*

CHAPTER
TWENTY THREE

"You have to remain focused on the targets," Alan said, irritated. "The aliens move like flies on a griddle."

He fought to keep his voice even as he studied the latest set of stats. The old hands - and it was strange thinking of men who were barely out of their teens as *old* - had done a good job, but the newcomers hadn't done anything like so well. It was a very different threat environment to the one they'd trained for, he had to admit, yet they *had* to adapt to the new world. The aliens wouldn't give them a chance to learn from their mistakes.

His eyes swept the briefing room. "This isn't a simulation where everything is hyped up a little, just to keep you on your toes," he added. "The alien craft truly *are* that good - and their point defence is a nightmare."

"It's too good," Flight Lieutenant Thomas Andrews said. He was one of the older pilots, nearly ten years out of the cockpit. "How are we meant to get a torpedo run through *that* level of firepower?"

"Keep dodging, granddad," Greene said. "They can't fill every last millimetre of space with plasma fire."

"They're certainly trying," Andrews snapped back. "It's starting to look like we need mass drivers, not torpedoes."

"I believe the boffins are working on them," Alan said. Mass drivers had been regarded as weapons of mass destruction for years and there had been a tacit agreement, amongst the Great Powers, not to build them. In hindsight, that might have been a mistake. A solid projectile might soak up plasma fire before it slammed into a target and punched right through the hull. "However, we have to make do with what we have."

He tapped the display. "Next time, I want Herring to cover Kipper as you push the offensive," he added. "And I expect *all* of you to work on your flying. Let the computers handle the firing. They're better at snap-shooting in any case."

"Perhaps some of us should take drugs," Greene muttered. "Their reflexes are dull…"

"At least we're trying," Andrews said. "You decided to clown around while we were flying into the teeth of enemy fire."

"Quiet!" Alan snapped, before a real argument could break out. "Like I said, we have to make do with what we have! And that means all of you working together. If you have a problem with it, complain to the Admiralty. I'm *sure* they will be glad to hear from you."

He sighed, inwardly, as his eyes swept the compartment. There *were* drugs that enhanced reflexes, but they tended to come with unexpected and unwanted side effects. Pilots were not allowed to use them, unless the situation was truly dire. Even now, Alan doubted the Admiralty would endorse their use, certainly not on a regular basis. The possible conse-quences were too bad.

"We'll resume our simulations in an hour," he said. "Get something to eat, then report back to the simulators. And be prepared to be flying for hours. Dismissed."

He watched the pilots leave, then sat back in his chair. "I feel old."

"You don't look a day over one hundred," Bennett said, dryly. He sat in the corner, reading a datapad. "And some of those pilots are older than you."

Alan nodded, shortly. The reservists were *trying*, but it was achingly clear that some of them had seen the reserves as a chance to earn a retainer while doing very little, while others weren't in the best physical state. They understood the importance of what they were doing - and the implica-tions of losing so many starfighters and fleet carriers - but their reflexes weren't up to standard. Normally, none of them would be allowed to fly anything more complicated than a shuttle.

This is the new normal, he told himself. *Get used to it.*

He glanced at the report on the datapad, forwarded from one of the pickets in the Asimov System. The aliens hadn't moved, after occupying a handful of systems near New Russia. It bothered Alan, more than he cared to admit. They had to be planning something, but what? It wasn't even clear if they could read and understand human datafiles. If they couldn't, they'd have to find their way to Earth through extensive survey work...

Don't count on it, he thought, sourly. *We don't dare assume they didn't manage to recover astrographic data.*

Not, he supposed, that it mattered. With care, the aliens could have surveyed most of human space over the last couple of years, without triggering any alarms. No one had been *watching* for aliens, after all. Any stray sensor contacts at the edge of a populated star system would be dismissed as vacuum fluctuations or sensor glitches, instead of an alien fleet. The aliens could have brought their forces all the way to Earth without being detected, if they knew where to go. He supposed that, if nothing else, was a sign the aliens didn't know anything about the internal astrography of the human sphere.

"We have three weeks to go," he said. "Do you think we have a chance?"

Bennett shrugged. "You're the CAG," he said. "What do *you* think?"

"I think we're going to take some pretty heavy losses," Alan said. He studied the starchart, thoughtfully. It wouldn't be long before they started to crawl through occupied space, making their way to their destination. "And they might be able to catch us while we're sneaking back."

"Worry about the mission first," Bennett said. "Extraction will come later."

Alan shot him an odd look. "Was that what they taught *you?*"

"We were always trained to balance pre-mission planning with improvisation and muddling through," Bennett told him. "There was always *something* that threw the plans out of sync."

"No battle plan ever survives contact with the enemy," Alan agreed.

"Quite," Bennett said. "And the man on the spot is the one best qualified to decide what to do."

Alan shrugged. He *was* the man on the spot, as far as he could tell, but he didn't feel as though he knew what to do. No, that wasn't quite accurate. He knew what he wanted to do, but he knew he couldn't do it. The older reservists were the only pilots available to reinforce his squadrons, while the younger ones went to fleet carriers or orbital bases. He understood the cold logic all too well. His pilots were expendable. And yet, he didn't like it. How could he?

Bennett rose. "Keep designing your simulations," he said. "And keep altering the parameters. You don't want them to get complacent."

"I doubt anyone will," Alan said. He held up the datapad. "Our most successful mission cost us two-thirds of our starfighters and three of the carriers. One *real* mission like that will be enough to ruin us."

"It depends, I suppose," Bennett said. "How much harm would you do to the enemy?"

Alan watched him go, feeling tired. There was no hope of actually *answering* that question, not when they knew next to nothing about the aliens. Would destroying a fleet carrier cost the aliens ten percent of their forces? Or five percent? Or one percent? How many fleet carriers did the aliens *have*? There was no way to know. And how badly would they be hurt if Alan wiped out a whole convoy? Again, there was no way to know.

And we're all expendable, Alan thought. He knew the Admiralty would happily sacrifice the entire flotilla if it killed an alien fleet carrier, but it was impossible to tell how badly that would affect the balance of power. There was a time when the term 'favourable loss rates' became meaningless. *We might wind up losing the war if the aliens can afford to trade fleet carriers for us.*

He stared down at the datapad for a long moment. It had only been a week...stats would improve, surely? But he knew there were limits. Starfighter piloting was a young man's game, not something for men who were old enough to be fathers...one of them was even a *grandfather*. There was a reason the military rarely recruited anyone older than thirty - and even *that* was a stretch. But the war took priority. Better to bring back the old fogies than waste younger pilots on what might be a forlorn hope.

That could be me, he thought, as he rose. *I might have been called back to the colours, even if...*

The thought cost him a pang. He'd tried not to think of what his life would have been like, if Judith hadn't cheated on him or if he hadn't killed her. Colchester made it hard to think of what might have been. And yet, now…he sighed. Would he have retired? He probably wouldn't have had a shot at a command chair, not when there were plenty of officers with better connections. But he might have gone into training or wound up flying a desk or…

He cursed himself, under his breath. Maybe he would have taken early retirement. Vets got preference, almost everywhere. He didn't have the best of educations, but he could have gotten into a training course or even found a job as a consultant. The big corporations liked having military vets on staff. It was easier to sell a starfighter design to the military if it had passed muster with someone who'd actually flown starfighters for a living. He could have watched his daughters grow up…he could have taken them to school, listened to their teachers, threatened their boyfriends…

They're too young to date, he told himself, firmly.

They won't stay that age forever, a little voice pointed out. *And they're not the babies you remember any more.*

He gritted his teeth. The in-laws hadn't been very good about keeping him informed. For all he knew, they were mistreating his daughters. It wasn't impossible…he shook his head, angrily. The in-laws might despise him, but they wouldn't harm his little girls. Jeanette and Alice were their daughter's children too. But not *knowing* was maddening. There hadn't been any response to his letter before the squadron had left Sol.

I might have to sue for visitation rights, he thought. *And that won't be easy.*

The hatch chimed. He looked up as Maddy stepped into the compartment. "I have the latest reports, sir," she said. Her uniform looked slightly mussed. "The new systems performed well."

"In simulations," Alan pointed out. He took the datapad and read the report, quickly. "We have to remember that simulations are not reality."

"Yes, sir," Maddy said. Her tone was so painfully polite that he *knew* she wanted to remind him not to teach his grandmother to suck eggs. "But they're as close as possible to reality."

Hah, Alan thought.

He passed the datapad back. "I'll go through it later," he said. "Right now, I have more simulations to run. Did the commodore set any time for live-fire exercises?"

"No, sir," Maddy said. "But we don't have much time to carry them out."

Alan nodded. The other escort carriers had to be having similar problems, then. In peacetime, the thought would have given him a certain amount of guilty amusement. A captain whose ship was at the bottom of the tables for two weeks running would be *sure* to feel the brunt of his admiral's displeasure. And while he knew it was important for everyone to train constantly, it was a relief to know they weren't the worst in the fleet.

But now we're at war, he thought. *And our very survival may depend on our comrades.*

"I'll check with him later, if we don't have a schedule by the end of the day," he said. Flying starfighters while they were sneaking through occupied space would be a good way to commit suicide. Starfighters were many things, but they weren't particularly stealthy. The aliens would have plenty of time to note their course and speed, then set an ambush. "Did you get a report from the sensor crews?"

"They report no major problems," Maddy said. "But they're unsure about alien sensors."

Alan sighed, crossly. The aliens had their sensor masks - cloaking devices, one wag had called them. They *knew* their sensor crews might have to find someone *else* using the sensor masks one day. And they knew enough about the sensor masks to pick out any weaknesses…tracking a ship in silent running might be easy, by comparison. Alan knew better than to assume the aliens *weren't* looking for ways to break their own stealth. It was what the Royal Navy would have done.

"We might be about to find out," he said. He rose. "I need to grab something to eat. Coming?"

Maddy nodded. "Yes, sir."

———

"Ping Anson," Abigail ordered. "Where *is* he?"

Poddy, wisely, didn't say a word as she keyed her console. Abigail watched her, reminding herself - sharply - that whatever had happened wasn't Poddy's fault. But she was damned if she wasn't going to chew

Anson out for being late. Freighter crews could be slapdash in places - she didn't care what her crew wore, as long as they did their jobs - but there were limits. Someone who was meant to be on the bridge at 1800 was damn well *meant* to be on the bridge at 1800.

The hatch opened. Anson stepped into the compartment. "Mum, I…"

Abigail rose. "Don't you *mum* me," she snapped. "Where *were* you?"

She waited, resting her hands on her hips. Her uncle had taught her that being late was unforgivable. There were standards that had to be upheld, whatever the situation. And there had been no emergency that would have distracted Anson from the bridge. She wouldn't have been so angry if she'd thought he had a *legitimate* reason to be late.

"I was…I lost track of time," Anson said. "I…"

"You mean you were in your bunk with Maddy," Abigail said. She allowed her voice to tighten. "Didn't you *know* you were meant to be on duty?"

Poddy made a faint sound. Abigail glared. Anson needed a chewing out, but it wasn't something that should be done in public. She glanced at her console, then nodded. Poddy could leave the bridge safely. The sensors would alert them if something required immediate attention.

"Poddy, go get something to eat, then have a nap," she ordered. "Do *not* be late for your next shift."

She watched Poddy hurry out the compartment, then switched her gaze back to Anson. "I don't give a good goddamn what you do when you're off duty," she said. It wasn't entirely true - Anson *was* her son, after all - but it was the sort of courtesy belter captains generally offered to their subordinates. "If you want to fuck a grown woman, or a man, or both at once, I don't care.

Anson winced. "I…"

Abigail spoke over him. "What I *cannot* tolerate is it interfering with your duties," she added, sharply. "And I certainly cannot tolerate it in *my son*!"

"Mum, I…"

"Stop mumbling," Abigail snapped. "Speak up! If I was Captain Bligh, you and Maddy would be floating naked in space with your underpants nailed to your head. Your great-uncle would probably have done something truly unspeakable to you. Tell me…what were you thinking?"

Anson flushed. "I wasn't thinking."

"Glad to hear you admit it," Abigail snapped. "Believe me, I *am* aware of all the jokes about blood rushing out of your brain and down to your dick when you see a pretty girl. And I don't fault you for having an affair while you're off-duty. But I *cannot* allow you to neglect your duties."

And perhaps allow you to actually fall in love with Maddy, she added, silently. She didn't really blame Anson for being embarrassed. It was one conversation *she'd* never had with her parents, or her uncle. There hadn't been any suggestion of someone *unsuitable* entering her life, not in a permanent way. Maddy, on the other hand, might not be a good addition to the family. *But you won't listen if I tell you to stop seeing her.*

"It was my fault," Anson said, stiffly. "And I stand ready to accept whatever punishment you order."

Abigail met his eyes. "You understand what would happen if the captain of this ship *wasn't* your mother?"

"Yes, Captain."

"Good," Abigail drew out the word as much as possible. "Fortunately, there are no shortage of compartments that need cleaning. Tonight, after your duty shift, report to Vassilios and he'll point you in the right direction. And, in future, be careful. I don't want to have to kick you off the ship."

"I understand," Anson said.

"Glad to hear it," Abigail said, sardonically. "And seeing you've managed to get to fourth base with Maddy…are you planning to *marry* her?"

Anson turned red. "Mum!"

"It's a valid question," Abigail said. She pointed a finger at him. "You have a position in the family, as well as shares in this ship. A fling is one thing" - she ignored the choking sound he made - "but a long-term affair is quite another. And, beyond that, does she understand that the affair might come to an end?"

"…I don't know," Anson said. "But I…I think *we* could handle it."

"Yeah," Abigail agreed. "But you do realise that you have obligations to the family? No one would blame you for putting them aside, but they do have to know where they stand."

She sighed. "Don't make your mind up now," she added. Lust was one thing, love - and a permanent relationship - was quite another. "But think about it before you get too involved."

And it may be too late for that, she thought, as she waved him to his console. *She's already distracting him from his duties.*

Her thoughts darkened. *And if she hurts him, I'll make damn sure she pays.*

CHAPTER

TWENTY FOUR

"Signal from the flag, sir," Maddy said. "We jump in five minutes."

Alan nodded, feeling a chill run down his spine. Making a combat jump into Alkaline felt off, somehow. The system was part of human space, occupied by nothing more dangerous than a handful of independent asteroid settlements. And yet...he shook his head. The system was no longer under humanity's control. If the last report was accurate, they were about to enter alien-held space.

He keyed his console. "Prepare for emergency launch," he ordered. Herring Squadron was already in the launch tubes, with Kipper's pilots waiting in the ready room. "Stand by for deployment..."

The timer blinked into existence on the display, counting down the minutes and seconds to jump. Alan gritted his teeth, feeling - again - the grim uncertainty of not being *sure* what was on the far side. Cold logic told him that the aliens *wouldn't* be waiting, ready to slam plasma fire or missiles into *Haddock's* hull, but his emotions weren't so sure. Perhaps the aliens *had* tracked them as they'd made their way towards the tramline. The far side would be the perfect place for an ambush, if the aliens knew precisely where they were going to appear.

"Ten seconds," Maddy said.

"Brace yourself," Alan ordered. The aliens *didn't* know where they were, let alone where they were going to appear. Commodore Jameson's random course changes should have seen to that, unless the alien sensors and stealth systems were better than the analysts assumed. "Here we go..."

He grunted in pain, feeling a fist slam into his belly as the starship jumped. No amount of fiddling with the drive had been able to lessen the jump shock, even though more modern ships barely provoked a reaction when *they* jumped. He forced himself to look at the display as the pain slowly ebbed away, watching grimly as passive sensors searched for enemy contacts. The only good news was that the enemy *hadn't* been lying in wait. They'd be dead by now if the aliens *had* been ready for them.

"Local space appears to be clear," Maddy said. "No contacts, no trace of enemy...*wait!*"

She paused. "Long-range sensors are picking up a distress beacon," she said. "It's from one of the colonies, orbiting the gas giant!"

Alan winced. The last report had stated that the aliens had simply stood off and blasted the colonies from a safe distance. But that had been weeks ago. If there was a distress beacon still active, it meant...what? Were there survivors? Or were the aliens hoping to lure unwary starships into their clutches? He had no way to know.

Maddy glanced at him. "Sir, will we go investigate?"

"That's the commodore's call," Alan said. He didn't envy the younger man. Whatever he did, *someone* would find a problem with it. It was a law of space that *everyone* had to respond to a distress call, even if it was from an unfriendly power. But if it was a trap, the flotilla would be blasted apart before it knew it was under attack. "I think we'll probably ignore it."

"You're right," Maddy said, a moment later. "Our orders are to continue to Tramline Four."

Alan nodded, torn between relief and a terrible kind of guilt. Being lost in space, being forced to watch helplessly as the oxygen gauge slowly ticked down to nothing...it was a nightmare, one he'd had countless times since he'd started training. Bailing out of one's starfighter alone was dangerous as hell, but waiting to be picked up by a SAR shuttle could be worse. Someone might mistake the lifepod for a mine and blast it without bothering to answer questions. And if the battle was lost, there might not *be* a SAR shuttle.

He sighed as he felt a dull quiver running through the ship. The memorial near Hamilton City on Luna contained hundreds of names, men and women who'd died during Britain's push into space. Some had died in the handful of clashes before the Solar Treaty had been worked out, but others had been lost to industrial accidents or simply crewed starships that had never returned. The thought of leaving the dying to die was horrific. If there were colonists left alive…

We have no choice, he told himself firmly. It didn't feel very convincing. *We cannot let the aliens lure us into a trap.*

"Silent running mode engaged," Maddy said. The lights dimmed, slightly. "Sensors detect very limited emissions from the other ships."

"Let's hope the alien sensors aren't much better," Alan said. Passive sensors were good, but they couldn't detect a stealthed alien ship. The alien wouldn't be emitting anything the sensors could pick up and report before it was too late. "But we should be well out of range."

He brought up the in-system display and studied it. The flotilla was slowly making its way towards the tramline, lurking at the edge of the system. It added *days* to their transit time - which would add up, by the time they reached their unnamed destination - but there was no choice. They could *not* run the risk of being detected. He frowned at the handful of icons orbiting the star, indicating the planets and larger asteroids. If the aliens *had* a presence in the system, it was beyond their ability to detect.

Which means nothing, he told himself. *They have ample reason to hide from us.*

"Order Kipper to stand down for an hour, then relieve Herring," he said. "We'll rotate the squadrons every four hours until further notice."

"Understood," Maddy said. She made a face. "No one is going to like *that.*"

Alan nodded, curtly. Being in a cramped cockpit was bad enough, even when one was flying through space. Being stuck in the launch tube was worse. The pilots couldn't even go to the toilet while they were on alert. They had to piss into the tubes…he grimaced. *That* was one detail that was normally left unspoken, during military awareness days. No one wanted to think about the practicalities when they were consumed with the glamour of flying through the inky blackness of space.

"They'll just have to cope with it," he said. He made a mental note to monitor the pilots as they waited. The younger pilots had the endurance to survive, but the older ones? eBooks and videos could only take them so far. "Inform me at once if anyone has problems."

"Aye, sir."

Alan tried to relax as the minutes slowly ticked into hours and the hours became days. It wasn't easy. The sense that they were being watched was growing stronger all the time, even though cold logic insisted that the aliens would have jumped them by now. Crew and pilots spoke in hushed voices, as if they feared the aliens could *hear* them. Alan pointed out, more than once, that sound didn't travel through a vacuum - in space, no one could hear them scream - but it didn't make a difference. He felt it himself, if he was honest. Even passing through the first tram-line and heading up a seemingly-useless tramline chain didn't make him feel any better. The aliens might have different ideas about what consti-tuted *useless*.

And if the boffins are wrong, this entire mission might be useless, Alan thought. It had seemed convincing, back at Sol. Now, countless light-years from home, the whole mission appeared a little more dubious. *We might be trapped at one end of the chain while they turn Earth to cinders.*

He paced the decks, trying to keep his people calm and focused. A couple of pilots got into fights and had to be chewed out, several more were caught making love in disused sections and yet another had a ner-vous breakdown that resulted in sedation and relief from duty. Alan wondered, sourly, just what the Admiralty had been thinking, when it had recalled the oldest reservists. Surely, a spot could have been found for them in the training centres. But then, most of their knowledge was a little out of date.

It was almost a relief, as they crawled across the third system, when Abigail called him into her cabin. Alan went, feeling a little trepidation. The last time he'd visited her cabin had been fine, but before then…half-drunken sex and confessions weren't his idea of fun. He braced himself as the hatch opened, unsure what he'd see. Abigail was sitting on the bed, pouring steaming water into two mugs. It looked reassuringly normal.

"It's been a while since we had a proper chat," Abigail said. She waved a hand towards the chair. "Take a seat. The tea should be ready in a moment."

"Thank you," Alan said, as he sat. The tea capsules tasted odd, to him, but beggars couldn't be choosers. Capsules took up less space - and lasted longer - than teabags, let alone tealeaves. "It *has* been a while."

He studied Abigail as she passed him a mug of tea. She looked tired and worn, dark rings forming around her eyes. Her shipsuit looked as though it hadn't been cleaned in weeks. He wasn't too surprised, to be honest. Every non-essential system on the ship had been shut down, just to minimise the risk of a stray emission alerting the aliens to their presence. Even the laundry had been closed. It was paranoia, perhaps paranoia taken to the bitter extreme, but there was no choice. He had no illusions about their chances if the aliens caught them in an ambush.

"I haven't been keeping up with your reports," he said. A polite lie - she hadn't been *writing* reports. "How are your crew coping?"

Abigail snorted, rudely. "You navy men and your reports," she said. "Why can't you just bury the aliens in paperwork?"

"I think most of our reports are electronic now," Alan said. He'd had the same thought himself, more than once. "But we can throw computers and datapads at the aliens if we run out of missiles and nukes."

"Perhaps," Abigail said. She smiled, thinly. It didn't quite touch her eyes. "The crew is coping, somehow. Luckily, onboard entertainments haven't been cut back *too* badly."

Alan nodded. There would probably have been a mutiny if they *had* tried to cut down on onboard entertainments, particularly when they were still running the simulators on a daily basis. He might just have joined the mutiny himself. Being able to lose oneself in an eBook - or a VR fantasy - might make the difference between enduring the slow crawl and cracking under the strain. Spacers tended to have a high boredom threshold, but there were limits.

"And Anson and Maddy have continued their relationship," Abigail added. "Does that concern you?"

"Not really," Alan said. "They're both adults - and they're not in the same chain of command. As long as it doesn't interfere with their work, I don't care."

He frowned, taking another sip of his tea. Maddy seemed smart enough not to play games during a war, but he could be wrong. The innocence she projected - the attitude that made him feel protective - could easily be a mask. And yet, she *was* smart. She would probably have gone far, if she hadn't decided it would be easier to steal from the navy's funds. The upper ranks would be forever closed to her - she wasn't a line officer - but she could have retired as a commodore if she was lucky.

"They're too young," Abigail said. "I don't think either of them are ready for a serious relationship."

Alan shrugged. He'd lost his virginity at sixteen. Besides, there was something fundamentally wrong about inquiring into the sex lives of two adults, particularly when their affair wasn't having any impact on *him*. He'd rebuke Maddy if it did, but...until then, he had no reason to say anything.

"See what happens after we get home," he said. "And after the war ends."

Abigail lifted her mug in silent salute. "What do *you* intend to do after the war?"

"I don't know," Alan said. He had few illusions. The Royal Navy might have recalled him to duty - and offered him a pardon - but he was hardly someone the navy would want to *protect*. They'd keep sending him on dangerous missions until the war ended or he was killed, whichever one came first. "The odds of survival are not high."

"We make our own odds," Abigail said. "And damned be the cold equations."

"They made me read that story in school," Alan said. He could remember it clearly. A girl had accidentally trapped herself on a spacecraft carrying medical supplies to a tiny colony. But there wasn't enough fuel on the ship for the supplies to arrive safely, unless the girl was ejected into space. And the girl wasn't a *bad* girl. She'd made a mistake, out of ignorance, and the universe demanded she pay for it. "I always found it depressing."

"Me too," Abigail said. She sounded odd, just for a second. "My uncle forced me to read it twice, then give him my impressions of it."

Alan lifted his eyebrows. "What did you tell him?"

"Oh, I came up with all sorts of answers," Abigail said. "I thought of a dozen precautions that could have stopped the crisis before it began. Even something as simple as a lock on the door might have kept the girl out. And it was written in the days before drive fields. Now, saving the girl would be a snap."

Her voice hardened. "My uncle told me that all the answers were useless. I was very hurt until he explained why. They were too late! The girl was already on the ship by the time someone realised there was a problem. Sure, the people in the story could prevent it from happening again, but it wouldn't save the girl. *Nothing* could save the girl."

She smiled, thinly. "The other moral, I suppose, was that making something foolproof is pretty much impossible. You can do everything reasonable - you can cover your ass so tightly that people think you're wearing nappies - and still get into shit because someone was idiotic enough to climb into a reactor core or test an emergency airlock."

"Or go playing on railway lines," Alan added. "Or something else equally dumb."

Abigail nodded. "You can't predict what someone will do, if that person is too ignorant or too stupid to understand what they're doing," she said. "All you can do is cover all of the bases as much as possible."

"Tell me about it," Alan said. "We can't even predict what the *aliens* will do."

"I suppose that makes sense," Abigail agreed. "If we can't predict what our fellow humans will do, what are our chances of predicting what the *aliens* will do."

She put her empty mug on the table, then shifted position until her legs were brushing against his. Alan froze, unsure what she was doing. Was it a silent invitation? Or was it meaningless? The cabin was small enough that they'd brush against each other if either one of them moved. He found himself unsure of what to do. They'd had sex before, but that had been different. Now...

Or maybe it's not that different, he thought. *We both want - and need - to relieve some tension.*

He leaned forward slowly, giving her a chance to pull away. Abigail was not the sort of person who'd have any difficulty in saying *no*. Besides, he half-remembered her arms wrapping around him. She wasn't the strongest person he'd met, but she was tough enough to hurt him. Or put him out completely, if she brought her knee up hard. Instead, she lifted her lips to his and kissed him. Alan felt a rush of arousal, mixed with a grim awareness that the alert could sound at any moment. They didn't have much time. Even so, he wanted it to be different.

His fingers struggled with her shipsuit, hastily undoing the clasps. Her breasts popped out, her nipples already hard. They pressed against his chest as she undid his suit, her tongue slipping in and out of his mouth. And then she was naked and he was naked and...she groaned, deep in her throat, as he slid inside her. It was all he could do to contain himself long enough for her to come too.

Afterwards, he lay on top of her on the tiny bunk. It wasn't large enough for them to be side by side. Abigail looked pleased, although it was hard to be sure. Like him, she had too many responsibilities to be distracted for long. He wondered, as he carefully climbed off her, just what the sex had *meant* to her. Did she have feelings for him? It seemed unlikely. He rather suspected she'd simply found him convenient.

"Thank you," Abigail said. She gave him a mischievous smile. "You're welcome to come back, when you're not on duty."

"Thank you," Alan managed. "You're...you're very blunt."

"I'm too old to be coy," Abigail said. She sat upright, her breasts bouncing in front of her. It was easy to tell she'd had children, yet...her body was still strong and healthy. Like most belters, a number of improvements had been spliced into her DNA. "And I'm too old to feel that sex and love are the same thing."

Ouch, Alan thought, wryly.

He checked his wristcom, then headed for the tiny washroom. There should be time for a quick shower before he went back on duty, if he was lucky. It shouldn't matter too much, unless the ship was attacked. But Maddy and the others knew not to wait for him if the aliens appeared out of nowhere and opened fire. They'd have to get the starfighters into space before it was too late.

And we still have two weeks to go, he thought. *And then...we'll find out if we're wasting our time after all.*

CHAPTER
TWENTY FIVE

"You know, we really ought to name this system something more interesting than IAU-4728," Anson said, as the flotilla slowly slipped away from the tramline. "Why don't we call it *Anson*? Anson is a lovely name."

"There's a settlement called Anson two jumps from Terra Nova," Poddy said. "Podkayne is a *much* better name."

"It also happens to be the name of a city on Mars," Anson pointed out. "Anson is a much better name."

"But also taken," Abigail said. "I don't *think* you're allowed to duplicate a name."

"Anson is a very common name in the belt," Anson insisted. "And Podkayne is quite popular on Mars…"

"Enough," Abigail said. "Concentrate on your work."

She watched the display, half-expecting something to appear out of nowhere. It was easy to see why the system had been classed as useless. There was simply nothing *in* the system, save for a handful of comets and asteroids. Perhaps someone would set up a black colony in the system, if there wasn't one already hidden in the comets. There was certainly no shortage of groups who wanted a private home, light-years from the Great Powers. Or maybe the aliens themselves had a base in the system.

"I'm not detecting anything obvious," Poddy said. "The long-range sensor arrays aren't detecting anything either."

"Which may mean there's nothing to find," Anson said. "This whole mission might be a gold asteroid chase."

Abigail shrugged. Belters talked about a legendary gold asteroid, but she'd always assumed it was just a story. Besides, it wasn't as if someone couldn't find traces of gold in more mundane asteroids. Gold was relatively cheap, in any case. Platinum and palladium were far more useful. A belter who found a source of either would be set up for life.

"Keep an eye on the sensors anyway," she ordered. "I want to know about it the *second* the aliens show themselves."

She leaned back in her chair, trying not to let her own doubts show on her face. The weak tramlines were clearly visible on the display, but what if the analysts were wrong? What if they *were* wasting their time? What if...she sighed, inwardly. The thought of waiting in the unnamed system until their supplies ran low, then returning to Earth to find a blackened cinder and Sol swept clean of life was a nightmare that no amount of work or sex could brush aside. She couldn't help worrying. If the analysts were wrong...

"Signal from the flag," Poddy said. A green icon flashed up on the display. "We're to hold position at Point Lovecraft and wait."

Abigail nodded. The tactic made sense...assuming, of course, that the aliens *could* use the weaker tramlines. Point Lovecraft was near a least-time course between Tramline Two and Tramline Three, close enough to allow them to adjust their position and far away enough to give them a chance to avoid contact if the alien convoy was too heavily defended. It made sense, but...she pushed her doubts away, savagely. They'd do their duty. The rest could take care of itself.

"Take us there," she ordered. "And watch your sensors!"

The hours crawled by with agonising silence as the tiny flotilla crawled towards Point Lovecraft. Abigail felt her eyes begin to hurt as she monitored the display, unsure if she wanted the aliens to show themselves or not. The flotilla might be out of place if the aliens sent a convoy through *now*, but at least it would be proof that the aliens could and did use the weaker tramlines. She wouldn't be so unsure of herself if she *knew* the analysts were right.

"Reaching Point Lovecraft," Anson said. He sounded tired. "Captain?"

"Hold position," Abigail said. It was foolish to expect a convoy to appear as soon as they arrived. She understood the realities of interstellar shipping, realities she assumed bedevilled the aliens too. "Anson, Poddy; call the relief crew, then get some rest."

"You too, Mum," Anson said.

Abigail nodded, curtly. There would be no time for sex, not now they were on full alert. Commodore Jameson was already launching stealth probes towards the weak tramlines, trying to ensure that the aliens were detected as soon as they made transit. And once they were detected, the flotilla could move to intercept.

"I'll sleep," she said. "And let us hope that the analysts were actually right."

———————

The howl of the sirens brought Alan out of bed, one hand grappling for a weapon that wasn't there as the sound grew louder. He glanced around, swearing angrily as he saw the red icons on the display. Long-range probes had indeed detected an alien convoy, the ships popping out of Tramline Two. He felt a shiver run down his spine as he grabbed his jacket and pulled it on. The proof that the aliens could indeed use the weaker tramlines was right in front of him.

Bennett landed beside him. "Go, go, go," he snapped. "Now!"

"No hurry," Alan said. He had no trouble calculating the vectors in his mind. "We have time."

He smiled, ignoring Bennett's grunt of annoyance. It would be at least three hours before the engagement, if there *was* an engagement. The probes hadn't detected any alien warships yet, but he'd be surprised if there were none. Even if the aliens didn't expect them to blockade the unnamed star, they'd be well aware that human forces would be trying to return to New Russia sooner or later. Hitting a convoy in the occupied system would be a good way to knock the aliens back on their heels.

And they know it as well as we do, he thought, as he opened the hatch and made his way down to the CIC. *They can't expect us to do nothing in response...*

"Seventeen freighters," Maddy said. "And five warships. The analysts believe that they're roughly akin to destroyers."

"Looks that way," Alan agreed. By tonnage, if nothing else, the alien ships were probably destroyers. But there was no way to know what surprises might be lurking within their hulls. A destroyer built within the last five years was a more effective combatant than one that dated back twenty years...or it had been, he supposed. The older starship would have carried more armour. "Are they expecting trouble?"

"I...I don't think so," Maddy said. "But I could be wrong."

Alan nodded, slowly. The alien ships weren't sweeping space with active sensors, but they weren't trying to hide either. He had no way to know if that meant they weren't expecting trouble or if they *wanted* it. There was a good chance that at least one or two of the freighters had been turned into a warship. Why not? *Haddock* had been turned into a warship. He studied the power readings, but saw nothing that might separate a converted warship from the rest of the ships. They simply didn't know enough about the aliens to make anything more reliable than guesses.

Commodore Jameson's face appeared in the display. "The aliens have arrived," he stated, addressing the entire flotilla. "They are proceeding along the projected course to Tramline Three. We will attempt to intercept them at Point Lovecraft-One."

Good thinking, Alan acknowledged. They'd have no trouble getting in and getting out, unless the alien freighters really were bait in a trap. But the sensor probes hadn't picked up any hint that there might be other alien ships in the system. *We can't keep second-guessing ourselves.*

He looked at the starchart, trying to parse out the weak tramline. Its destination appeared to be a star five light years away, but it was hard to be sure. Gravimetric tracers weren't always accurate, for reasons the boffins had never been able to put into words. There were a couple of tramlines that went to the wrong stars. He didn't know anything about the target star. The files insisted that humanity had never visited it. God alone knew how important it was to the aliens.

A big fleet base or just another waypoint? He sighed, dismissing the thought. *There's no way to know until we crack the secret of using the weaker tramlines.*

"I've forwarded movement orders to you now," Commodore Jameson said. "Please remember to avoid *all* unnecessary emissions. One sniff of

212

our presence and they'll react badly. Starfighters will be launched on pow-ered-down trajectories at 1900 precisely, unless matters change."

"Two hours," Maddy said. "Hell of a risk, sir."

"It has to be done," Alan told her. He studied the roster for a long moment. The pilot who'd had a nervous breakdown was still in a secluded cabin, unable to take up his duties. "Inform Wing Commander Savage that I'll be taking Jefferson's place."

Maddy looked up, sharply. "Sir?"

"The flag can handle starfighter operations," Alan said. He'd run Maddy through a whole series of drills, just to make sure she could take the CIC if necessary. It wouldn't happen on a fleet carrier, but *Haddock* was no fleet carrier. "And if you have to issue orders, you can issue orders."

"I can issue orders to you," Maddy said, lightly. "Sir…"

"See to it," Alan said. He checked the timer. "And inform the remain-der of the pilots that we'll start launching procedures in two hours."

He sighed as he started to check the reports from the maintenance staff. The starfighters were all ready to go, thankfully. He'd seen plenty of flights when one or more starfighters developed a minor technical fault and had to turn back, even though the pilot should have been able to continue to fly. He supposed that had changed, now that they were at war. It was more important to get the starfighters into space than repair a tiny fault.

Except a tiny fault might become a big fault, if left alone, he reminded himself. *And if it becomes much worse, the starfighter might be lost completely.*

Maddy gave him a droll look. "If you don't come back," she said, "do I get your cabin?"

"Only if you don't mind sharing with Bennett," Alan said, sarcasti-cally. He looked around, half-expecting the big man to be lurking in the shadows. But there was no sign of him. "If I don't come back, declare yourself the CAG and do a bloody good job."

He smiled as he headed for the hatch. Maddy wouldn't have an easy time of it, particularly as she hadn't been a starfighter pilot herself. Savage or Whitehead might have to take over, although *that* might be tricky if they were needed outside. The Royal Navy had experimented with two-seater command starfighters, but none of them had proven particularly successful. He smiled, again, as he remembered the drills. The concept had been sound, but the double-sized starfighters had been easy for the enemy to pick out and target for destruction. And then the whole formation had started to come apart.

Savage met him outside the launch tubes. "You'll be taking orders from me, sir."

"I know," Alan said. He outranked Savage, but Savage *was* the squadron CO. Technically, Alan should take command; practically, Savage should *remain* in command. The Admiralty would probably pitch a fit, if they noticed that Alan declined a command that should have been his, but he found it hard to care. "Just slot me into Jefferson's place."

"I feared the old fart didn't have it in him to last the course," Savage said. He looked down at the metal deck. "Are we really *that* desperate, sir?"

"You were at New Russia," Alan said, grimly. Twelve fleet carriers, two of them British, had been wiped out in less than ten minutes. It would be a long time before such losses could be replaced, if the aliens gave them time. "What do you think?"

He couldn't help feeling a thrill as he walked into the launch bay. Jefferson's starfighter was already waiting for him, a spherical form bristling with weapons and sensor nodes. Two torpedoes sat under the cockpit, resting in makeshift cradles. It looked ungainly, certainly when compared to the hypersonic fighters the RAF flew on Earth, but he knew just how agile the design was in a battle. Besides, the RAF was living in a fool's paradise. The aliens would have no trouble blasting stealth hypersonic aircraft out of the air, if they captured the high orbitals. Only bloody-minded stubbornness had kept the RAF from being folded into the army or navy long ago.

Although there still is room for patrol craft on the waters, he reminded himself. He'd considered the border patrol as a career, before settling on the navy. *And there may be room for the RAF too.*

Savage glanced at his wristcom. "Does your shadow know you're taking a starfighter into combat?"

Alan winced, despite himself. Savage knew…well, he knew *something*. The only real question was why he'd kept his mouth shut. Perhaps he'd reasoned that Alan had done something remarkable to earn a bodyguard, rather than a prison warden. Or maybe he simply understood that the job needed to be done. Alan was in a better state, thanks to Colchester, than some of the reservists. His services couldn't be discarded in a hurry.

"I dare say he'll find out, sooner or later," Alan said. Bennett would go to the CIC when the shit hit the fan, of course. And Maddy would tell him what had happened. "It doesn't matter."

He changed into a flight suit, then scrambled up the ladder, gritting his teeth as he secured the oxygen feed and waste tubes. It wasn't embarrassing, certainly not after flying starfighters and then being in jail, but it was still annoying. He'd heard stories about pilots who'd been killed because they'd been distracted while fiddling with the waste tubes. And some of the stories were actually true. The starfighter powered up a moment later, allowing him to check the live feed from the carrier's sensors. There was no hint that the aliens knew they were there. Their ships were still proceeding along the projected course.

"Prepare for launch," Savage ordered, as the timer reached zero. "Here we go."

Alan braced himself as the starfighter moved forward, into the launch tube. A faint sensation ran through the craft as the catapult powered up, followed by a sudden rush of pressure that forced him back into his chair. He took control of the starfighter as the dull interior of the launch tube was replaced by glowing stars, each one burning brightly against the darkness of space. The gas jets hummed to life, slow bursts correcting his course. It was almost pathetically slow, compared to their normal speed, but it had one great advantage. The gas jets were almost completely undetectable.

And we're falling right towards the aliens, Alan thought. He felt a moment of grim satisfaction, mingled with fear. He'd always felt nervous before an engagement. *And they don't have the slightest idea we're here.*

The laser link hummed to life, a command network that relayed messages from starfighter to starfighter. Savage might lose direct contact with one of his craft, but the others would relay the message anyway. It was complex, more complex than he preferred, but there was no choice. The laser network was also completely undetectable, unless the aliens somehow stumbled across one of the laser beams. It wasn't entirely impossible, but the odds of the aliens getting that close without detecting the starfighters anyway were too low to calculate.

He sucked in his breath as the alien ships grew closer. A handful of analyst reports popped up in front of him, speculating on everything from tonnage to point defence capability. Alan wasn't too surprised to note that there was nothing remotely *certain* about anything the analysts said. They couldn't determine too much about the alien craft until the aliens showed their mettle.

New attack vectors popped up in front of him. He nodded in acknowledgement. Jameson might be young, but he - or his subordinate - was doing a good job. The vast majority of the starfighters would attack the destroyers, hopefully clearing them out of the way before the freighters could be attacked and forced to surrender. He wasn't sure if *that* was a good idea, even though he understood the vital need to capture samples of alien technology. So far, no one had managed to actually communicate with the aliens…he wasn't even sure it was *possible*. Telling the aliens they could surrender - and that they wouldn't be mistreated if they surrendered - was not going to be easy.

Here goes nothing, he thought.

The alien craft came closer. Passive sensors couldn't tell him *much* about the craft, but he'd seen some of their warships at New Russia. There was something oddly *melted* about the alien designs, although he had to admit that it could just be their sense of aesthetics. Anyone who judged humanity by a fleet carrier would assume that the human race had *no* sense of elegance. And yet…a handful of new pieces of information flashed up in front of him. The aliens were running their active sensors, sweeping space for threats. It wouldn't be long before they detected the starfighters.

But they couldn't be expecting to contact us here, surely? The thought nagged at him as he jostled the fighter into position. *If they know we can't use the weaker tramlines, they might assume that we'd see no value in this system. And they might be right.*

He felt sweat trickling down his back as they reached the point of no return, the point when detection was effectively a mathematical certainty. They were committed now, committed to pressing the offensive at all costs. There was no way to retreat…he wished, suddenly, that he'd written to his daughters sooner. Perhaps they could have exchanged v-mails…

The display flared red, just for a second. They'd been spotted.

"All squadrons, break and attack," Jameson ordered. "I say again, break and attack!"

CHAPTER
TWENTY SIX

"Damn, they're fast," Greene said. "They're turning towards us already."

"As you were," Savage snapped. "Prepare to engage the enemy!"

Alan gritted his teeth as the starfighter came to life, active sensors seeking out targets as the drive powered up. Greene was right. The alien ships *were* reacting quickly, the warships rapidly putting themselves between the incoming attack and the freighters. He would have respected their bravery if he hadn't known they'd slaughtered tens of thousands of spacers at New Russia. As it was, he wanted to blast them all to dust before they had a chance to kill him.

"Lock onto your designated target and follow me on my mark," Savage ordered. An enemy destroyer blinked yellow, indicating that it was the primary target. "Mark!"

The starfighter twisted, then slid into its slot as the squadron fell into attack formation. Alan keyed his torpedo launchers, programming them to fire automatically when the starfighters reached attack position, then followed the rest of the pilots straight towards the alien starships. Their target opened fire, plasma bolts lashing out towards the starfighters. The odds of hitting anything were low, Alan noted, but it did keep the human pilots from closing their ranks. Perversely, it might well work against the aliens.

He studied the firing pattern as the starfighters ducked and weaved, careful not to make their trajectories predicable. The aliens didn't seem to have any sort of precise targeting system, although he couldn't tell if they thought it was pointless - given how many plasma bolts they could put into space - or if the plasma guns simply weren't very accurate. It might well be the latter, he thought, but it might not matter. Two starfighters vanished from the formation as they were struck by plasma bolts, one spinning out of control an instant before exploding. It didn't look as though the pilot had managed to bail out in time.

The alien craft grew closer, taking on shape and form in the display. He couldn't help thinking it was thoroughly alien, even though it wasn't that different to something humans would build. The hull definitely looked melted, the handful of sensor blisters and weapons mounts practically worked into the metal. He wondered, as they slipped into engagement range, if the aliens would have problems repairing their ships. Human ships were designed to make it easy for the engineers to replace a destroyed sensor node, but the alien ships seemed a little more complex. It struck him as odd, more of a civilian than a military attitude. But then, given their weapons and firepower, it was unlikely to matter. Anything that pounded the alien hull would probably destroy it.

And yet it still seems oddly elegant, he thought. *If we could actually talk to them...*

He cursed under his breath as the aliens doubled and redoubled their fire, jinking the starfighter randomly as they flew closer and closer. The analysts had suggested that firing torpedoes from point-blank range would work better than firing as soon as they came into range, but the analysts weren't flying the starfighters. Normally, it took a special kind of incompetence to actually crash into an enemy starship, yet now...he felt sweat trickling down his back as they slipped closer to the alien hull. To die because he'd accidentally crashed - or steered right into a plasma bolt - would be embarrassing as hell. The only consolation was that he wouldn't survive the impact.

"Firing now," Savage snapped.

Alan felt his starfighter jerk, the automatic systems launching the torpedoes as soon as they reached the designated range. He yanked the starfighter away, spinning back into interplanetary space; the alien ships fired a handful of bursts after him, but concentrated on taking out the torpedoes. Twenty-four had been fired, only three made it through to strike the alien hull. But the warheads were more than powerful enough to punch through the metal and explode inside the hull. Moments later, the alien ship exploded into a ball of expanding plasma.

"Got the bastard," Greene carolled. "We killed the fucker..."

"Form up on me," Savage ordered. "And prepare to cover the second wave."

Alan nodded and took a quick glance at the overall status display. Two of his pilots had been killed, both old reservists. He winced, feeling a twinge of bitter guilt. They'd trained hard, but they really shouldn't have been anywhere near a starfighter cockpit. Technically, *he* shouldn't be flying too. He *was* pushing the upper limits quite sharply. But there was no choice.

And we killed all five destroyers, he thought. He smiled, coldly. Whatever else happened, they'd proven that the alien ships were not invincible. *Serve the bastards right.*

He took the starfighter into formation and watched as the second wave advanced on the alien freighters, broadcasting messages inviting the aliens to surrender. There was no way the aliens *couldn't* detect the messages, Alan was sure, but they didn't seem inclined to actually respond. Instead, they were firing at any human craft that came within range. Their freighters were clearly armed and ready to continue the fight.

And we don't have much time to force them to surrender, Alan reminded himself. There was no way to be *certain* that alien reinforcements weren't on the way. The aliens could easily have sent a message to a ship sitting on the tramline. *They might think they can hold out long enough for relief to arrive.*

Jameson's voice echoed through the command link. "Close to engagement range and finish them," he ordered. "I say again, close to engagement range and finish them."

Alan nodded, curtly. Jameson hadn't sounded pleased. Alan didn't really blame him. They *did* have orders to capture alien technology - and living aliens - and ordering the freighters destroyed was a tacit admission that the orders couldn't be carried out. It might come back to haunt Jameson too, Alan reflected. A *smart* admiral would understand that Jameson had been in an impossible position, but Alan had met senior

officers who appeared to have been lobotomised. And there were politicians who'd question the decision too.

He took the starfighter forward, falling into formation as they roared
towards the alien freighters. They didn't look *that* different to humanity's
designs, he noted; indeed, there was a crudeness about them that surprised him. But then, there was no indication that the aliens didn't have
the same logistical requirements as humans. They had to load and unload
their freighters as quickly as possible too. Elegance was very much a secondary concern.

The freighters kept firing as the starfighters slipped closer, spraying
plasma bolts like machine gun fire. Alan jerked the starfighter up and
down, jinking from side to side as the fire intensified. Playing decoy wasn't
his idea of a good time, but the aliens probably couldn't tell the difference
between the starfighters that still had torpedoes and those that didn't. One
by one, the torpedo-armed starfighters slipped into range and opened fire.
The enemy ships began to die.

Alan frowned, despite himself, as their icons vanished from the display.
He had no qualms about killing enemy warships - he intended to make sure
that a destroyer silhouette was painted on the starfighter, when he got back
to *Haddock* - but destroying freighters was different. The aliens didn't really
have a chance. And yet, each freighter destroyed would slow their offensive
against Earth...he hoped. He cursed, again, the sheer lack of useful intelligence. There was no way to know just how big an impact they'd actually *had*.

The last of the alien freighters exploded into fire. The human starfighters were suddenly alone. Alan studied the display for a long moment, but
as far as his sensors could tell the entire system was deserted. And yet...he
shook his head as Savage started issuing orders, directing the starfighters
to return to their mothership. The aliens would deduce that *something* bad
had befallen their convoy, sooner or later. It wouldn't be too hard for them
to work out what had actually happened.

Which raises an interesting question, Alan thought. *Will they start
hunting for us? Or will they just resume their drive on the inner worlds -
and Earth?*

He dismissed the thought. They'd won a victory. A tiny victory, to be
sure, but a victory nonetheless. It was worth celebrating, he thought. And

when the news reached home, all of humanity would have something to celebrate. It wouldn't take the media too long to turn their brief engagement into a triumph resembling the Battle of Islamabad.

But losing seventeen freighters wouldn't stop us, he reminded himself, firmly. *Our victory may not slow the aliens down very much at all.*

———

"Captain, the starfighters are returning to their ships," Poddy said. "We lost three…"

Abigail nodded, curtly. Three starfighters…cold logic told her it was an acceptable price, for what they'd accomplished, but she'd never been happy with that sort of logic. She certainly didn't consider her ship and crew expendable, even though she was fairly sure that the Royal Navy *did*. They wouldn't have given her the dregs of the service - criminals, delinquents, aged reservists - if they'd had any faith in *Haddock's* ability to do anything more than soak up enemy fire.

"Keep a very sharp eye on your sensors," she ordered. "And keep the laser links to the drones."

"Aye, Captain," Poddy said. She tactfully *didn't* point out that it wasn't the first time Abigail had given that order. "Local space appears to be clear."

"No one here, but us chickens," Anson put in.

Abigail ignored him as the starfighters slowly returned to her ship. It was slow, too slow…she knew they'd be in real trouble if they had to rearm their starfighters during a battle. Her engineers had come up with a handful of hacks, but they hadn't been able to shave more than a couple of minutes off the procedure. Anything better would require them to tear apart the hull and rebuild it from scratch.

The purpose-built designs will be better, I'm sure, Abigail thought. The Royal Navy had actually consulted her and the other captains, although she had no idea how seriously they'd taken her comments. *They're really nothing more than flight deck, drives and tiny living quarters.*

"Signal from the flag, Captain," Poddy said. "We're to withdraw to Point Theta. The shuttles will search for traces of alien life and technology."

"Not much chance of finding anything," Anson grunted, as he powered up the drives. "Those ships got vaporised."

Abigail nodded. The aliens didn't seem to have launched lifepods, although they *had* had time to abandon ship. Perhaps they'd been terrified of falling into human hands. Or perhaps they simply couldn't endure human environments. It was hard to imagine a creature so radically different from humans that it couldn't survive on her ship, but she knew it was possible. She'd certainly had problems on some of her postings. There had been commanders who liked the heat and others who seemed to think they could save money by lowering the temperature.

And some who were too fearful of what might happen if they tried to change things, she reflected, ruefully. The older ships were marvels of engineering - and serving on one was a learning experience - but they had their problems. God alone knew how the crews kept them running when half the technology was nearly a century old and the rest cobbled together from a dozen different sources. *They often flirted with disaster because they couldn't pay to upgrade the whole system.*

She leaned back in her chair, keeping a wary eye on the weak tramline. It was pointless - and she knew it was pointless - but she didn't want to look away. The aliens could be much closer, hidden under their sensor masks. Or...she sighed, watching grimly as the remaining starfighters altered course to land on her flight deck. She couldn't help feeling ambivalent about that, even though she had no intention of abandoning her pilots in interplanetary space. It was a reminder that *Haddock* could not *hope* to outrun the alien starfighters, if - when - they came after her.

"The last of the starfighters has landed, Captain," Poddy said.

"Very good," Abigail said. "Ensure they're ready to launch again as soon as possible."

"Aye, Captain."

Abigail nodded. Normally, she could make estimates of how long it would take the enemy to respond, but there was no way she could do that when she had no idea what was on the far side of the weak tramline. An alien fleet base? Or just another transit system? She tossed vectors around in her head, considering the possibilities. But she couldn't come up with anything beyond wild guesses. There was certainly no way she could take any of them for granted.

We need to figure out how to ride those tramlines ourselves, she thought. *And then we can go see what might be lurking on the far side.*

The possibilities were endless - and so were the dangers. There were stars near Sol no one had ever visited, simply because there were no usable tramlines that led to them. They had planets, but those planets were effectively out of reach. The only way to *get* to them involved travelling at STL speeds, which would mean at least a decade spent in transit before reaching the star. And some of those planets were habitable. Who knew *what* could be lurking there?

She frowned. It was easy to come up with a mental image of two races sharing the same general region of space, but being utterly unable to actually meet. Perhaps the aliens humanity had encountered lived right *next* to Sol...she shook her head, dismissing the thought. The giant telescopes and sensor arrays assembled near the edge of the solar system would have picked up radio transmissions, if there were any to detect. If there were intelligent races on the inaccessible worlds, they didn't have anything resembling modern technology.

They might have evolved beyond it, she thought. *Or they might never have developed it at all.*

She sighed, dismissing the thought. There was no point in speculation. No one was going to pay for an STL exploration ship, not when there were hundreds of stars and planets within easy reach. The inaccessible worlds would remain inaccessible, as far as humanity was concerned. Any threat they presented would have to cross the gulf of interstellar space...

...Unless the aliens found a way to use the weaker tramlines.

Worry about it later, she told herself, as she returned her attention to the display. *You have too many other problems right now.*

―――――

"Nice shooting, sir!"

"Thank you," Alan said, tiredly. Greene meant well, Alan was sure, but right now he wasn't in the mood for dealing with an overgrown adolescent. "Your shooting was pretty good too."

He shrugged as the pilots congregated in the ready room. Three chairs were empty, a grim reminder that three pilots were dead. Alan couldn't help feeling a stab of guilt. He hadn't realised that they'd lost a third pilot until the engagement had been over. Somehow, not noting the pilot's passing felt wrong. But there was no point in fretting about it.

"Grab something to eat, then rotate through the bunks," he ordered, raising his voice to be heard over the boasting. Everyone wanted to claim credit for destroying the alien ships, although it was difficult to be sure who'd fired the fatal shots. Post-battle analysis *might* point to the shooter, but their torpedoes might not have gotten through if the aliens hadn't been occupied shooting everyone else's torpedoes out of space. "We may have to deploy again at very short notice."

"Aye, sir."

Alan caught Savage's eye as the pilots resumed their bragging. "I have to go to the CIC," he said. "If the alerts sound, get the squadrons ready for launch."

"Of course, sir," Savage said. "Do you want to work out who actually killed the ships?"

Alan shook his head. Commodore Jameson *might* want to reward the shooter, but it was better for the pilots that they thought of it as a team exercise. Hell, it had *been* a team exercise. He understood the urge to gloat about scoring a direct hit, particularly on such a tough target, but it would only cause trouble. *Everyone* had made a valuable contribution to the mission.

And we all deserve medals when we get home, he thought, taking one last look at the empty chairs. *But will we get them?*

He felt a pang as he walked down the corridor. Three more pilots were dead, two men and a woman who should never have been in the firing line. And yet, they'd stepped up to serve when the call came. It was hard not to respect them, particularly when they probably wouldn't have had any trouble convincing a medical board that they weren't fit for active service. Better to put them behind a desk while the younger men took the field. But they'd decided to fly starfighters...

"They deserve to be honoured," he muttered. They'd hold a wake, if they ever had the chance to go to a pub. Surely, the crew wouldn't be slapped back into lockdown after their famous victory. "And they *will* be honoured."

He stepped into the CIC. Maddy was sitting in front of her console, watching the live feed from the shuttles, while Bennett was leaning against the bulkhead. Alan half-expected a reprimand - or worse - but Bennett merely nodded curtly. There was no way to know if Bennett thought he'd done well or if he was disappointed that Alan hadn't managed to get himself killed.

"The shuttles aren't finding much," Maddy reported. "There are a handful of traces of biological matter, apparently, but it's beyond reconstruction."

"Unsurprising," Alan said. A couple of the freighters had contained *something* dangerous, judging by how violently they'd exploded when they'd been hit. "We walloped those ships pretty hard. I think…"

The alarms started to howl. "Shit!"

"Yes, sir," Maddy said. A red icon appeared on the display. "Enemy fleet carrier, inbound!"

CHAPTER
TWENTY SEVEN

"Fuck," Poddy said. "Captain, an enemy fleet carrier just jumped out of the tramline."

"Don't panic," Abigail ordered sharply, as five red icons appeared on the display. It was hard not to panic herself. Her most pessimistic estimates - guesses, really - had suggested they'd have several hours before the aliens managed to mount a counterattack. But now there was an enemy fleet carrier and four smaller ships bearing down on them. "They won't be on us for at least an hour."

Unless their drives are better than we think, she told herself. She was still stunned by just how quickly the aliens had managed to react. Was it a stroke of bad luck? The alien fleet carrier might have been on its way to New Russia before the convoy was attacked. *Or do they have a way to send messages at FTL speeds?*

Her blood ran cold as she considered the possibilities. Normally, the only way to get a message from one star to the next was a relay chain. A starship would jump through the tramline and beam the message to its destination - or to another starship, waiting near the *next* tramline. There was an entire network of courier boats designed to do nothing more than hopping backwards and forwards along the tramlines, delivering messages as quickly as possible. But if the aliens really *did* have a way to send messages at FTL speeds, the war might be on the verge of being lost.

She shivered. It took far too long to send a message from New Russia to Earth, long enough that the message might be out of date by the time it reached its destination. The Admiralty couldn't hope to micromanage the war...and *trying* would impose so many delays that the war might well be lost while the navy was waiting for orders. But if the aliens *could* send messages at FTL speeds, their high command could hear about problems - and issue orders - in real time. They'd react instantly to any setbacks along the war front...

Commodore Jameson's face appeared on the display. "It appears that we've outstayed our welcome," he said. "I'm recalling the shuttles now. Once they've returned, we'll go into silent running and head straight for the tramline."

Abigail nodded, running through the possibilities in her head. If it was a coincidence, if they'd simply had a stroke of very bad luck, it might take the aliens some time to notice that their convoy had been destroyed. The shuttles weren't stealthy, but the aliens might not think they had any reason to *look* for them. But if the aliens *had* been alerted - somehow - the flotilla was in deep trouble. There would be no time to evade contact before the aliens landed on them with both feet.

She calculated the odds, quickly. If the aliens didn't know to look for them, they might just get away...

The display bleeped an alarm. "The alien ships have altered course," Poddy reported, grimly. "They're heading our way."

"Fuck," Abigail muttered. "How long until the shuttles return to the flag?"

"Two minutes," Poddy said. "They didn't find anything interesting."

She broke off as new updates flashed up on her screen. "The flag's sent flight vectors, Captain," she added. "We're leaving now."

"Very good," Abigail said. She brought the vectors up on her screen and studied them. The flotilla would fly a predictable course until the shuttles were back onboard, then alter course sharply to throw off pursuit. If, of course, the aliens didn't get close enough to follow them through the course changes. "Anson, get us moving."

"Aye, Captain."

A low shiver ran through the ship as the drives engaged. Abigail gritted her teeth, watching grimly as the equations narrowed sharply. Either they put enough distance between themselves and the enemy ships to sneak back home or they didn't, in which case they'd be overwhelmed and destroyed. The aliens presumably knew, too, that the flotilla would have to use Tramline One. They'd certainly know how the fleet intended to make it home.

And that gives them options, even if they lose track of us completely, she thought.

"The shuttles have been recovered," Anson said. "Silent running... now."

For what it's worth, Abigail thought. She would have sold her soul for a sensor mask, let alone a proper cloaking device. The aliens might *just* be able to track them. *And if they find us without using active sensors, they'll take us by surprise.*

"Altering course," Anson said. The display updated, yet again. "This course will add an extra week to our journey home."

"It can't be helped," Abigail told him, bluntly. Thankfully, the aliens didn't seem to have noticed the course change. "Better to be a week late than dead."

"Unless Earth has been destroyed while we're up here," Anson said. "They might have stomped the groundpounders flat by now."

"Concentrate on your job," Abigail ordered. "You can argue about politics later."

She sighed. There were belters who sometimes wished the homeworld would vanish. God knew there were no shortage of radical groups that believed Earth would eventually occupy the belt, unless the belters struck first. But she knew they'd miss Earth if the homeworld was destroyed... assuming, of course, the aliens didn't attack the belt afterwards. Earth - and the orbital halo of industrial nodes - was still the main source of everything from communications lasers to drive field components. Losing the orbital industries alone would probably cost humanity the war.

And there's no way to know what might be happening core-wards of here, she thought. *For all we know, we're the last of the human race.*

It wasn't likely, she knew. There were nearly a hundred colony worlds, from Britannia and Washington to New Penn and Pasadena, and literally thousands of asteroid settlements. The aliens might be bent on genocide, but the logistics of exterminating the human race would tax even *their* capabilities. No, they weren't the last of humanity. But she couldn't help worrying about what might have happened over the last month.

Poddy swore. "Captain, the alien ship just engaged her stealth systems!"

Abigail glanced at the display and swallowed a curse of her own. The alien fleet carrier had vanished. So had her five escorts. Instead, there was a rapidly-expanding red sphere showing where the fleet carrier *might* be. And even that might not be accurate. If the alien starships could move significantly faster in realspace than their human counterparts, the wretched carrier might already be outside the sphere.

And are they coming after us, she asked herself, *or are they racing straight for the tramline?*

She puzzled it out, carefully. If the aliens *did* have a solid lock on the flotilla, the fleet carrier would have no trouble breathing down their necks. Given their stealth systems, the aliens might get very close indeed before they were spotted, allowing them to launch starfighters at short range and obliterate the flotilla without trouble. But if the aliens didn't... where would they go? The tramline, perhaps. They'd know that *Haddock* had to use the tramline. But the tramline was immense.

Commodore Jameson's face appeared, again. "We'll alter course in thirty minutes," he said, slowly. "It will give us some extra room to manoeuvre, if they are chasing us."

Abigail nodded. "I suggest dropping a stealth probe," she said. "It might alert us if they're coming up our tail."

"Good thinking," Jameson said. He rubbed his forehead. "We will get through this, somehow."

"Yeah," Abigail agreed.

She turned her attention back to the interplanetary display and frowned. The red sphere was now so vast that it was effectively meaningless. Alien carriers were larger than their human counterparts, but they were still tiny on an interplanetary scale. And it could be anywhere. She wished she knew where the bastard was, even though she knew the aliens might be right behind her. Not knowing was worse than seeing the enemy ship coming right at her. Her lips twitched in cold amusement. She'd change her mind if she actually *saw* the ship closing for the kill.

"Poddy, maintain a passive sensor watch at all times," Abigail ordered. "I want to know about it the *second* that wanker shows himself."

"Understood," Poddy said. She sounded very young, all of a sudden. "They can't get too close to us without being detected, can they?"

Abigail shrugged. They just didn't know. The flotilla couldn't use active sensors without revealing its location, so it was quite possible that the aliens might get very close without being detected. But it was also possible that the carrier had headed straight for the tramline instead. Or deployed its escorts to locate the flotilla while it remained in the rear, waiting for the chance to kill. Or...there were just too many possibilities.

"I hope not," Abigail said. She wished, not for the first time, that she'd sent Poddy back to the family before *Haddock* departed. Poddy was young, too young. Her daughter would never have forgiven her, but at least she'd be alive. Abigail could have coped with Poddy's hatred if she knew the girl was alive. "I'm sure you'll see him if he gets too close."

She kept the rest of her thoughts to herself. The alien carrier could launch its starfighters in one massive wave, while the escort carriers could only dribble them into space. Five escort carriers and their starfighters would be outnumbered anyway, but she doubted the aliens would let them have time to deploy all their craft. Why *would* they?

They wouldn't, she thought. *If they were interested in a fair fight, they'd have used different weapons at New Russia.*

———

Alan sat up, cracking his head into the overhead bunk. He swore, loudly.

"You swear like a little girl," Bennett said, from somewhere over his head. "I've heard worse in locker rooms."

"So have I," Alan growled. He felt awful, as if he hadn't slept at all. His body protested as he swung his legs over the side of the bunk and stood. "We're still alive, aren't we?"

Bennett snorted. "For a given value of *alive*, I suppose," he said. "Or do you think this is hell?"

Alan swallowed several nasty remarks as he checked the display. The computers had to be on the blink. According to them, he'd had five hours of sleep, but his body insisted that he'd barely slept…if, of course, he'd slept at all. His eyes felt scratchy, as if he'd been sleeping in sand. He stumbled into the shower and turned on the water, cursing again as icy cold liquid cascaded down on his head. Thankfully, it helped clear his mind.

"My grandfather served on a submarine," Bennett said, once Alan was out of the shower and getting dressed. "I think I know how he felt now."

"I think I know too," Alan said. "But at least he wasn't too far from home."

He looked at the interplanetary display and scowled. There was an alien fleet carrier and four escorts somewhere within the system; perhaps alarmingly close to them, perhaps on the other side of the dim red star. Or…he wanted to believe that the aliens had simply turned around and left the system, but he knew better. It was what he *wanted* to believe, after all.

Five days, he thought. *Five days of sneaking towards the tramline, turning tail every time we pick up even a hint of their presence. And the hell of it is that we don't know if we're detecting them or random fluctuations in space!*

He pulled his uniform on, then headed to the hatch. Bennett made no move to follow him, something Alan suspected had more to do with a desire to rest than trust. It wasn't as if Alan had anywhere to go, anyway. Bennett would probably stay closer to him once they were back at Sol. If, of course, they made it home.

The CIC was quiet. Maddy was sitting at her console, looking half-asleep. Alan cleared his throat as he entered, making her jump. She was lucky she wasn't in the army. No one would complain - much - if a sergeant beasted a soldier who'd fallen asleep on watch. But then, nothing had happened. He skimmed the feed, just to be sure. The flotilla was steadily approaching the tramline, every passive sensor listening for trouble. If the aliens were nearby, there was no sign of their presence.

And they won't be able to tell when we leave the system, he thought. *Unless they're close enough to see our hulls.*

He made a face as he sat down, quietly dismissing Maddy to her bunk. A couple of pilots had argued that the alien carrier had already left the system, pointing out that the aliens *had* to know that searching for *Haddock* was a waste of time. Alan hadn't been so sure. The aliens probably wanted a little revenge…and following *Haddock* down the tramlines to Alkaline would give them a chance to take it, without delaying their arrival at New Russia too much…

The tramline grew closer as the flotilla inched towards it. Alan felt his heart starting to pound, knowing that the aliens would *have* to make a move now…if they wanted to overwhelm *Haddock* and the rest of the ships. If, of course, they were there at all. He kept a wary eye on his sensors, one hand ready to sound the alert and start launching starfighters. But nothing materialised as they crossed the tramline.

He gasped in pain, doubling over as an invisible fist slammed into his stomach. It was hard, very hard, to keep from throwing up. He forced himself to swallow, time and time again, as he straightened. The display had blanked, but was rapidly filling up with new data. There was no sign of any alien ships. He reminded himself, again, that that meant nothing. The aliens might have crossed the tramline ahead of them and started plotting an ambush.

"We will proceed as planned," Commodore Jameson said, once the flotilla was well away from the tramline. "Hopefully, we'll stay well away from any enemy ships."

Alan nodded, grimly. It would take three days to cross the second system, then another four days to cross the third…it would take nearly two *weeks* to reach Alkaline, let alone the American base at Coralline. If they were lucky, they'd find safety there; if they weren't…they might reach the base, only to discover that the aliens had sliced it to ribbons and moved on to destroy Earth. God knew the Americans hadn't designed the base to serve as anything more than a basic maintenance and resupply facility. In hindsight, the American-Russian agreement not to fortify the system beyond the basics looked like a dreadful mistake.

New Russia was heavily fortified too, Alan reminded himself, as he ordered half his pilots to return to their bunks. *And the aliens had no trouble blasting their way into the high orbitals.*

He took a long breath, then settled back to wait. If they were lucky, nothing would happen before they reached the base. And if they weren't lucky…they'd just have to deal with whatever happened. And they *had* hurt the aliens. If nothing else, they'd taught them that humans had teeth.

It might just slow them down, Alan thought. *And if it buys us time, it was worthwhile.*

———

Abigail was used to monotony, but she'd never had to cope with the twin sensations of being bored *and* hunted at the same time. Normally, there was no shortage of maintenance work to do - and eBooks to read, and videos to watch - but now she found herself pacing the decks as the days turned into weeks. Crawling back home felt *wrong*, somehow, even though she knew all too well what would happen if the aliens got a sniff of their location. It was something she couldn't escape, no matter what she did. Even sex provided no solace as the reality of their position crashed down on her, once again, during the afterglow. By the time they finally reached the Alkaline Tramline, she felt like a nervous wreck.

And we haven't even caught a sniff of the aliens, she thought grimly, as she sat on the bridge and watched her crew preparing for the jump. *They might not even be in the same star system!*

She dismissed the thought as the timer started to count down to zero. There was very little chance of the aliens *not* having a presence in Alkaline, even if it was just a handful of picket ships monitoring the approaches to New Russia. The odds of being detected were higher than they'd been since they left the unnamed star system. And yet…cold logic insisted that the odds were very low, but she felt otherwise…

"Jumping in three," Anson said. "Two…one…*jump!*"

I'm getting too old for this, Abigail thought. She bit her lip to keep from gasping in pain. *We need to replace those drives.*

She scowled as the sensation slowly faded away. She was no stranger to physical pain - she'd been in her fair share of fights as a younger woman - but there was something about the jump-shock that bothered her. It wasn't the pain, she thought, so much as the sense there was something fundamentally *wrong* about it. And it was growing worse as they put more and more stress on *Haddock's* drives.

Alarms howled. "Report!"

"Picking up a contact," Poddy snapped. A red icon flashed into life on the display. "One enemy ship, far too close to us!"

Abigail swore. An enemy ship…a cruiser, judging by the tonnage. Not the fleet carrier, thankfully, but something that could bring the fleet carrier down on their heads. And the ship was too close for comfort. The odds of not being seen were very low…

"She's turning towards us," Poddy said. "Captain, the flag is ordering us to launch starfighters."

"Deploy starfighters," Abigail ordered. "Point defence, stand by!"

CHAPTER
TWENTY EIGHT

"Stand by for launch," Savage said. "Go!"

Alan gritted his teeth as the starfighter was hurled out of the launch tube and into interplanetary space, the drive field coming online and taking control the moment the craft was clear of the carrier. There was no point in trying to hide, not this time. The enemy cruiser was far too close to miss them…he wouldn't have doubted that the wretched ship had seen them, even if the crew had played dumb. It was just too close to *avoid* seeing the human ships.

They must have caught a sniff of us in the last system, he thought, as the starfighters fell into their ragged formation. *And then they set an ambush…*

He forced himself to think, hard. The aliens clearly hadn't had *much* time or they would have deployed the fleet carrier…unless she was nearby, hidden under a sensor mask. But Commodore Jameson had already deployed a web of sensor drones to search for the enemy ship. She couldn't be *that* close to the flotilla or she would have been spotted by now.

"I want one pass," Savage said. "Hit the bastard with everything you've got."

Alan nodded as the alien cruiser came closer. Oddly, it wasn't spitting plasma fire in their general direction. He would have wondered if it was a human ship if he hadn't seen the telltale signature of an enemy drive field. And, as their sensors picked out more detail, it became clearer that the 'cruiser' was a scaled-up destroyer. The melted hull design was unmistakable.

"Their targeting sensors are coming online," Savage said. "Break and attack...*now!*"

The enemy ship opened fire a second later, directing a hail of plasma fire towards the incoming starfighters. Alan wondered, as he fought to keep his starfighter on a steady course while evading the enemy fire, if the cruiser was *designed* to stand off starfighter attacks. She didn't look to have any heavy weapons, nothing designed for ship-to-ship combat...perhaps the aliens thought the plasma guns would be enough to handle a capital ship too. It offended Alan's sensibilities, but he had to admit that the aliens might well be right.

"Torpedoes away," he snapped, as the automated systems launched the projectiles. "Taking evasive action..."

He cursed as he watched both torpedoes evaporate under enemy fire, an instant before Greene's torpedoes slammed into the enemy hull. An explosion staggered the ship, but the cruiser somehow held itself together until four more torpedoes lanced into the damaged area and exploded with staggering force. Alan allowed himself a sigh of relief as the enemy ship disintegrated, then slowly turned his craft back towards the carrier. If they were lucky - really lucky - they might just be able to make it halfway to the tramline before the aliens showed themselves.

A red icon materialised in the display. "Shit," Greene swore. "Where the hell did *he* come from?"

Alan frowned. "A starfighter," he said. It was a different design to the ones they'd faced at New Russia, but it couldn't be anything else. "The carrier must be nearby."

He ran through the vectors in his mind. The starfighter was too far from the flotilla to be easily intercepted, but too close to be evaded. And *that* meant the carrier couldn't be too far away either. The aliens had definitely picked up a sniff of them in the last system, then. It wouldn't be long before the flotilla was under heavy attack.

"The flotilla is altering course," Savage said. "We're to serve as CSP until we're relieved."

If we last that long, Alan thought.

He shook his head. Commodore Jameson had switched the flotilla to a least-time course, heading straight towards the tramline. It made sense, as long as they couldn't get rid of their damned shadow, but he couldn't help thinking that it was predictable. The aliens might plant themselves between the flotilla and the tramline and force them to punch through if they wanted to escape.

"We may die, but we'll claw the bastards good and proper," Greene said. He sounded disgustingly cheerful. "And they won't have a hope of getting away from us."

Alan opened his mouth to make a sarcastic remark, then closed it again without saying a word. Greene knew the odds. They all knew the odds. And if pretending to be cheerful was how Greene coped...well, Alan wouldn't begrudge it.

"We're not trapped in this useless system with them," Flight Lieutenant Patsy Govan put in, dryly. "They're trapped in this useless system with us."

"It was more impressive when that actor said it," Savage commented. Red icons flashed to life on the display. "Here they come..."

Another red icon materialised. Alan sucked in his breath, silently thanking God for small mercies. The alien carrier had been caught out of position, forcing the aliens to chase the human ships rather than block their way out of the system. It was a far from perfect situation - the aliens could wear them down, piece by piece - but at least the human ships didn't have to run a deadly gauntlet.

But they could summon reinforcements from New Russia, he thought, grimly. Abigail had raised the possibility of the aliens having an FTL communicator, but there was a more mundane solution. The aliens could have simply sent one of their ships along the weak tramline to New Russia, cutting two weeks off their transit time. *For all we know, the carrier we're facing now isn't the carrier we saw earlier.*

"Don't let them reach the ships," Savage snapped. "Those carriers are our only way home."

Alan nodded to himself, then gunned the drives. The alien fighters were already firing, snapping off plasma bursts in all directions. He allowed himself a flicker of relief at the proof his assessment of their targeting wasn't too far off, although part of him noted that it didn't really matter. And then he fired his guns at an alien fighter and watched it explode...

Kill now, think later, he told himself. The alien craft were *fast* little buggers. Some of them had broken through the CSP, despite some brave and skilled flying. *If you don't kill them now, Alan, there won't be a later.*

———

"They're entering engagement range now," Poddy said.

"Get the rest of those fighters out," Abigail snapped. Calling some of them back had been a mistake, clearly. "And open fire with point defence!"

She gritted her teeth as the alien craft swooped down on *Haddock*. Their targeting still wasn't very good, but it didn't matter. Two alien fighters died, an instant before the first plasma bolt burned into her hull. Alarms sounded, muting rapidly as the situation was assessed. It was hard to be sure, but the makeshift armour had definitely done *some* good. There was damage, yet…not as much as she'd feared. A third alien fighter was picked off as the pilot swung around, clearly looking for somewhere a little more vulnerable. He might have gotten lucky if he'd targeted the flight deck.

Her console bleeped. "The armour held, Captain," Drakopoulos said. "But repeated hits will wear it down."

"Understood," Abigail said, sharply. "I'll tell them not to shoot at us, all right?"

"That would be good," Drakopoulos agreed. His voice was so dry she couldn't tell if he was joking or not. Probably…he knew, as well as anyone else, that the aliens didn't seem to accept surrenders. "I suggest…"

The ship rocked, violently.

"Direct hit, lower hull," Poddy snapped. "They tore away a chunk of the armour."

"I'll get teams on it," Drakopoulos said. "It might give us some time."

Abigail doubted it. The engineers were good - and they'd practiced patching cracks in the hull - but there was no way they could repair the armour. And the aliens probably knew it. If they fired into the hull breach, they'd tear *Haddock* apart even if their plasma bolts didn't find something explosive. And yet…it might just give them a few more minutes of life…

"Captain," Poddy said. "*Rackham!*"

Abigail swung around as a new icon flared up in the display. HMMS *Rackham* was under heavy attack, a dozen alien starfighters pouring plasma fire into her hull despite the best efforts of the CSP. A second later, the escort carrier exploded into a ball of expanding plasma. The alien starfighters seemed to pause, just for a second, before heading back to their carrier. It looked as though they were withdrawing.

She frowned in disbelief. The *human* starfighters needed to return and rearm, but the aliens? They didn't *need* to rearm. But they were operating at quite some distance from their carrier…perhaps their life support pods were running out. Or…

"Get the starfighters rearmed," she ordered, curtly. She had no idea how long it would take the aliens to swap out their life support pods, but she'd bet good money that a purpose-built fleet carrier could do it faster than *Haddock*. "They'll be back."

————

Alan felt tired, desperately tired.

The alien starfighters had returned to their carrier - for whatever reason - and then resumed the offensive, sweeping in from the rear and blasting through the CSP as the human pilots struggled to counter them. They seemed to be showing a new sensitivity to losses - perhaps because the human point defence was getting better - but that didn't appear to be slowing them down very much. Another escort carrier had been destroyed and a third had taken heavy damage. Alan doubted the ship could remain in formation for much longer.

"They're playing with us," Greene snapped. "We should go after them!"

"Bad idea," Alan said. He allowed his voice to harden. "We cover the flotilla."

He scowled. He understood Greene's frustration all too well. The alien fleet carrier was keeping her distance, but Alan had no doubt that her CSP would be enough to deflect any attack by his remaining starfighters. It was possible that they'd *planned* to lure his starfighters into a trap, if the fleet carrier mounted as much point defence as her size suggested. Or maybe they were just concerned about taking too many losses.

Or maybe they're just trying to wear us down, he thought. At least one of the pilots had been killed because he hadn't been able to react fast enough. Herring Squadron had lost five pilots in quick succession when the aliens caught them on the hop. *If this goes on, my people aren't going to be in any state for anything.*

He checked the display as the remaining alien craft fell back, heading straight towards their carrier. They didn't seem to be *worried* about pursuit, damn them. They'd have plenty of time to rearm while the remainder of their squadrons pushed the offensive against the human flotilla. The bastards could probably have a nap too, damn them. His pilots wouldn't have a chance to rest...

...And his thoughts were wandering. He concentrated, working out the trajectories. The flotilla was pushing its drives as hard as it could, but they wouldn't be able to reach the tramline to Coralline in less than seven hours. Sooner or later, he would *have* to pull his people out of their cockpits for a rest, unless he authorised the use of stimulant drugs. But if he did, there was a good chance that there would be nasty side effects.

And I'll probably be hauled in front of a court-martial board, he thought. Using stimulants was *dangerous*. And yet, he couldn't see any other choice. *They can hang me if I get the ship home, but at least I'll have gotten the ship home.*

He took a moment to assess the remaining squadrons. The original formations had been smashed beyond repair, thanks to the aliens. He - and the other remaining commanders - had been forced to reorganise on the fly, tearing apart some of the squadrons to keep the others at full strength. It said a great deal about the situation that the complaints had been muted, even though starfighter pilots were proud of their squadrons. Everyone knew they were on the brink of obliteration.

"Herring Squadron is to rearm," he ordered. His mind wondered, absurdly, if Herring Squadron was still Herring Squadron, if two-thirds of the pilots had come from other formations. "And the pilots are to take stimulants before launching again."

There was an immediate howl of protest from a handful of the pilots. They knew the dangers, particularly when there was no time to tailor the stimulant injection to each individual flyer. But they also knew the dangers. They were reaching the limits of their endurance. It wouldn't be long before the aliens resumed the offensive. And then...

Alan sighed. He felt bone-weary, so tired that he just wanted to close his eyes and sleep. His eyelids felt heavy. But he had to remain awake. Hopefully, there would be time to rotate the other starfighters through the carriers one final time. He didn't want to take the stimulants himself, but...but he knew he had no choice. None of them did.

Thankfully, they had just enough time for him to rotate his squadron through before the attack started again.

"Captain Chester is warning that he might have to break formation," Poddy said. "His drive nodes are overheating."

"Tell him to stay with us as long as possible," Abigail said. Overheating nodes were dangerous, but alien plasma fire was worse. Besides, *Sirius* could still launch and recover fighters. The flotilla could not afford to lose another escort carrier. "And see what we can do to cover her."

She sucked in her breath. Commodore Jameson had given orders that cripples had to be abandoned - a sign that the situation was truly desperate - but surely he knew they couldn't afford to lose *Sirius*. And yet, the entire flotilla would be at risk if they slowed long enough for Captain Chester to make repairs. She closed her eyes for a long moment, remembering the days they'd spent together as friends and lovers. Captain Chester didn't deserve to die.

None of us deserve any of this, she thought, as the alien starfighters swooped down once again. This time, they seemed more inclined to target the warships than the battered escort carriers. She had no idea what the aliens thought they were doing - unless they had concluded that the escort carriers couldn't possibly escape in time - but she was grateful for the small respite. *All we can do is keep fighting and hope for the best.*

There were warnings, strict warnings, about abusing military-grade stimulants. Alan had heard all the cautionary tales during basic training and
he'd taken them to heart, even though he'd suspected that some of the stories were exaggerated. The horror stories he'd been told had never seemed
quite plausible. Now...his heart was thumping in his chest, his veins felt as
if they were on fire and his senses felt almost preternaturally sharp.

Be careful, he told himself. His starfighter suddenly felt achingly slow
as he blew away two alien craft in quick succession, his reflexes boosted
beyond human norms. *What you're feeling isn't real.*

It was hard, very hard, to believe it. The alien craft were moving in
slow motion, barely able to avoid him as his guns fired snap-shots into
their cockpits. Alan felt as through his starfighter was part of him, at once
alarmingly fast and terrifyingly slow. He knew it was an illusion caused by
the drug, but he didn't quite believe it. It was impossible to keep a clear
head when the stimulant was pounding through his system...

...And then the aliens started to fall back.

Alan almost threw caution to the winds and charged after them. The
humans were outnumbered, but not outgunned...right? It took everything he had to keep his body - his starfighter - from giving chase. He had
to repeat his orders several times before the other pilots fell back to cover
the flotilla. And the alien carrier was retreating...?

It was a trick, Alan told himself. But what was the point? The drug
made it hard to think clearly, but he knew the aliens had *had* them. One
or two more passes and the entire flotilla would have been wiped out. His
pilots were in no state for a long engagement, even with the drug. And
an engagement that lasted too long would see his pilots suffering from
withdrawal effects. They'd be doomed.

We were doomed, he thought.

"They're running?" Savage asked. His voice sounded thick, as if he
was talking and eating at the same time. "Where are they going?"

"Fucked if I know," Alan said. It wasn't something he would have said
normally, not over an open link, but the drug made it hard to give a fuck.
His mind was spinning out of control. "I...they *had* us."

"All pilots, return to your ships," Commodore Jameson ordered. "We'll
slip back into silent running."

And hope they don't have a stealthed ship following us, Alan added, silently. *We're not in any state for a fight.*

———

"Ah...the pilots are in no state for anything," Poddy reported. "Maddy says the stimulants will take time to work their way out of their system."

"Understood," Abigail said. She had enough experience with stimulants to be wary of them. Military-grade drugs were supposed to be good, better than anything you could get on the civilian market, but they came with a high price. Her lips quirked. "Tell them to get well soon."

"Aye, Captain," Poddy said.

Anson looked up. "Why did they run?"

"I don't know," Abigail said. She studied the display for a long moment. There was nothing. No wave of human starships crashing through the tramline, no invasion force on its way to New Russia...it made no sense. "Perhaps we'll never know."

"That's not very satisfactory," Anson muttered.

"Yeah," Abigail agreed. "But sometimes the real world isn't very satisfactory either."

CHAPTER
TWENTY NINE

"You got very lucky," Admiral Thomas Grant said. The American looked pleased, yet worried. "Do you know what happened while you were gone?"

Alan shook his head. He wasn't in the mood for games. His head felt as though Bennett had used it as a punching ball, repeatedly. He hadn't felt so bad since his first experiments with alcohol, back when he'd been fourteen. In hindsight, the hangover had been worse than the punishment the headmaster had handed out. Now...part of him just wanted the American to shut up. Grant was far too fond of the sound of his own voice.

Commodore Jameson was politer, somehow. "We just broke through to Coralline," he said, in a very diplomatic tone. "We've been out of touch for nearly six weeks."

"A carrier - *your* carrier - stopped an alien offensive dead," Grant said. "*Ark Royal* met the enemy in battle and crushed them."

"Crushed them?" Alan stared in disbelief. "We won?"

"You won," Grant said. "The aliens lost at least four fleet carriers in the engagement. They haven't probed our defences since."

Alan looked at Jameson, who seemed equally surprised. They'd known that *something* was going to happen that might distract the aliens, but *Ark Royal?* Alan had always assumed it would take longer to get the old carrier back into service. God knew the ship was over seventy years old. But it explained, at least, why the aliens had been so reluctant to risk losses. They'd been taught a sharp lesson.

"I'm very glad to hear that," Jameson said. "And I hope you're glad to hear of our success."

"I'm less pleased to have confirmation they can use the weaker tramlines," Grant said. The American furrowed his brow. "They can bypass our defences here any time they like."

"The threat is far from over," Jameson agreed. "But at least we have proof we can *hurt* the bastards."

"God be praised," Grant said.

Alan nodded. Coralline had been reinforced heavily over the past two months, but it didn't take a genius to know the defences weren't strong enough to stand off the aliens. New Russia had been more heavily defended, for crying out loud! The combined fleet in the system knew what it faced, now, but knowing wasn't even *half* the battle. If the aliens wanted Coralline, they could take it. The only upside, as far as he could see, was that Coralline might distract them from Earth.

Except they don't need to go through this system to reach Earth, he reminded himself. *And even if they do, they can avoid the defenders with ease.*

Grant leaned forward. "My analysts are very glad for the data you brought," he said. "And we've already started updating our training modules. However, where do you intend to go now?"

"I believe we have to return to Earth," Jameson said, after a moment. "I can transfer a number of pilots, if you need them."

"I think you might need them more," Grant said. "Your ships took one hell of a beating."

"It would have been worse if they'd bored in for the kill," Alan said. He wasn't keen on the idea of giving up his remaining pilots, but he could see the logic. Grant's forces were far too close to New Russia for anyone's peace of mind. "They really were concerned about taking losses."

"Mass drivers gave them one hell of a shock," Grant said. He jerked a finger towards the bulkhead. "I've got teams putting together some mass drivers of our own, for the base...building them from scratch is going to be a slow process, it seems. We stockpiled the components back home, apparently, but they've all been reserved for Earth."

Which is technically a breach of the treaty, Alan thought. *But Britain probably did the same thing.*

"Understandable," Jameson said. "Earth is the point-failure source for the entire human race."

"Not so comfortable for us," Grant said. "I'll forward you a copy of the latest set of updates, Commodore. As far as we can tell, local space between Coralline and Earth is clear...but that proves nothing, as you know. Watch yourselves. We can't be the only ones who thought of raiding freighters to slow the bastards down."

Alan looked up. "Are there other raiding parties heading into alien space?"

"I believe so," Grant said. "But the reports were short on detail."

"All the Great Powers were converting freighters into escort carriers," Jameson said. "I dare say they'll be sending raiding parties in all directions."

"Anything to keep the bastards off-balance," Grant agreed. "And, again, congratulations."

Jameson took the hint and rose. "Thank you for your time, Admiral," he said. "And thank you, very much, for your assistance."

"I wish I could do more," Grant said. "But I have to keep stockpiles in reserve for the warships."

Alan nodded, curtly, as they walked through the hatch. The Americans had been generous, but they hadn't had much to give. Grant was right to reserve supplies for his ships, although Alan was sceptical of their combat value. A ship like *Ark Royal* would be - had been - far more effective against the aliens. The modern fleet carriers were little more than target practice. It had been easy to see the engineers bolting armour to hulls as *Haddock* and her remaining consorts approached the orbital base. Alan was surprised the aliens hadn't pushed the offensive against Coralline as soon as they'd finished wiping out the MNF at New Russia.

There aren't many other military bases between Earth and New Russia, he thought. *But this one may actually be a drain on our strength.*

The American base felt strange, compared to a British installation. It had the same prefabricated gray bulkheads, but it had a sense of being bigger - far bigger - that its British counterparts. The Americans had always liked large structures - American carriers were the largest in space - yet it struck Alan as a little extreme. Perhaps the Americans had hoped to expand the base all along, if the tensions between the Great Powers eventually led to war. Or maybe they'd just wanted somewhere with plenty of living space. The skeleton crew would have had plenty of room, before the war. Now...

There was an odd sensation in the air, relief mingled with desperation. Alan understood, even though it was something he would have struggled to put into words. The crew *knew* how vulnerable they were, after New Russia. They'd *known* their base wouldn't have lasted long, if the aliens had come knocking. The aliens would have obliterated the mobile force, then turned their attention to the fixed installations. And yet...now...they knew that the aliens *had* received a bloody nose. They were not gods. They could be beaten.

But the base itself was still vulnerable. Alan had no illusions, as much as he might wish to cling to them. *Ark Royal* was nowhere near Coralline - he thought - and her closest American counterpart had been chopped up for scrap twenty years ago. The aliens would reassess the situation, he assumed, and then resume the attack. *Ark Royal* was effectively unique. It would take time to retool the shipyards to produce a whole new generation of armoured carriers. The aliens could still win the war.

At least we kept an armoured carrier in service, Alan thought. *If the Americans had kept theirs...*

Jameson cleared his throat, loudly. Alan jumped, cursing himself. His superior had been saying something...and he hadn't been paying attention.

"I'm sorry, sir," he said. There was no point in claiming that he *had* been listening. "I was miles away."

"Light-years, no doubt," Jameson said. He sounded amused, rather than irked. "I trust the starfighter squadrons are ready for deployment?"

"Yes, sir," Alan said. He'd found himself *de facto* CAG for the remaining ships, somewhat to his surprise. But then, the original squadrons had taken one hell of a pounding. He didn't think there was much point in

trying to reconstitute them, at least until they received some new starfighters and pilots. "We will be rough around the edges, but we're ready to fly."

"Hopefully, we won't encounter anything dangerous before returning
home." Jameson mused. "But if we do, I want to be ready."

"Yes, sir," Alan said. He couldn't disagree with the sentiment. "And
what will we do when we get home?"

Jameson smiled. "Be honoured as heroes, I imagine," he said. "And
then we'll be sent straight back out again."

Alan sighed as they reached the shuttlebay. It was easy to forget, at
times, that his career was a sham. There would be no future for him once
the war was over...not in the navy, in any case. He'd be pardoned, but
then...he shrugged. There was no guarantee of bare survival, let alone
victory. He'd worry about post-war life when the war was over.

"We'll depart in five hours," Jameson said. "That should give the pilots
enough time to rest, I think."

"And the crews too, sir," Alan said. He understood the younger man's
thinking, though. The starship crews worked in shifts, but the starfighter
pilots didn't have that option. "I think we'll be ready to go, once repairs
have been completed."

"Very good," Jameson said. "And tell everyone about *Ark Royal*. I
think we need some good news."

"Yes, sir."

"The damage isn't as bad as I thought," Drakopoulos said. "But the armour
was weakened quite badly in a dozen spots and several plasma bolts
wreaked havoc underneath it."

"Ouch," Abigail said. They floated together outside the ship, examin-
ing the scorched and blackened hull. "Can we make repairs?"

"Not without some replacement parts, which the fleet base doesn't
appear to have," Drakopoulos said. He sounded as if he didn't believe
it. It wasn't uncommon for naval bases to deny supplies to independent
freighters, although the war should have put all such considerations aside.

"The real problem is that we overworked some of the drive nodes. I've replaced two of them, but we don't have any more spares."

Abigail frowned, considering. "Doesn't the fleet base have anything suitable?"

"Not for us," Drakopoulos said. "They did offer a couple of modern nodes, but they'd need to be reconfigured before we could use them. Better to crawl home, I think."

"Point," Abigail said. "As long as we can *make* it home."

"As long as we don't overstress the drive nodes, we should be fine," Drakopoulos assured her. "And if we are attacked…well, we'll have other things to worry about."

Abigail nodded as she studied the mess the aliens had made of her hull. The damage was largely cosmetic, but…she knew they'd been lucky. If the aliens had ignored their losses and pressed the offensive, they would have finished off the flotilla before the human ships had managed their escape. And then…she told herself, firmly, not to look a gift horse in the mouth. The aliens had come far too close to smashing the entire flotilla.

She sighed, inwardly. She loved EVA, but now…she turned the suit, taking a moment to survey the endless sea of stars. It was easy to believe why so many people worshipped them, but…they were also terrifying. They had glowed in the darkness for millions of years before she'd been born and would still be glowing, millions of years after she was gone. And who knew how many other threats were lurking amidst the stars?

"I've replaced a number of the smashed point defence guns," Drakopoulos added. "They don't seem to have *intended* to target them, which is why so many of the weapons survived, but I expect that'll change in the next encounter. They might have more respect for our armour by then. Thankfully, the datanet modifications kept it up and running while all hell broke loose. This time, there were no coordination gaps."

"Just a shame we didn't have any more ships to coordinate *with*," Abigail muttered. The flotilla had been badly hurt. She was sure the news broadcasts would say otherwise - and, from a tonnage point of view, they might be right - but she couldn't avoid thinking that their next mission would be their last. They'd been lucky to survive. "I don't suppose you can whip up a superweapon in your spare time?"

"I *might* be able to devise a planet-cracker," Drakopoulos said. "Do you think that would help?"

"I think I'd prefer a super-laser," Abigail said. "Or a FTL communications device."

"I'll get right on it," Drakopoulos promised. "Right after I devise the teleporter, the stress-free jumper and the latest bread-slicer."

Abigail laughed, even though she knew it wasn't really funny. She was pretty sure that research programs across the belt - and on Earth - had been kicked into high gear, with money being thrown at everything that looked even *remotely* as though it would produce a serviceable weapons system, but she had no way to know what would turn into usable hardware. Most of the *really* interesting programs were highly classified, although some of the datapackets she'd scanned had talked about a handful of far-out possibilities that would reshape the universe if they ever became reality. She couldn't help thinking that their unclassified nature wasn't a good sign.

It might scare the aliens, if they start picking up transmissions about wormhole generators and tramline-free FTL travel, she thought. *But do they even bother to pay attention to our broadcasts?*

She shrugged as she rotated in space, then jetted towards the nearest hatch. The aliens probably *did* pay attention to human transmissions, although there was no guarantee that they'd understand a word. There was certainly no sign that they were inclined to actually *talk* to humanity. And yet, even if they understood human languages perfectly, would they actually be able to comprehend what they were hearing? Abigail had enough problems understanding groundpounders - and groundpounders were human too - that she doubted the aliens could make heads or tails of human slang. A word could mean something specific in one place and something completely different somewhere else.

The hatch opened smoothly, allowing her to float into her ship. She felt a mild sense of disorientation as the gravity field reasserted itself, pulling her feet down to the deck. The hatch closed behind her, the telltales slowly flickering from red to green as a standard atmospheric mix was pumped into the chamber. She removed her helmet as the inner hatch swung open, removing the rest of her spacesuit as she walked into the antechamber. Her fingers automatically tested the suit - twice - as she hung it up for later use. She'd had the importance of testing everything drilled into her from the very first day she'd shipped on a merchant ship.

And uncle was always good at leaving little faults for me to find, she recalled. *And missing one could have landed me in real trouble.*

She shivered as she remembered believing, just for a second, that she'd donned a punctured suit. None of the faults had been lethal, but they'd always been alarming. Her uncle had believed - firmly - that it was better for her younger self to have a little scare before she tried something without a safety net. She supposed he'd been right, although she hadn't liked it at the time. It wasn't something she'd really understood until she'd had children of her own and discovered, the hard way, just how inquisitive toddlers could be. The time she'd caught Anson experimenting with the airlock had almost given her a heart attack. After that, she'd made sure to educate her children as quickly as possible. They lived in a very dangerous environment.

Her wristcom chirped as she made her way to the bridge. "Captain, Commodore Jameson wants to ship out in four hours," Alan said. He sounded tired, but happy. "And I have a very special briefing for you."

"We should be able to depart on time, but we'll be slower," Abigail said. She made a mental note to see what else they could requisition from the Americans. The Americans might just have some *real* food for the starship's crew. "What about your pilots?"

"They should be recovered by then," Alan said. His voice didn't suggest that he was particularly confident. "None of us feel great, of course, but we survived."

You just wish you hadn't, Abigail finished, silently. She'd only used stimulants twice and, both times, she'd felt as though she had come very close to dying afterwards. And those had been *civilian* stimulants. The military drugs were supposed to be worse. *We didn't have a choice.*

She cleared her throat. "Will they be up to flying?"

"I hope so," Alan said. "But right now, they're either having a rough sleep or communing with the god of the porcelain throne."

"I know the feeling," Abigail said. She'd felt terrible after using stimulants. "Make sure you get some rest yourself. I'll speak with you before departure."

"Understood," Alan said.

He closed the connection. Abigail looked down at her wristcom for a long moment, thinking hard. Ideally, she would have preferred to remain at Coralline long enough for her crew to recover and to carry out some more repairs. But there was a very good chance the aliens would mount an attack within the next few days. They *had* to be hopping mad after losing so many freighters, even if they were reluctant to press the offensive against the flotilla. She didn't know what it meant, but she hoped it was good news. God knew humanity *needed* some good news.

And we did score a victory, she told herself. Losing so many freighters would hamper the aliens as they prepared for the next offensive. There was no way to know *just* how badly they'd hurt the aliens, but they *had* hurt them. *Jameson probably wants to get home to tell everyone about our great victory.*

She smiled, wryly. *And who could possibly blame him?*

CHAPTER
THIRTY

"Well," Anson said. "Nothing *seems* to have changed."

Abigail frowned as they slowly made their way towards Tallyman. Sol seemed more industrialised than ever - she could see a number of new production nodes in the belt - but several more asteroid settlements had apparently vanished from the display. She hoped that meant they'd gone dark, rather than being attacked or otherwise abandoned. There didn't *seem* to be any missing military installations. That was a good sign, she supposed.

"I'm picking up a detailed newspacket," Poddy said. "*Ark Royal* did smash the bastards!"

"We knew that," Anson said.

"It's good to have confirmation," Abigail reminded him, dryly. Three weeks in transit had given them plenty of time to speculate on just how badly the story had been exaggerated by the media. Humanity *needed* a victory, needed one desperately. It wasn't hard to believe that *Ark Royal's* great victory might be nothing more than a damp squib. "Poddy, transfer the datapacket to my console."

"Yes, Mum," Poddy said. Her console bleeped. "And we have new orders. We're to orbit Tallyman and…"

She paused. "Apparently, we're getting *leave!*"

Anson punched his fist in the air. "Sin City, here I come!"

"I'll come too," Poddy said. "I…"

"You're too young to go to Sin City," Abigail said, firmly. Ideally, she would have barred Anson from going too, but he was too old for her to dictate his every move. "You can go to Ceres or Orion's Belt or…"

"Aw, Mum," Poddy protested. "I'm *nearly* sixteen!"

"And you have to be at least *eighteen* to get into Sin City," Abigail reminded her. "Don't worry. You can make supercilious remarks when Anson comes back, so drunk he doesn't remember his own name."

She frowned as she pulled the message up on her screen. "We only have four days *guaranteed* leave," she added. "Anson might want to go to Ceres too."

Anson looked mutinous. Abigail shrugged at him. He was old enough to decide if he wanted to spend a day in transit, two days having fun and then *another* day in transit just to get back to his ship. It wouldn't be held against him if *Haddock* had to leave in a hurry and he couldn't get back in time, although he would be in deep shit if he failed to get back before their planned departure date. But then, they didn't have one yet. Four days of leave was a good sign the navy didn't have any plans for her ship, she considered. It might also be a sign that the navy understood that *Haddock* was in no fit state for combat.

Which is surprisingly understanding of them, she thought. *The next mission is going to be really bad.*

Abigail keyed her console. "All hands, attention," she said. "We have been guaranteed four days of leave, starting from the moment we reach Tallyman. Let me know what you plan to do so I can arrange watch schedules. If you want to stay on the ship…"

She paused. Normally, people who stood watches while the ship was docked were paid time and a half, but she doubted the *navy* would authorise the expense. It wasn't as if they were going to war. If nothing else, the bureaucrats would probably hesitate to pay…she sighed in irritation. Life would be a great deal easier with a regular navy crew. But she knew she probably wouldn't have been able to endure a naval career.

"If you want to stay on the ship, I'll try to organise the standard bonus," she added. "But I can't promise anything. I suggest you make your plans on the assumption that there will be no extra pay."

"Ouch," Anson muttered.

Abigail closed the channel, then gave him a sharp look. "Just remember that you don't have unlimited funds," she said, warningly. "And *don't* get into debt on Luna. They're right bastards about collecting money they're owed."

Anson looked unconcerned. "I'll be fine."

"Make sure you are," Abigail said. "And if you're late back to the ship, I'll have you scrubbing the decks for hours."

"Perhaps you should take Maddy somewhere nice," Poddy suggested. "I'm sure she'd like to see Ceres."

"She might like to see Sin City too," Anson said. "I haven't asked her."

"Then perhaps you should," Abigail said. She glanced at the display. "You have around three hours to make up your mind."

———

"I've been called to the station," Bennett said. He looked around their cabin, then back at Alan. "I trust you'll be staying here?"

It wasn't really a question, Alan knew. He hadn't really expected shore leave, particularly not to a place where he *could* desert. The belters weren't very accommodating to demands that they find and return naval personnel who preferred to make a life in the belt than return to Earth. There *was* a war on, but he found it hard to believe that the belt had changed that much. They were *very* independent minded.

"I have plenty of reports to write," he said. He'd written a full report - and included some analysis - during the long crawl home, but he knew from grim experience that the Admiralty would come back with a whole list of questions. Most of them would be impossible to answer, yet...yet he'd be expected to try. "What about yourself?"

"I will probably have no time for shore leave," Bennett said. He didn't seem particularly disappointed. "But we will see."

Freak, Alan thought, unpleasantly. *I bet you liked school too.*

He shook his head, crossly. Shore leave - even very basic shore leave - was vitally important, if only because it kept the crew from going insane. Several months trapped on the same ship, with the same faces...even the best crew in the navy would have problems, after a month or two had gone by. He found it hard to believe it was any different in the army. No matter how much you liked your fellows, it was only human to want a break from time to time. And he was stuck on the escort carrier…

You could be back in jail, he reminded himself, sharply. His cell had no prospect of a sudden and violent death, but the disadvantages outweighed the advantages. *You didn't get regular sex in your cell, did you?*

Bennett gave him a sharp look - as if he knew precisely what Alan was thinking - and then turned and walked through the hatch. Alan watched him go, thinking uncomplimentary thoughts. Bennett seemed more inclined to relax while they were underway, assuming - probably correctly - that there was nowhere for Alan to run. But it was still galling to have an escort everywhere he went.

He picked up his datapad and checked the inbox. The news services he'd subscribed to after his release from jail had forwarded all their updates to him, stretching back over six long weeks. He skimmed the headlines automatically, looking for interesting articles. *Ark Royal's* victory had been decisive, apparently. Reading between the lines, it was easy to see how the good news had been spun to obscure the bad. The aliens had occupied two more systems - he had to bring up a starchart to check where they were - and opened up two other possible ways they could advance towards Earth.

The really good news is that they don't have an FTL communicator, he thought. Seen in hindsight, the aliens might have made a mistake. Their feints were wasted effort, now the main offensive had been turned back. Perhaps their local CO had scented weakness and taken advantage of it. *I wonder if that means the enemy has already pulled back from those systems.*

A new set of updates blinked up in his datapad. The Admiralty was stealing half of his pilots and reassigning them to fleet carriers. Alan gritted his teeth in irritation. It had taken three weeks to batter the makeshift squadrons into some semblance of order and now they wanted him to do it all over again? But he couldn't really blame the higher-ups. His pilots had seen the aliens and survived. They *knew,* deep inside, the lessons simulators couldn't teach. It would be better to ensure that their knowledge

- and experience - was spread as widely as possible. But it didn't stop it being annoying.

He forwarded the updates to the squadron leaders - they'd have to decide who to reassign - and then clicked through the next set of messages. Some bureaucrat probably needed to be shot, he thought. Quite why they thought *he* needed to read a thousand minor updates for everything from fleet carriers to tiny shuttles was beyond him. Someone was covering his ass, making sure he couldn't be accused of *not* sharing data. But there was so *much* data that there was no way he could read it all.

At least they're improving the purpose-built escort carrier designs, based on our experiences, he thought, as he scanned one message. *That ship might actually be dangerous, given half a chance. She could certainly get her fighters into space quicker if she came under attack.*

His datapad bleeped. New messages - three *personal* messages - had just been downloaded from Tallyman. Alan swallowed, hard. No one would send him a *personal* message, apart from his daughters. And the in-laws, he supposed, although he rather suspected *they* would prefer to have nothing to do with him. The delay nagged at his mind. Someone on Tallyman had probably reviewed the messages ahead of time, just in case it was a 'Dear John' situation. He supposed the simple fact that the messages had been forwarded to him - after they'd been read - was a good sign. No one had turned up to provide 'counselling.'

Not that they'd bother to counsel me anyway, he thought darkly. *I'm a murderer, not an innocent young crewman on his first cruise.*

He reached out a finger, then stopped. His heart was pounding frantically. Did he really want to know? He wasn't sure he *wanted* to open the messages. He hadn't felt so nervous since he'd opened his exam results, decades ago. And *then* he'd been sure he'd pass, although he doubted he'd get full marks. He'd spent too much time playing football and too little time studying. He knew he'd get far enough to enter the starfighter training program and that had been all that mattered. But now...

His finger hovered over the first message. The header had already downloaded, informing him that it was a text-only message from Robert Foster. Judith's father...Alan told himself, firmly, that it was time to be brave. Robert Foster had never liked him, but surely he wouldn't deny his grandchildren the right to communicate with their father. It was illegal to deny a man access to his children, unless there was ironclad proof of abuse.

Murder is also illegal, a dark voice pointed out at the back of his mind. *And he has every reason to hate you.*

He tapped the message icon. It unwrapped, revealing a short message. Alan leaned forward, eagerly. He couldn't have looked away if his life had depended on it.

I won't mince words. You killed my daughter. Whatever she did, whatever you think she did, you killed my daughter. You ensured that her children - your children - had to grow up without a mother. You should rot in jail for the rest of your life. But it seems you have somehow managed to wrangle your way out ahead of time.

I do not want you contacting your children. But it seems I cannot deny you. Very well - you may contact them via the datanet, on the clear understanding that every message you send will be read by me and my lawyers. You are explicitly forbidden to contact them via videochat or visit them in person. Any attempt to do so will result in the police being called and you being returned to jail. I will not hesitate to demand an injunction if you behave in a manner I deem inappropriate.

Ideally, my granddaughters would not have any contact with you until they were old enough to make up their own minds. However, it seems that I have no choice. Rest assured, I will put their safety and security ahead of any of your rights.

Alan clenched his fists. The bastard talked to him like that...the bastard *dared* talk to him like that? How dare he? Robert Foster had never liked him. He'd never given much of a shit about the lower-class yobbo his daughter had married. And now...

You did murder his daughter, a little voice pointed out. *I'd say his concerns were fully justified.*

Shut up, Alan thought, savagely.

The next message was a video file. Alan reached for the icon, then hesitated. What if…what if the in-laws had turned his daughters against him? What if…

You murdered their mother, the little voice said. *I don't think they'd need to bother.*

He forced himself to take a deep breath. It would be easy, very easy, to simply delete the messages and walk away. They were better off without him. And besides, the odds of him surviving long enough to earn his pardon and freedom were very low. It would be difficult to win a battle for custody, particularly after he'd spent so much time in jail. God knew the in-laws had money to fight and win a court case.

But they were his *children*. He couldn't walk away from them. His finger tapped the icon almost before he knew it.

A young girl appeared in front of him. Alan stared in disbelief. The brown-haired girl was a stranger. Who was she? Had Robert Foster somehow hired an actress to pretend to be one of his daughters…no, he was being stupid. It had been nearly five years since he'd laid eyes on his oldest child. Jeanette was twelve now, not seven. Of *course* she'd look different. The uniform she wore - a red blazer, covering a red shirt - told him that she was attending a fancy private school. Only the very rich could afford to spend so much money to look like a wally as they walked to and from school.

It could be worse, he thought. *She could have a straw hat and boater.*

"Dad," Jeanette said. "I…"

Alan felt his heart skip a beat. It *was* Jeanette. The voice was the same, the mixture of Glaswegian Scot and Yorkshire that had characterised his daughter, back when she'd been nine. The Glaswegian had slipped slightly, part of him noted. He hoped that wasn't a bad sign. It wasn't uncommon for kids to be bullied because they sounded funny, a holdover from the Troubles that had never quite gone away. He clenched his fists at the thought, remembering some of the assholes he'd met in the borstal. The surge of anger - and protectiveness - surprised him. If some fucking wanker of a kid picked on his daughter, that wanker was going to be eating his meals through a straw for the rest of his life. And if his daughter's teachers couldn't impose discipline, they'd be dead too. He'd go back to jail - quite happily - if it meant his daughter was safe.

"Dad," Jeanette said, again. "I don't know what to say."

Because your grandfather was probably listening, Alan thought. There was no sign of anyone else within the pickup, but that meant nothing. *And because...*

"I miss you," Jeanette said. "But I miss Mum too. When they told us...I wanted to pinch myself. I hoped I would wake up and discover that it was just an awful dream. But it wasn't, was it? I...my father murdered my mother."

Alan felt his heart sink. His in-laws hadn't told their granddaughters the truth, then. But what did it matter? Alan had killed their mother! *They* didn't care about his reasoning, let alone his excuses. How could they? They wanted their mother back!

"I don't know what to say," Jeanette said. "I wanted to write to you, afterwards, but Granddad wouldn't let me. He said we would do better to forget you. And yet, I can't forget you. I want..."

Tears glistened in her eyes. "I want you back. I want Mum back. I want..."

She rubbed her eyes. "Keep messaging us, please," she said. "But I don't know..."

The screen went blank. Alan jerked. That - that - was the end of the message? It certainly *looked* like there was nothing further. He wondered, sourly, if the in-laws had fiddled with the recording. Robert Foster was hardly a technophobe. It wouldn't be that difficult to edit the video. Or simulate an entire conversation, if necessary. It had been so long since he'd laid eyes on his daughter that any flaws in the simulation could easily be explained away.

Or that might be her, Alan thought. He didn't want to open the third message, not now. And yet, he knew he had no choice. *She has every reason to be conflicted.*

He looked down at his hands. She'd had no reason to hate him, let alone fear him, until someone had told her that he'd murdered her mother. He hadn't been an abusive father...he hadn't even smacked her when she was naughty. It was natural for her to feel conflicted, but this was bad...

It would be easy to kill himself. He wanted to kill himself. Bennett hadn't allowed Alan a gun, but there were plenty of ways to commit suicide on a starship. Rigging the airlock to allow him to leave without a spacesuit would be easy. And yet, part of him refused to just give up. He had duties towards his children as well as rights.

"It will take time," he muttered, grimly. He keyed his datapad, setting it up to record a new message. "All I can do is be patient."

CHAPTER
THIRTY ONE

Alan looked…different, Abigail decided, as they rode the shuttle to the asteroid base. It wasn't something she could put her finger on, but it was there. They'd both been too busy over the last few days to sit down and chat, something that made her wonder if she should have been paying more attention to him. They hadn't even had time to go to bed together.

She pushed the thought out of her head as they docked and followed the marines through the network of corridors. Tallyman seemed to have expanded since her last visit, a sign the escort carrier program was actually working. She guessed that their success had to have convinced the Royal Navy to start converting more freighters, although she suspected they'd eventually reach a point of diminishing returns. There hadn't been enough freighters plying the spacelanes even *before* the war.

"Ah, Captain Harrison," Jameson said, as they entered the briefing compartment. "Thank you - and Commander Campbell - for coming."

"You're welcome, sir," Abigail said. She had to admit Jameson had put his own life on the line, just to prove that the escort carrier concept was workable. "Thank you for the repair crews."

"It's in the Royal Navy's interest to see that your ship is turned around as quickly as possible," Jameson told her. Four new captains, all strangers, entered the room. "Please, take a seat. We'll start as soon as everyone's arrived."

Abigail looked at Alan, then led the way to a seat close to the projector. She sat and watched the newcomers, wishing she had a moment to talk to Alan privately. If something was bothering him, she wanted to know about it before it exploded in her face. But she doubted she'd have the time. It was starting to look as though they would be shipping out within the next few days.

Or sooner, she thought. The four days of leave had never been extended. She'd had to reprimand two of her crew for grumbling about not being able to get to Titan and back in four days. *The navy probably want us to leave this afternoon.*

The hatch hissed closed. "Thank you all for coming," Jameson said. "As I'm sure you're all aware - from the briefing notes I forwarded to you - our enemies have been given a bloody nose. Our best guess - at the moment - is that they're reassessing their plans, following some unexpectedly staunch resistance. These are just guesses, to be fair, but they do make a certain kind of sense."

"A certain kind of *human* sense," Alan muttered.

Jameson proved to have sharp ears. "Correct," he said. "Their idea of smart military tactics may be completely alien to us. However, so far their planning appears to follow a sensible - and entirely understandable - pattern. Lure our ships into a killing zone, test themselves against the ships - and then make an attack on Earth, when our ships proved incapable of stopping them. Thankfully, we stopped that attack dead in its tracks."

Abigail nudged Alan. "Busted."

"The Admiralty is currently looking at a number of options for taking the offensive and - again - winning time for refitting our fleets," Jameson said. He keyed a switch. A holographic starchart appeared in front of them. "As you can see, the aliens have been moving towards Aquitaine - a French-ethnic colony only three jumps from New Russia - with the obvious intention of forcing us to split our defences. As Aquitaine is under threat from two separate tramlines - and its fall would open up several other possible routes core-wards - we have a strategic interest in not allowing it to be occupied."

"And a political interest too," a captain said.

"Correct," Jameson agreed. "Politically, allowing Aquitaine to fall would lead to a major political crisis. And, as the system has a small industrial base, we have a vested interest in not allowing the aliens to destroy it.

I believe the French have already started to convert their industrial nodes to war production, but it will take time before new weapons and starfighters start rolling off the assembly line.

"It has therefore been decided, at the very highest levels, that we will make a serious attempt to reinforce the system before it can be invaded. Your ships will be charged with protecting a convoy to the system, then taking part in the defence - and, perhaps, a little aggressive raiding. We might well be able to give the aliens another bloody nose."

Or get our ships blown up, Abigail thought coldly.

"The convoy is already being organised," Jameson said. "Assuming that everything goes according to plan, we'll be leaving tomorrow morning. I had hoped for a longer period of downtime, but" - he shrugged, expressively - "it was not to be."

He paused. "Do you have any concerns?"

Alan stuck up a hand. "We will have hardly any time for squadron training, let alone integration," he said. "I have seven pilots under my command who served on *Haddock* during our last engagement. The remaining pilots are either reservists or maggots who've been rushed through the final stages of basic training. Frankly, sir, we need more time in simulators before we start flying actual *starfighters*."

"I am aware of the problem," Jameson said. "However, we are very short of experienced personnel."

Alan didn't look pleased, but he didn't say anything further. Abigail glanced at him for a moment, wondering if *that* was what was bothering him. Alan had trained two squadrons - four, practically - and now he was faced with the task of doing it for the third time. She could understand how that might gnaw on him, particularly given the loss rates. Sooner or later, Alan's luck would run out...

And mine too, she thought grimly. *A few more plasma bolts in the last engagement and my ship would be nothing more than atoms.*

"We are also short of commanding officers," Jameson said. "We have a number of officers who are desperate to move up, but very few of them have any experience in commanding and operating fleet carriers. Therefore, it has been decided that Captain Harrison will receive a brevet promotion to *commodore*, effective immediately."

Abigail blinked. "Me?"

"You will assume command if something happens to me," Jameson said. "I don't know if the French will recognise a brevet promotion, Captain, but you'll definitely have command of the flotilla. It should help limit the command disputes that plagued some of the other early engagements."

"Congratulations," Alan muttered.

Commiserations might be more in order, Abigail thought. Herding bel-ter captains was like herding cats. Some of her new subordinates would understand the importance of a unified command, others would resent her newfound prominence. *Even if I never have to take command, it will make life difficult.*

"I'm sorry for the late notice," Jameson said. "If it was up to me, there would be a longer gap between missions. But right now…England expects that everyone will do their duty."

"Duly noted," Abigail said, calmly.

Jameson dismissed the audience, then hurried through the hatch before anyone could ask him any further questions. Abigail rolled her eyes at his retreating back, then led Alan back to their shuttle. She'd never liked pointless social chatter and she had no intention of talking to any of the other captains, not when half of them were probably feeling resentful and the other half indulging in some *Schadenfreude*. Besides, she was too old to feel obliged to spend time with people when she didn't *need* to do anything of the sort.

"So," she said, once they were back on the shuttle. "What's bothering you?"

Alan gave her a surprised look. "You can tell?"

"I've been a daughter, a wife and a mother," Abigail said. She leaned back into her chair as the shuttle started to move, undocking from the asteroid and heading back to *Haddock*. "I know how to read a man, Alan. What's bothering you?"

Alan half-covered his face with his hand, just for a second. "I've been exchanging messages with my eldest daughter," he said. "We've been… we've been chatting. The in-laws have been reading over her shoulder."

Abigail lifted her eyebrow. "Do you blame them?"

"Not really," Alan said. "But it is annoying."

"Put up with it," Abigail advised. If a belter had murdered his wife, he'd be executed. The belt didn't tolerate murderers. Alan might not be a monster, but he'd still crossed the line. "I don't think you have any room to complain about them reading your mail."

Alan's eyebrows furrowed. "Tough love?"

Abigail shrugged. "I grew up in a place where the slightest mistake could get me killed," she said, dryly. "You *know* that. I was taught harsh lessons as a child and I taught them myself to my children, because the alternative was them fucking up when I wasn't there to catch them. Sometimes you have to let children make mistakes…and sometimes you have to keep a close eye on them, so those mistakes aren't disastrous."

She shrugged, again. "What are they saying?"

"They seem to be in two minds," Alan said. "There are times when they want to talk to me and times…and times when they seem to want to have *nothing* to do with me. And how can I blame them for that?"

"I don't suppose you can," Abigail said. Losing a mother was bad enough, but losing a mother because the *father* had murdered her…she couldn't imagine it. She'd grown up with the grim knowledge that she could die at any time, yet…death had been an impersonal force of nature. One didn't need malice to kill. "Just…give them time. Record a final message for them before we leave."

Alan shook his head. "We don't have time to get ready before we leave."

"And Jameson told you to suck it up," Abigail reminded him. "I don't think we have much of a choice."

"No," Alan said. "We don't."

———

Alan would have brooded more over the unfairness of it all if there hadn't been so much to *do*. The new pilots had to be briefed - he felt as though he could give the speech in his sleep now - and then assigned to bunks and their bags searched for contraband. He knew he should be trying to get to know his new subordinates, but he didn't want to allow himself any more ties to them. Too many of his former subordinates had died in the brief, savage engagements for him to feel inclined to get to know their replacements. He knew that too many of the newcomers would be dead before too long.

Training is getting shot to hell, he thought, bitterly. The Royal Navy normally trained its pilots in four classes, but the first and second classes had already been rushed into service. They knew how to fly - he'd give them that much - yet they were lacking in so many other ways. And while he wasn't a *keen* proponent of military etiquette, he knew there were plenty of other fields of study. *Half of them can barely tie their own shoelaces without help.*

Maddy stepped into the briefing room, holding a datapad in one hand. "A couple of pilots were caught with alcohol," she said. "Officer Bennett sent me to ask what you wanted done with the bottles."

Alan considered a number of answers, none of them really useful. "Tell him to pour the bottles into the head," he said, bluntly. "We may as well run it through the recyclers."

"Aye, sir," Maddy said. She glanced down at her datapad. "They were new pilots, not the old hands."

"Old hands," Alan repeated. It was funny, but...he felt too depressed to laugh. "How long have we been on this ship?"

Maddy looked puzzled. "Ah...four months, roughly," she said. "That's about right, sir."

"Feels longer," Alan said. He leaned back in his chair. "There was a time when you would still be considered a newcomer until you'd served at least a year in a squadron. Wasn't there?"

"Yes, sir."

"And now there are old hands who might as well be in diapers," Alan continued. "Or at least have only been flying for three or four months."

"And others who returned to the colours," Maddy said. "They're not exactly *new*."

Alan scowled. There had been no way to avoid the simple fact that most of the older pilots had been killed. They simply hadn't been up to the demands of modern warfare. He wanted to order everyone over the age of thirty out of the cockpit, but he knew he'd never be allowed to make it stick. The Royal Navy had more starfighters than it had pilots. Once upon a time, everyone had assumed that producing more starfighters would be the bottleneck, if full-scale war broke out. In hindsight, that assumption was starting to look foolish.

And besides, everyone over the age of thirty would include me, he thought. *I'd have to pull myself out of the cockpit.*

He looked down at his hands for a long moment. Was there blood on his pale skin? Or was it just an illusion? He blinked. The shadow vanished. He was too tired, he told himself. He was starting to see things. The drugs had long-since worn off, but tiredness seemed to follow him wherever he went...

Maddy cleared her throat. "Sir?"

"Tell Bennett to pour the alcohol away," Alan said. "And then report back here. We have a training schedule to work out."

"Yes, sir," Maddy said.

Alan looked down at the datapad as Maddy left, the hatch hissing closed behind her. Nineteen new pilots, thirteen of them yanked out of the training centre before they'd managed to acquire even a *gleam* of polish. Alan checked the comments on the first file and allowed himself a moment of relief as he realised the instructors had thrown a fit, then rushed to prepare the pilots as much as possible. And yet, he knew from grim experience that the instructors hadn't had a hope of actually succeeding. He was commanding children, *children*!

"They're not exactly babies," he told himself, firmly. "Just... inexperienced."

He scowled. Once, years ago, he'd watched bootleg copies of *Star Fighter Maverick*. The series had been banned, which had been part of the reason he'd wanted to see it. And yet, he'd found it impossible to understand *why* it had been banned in the UK until he'd reached adulthood. The characters were the sort of rogue agents who did well on movie screens, but were loathed and detested in the actual military. Not following orders was considered a Bad Thing, unless one had a very good excuse. A *real* pilot who pulled half the shit Maverick had done would have been tossed out long ago.

Putting the thought aside, Alan started to compose a final message to his daughters. He hoped - prayed - that Jeanette would be allowed to see it, although he had a sneaking suspicion that not all of his messages were getting through. Jeanette's replies hadn't answered some of his questions, making him wonder…he sighed, knowing it would take a miracle for him to survive the war. If he survived, maybe he could start again. But that wouldn't be easy.

Maddy returned, looking amused. "They weren't pleased, sir."

"I bet they weren't," Alan said. He put the incomplete message aside for later. "I just hope they got the message."

"It was expensive, apparently," Maddy added. "They want their money back."

"A likely story," Alan said. "Tell them to take a sexual travel package."

He snorted. What sort of idiot did the newcomers think he was? It was vaguely possible that some young fool had blown his paycheck on a bottle of aged whiskey, but rather more likely that he'd purchased a bottle of shipboard rotgut. No one in their right mind risked bringing anything they didn't want to lose on deployment, even though the odds of it getting stolen were very low. The odds of getting something lost or broken were much higher. He'd made sure only to bring *copies* of his family photographs with him.

"Bennett already did," Maddy said. "They weren't pleased about that, either."

"Good," Alan said. "Now, the pilots have all been assigned to their squadrons. Training will begin within the hour…"

———

"Should I be addressing you as *Your Majesty* now?"

"That depends," Abigail said. She wasn't in the mood for Anson's sense of humour. "Are we ready to depart?"

"More or less," Anson said. He cleared his throat, perhaps picking up on her feelings. "All decks have checked in."

"And the pilots are training," Poddy added. "I think they'll be busy for a while."

Abigail nodded, curtly. It was hard to believe that Poddy had more experience than some of the newbie pilots, but…groundpounders were strange. Their children were wrapped in cotton wool until they were almost too old to learn from their own mistakes. Alan would knock them into shape before they actually encountered something dangerous. If not…

She put the thought aside. "Bring the drive field online," she ordered. Commodore Jameson had already ordered the convoy to be ready to depart. "And take us into our position."

"Aye, Captain."

Abigail leaned back in her chair as a dull quiver ran through the ship. The repair crews had done a good job, but it was hard to be sure that everything was perfect. All their checks and rechecks insisted that they were ready, yet…she couldn't help feeling unsure of herself. It felt as though something was about to go wrong.

You're imagining it, she told herself, firmly. *You checked everything yourself before we started to power up the drives.*

"Signal from the flag," Poddy said. "The convoy is to depart as planned."

"Well," Abigail said. "Let's not keep him waiting, shall we?"

CHAPTER
THIRTY TWO

For all of Abigail's misgivings, no trouble materialised as the convoy crossed the Terra Nova System, nor after it had started up the long chain towards Aquitaine. If there were any alien ships within the core systems, they kept their distance from the convoy. She honestly wasn't sure if the absence of alien contacts was a good thing or not; on one hand, the convoy couldn't hope to stand off a really determined attack, but - on the other - it suggested the aliens might have other priorities. They'd taken a bloody nose, yet that would force them to retake the initiative as soon as possible. They wouldn't want humanity to take the offensive itself.

She paced her decks, chatting to crew and passing time with starfighter pilots. The latter were surprisingly young, young enough to worry her. It was far from uncommon for youngsters to start work early, in the belt - Abigail herself had been thirteen when she'd shipped out for the first time - but the starfighter pilots managed to combine the bravado of teenagers with the ignorance and inexperience of preteens. She couldn't help finding them a little disconcerting. Poddy was fifteen and *she* was far more experienced than any of the new pilots.

"None of them went to space before being accepted for training," Alan said, when she commented on it one night. "And they haven't even had the full training period before being ordered into a real cockpit."

Abigail wondered, as the days slowly turned into weeks, just how much of a fuss a *naval* captain would have made if he'd had such under-trained pilots dumped on him. A big one, she assumed. Fleet carriers couldn't afford to deploy inexperienced pilots...although, she admitted sourly, they also had better facilities for training the newcomers before they were launched into space and told to fight. It would have been better, she thought, to recruit volunteers from the belt. Belters might have problems coping with military discipline, but that only meant they'd fit in amongst the other starfighter pilots. *They* seemed to have problems with discipline too.

She ran her crew ragged, going through drill after drill as they moved further from the core worlds. Combat drills, damage control drills...she wanted to be ready, if - when - the enemy showed themselves. The new components seemed to mesh perfectly with the older systems, something that worried her more than she cared to admit. Normally, there were all sorts of compatibility problems. Technically, it was possible to wire French or Russian components into a British-designed network, but she knew from experience that it wasn't always easy to get them to work together. She would sooner have handled a dozen problems while they were installing the new components than deal with a single systems failure during an engagement.

Paradox - a star system towards the end of the tramline chain - was surprisingly barren, save for a handful of asteroid and lunar settlements that were either independent or fuelling stations for one or more or the Great Powers. But then, most systems along the chain weren't much better. Aquitaine had been a lucky find, if the files were to be believed; there hadn't been any reason to think there was an Earth-like world at the end of the tramline chain. She suspected that some groundpounder had been dangerous incompetent, given that Aquitaine wasn't *that* far from Earth. One of the giant space-based telescopes should have picked up a habitable world *decades* before the survey ship had stumbled across it. Maybe Aquitaine had been behind its primary star at the time. God knew there was nothing else particularly extraordinary about the system. The French had turned it into a colony and developed it over the last seventy years. They hadn't done a bad job, she admitted, if one *wanted* to live on a planetary surface. The groundpounders were blind to the simple fact that *true* civilisation was only possible in space.

It may be safer to live on the ground, she thought, although she'd read enough horror stories about Earth to feel otherwise. Murder, rape...even in the civilised countries, the crime rate was terrifyingly high, compared to the belt. *But living planetside is also conducive to laziness.*

Abigail was inspecting the crew quarters when the alarms started to howl. She jumped, then hurried to the bridge. The enemy had been detected, then. She'd made it clear that alarms were *not* to be sounded unless the long-range sensors had picked up enemy activity. Given how many weak tramlines threaded through the Aquitaine Chain, she was surprised they hadn't encountered the aliens weeks ago. But then, the aliens were probably more interested in probing towards Earth than harassing Aquitaine.

Their tramlines change everything, she reflected, as she stepped onto the bridge. Red icons sparkled on the display, heading towards the convoy. *They can cut their journey times down sharply, then appear in systems that should be safe.*

"Anson, report," she snapped.

"Enemy starfighters, coming at us on attack vector," Anson said. "They'll be within firing range in seven minutes. Commodore Jameson has ordered our starfighters to launch."

"They must have a carrier," Poddy added. "But I can't find the wretched ship!"

Abigail sat down. "They may be operating at extreme range," she said. "But keep a close eye on the sensors anyway."

She frowned. New orders were popping up in her display. Commodore Jameson wanted the convoy to alter course, turning away from the alien starfighters. Outrunning the tiny bastards wasn't an option, but it was quite possible that the aliens were operating right at the edge of their range. The human ships might manage to put enough space between them and the alien mothership to force the aliens to back off. Unless they were feeling suicidal, of course...

Or unless their carrier is a great deal closer, she thought. *They could get very close to us under a sensor mask.*

"There are only sixty starfighters within detection range," Poddy said. "Where's the rest of them?"

Abigail's lips twitched. "Don't complain," she said. "I dare say we'll see them soon enough."

She allowed herself a moment to contemplate the possibilities as the alien starfighters converged on the convoy. The aliens might have been using their starfighters to search for the human ships, spreading them out to maximise their chances of finding their targets, or they might simply have gotten lucky. They *had* to have caught a sniff of the convoy at some point, she suspected. Perhaps an alien scout picked up the ships as they crossed the last system, then shadowed the convoy until an ambush could be organised. Commodore Jameson had already taken that possibility into account. His ships were launching recon drones to expand their sensor range.

Not that it matters now, she thought. *They did manage to ambush us.*

"Contact in two minutes," Poddy said. "The second starfighter squadron is launching now."

Abigail felt an odd pang. Poddy sounded like a seasoned professional, rather than an excitable young girl. She'd never been allowed to be as footloose and fancy-free as a groundpounder girl - *they* were allowed to be childlike until they turned twenty, an absurdity that made little sense to anyone who grew up on the belt - but she'd still had her childish moments. Hell, Abigail *expected* her to mature as she served on the ship. Now...

Think about it later, she told herself. On the display, the red icons were falling into attack position. *Right now, you have other things to worry about.*

———

"Herring Squadron is taking its time," Maddy said, tartly. Her voice echoed oddly in the quiet CIC. "They're not going to be deployed by the time the attack begins."

Alan nodded, grimly. The alien attack had caught them by surprise - and, as much as he'd drilled his pilots over the last two weeks, they'd still been slower to deploy than he would have preferred. They'd be in real trouble on a fleet carrier - he knew captains who would have called him up for the express purpose of tearing him a new arsehole - but right now they had worse problems. A starfighter trapped inside the carrier when the aliens attacked would be helpless, utterly unable to defend itself. And the aliens might be smart enough to target the flight deck *first*.

Not that it matters that much, he reminded himself. *Our armour isn't that good.*

He resisted the urge to contact the flight deck and order them to expedite. They were moving as fast as they could. And yet...he wished, suddenly, that he'd taken a starfighter himself, rather than remaining in the CIC. He'd certainly *planned* to take a place in the rotating CSP, just to keep his hand in. But there was no time to take a starfighter now. The flight crews would prep his craft after the remaining starfighters were launched...

"Enemy craft entering attack range now," Maddy reported. "They're engaging the CSP."

Alan studied the display, watching the interplay of green and red icons. It looked remarkably bloodless, almost like a computer game rather than something *real*. It was easy to forget that each of those icons represented a starfighter and its pilot, that each icon that blinked out of existence meant that a living being - human or alien - had died. He remembered the vague reports from *Ark Royal* about the aliens, reports that suggested the aliens were roughly humanoid. And yet, they were still faceless. That bothered him more than he wanted to admit.

"The first wave is breaking through the CSP," Maddy said. "Their second wave is trying to pin the CSP in place. Commodore Jameson is ordering the CSP to move to engage the first wave."

Nothing wrong with their tactics, Alan thought. The alien starfighters were swooping down on their targets, choosing to engage the freighters rather than the escorts. It was a good sign, he told himself. The aliens wouldn't have ignored the escorts if they'd had enough forces to crush the escorts, then destroy the convoy at leisure. *And they might just be in for a surprise.*

The aliens opened fire, savaging a pair of medium freighters. A moment later, a number of alien fighters vanished as the freighters opened fire with their point defence. The aliens seemed to hesitate, caught by surprise. Alan wondered, feeling a flicker of amusement, just why they *were* surprised. *Their* freighters were armed. Normally, human freighters didn't carry weapons - space pirates were the thing of trashy fiction, not real life - but it hadn't been hard to bolt a few weapons mounts to their hulls. The Admiralty had been desperate for something - anything - that might give the freighters a chance to survive...

"The CSP is driving the aliens back," Maddy said. "But their second wave is heading straight for the freighters..."

She sucked in her breath. "Tomlinson is ignoring orders!"

Alan looked up. "What?"

The display centred on a single starfighter. Flight Lieutenant Alex Tomlinson was engaging an alien craft, battling backwards and forwards instead of following his wingmates to cover the freighters. Alan swore, harshly. The impulse to test himself against an enemy pilot, one-on-one, was understandable, but utterly out of place. Breaking formation in the midst of a fight was a court-martial offence. Tomlinson...was too young, too inexperienced, to understand.

"Order him back into formation," Alan snapped. The alien pilot seemed inclined to accept the challenge...Alan couldn't tell if the alien felt he had no choice, or if he was simply keeping Tomlinson away from his comrades. The aliens didn't actually have a numerical advantage. Their weapons just suggested they did. "Now!"

"Aye, sir," Maddy said. "I...he just *hit* the bastard!"

"Very good," Alan snapped, crossly. "And now...tell him to get back in formation."

He took a long breath, calming himself. Whitehead was going to give the young fool the chewing out of a lifetime, then Alan himself would have a go. Technically, it was Whitehead's responsibility, but Alan knew he might need to drive the lesson home. The youngster was too young to understand that his little quest for glory - and he'd be feted as a hero, back home - might have cost lives.

And then we have to tell him that, without breaking him, Alan thought. *That isn't going to be easy.*

"*Monty* has been destroyed," Maddy reported. "*Bad Penny* has taken heavy damage, but her captain insists that she can still fly."

Alan winced. In the short term, losing the freighters wasn't a problem; in the long term, it could be disastrous. The forces deployed along the front line *needed* those supplies, the supplies the aliens had just destroyed. And the aliens would come back, time and time again, until the convoy was wiped out. Everything depended, now, on breaking contact before the enemy managed to mount a second attack.

"The enemy craft are breaking off," Maddy said. "Squadron COs are requesting permission to give chase."

"The Commodore will have to make *that* decision," Alan said. "We don't know what might be lurking in the darkness."

He studied the display for a long moment. The alien starfighters appeared to be flying into empty space, but *something* had to be lurking there. A fleet carrier? Or an escort carrier? It was hard to believe that the aliens might not have come up with the concept themselves, yet - even if they hadn't - they'd certainly seen *human* escort carriers in action. He wondered, idly, how long it would take the aliens to convert their freighters into escort carriers, then decided there was no way to know. It hadn't taken the Royal Navy long to convert *Haddock* and her sisters into makeshift carriers, but most of the components had been produced years ago and stored until they'd been needed. The aliens might be starting from scratch.

"Signal from the flag," Maddy said. "We're to change course to evade the aliens."

Alan nodded. Assuming the aliens *did* have a fleet carrier nearby, it wouldn't be long before they resumed the offensive. And if they didn't...he contemplated the possibilities. There had to be a starfighter base of *some* kind within the system. But that didn't matter, he told himself grimly. The important thing, right now, was to break contact and try to sneak to their destination without being detected. Again.

"Recall Herring Squadron, then order Kipper to take position on the hull," he said. "I want Herring ready for immediate turnaround."

"Aye, sir."

"And then inform Whitehead that I want to speak with him, once he's turned his ships around," Alan added. "I'll see him in the ready room."

"Aye, sir."

———

"They're out there, somewhere," Poddy said. "But where?"

"Maybe they lost us," Anson said. "Or maybe they're planning something *really* bad."

Abigail kept her thoughts to herself. Assuming the convoy was being shadowed, Commodore Jameson's course changes shouldn't have kept the aliens from launching another attack. But no attack had materialised. It suggested, very strongly, that the aliens *weren't* shadowing the convoy. Perhaps the alien scout had just pulled back when the attack began, only to lose the human ships when they altered course. It was possible. Using its active sensors to hunt for targets would reveal its location to passive sensors...

And we'd send our starfighters after him, if we saw him, she thought. So far, the recon probes hadn't picked up anything worth mentioning. *He has to know that too.*

She glanced at the report from the flagship. Two freighters destroyed, a third badly damaged...it didn't look good. Thankfully, the third freighter wasn't radiating anything that might lure the aliens or the convoy might have had to abandon her to her fate. The only good news was an assessment by an analyst that suggested the aliens had actually been operating at extreme range, hence the brevity of their attack. But she wasn't sure how to take it. The Royal Navy's analysts, in her option, appeared to be paid by the word. They certainly didn't bother to use one word when three would do.

At least these analysts are sharing the danger, she reminded herself. *They know better than to make foolish mistakes. Or to draw unsupported conclusions and present them as certainties.*

"Keep us on course," she ordered, pushing her doubts aside. It would be four days before they could pop through the tramline, thanks to the course change. There hadn't been any choice. If the aliens really *had* lost the convoy, their best bet was to take up position along a least-time course to the tramline and wait. "And alert me the moment they show themselves."

"Aye, Captain," Anson said.

Abigail settled back into her chair and told herself, firmly, to wait. She'd done everything she *could* do, now the aliens had shown themselves.

And yet...a few hours of watching and waiting would take their toll. The aliens would force them to play hide and seek all over the system if they resumed their offensive now. She yawned, despite herself. Tiredness was going to wear her down.

It'll get to all of us, she thought. She'd have to leave the bridge eventually, just to get some sleep. The others would have to do the same. And yet, she didn't want to leave her ship in someone else's hands when the aliens resumed the offensive. It would feel like she was neglecting her duties. *We only have four days to go.*

She rubbed her forehead. Four days...they'd already burned up some of their fuel and ammunition. And the more the aliens pressed the offensive against the convoy, the more the defenders would burn through their supplies. It might not be too long before they were effectively defenceless. And then the aliens would close for the kill.

And she tried not to think about what would happen if - when - the aliens forced them to change course again.

CHAPTER
THIRTY THREE

"Tell me something," Alan said, as he studied the younger man. "Do you understand how foolish you were?"

The youngster looked torn between rebellion and a desperate desire to brace a non-existent bulkhead. Alan couldn't help thinking of someone wearing his father's uniform, rather than one he'd earned in his own right. Alex Tomlinson was nineteen, according to his file, but he barely looked old enough to shave. He certainly *didn't* have the military bearing. Alan rather thought he looked like a civilian playing at being a military officer.

"Ah...Commander Whitehall made it clear, sir," Tomlinson said. He sounded young too, his voice carrying very definite traces of Sussex. "I should have stayed in formation."

"Correct," Alan said. "You were lured out of place. If they'd had more starfighters, young man, they would have either dogpiled you or punched through to hit the freighters. I am aware" - he held up a hand before Tomlinson could say a word - "that it isn't always *easy* to avoid a dogfight. However, you had other priorities and you should have stuck to them."

He allowed his voice to harden. "Not to be repeated, clear?"

"Clear, sir."

"Good," Alan said. It didn't *look* as though Tomlinson's wingmates had decided to indulge in a little barracks-room justice, thankfully, but none of the older hands would be very pleased. *They* knew the dangers, even if Tomlinson was too inexperienced to see them. "I expect you to spend the next two days going through the engagement in the simulators. And consider yourself lucky that there's no time to beach you."

"Yes, sir," Tomlinson said.

Alan eyed him for a long moment, then pointed a finger at the hatch. "Don't force me to take notice of you again," he ordered. "Dismissed."

He watched Tomlinson slowly walk to the hatch, his gait suggesting that he wanted to run for his life. It would hardly be the first time Tomlinson had been in trouble - his file suggested that he'd been a handful at school - but it might well be rather more significant than a short, sharp encounter with the headmaster's cane. His permanent naval record had already been updated to reflect his mistake, although Alan - and Whitehead - wouldn't set anything in stone until the end of the deployment. It was still possible that Tomlinson would do something to redeem himself.

Or get killed in a later engagement, Alan thought. *None of us might make it back to Earth.*

He leaned back in his chair and studied the near-space display. Aquitaine was a beautiful world, a blue-green orb floating against the darkness of interplanetary space. The French *had* done well for themselves, he conceded. Seventy years of intensive development had led to a number of cities, small communities and a thriving orbital industry. He rather suspected the colonists were more French than the French - he'd heard that the colonists on Britannia prided themselves on being more British than the folks back home - but it hardly mattered. It was better to have a national identity than a melange of ethnic communities that disliked and distrusted their fellows. A great deal had been lost, during the Troubles, but a great deal more had been preserved.

And the aliens are already raiding the system, he reminded himself. The convoy had been attacked twice more during the voyage, once in the Aquitaine System itself. *Two tramlines that lead towards occupied space and the aliens appear to be raiding through both of them.*

He brought up the starchart and studied it for a long moment. The alien raiding patterns were odd, to say the least. A reflection of their concerns about taking heavy losses - Aquitaine was important, but hardly a vital target - or something more subtle? Perhaps they wanted the raiders to report back to higher authority between raids…it certainly seemed to make sense. *And* it proved the aliens didn't have an FTL communicator…

His wristcom bleeped. "Alan," Abigail said. "Commodore Jameson has requested that we join him for a holoconference."

Alan frowned. He'd been hoping for a trip to the orbital station. There probably wasn't any time to go down to Aquitaine itself, but visiting the station would have given them a chance to eat something that hadn't been recycled or preserved for months or years before consumption. Or…he shook his head. He couldn't blame Jameson for wanting to keep the ships fully manned. The aliens hadn't probed the orbital defences yet, but everyone knew it was just a matter of time.

"We'll take it in the CIC," he said, rising. "I'll see you there."

He took one last look at the near-space display - reassuringly clear of alien starships, although he knew that meant nothing - and walked through the hatch. A pair of crewmen were working on an open access panel, replacing a datanode that had been showing signs of failure during the brief engagements. Alan stepped past them, raising his eyebrows as he saw Maddy and Anson slipping out of her cabin, hand in hand. He didn't really care what they did when they weren't on duty, but they *were* in a war zone. The aliens might attack at any moment.

And you spent last night fucking Abigail, he reminded himself, sharply. *Who are you to complain?*

He dismissed the thought as he stepped into the CIC. The consoles were unmanned, something that would never have passed muster on a fleet carrier. But a fleet carrier had enough trained crew to keep the consoles manned at all times. Alan took a seat, tapping his ID code into his console. A list of updates blinked up in front of him, none of which appeared to be urgent. The French CO didn't seem to have any real idea of what he wanted to do with the convoy's escorts, now they were here. He smiled at Abigail as she stepped into the compartment, closing the hatch behind her. Perhaps that had changed.

Commodore Jameson's face appeared in front of them, a handful of other faces appearing briefly and then fading into the background. Alan kept his face impassive with an effort, remembering some of the holoconferences he'd attended as a young man. The compartments had been large enough to maintain the illusion that everyone was in the same space, even though they'd *known* it wasn't true. Now…Jameson looked small and the others wouldn't even register as long as they kept their mouths shut.

"The French are very pleased to see us," Jameson said, without formalities. "They've requested that we launch a raid through Tramline Two into Yeller, where the enemy forces have apparently established a base. They believe we can make a significant impact if we take out the fuelling station before it can be used to support a major thrust against Aquitaine."

"I'd be surprised if the station was *that* important, sir." Captain Hamline's face flashed into existence. "Their drives are, if anything, more advanced than ours. They wouldn't need any additional reactor mass or HE3 for quite some time."

"And yet, they have established a mining station near the gas giant," Jameson said. "That much is indisputable."

"Yeah, so let the French go take it out," Captain Malone said. "This isn't a job for escort carriers."

"The French have two fleet carriers," Jameson said. "And neither one can be risked on *this* operation."

Alan frowned as he brought up the starchart and studied the tramlines. A mining station in Yeller made a *certain* amount of sense, although he doubted that taking it out would impede the aliens for longer than a few weeks…if at all. Humanity's fleet trains could and did transport HE3 through the tramlines, if necessary. It wasn't particularly economical, yet it was doable. Taking out the mining station might annoy the aliens - and it might remind them that humanity wasn't dead yet - but he couldn't imagine it actually *stopping* them.

"This is a precursor to a potentially larger operation," Jameson added. "However, the second operation will not start until the first is completed."

Abigail leaned forward. "What *is* the second operation?"

"Classified," Jameson said. "What you don't know you can't tell."

Alan glanced at Abigail. She didn't look pleased. He didn't really blame her, although he understood Jameson's concerns. The Great Powers wouldn't mistreat prisoners from the other Great Powers, but there was no reason to believe the aliens would follow the same rules. Besides, those rules only applied to honourable combatants. No one would bat an eyelid if a terrorist or insurgent was tortured to force him to talk. All the old decencies had been forgotten long ago.

We really did lose something, didn't we? Alan looked down at the console, trying to keep his face impassive. *But we couldn't have won while keeping one hand tied behind our backs.*

Jameson was still speaking. "We'll jump into the Yeller System under full silent running, then proceed towards the target. If it looks clear, we'll strike and obliterate the mining station before retreating to the tramline. If the defences are too strong, we'll fall back...hopefully, without them ever knowing we were there."

"It sounds very simple," Abigail muttered.

"Plenty of room for something to go wrong," Alan muttered back. There was nothing *wrong* with the picture, as far as he could tell, but...he shook his head. The aliens had established a mining station they didn't need, in a system that was literally one jump away from an enemy naval base. Put that way, it was starting to look like a trap. "What are they doing?"

He cleared his throat. "How do we know this isn't a trap?"

"We don't," Jameson said. "The analysts are unsure why the aliens bothered to establish a mining station in the first place. Yes, it is possible that it *is* a trap. And yet, we have to spring it."

"I don't like that logic," Captain Hamline said. "Are we planning to try to *capture* the mining station?"

Jameson shrugged. "It depends," he said. "If local space appears clear, we may try to land on the station. But if it doesn't...we'll probably launch kinetic projectiles at the installation from a safe distance."

And pray that our estimates of a safe distance aren't grossly inaccurate, Alan added, mentally. *If this is a trap, they'll want to make sure we're too deep within the system to escape before they close the jaws.*

"Capturing the station does add a few more variables," Malone offered. "Has there been any progress in talking to the bastards?"

"Nothing," Jameson said, curtly. "*Ark Royal* did capture scraps of alien computer nodes, so *something* might have been devised" - he shrugged - "but if it was, I don't know about it. We have no way of guaranteeing that they'll hear, let alone understand our messages."

Abigail nudged Alan. "You'd think they'd understand the basics, if nothing else."

Alan shrugged. There had been countless attempts to devise a first contact package that would allow both sides to build up a basic vocabulary before moving on to more advanced concepts. But none of the packages had been *tested* properly until the first interstellar war had actually broken out, whereupon they'd proven completely useless. As far as anyone could tell, the faceless aliens had no interest in anything, but war. The analysts were sure they had *radio* - they *must* have radio - yet they'd shown no response to human transmissions. It was hard to escape the sense that humanity was in a war to the death.

Perhaps they think the galaxy really isn't big enough for both of us, he thought.

It wasn't a pleasant thought, so he contemplated it for a long moment. If the aliens ruled the spiral arm, humanity might be grossly outnumbered; if the aliens ruled the whole galaxy, humanity might be so badly outmatched that the aliens could simply smash their way to Earth with the high-tech equivalent of human wave attacks. But all the evidence suggested that the aliens weren't *that* numerous, even if they were advanced. Perhaps there was another threat on the far side of alien space, something that kept the aliens from expanding away from humanity. Or perhaps they simply didn't have any tramlines leading away from the human sphere...

"We will depart tomorrow morning, then head straight for Tramline Two," Jameson concluded. "Naturally, we'll slip into silent running as soon as we are well away from Aquitaine. We don't want them following us through the tramline."

Unless it really is a trap, Alan thought. *But they've gone to a great deal of trouble just to snag a handful of warships and expendable escort carriers.*

He winced, inwardly. The Admiralty had made it clear that they considered the escort carriers to be expendable. Jameson wasn't a bad guy, but his superiors would happily expend the ships under his command to buy time for Earth. Or Aquitaine, in this case. Alan didn't blame the French for wanting to give the aliens a bloody nose, but the whole situation bothered him. What *were* the aliens doing?

The starchart glowed in front of him. Alan studied the tramlines, trying to parse out their reasoning. The aliens might be alien, but their military logic couldn't be *that* alien...could it? So far, everything they'd done spoke of a cautious mentality, one unwilling to take unsupported leaps into the dark. They'd only launched a thrust at Earth after becoming convinced that the defenders couldn't stand in their way.

Perhaps they use the mining station for something else, he thought. *But what?*

Jameson answered a few minor questions, then ended the briefing. Alan listened, then read the formal orders as they popped up in his inbox. They were surprisingly vague, although he supposed they did come from a foreign officer who wouldn't be accompanying the flotilla on its mission. Jameson would need a great deal of latitude in interpreting his orders, depending on what they found on the far side of the tramline. Alan read the orders a second time, then forwarded them to his subordinates. They'd need to prepare themselves for the coming engagement.

He keyed his wristcom. "I want all of our pilots and flight crews to get at least nine hours of rest," he said. Standing down would be risky, given how regularly the aliens had been probing the system, but there was no choice. The French could cover the flotilla long enough for his pilots to jump out of their bunks and sprint to the flight deck. "We'll be jumping through the tramline into hostile space."

Abigail caught his arm. "What do you think of the mission?"

"I think it's risky," Alan said, as she led him towards the hatch. "It looks far too simple."

"And it could be a trap," Abigail said. "If that's a fuelling station, Alan, what is it fuelling?"

Alan followed her along the corridor, thinking hard. He had no answer. Starfighters used power cells - there was certainly no indication that the aliens thought differently - and starships used fusion plants. HE3 was vital for fusion, of course, but...he shook his head as they reached her cabin. The aliens were either producing far more HE3 than they could possibly need, which wasn't entirely impossible, or they were up to something. But what?

"It could be anything," Alan said, as the hatch hissed closed. "A super-weapon of some kind, perhaps...maybe a giant laser. Or a scaled-up plasma cannon. Or..."

Abigail smiled, rather tiredly. "Or a mass driver to propel HE3 capsules from the gas giant to a pick-up point," she said. "You could be over-thinking it."

"...Maybe," Alan said.

He silently gave her credit. It *was* the simplest explanation. But if the aliens had known about mass drivers, why had *Ark Royal's* weapons been such a terrible surprise? He found it hard to believe that they couldn't imagine just how destructive a mass driver could be. The human race had worried about accidentally striking Earth a long time before the first cloudscoops had been constructed around Saturn.

"It still raises the question of precisely where the HE3 is *going*," he mused. "It isn't as if they need to ship it from system to system."

"And you are being an idiot," Abigail said. Her fingers started unfastening her shipsuit, revealing her breasts. A moment later, she was naked. It was easy to tell that she'd removed all the hair below her neckline. "I didn't bring you here to discuss the aliens, you know."

Alan flushed. He couldn't help staring at her, even though it was hardly the first time he'd seen her naked. Abigail was...hard. Maybe not physically, although her muscles were clearly visible as she flexed her arms, but mentally. She knew what she wanted and reached for it, without any sense of vulnerability. It was easy to believe that she'd grown up in a very different society. None of the girls he'd known - and dated - on Earth had the same casual attitude to sex. Even the girls everyone had called sluts hadn't been *quite* so brazen...

"I..."

"I brought you here to forget the aliens," Abigail said. She leaned forward, her bare breasts brushing against his chest. "And I think you want to forget them too."

Alan opened his mouth. "I..."

Abigail kissed him, hard. There was no *love* in the kiss, just a desperate passion...and, perhaps, a determination to forget the universe, just for a few short hours. Alan felt his body stir as her hands pulled him closer, undoing his fastenings. It meant nothing to her, he was sure, and yet...

Enjoy it while it lasts, he told himself. It wasn't as if they had a future together. Or, perhaps, any future at all. *Eat, drink and be merry, for tomorrow might be our last day.*

CHAPTER
THIRTY FOUR

"Jump completed, Captain," Anson said.

"No sign of enemy activity," Poddy added. "We appear to have made it through the tramline without being detected."

Abigail frowned. "Keep an eye on your sensors," she warned. "You know how stealthy those bastards can be."

Commodore Jameson's face appeared in the display. "We will proceed towards our target in silent running," he said, "and hold position at the planned waypoint."

"Understood," Abigail said.

She watched, grimly, as the tiny flotilla slowly made its way into the system. It was not, under normal circumstances, the sort of system that would attract a great deal of attention from the groundpounders, but *she* could see the value in it. A large gas giant and literally *millions* of asteroids…? The belters would see such a system as prime real estate. A handful of settlements had already been established, all of which had either gone silent or been smashed by the aliens. She ground her teeth in silent fury. The settlers probably hadn't even known there was a war on when the alien ships had entered the system and opened fire.

Time ticked away, slowly. There was no sign of any industrialised presence in the system at all, not even an alien starship. She forced herself to remain seated, keeping a wary eye on the display. Was it a trap? Or were the aliens merely following the dictates of whatever they had that passed for logic. Perhaps…perhaps they'd expected the war to be over by now, allowing them to settle where they liked. She'd certainly heard plenty of stories of groundpounders - and belters too, if she were forced to be honest - who'd counted their chickens before they'd hatched.

If it is a trap, it's an odd one, she thought. *They have no way to know when we might come knocking.*

Poddy's console chimed. "I've got the mining station," she said, as a red icon appeared on the display. "It looks roughly comparable to a Type-XI cloudscoop."

Abigail leaned forward as data started to trickle into her console. It was hard to be sure - they were operating at the limits of sensor range - but the alien station *did* look strikingly similar to its human counterpart. But then, there was little *reason* for it to be different. A long thin tube, reaching down into the gas giant's atmosphere; an orbiting station, anchoring the tube high above the gas giant, surrounded by fragile inflatable bags. There would be systems designed to reel in the tube or simply lift it out of the atmosphere, if the gas giant's storms grew too strong for the construction to handle. It was understandable...and yet, there were some elements the sensors couldn't identify. The energy signature was surprisingly high.

She tapped her console. "Vassilios, any ideas?"

"I think they installed a pair of fusion generators in orbit," Drakopoulos said. The Chief Engineer sounded bemused. "I don't understand the *need*, Captain. Their power requirements can't be *that* high."

"Unless it's a superweapon emplacement," Anson suggested. "It could be a hyperspace cannon designed to blow entire *planets* out of orbit."

Drakopoulos made a rude sound. "There's nothing to suggest that the aliens have anything *like* that sort of power," he said. "And I *assure* you, young man, that they wouldn't *need* anything like a hyperspace megagun if they *did*. They could just fly to Earth, stomping anything that got in their way, then demand surrender. There's no need to build a wasteful superweapon when you can use something simpler to get what you want."

"Ouch," Anson said. "So, what do you think it *is* for?"

"I don't know," Drakopoulos said. "Its only purpose, as far as I can tell, is to generate vast amounts of power. But what are they doing with it? I don't know. They *could* be beaming it across space, I suppose, but they certainly have the tech not to need to beam power anywhere...Captain, I am stumped. They don't *need* that thing. We might as well install wooden oars on starships."

Abigail rubbed her forehead. There *had* been installations - solar power satellites - that had beamed power down to Earth, once upon a time, but they'd been retired when fusion power had entered the mainstream. The satellites had been ridiculously vulnerable, if she recalled correctly. Jostling between the Great Powers had put a number of them out of action before the Solar Treaty had been worked out. And then fusion power had rendered them outdated anyway. The aliens had fusion too, didn't they?

They must have, she told herself. *They wouldn't need HE3 if they didn't have fusion power.*

"They might be trying to ignite the gas giant," Anson speculated. "It's supposed to be possible."

"A great many things are supposed to be possible," Drakopoulos snapped. "Let's see, shall we? Jupiter, one of the largest gas giants in explored space, simply doesn't have anything like the mass it needs to turn into a star. And dumping excess mass into the planet would be pretty much impossible, unless we're prepared to spend thousands of years doing it. And then we'd have to somehow start a fusion process that would turn the gas giant into a star...yeah, it's theoretically possible. Practical? Not a hope in hell."

"And they wouldn't be trying to ignite a gas giant anywhere near our territory," Abigail added. "Any top secret projects of theirs would be carried out on the other side of their space."

"This system *was* surveyed years ago," Poddy agreed. "We couldn't have missed the alien presence."

"Unless it was noted, logged and classified," Anson countered. "The groundpounders put a hell of a lot of effort into building up their navies, didn't they?"

Abigail resisted the urge to roll her eyes like a schoolgirl. The belters *had* been muttering about the vast expenditure on interstellar battle fleets - and wondering if the groundpounders had known about the aliens a long time before Vera Cruz - but she doubted it. Yes, they had built powerful space navies; yes, they had prepared for war...and yet, groundpounders had never needed excuses to go to war with each other. They simply didn't grasp that there was enough for everyone, if they made full use of space. But then, the aliens didn't seem to grasp it either.

"Signal from the flag," Poddy said. "We're to hold position at the RV point and prepare to attack."

"Understood," Abigail said. "I..."

An alarm chimed. "Report!"

"We have a contact, bearing...it came from Tramline Four," Poddy snapped. "One of the weaker tramlines!"

"And one that leads to Paradox, if the astrographers are right," Abigail mused. "I wonder..."

She looked down at her console, silently calculating vectors in her head. Assuming the alien contact hadn't changed course, it *had* come directly from Paradox. And that meant...

The mystery fleet carrier? The contact didn't *look* like a fleet carrier, but that didn't prove anything. *Or something more akin to our escort carriers?*

"Orders from the flag," Poddy said. "We're to prepare to launch fighters at Point Alpha, then engage the fuelling station with mass drivers."

"Understood," Abigail said. "Inform the CIC, then prepare to launch fighters."

"Aye, Captain."

———

Alan hated himself for thinking it, but there was one advantage to Flight Lieutenant Ronald Dennison getting himself blown into atoms. It had opened up a slot in Herring Squadron, a slot he could fill. It wasn't as though he *had* to be in the CIC, not when there were four other escort carriers and Commodore Jameson's warships. Having a spare starfighter in open space might make the difference between a successful engagement and inglorious defeat.

He braced himself as the starfighter was rocketed out into space, the drives coming online a second later. Two-thirds of their entire starfighter strength was aimed directly at the alien ship, the remaining third held in reserve...moments later, kinetic projectiles appeared on the display as they were fired towards the cloudscoop. Jameson had clearly given up on his stated intention to try to convince the aliens to surrender. Unless the cloudscoop was something truly fantastical, it was doomed. No human cloudscoop could alter position fast enough to avoid a spray of kinetic projectiles.

And even if they did manage to alter position, we'd just throw more rocks, Alan reminded himself. Mass drivers weren't *that* effective against starships, once the ships knew what to watch for, but they were lethal against unmoving targets. *It isn't as if we have a shortage of space junk to throw at them.*

The alien starship slowly - very slowly - started to take on shape and form. It was an odd design, something so strange that the warbook seemed unable to determine if it was a warship or a freighter. Alan eyed it warily, checking and rechecking the torpedoes slung under his starfighter's stubby little wings. *Haddock* would be hard to pin down too, at least the first time the aliens encountered her. Now...now they presumably knew how to pick out an escort carrier from the freighters.

New icons - red icons - flashed to life on the display. "Starfighters," Whitehead snapped. "I say again, starfighters!"

"Squadrons One through Four, break and attack," Jameson ordered. "Squadrons Five and Six, engage the enemy starship!"

Tomlinson will be happy, Alan thought wryly, as he twisted his starfighter into an evasive pattern. *Finally, a chance to dogfight without getting a new asshole torn for his pains.*

The enemy starfighters were already firing, blasts of plasma tearing through space. Alan yanked his starfighter through another series of evasive manoeuvres, counting on the computers to fire whenever they saw a clear shot. The aliens were good, part of his mind noted. They weren't staying exposed long enough for reflexes - even electronic reflexes - to be sure of a hit. He punched through the alien formation, then concentrated on luring the alien pilots into a series of dogfights. It would keep them busy long enough to allow the other human starfighters a chance to take out their carrier.

"Tomlinson, I hope you're watching this," Alan said. "You nearly made *their* mistake."

"Told you so," Greene carolled. "Watch your back!"

Alan nodded, twisting his craft away from an alien starfighter and taking advantage of the brief exposure to fire on a second enemy fighter. It exploded into dust, allowing him a moment to fly free. The remaining squadrons were already launching their torpedoes against the alien starship, slamming five bomb-pumped lasers into its hull. Alan whooped - he couldn't help himself - as the alien ship exploded. Whatever else happened, the alien starfighters wouldn't be going home.

"It was probably a modified escort carrier," one of the analysts said. "I don't think it was designed to handle long-term deployments."

"Later," Alan snapped. It was fascinating, but he needed to concentrate. The aliens had lost their ticket home, which meant...he cursed under his breath. They didn't have anything to lose. "Watch them!"

The alien starfighters rotated and roared towards the flotilla. They were fast, Alan noted, as he gunned his engines in response. *Very* fast. They screamed towards the flotilla, firing madly into the heart of the human formation. The flotilla returned fire, blasting away at the incoming craft with point defence, but it wasn't enough. Alan barely had a second to realise that the alien craft were going to ram HMS *Daring* before four starfighters slammed into the destroyer's hull, blowing it into an expanding cloud of plasma. A fifth struck HMMS *Butcher's* flight deck, rendering it useless. Alan groaned. They were going to have to rotate two entire squadrons through the remaining fleet carriers, unless the engineers somehow managed to repair the flight deck. But it looked as though they'd need a miracle...

"Objective complete," Jameson said, as the last of the enemy starfighters was blown out of space. "I say again, objective complete."

Alan frowned. The mining station was gone...he looked at the records and felt his frown deepen. There had been a *big* explosion when the kinetic projectiles had struck their target, vaporising most of the station. The remains of the tube had fallen into the gas giant, where it would either be torn apart by the storms or crushed by the planet's gravity. Whatever secrets the station had been hiding were gone, now. There was nothing for the boffins to examine...

"All ships, resume silent running as soon as the starfighters have returned to their carriers," Jameson ordered. "We'll depart once they've all been recovered."

And start crawling out of the system, Alan thought. The mystery nagged at his mind, refusing to leave him alone. What - *what* - had the aliens been *doing?* It was still bothering him as he landed on the flight deck and handed the starfighter over to the ground crew. *What were they trying to do?*

"They think it was an escort carrier of some kind," Maddy said, when he entered the CIC. "I forwarded their report to you."

Alan nodded his thanks and sat down to read the report. Thankfully, Jameson's analysts weren't as verbose as the analysts on Earth, but still… the aliens had somehow crammed six squadrons of fighters into a hull that hadn't been *that* much bigger than *Haddock*. He couldn't help wondering just what sort of conditions the aliens *liked*. Naval crews were used to being cramped, but there were limits. Putting so many crews into such a small space would cause mutinies. He'd probably join them.

A low quiver ran through the ship as she picked up speed, heading back towards the tramline on a dogleg course. If there were alien reinforcements on the way…he looked back at the datapad as the pieces suddenly fell into place. The whole mining station had actually been a power generator, storing power for alien starfighters! They used power cells, like humanity, but theirs were far more efficient. The more he looked at it, the more he was sure he was right.

They'd need to be, if they're superheating plasma for their guns, he thought. His hands danced over the console, sketching out the concept for the analysts. *They might need to recharge their batteries after every encounter.*

The whole system struck him as a little makeshift. He almost gave it up as a bad idea when he remembered just how many limitations *Haddock* had, compared to a fleet carrier. Or even one of the proposed purpose-built *escort* carriers. The aliens might just have been - no, they would be - desperate to produce additional carriers as quickly as possible. They'd converted a freighter into a carrier, then rigged up a prefabricated cloud-scoop to provide additional power.

And then they raided through the tramlines, he told himself. *They must have been very sure they'd take Aquitaine.*

He sent the report to the analysts, then turned his attention to the in-system display. Interplanetary space seemed empty, which suggested they'd managed to get in and out before any alien reinforcements arrived. And yet...he wondered, as he studied the tramlines, just where the aliens were basing themselves. If they had systems that could only be reached through weak tramlines, they could deploy all of their forces without having to worry about human counterattacks. Coming to think of it, they probably had a rough idea just how long it would take humanity to duplicate their modified Puller Drives.

Not as long as they think, he thought. *We know they can use the weak tramlines - and knowing is half the battle.*

"Captain," Poddy said. "Long-range sensors are detecting two alien carriers and a number of escorts, heading directly towards the gas giant."

Abigail tensed as new icons appeared in the display, surrounded by red spheres to remind her of the time delay. The alien ships could be anywhere within the spheres...thankfully, they weren't heading towards the human ships. And that meant...what? A direct attack on Aquitaine? Or reinforcements for Yeller that had arrived too late? She suspected they would probably never know. The alien ships didn't seem to know where the human ships had gone after the brief, savage engagement.

"Keep an eye on them," she ordered. It would take hours for the aliens to catch up with the flotilla, which meant...they might just head straight to Aquitaine instead. Or go back to wherever they'd come from. Losing the fuelling station wouldn't impede them *too* much, unless their power cores were primitive. She found that rather hard to believe. "Anson, ETA tramline?"

"Forty minutes," Anson said. "They *could* be trying to distract us..."

Abigail doubted it, but she kept an eye on the sensors anyway. Most experienced spacers would know better than to try something so clever that it was effectively impractical, yet there was no shortage of inexperienced groundpounders out there. She wondered, absently, if the aliens drew lines between spacers and groundpounders, or if they were nothing more than spacers. They certainly seemed *used* to operating in three dimensions.

But if they're spacers, why would they want our worlds? It puzzled her. There were reports suggesting that the aliens had definitely landed on New Russia, primarily along the planet's coastlines. And yet, there appeared to have been very little actual contact. *What do they have to gain?*

She pushed the thought out of her mind. They'd sneaked into an enemy-held system, blasted a target and - for good measure - taken out a makeshift enemy carrier. It wasn't a *great* victory, certainly not compared to *Ark Royal*, but it was something. The enemy had been given a bloody nose...

...And who knew? It might *just* be enough to convince them to sue for peace.

Except we took out a minor station and an expendable ship, she reminded herself. *That isn't going to slow them down for long - if at all. The war is very far from over.*

CHAPTER
THIRTY FIVE

Alan couldn't help disliking Admiral Louis Delacroix on sight.

It wasn't the man's general appearance, which was so neat and tidy and absolutely perfect that he was tempted to believe that Delacroix had never flown anything more dangerous than a desk. Alan had looked up Delacroix's record and discovered that the older man had a reasonably long and honourable career, including two fleet carrier commands. And it wasn't that the admiral was French, either. The French military had a long and respectable history, ranging from the Hundred Years War to the Paris Intifada, where it had saved the country from decades of political mismanagement. It was...

He presents himself as a dashing military officer, Alan thought. He'd been told, years ago, that one could have good units or ones that *looked* good, but never units that were both at once. Perhaps it was just the old prejudice against someone who spent far too long on their appearance rearing its ugly head. He was too old to waste time making himself look fashionable. *And it makes him harder to take seriously.*

Admiral Delacroix stood in the centre of the briefing room, waiting for the last of his senior officers to take their places. Alan stood next to Abigail, behind Commodore Jameson. He wasn't sure why *he'd* been summoned, unless the French were feeling paranoid about communications security. Too many officers were going to be away from their command decks for the next few hours, giving the aliens a priceless opportunity if they wanted to attack. A holoconference would have made much more sense. But he supposed Delacroix wanted to meet them all in person, at least once. A trickle of multinational reinforcements had made their way into Aquitaine, but almost none of it had been planned. Delacroix didn't know any of his new subordinates personally.

"Thank you for coming," Delacroix said, as the hatch slammed closed. He spoke perfect English, like every other naval officer, but there was a twinge of Paris to his voice. Perhaps he was one of the nationalists who resented English's predominance throughout the human sphere. "We have much to discuss."

He paused for dramatic effect. Alan resisted - barely - the temptation to roll his eyes.

"Over the last two weeks, we have carried out a number of scouting and raiding operations to determine precisely where the aliens have based themselves," Delacroix continued. A starchart flashed into existence, floating over his head. "As you can see, the aliens have secured Bavaria and sent raiding parties into Talofa and through the tramline into Aquitaine. We believe the aliens have actually *landed* on Bavaria, but we don't have any contact with the colonists on the ground. It is quite possible that they've been slaughtered."

Or dispersed, Alan thought. The colonists *should* have had some warning. *They might have slipped away from the colonies before the aliens arrived.*

"Intelligence estimates that the aliens intend to thrust through the tramlines and into Aquitaine once they have sufficient force," Delacroix informed them. Red arrows appeared on the display. "Destroying the task force - and the orbital installations - will give the aliens a chance to secure the whole sector, even if they don't land on the planet itself. The only thing delaying them, we believe, is the recent defeat they suffered. Right now, they're reassessing the situation."

We think they're reassessing the situation, Alan thought. *Ark Royal* was powerful - and her existence had come as a complete surprise to the aliens - but she was only one ship. The aliens still had a significant advantage, particularly when *Ark Royal* was hundreds of light years away. *The aliens still pack one hell of a punch.*

Delacroix smiled. "This gives us the opportunity to take the offensive and liberate Bavaria," he informed them. "The majority of the task force will proceed directly through Talofa and slip into Bavaria, whereupon the aliens will be engaged and destroyed. Any alien installations on the surface will be captured or bombed from orbit, depending on the exact situation. Ideally, we'll finally have a chance to capture live aliens - or, at least, video footage of our enemies. Once the system is liberated, we'll rescue as many colonists as possible and fall back to Aquitaine. We will make no attempt to hold the system permanently."

Because that would pin our forces in place, Alan thought. *And the system itself is largely worthless.*

He frowned, considering the options. He'd been - he *was* - a starfighter pilot. Aggression had practically been drummed into him at the academy. He'd been taught to take the offensive at all times. And yet...they weren't risking a handful of starfighters or even the escort carriers, but two fleet carriers and their escorts. He hated to admit it, yet there *was* such a thing as being *too* aggressive. Too much was at stake if Admiral Delacroix took his entire fleet to Bavaria.

And yet, he could see the admiral's logic. Humanity *couldn't* just sit around and wait to be hit, not when the aliens still had plenty of advantages. Taking the offensive and knocking them back on their heels might just give humanity a chance to win - or, at least, enough breathing space to put newer weapons and defences into mass production. He'd read enough reports suggesting that there *were* options that allowed humanity to feel some hope for the future, if humanity had time. And, if their intelligence was accurate, Admiral Delacroix would have a numerical advantage. It might just be big enough to tip the scales in his favour.

"I admit there are dangers," Delacroix said, in response to a question from one of his newer subordinates. "However, there are also dangers in doing nothing."

There was a long pause. "The task force will depart tomorrow morning," he said. "I would prefer to keep the mission - and its objective - a secret, but unfortunately that isn't going to be possible. Still, we'll have a complete communications blackout from the moment this conference ends. All outgoing messages will be stored in buffers until the fleet departs."

Alan nodded. He wasn't inclined to believe the panicky reports of alien shapeshifters or humanoid androids capable of impersonating living humans, but…there *was* a very real danger that the aliens could pick up and translate human transmissions. A single leak would be enough to doom the operation, if the aliens had a clue where the fleet was going. They could mass their forces to meet Delacroix or simply avoid battle, forcing him to choose between inglorious retreat or permanent stalemate.

"You'll receive your specific orders this afternoon," Delacroix informed them. "We'll start drilling as a unified task force as soon as we cross the tramline into Talofa. It won't be enough, but we'll just have to cope. Time is not on our side."

No, Alan agreed silently. *Time is definitely not on our side.*

"If you have questions or concerns, please don't hesitate to bring them to me," Delacroix finished. "Until then…good luck to us all."

Alan glanced at Abigail as a handful of officers started firing questions at Delacroix. He had questions and concerns of his own, but he was too junior to say them in front of so many senior officers. Commodore Jameson probably had the same concerns himself, ones that would need to be raised before they left Aquitaine. They'd have to discuss the matter when they returned to *Haddock*.

"It looks like a workable plan," Abigail muttered. "Why do I have a bad feeling about it?"

"Probably because it hinges on too many unknowns," Alan muttered back. He could see Delacroix's point, but…he couldn't help thinking that the older man might have read too much into the intelligence reports. The aliens *might* be reassessing the situation or they might have decided they could still win or…it was hard enough to predict how *humans* would react in any given situation. Predicting the aliens was almost impossible. "On the other hand, Delacroix has enough sense to back off if it's clear we can't win."

Unless we get mouse-trapped, he thought. *There are too many possibilities.*

The thought chilled him to the bone. The aliens might just wait until the task force was too deep within the target system to withdraw, then close the jaws of their trap. If, of course, there *was* a trap. The aliens would probably have a few hours of warning - Alan doubted the fleet could leave Aquitaine and slip through Talofa without being detected - but would they have long enough to devise and prepare an ambush?

"And what," Abigail asked, "if you're wrong?"

"Then we fight to the death," Alan said. It wasn't a very comforting answer - and the sharp look Abigail shot him suggested she wasn't very happy with it - yet there weren't any other options. Commodore Jameson presumably had veto power over his ships being involved in the battle, but *using* it without a *very* good reason would spark off a diplomatic crisis. "And yet, the plan does seem workable."

"We shall see," Abigail said.

Delacroix dismissed the meeting. Commodore Jameson turned to look at them as the gathered officers headed for the hatch.

"We'll discuss this later, over the laser link," he said, shortly. "But yes, the plan does seem workable."

Alan was too old to be embarrassed at being overheard. "Yes, sir," he said. "On the other hand, the risks..."

"Are manageable, apparently," Commodore Jameson said. He rose, nodding towards the nearest hatch. "And Delacroix himself will be in command."

Hah, Alan thought.

It was something, he supposed. He'd seen too many desk jockeys issue orders that were - at best - impractical, if not borderline suicidal or simply impossible. Delacroix was too experienced an officer for that...and *his* arse was on the line too. And yet, Delacroix had plenty of reason to interpret the data in his own favour. Captain Theodore Smith had been practically *drowned* in decorations from all over the world. Delacroix might want some of that glory for himself.

"And besides, we can't just sit here," Jameson added. "Taking the offensive may just convince the aliens that they've bit off more than they can chew."

———

Abigail hadn't been too pleased when she'd heard the mission orders, although she had to admit - ruefully - that she was in no position to disagree. The operation seemed workable, yet alarm bells were ringing in her head. Perhaps it was the grim awareness that they'd already had far too many brushes with death…or, perhaps, it was the remembered slaughter at New Russia. The aliens were just too powerful to take lightly. She spent the shuttle ride back to the ship thinking of possible options, but nothing came to mind. There didn't seem to be any way to avoid the mission.

And besides, we might make the difference between victory and defeat, she thought. *Haddock* had faced the aliens before, which was more than could be said for either of Delacroix's fleet carriers. *We know the dangers even if the naval crews don't.*

She shook her head as they docked at the airlock. The naval crews couldn't be faulted for underestimating the alien threat before New Russia, but they had no excuse now. They'd all seen the records from the battle, they'd all watched in horror as the fleet carriers were torn apart by alien starfighters. The French would have bolted extra armour to their hulls, she was sure, but it might not be enough to save their ships. And yet, Delacroix thought he had an ace or two up his sleeve. Abigail hoped he was right.

There's at least one other alien fleet carrier nearby, she thought. It was possible that the alien starship had been ordered back to New Russia, but they couldn't *count* on it. *Who knows where that ship is now?*

Anson and Maddy met them at the hatch. "Mum," Anson said. "Can we talk to you?"

Abigail eyed him for a long moment. "I suppose," she said, although she had a feeling it wasn't a conversation she wanted to have. "We'll talk in my cabin."

She bid goodbye to Alan - he'd have to brief his pilots, then start training simulations - and led the way along the corridor. There was only one reason Anson and Maddy would want to talk to her together, unless…she hoped she was wrong, even though she had a nasty feeling she was right. She cursed under her breath as she opened the cabin, motioning for them to sit on the bed. There just wasn't enough *room*. She promised herself, silently, that she'd arrange for bigger cabins if she ever bought another ship. But then, that would mean reducing the space that would otherwise be devoted to storage…

"Here I am," she said, closing the hatch. She thought about offering tea, then decided against it. "What do you want to talk about?"

Anson exchanged a glance with Maddy, then looked at Abigail. "We would like your permission to wed," he said. "We…"

Abigail barely heard the rest of the sentence. They would *like* her permission to wed? Of course they'd *like* it, but they didn't *need* it. Anson was her son, not one of her husbands. It wasn't *her* place to forbid the match, even though she doubted Maddy would make a good wife. There were some mistakes that Anson had to make on his own.

She looked at Maddy. "Are you pregnant?"

Maddy coloured. Her face was almost as red as her hair. "No, Captain," she said. "I…I do have the implant, you know."

"I didn't know," Abigail said, truthfully. "I'm glad to hear that you were careful."

Anson shot her a sharp look. Abigail ignored it. Birth control implants were freely available in the belt, but they weren't so common on Earth. It hadn't been *that* long since the Great Powers had been doing everything in their power to encourage their citizens to have as many children as possible. The Royal Navy wouldn't want its crewwomen getting pregnant while on active duty, but she didn't really expect groundpounders to go for the logical solution.

And besides, Maddy was in jail, Abigail thought. If half the stories about groundpounder jails were true, it was easy to see why so many people were desperate to avoid them. *The implant might have expired before she was offered the chance to serve her country instead.*

"We have discussed it," Anson said. "If you're unwilling to accept us as a married couple, we can jump ship when we return to Earth and find other employment…"

"Which won't be so easy in the middle of a war," Abigail pointed out. *Anson* wouldn't have any trouble finding a freighter willing to take him on, under normal circumstances, but Maddy was a whole other story. It would be hard to find a freighter prepared to take both of them. And, of course, there was a war on. "The Navy might class you as a deserter."

"I'm not a naval officer," Anson pointed out.

"Technically, you are," Abigail said. "And *she*" - Abigail pointed a finger at Maddy - "very definitely *is* a naval officer."

She met Maddy's eyes, silently daring the younger woman to lie to her. "Did you tell him about your past?"

"Yes, Captain," Maddy said. There was no hint of a lie in her expression. "I told him everything."

"Oh, *goody*," Abigail said.

"Mum," Anson said. "How many Belters would be arrested if we enforced groundpounder law?"

Touché, Abigail conceded. "Too many," she said, out loud. "But are you sure - are you both sure - that you want to get *married*?"

"Yes," Anson said.

Abigail sighed, inwardly. God knew she'd made some relationship mistakes in her life, but she'd never fallen in love with a convicted criminal. She might be sharing her bunk with Alan, yet she wasn't in *love* with him. Of course not. Sex and love were two different things and she was too old to pretend otherwise. The relationship wouldn't last past the end of the war.

She took a long breath. "Then *listen*," she said. "Sex is one thing. Marriage is quite another. You will be sharing your lives with each other - and others, if you open the marriage. You will discover - *both* of you will discover - that you will have to change to accommodate your partner. You will *also* discover that your partner has habits you won't like, habits that can - that will - become maddening after a few months of sharing lives. And you will discover that a marriage cannot be so easily dissolved as a sexual relationship, particularly if you have children."

Her lips twitched. "Your father has a habit of singing in the shower," she added. "I used to feel as though he was deliberately torturing me."

Anson flushed. "Mum!"

"And your Uncle Mattie likes spicy food that no one else can eat," Abigail said. "And those are *minor* problems. You may discover that there are bigger ones when you live together."

She looked from Anson to Maddy and back again. There wasn't any point in forbidding the banns, not when Anson was clearly determined to go through with it. He was stubborn, something he'd inherited from both of his parents. And while Maddy wasn't a suitable bride, there was no point in harping on that now. Who knew? Perhaps she'd do better after the war. She'd certainly get her pardon and discharge when the navy no longer required her services.

And Anson is right, she thought. *Quite a few Belters ran away from Earth.*

"I am required to give you a week to consider," she said. It was true enough. "And if you still want to get married, I will give you my blessing. And I will even perform the ceremony."

She took a breath. "But right now, I believe you have work to do," she said. "We'll be leaving in a few hours."

"Aye, Captain," Anson said.

CHAPTER
THIRTY SIX

"Transit complete, Captain," Anson said. He sounded reassuringly normal, for all that they'd been discussing his marriage only a few scant hours ago. "The task force has jumped with us."

"Laser links establishing…now," Poddy added. The display rapidly started to fill up with green and blue icons. "No enemy targets within detection range."

Abigail nodded, stiffly. Admiral Delacroix had led the task force through the tramline and across Talofa with a speed she could only admire, even though it had pushed her drives to the limit. It wasn't particularly stealthy, but the odds of the aliens *not* having Aquitaine under some form of surveillance were incalculably low. They'd see the task force depart and either deduce its target or take advantage of its absence to strike at Aquitaine.

And Bavaria is a poor trade for Aquitaine, she thought. *The aliens would probably be happy to swap, if they realised that was an option.*

"Signal from the flag," Poddy said. "The task force is to advance on the target at once."

"Understood," Abigail said. "Helm, keep us in formation."

"Aye, Captain," Anson said.

Abigail leaned back in her command chair, trying to ignore the discomfiting feeling in her stomach. There was no sign of a trap, but that was meaningless. Bavaria was largely worthless, unless the aliens genuinely wanted human slaves. The aliens might have seen the task force coming and withdrawn or...there were just too many options. And far too many places for an alien fleet to hide. And yet...

Her eyes crept to the display. Admiral Delacroix wasn't being foolish, even though Abigail thought he was overconfident. The task force was ringed by sensor probes and pickets, watching constantly for stealthed enemy ships. There was no way the enemy would get an attack force into range without being detected, although she doubted the sensor probes would give the task force *that* much warning. The aliens would have plenty of time to get into position. Or simply to form a blocking formation and dare the humans to try to punch through it.

Bavaria itself was a blue icon on the display, well within the life-bearing zone. The system was still in the first stage of development, but there *should* have been a cloudscoop and a handful of mining stations...there *had* been, she knew. The aliens had blasted them out of space when they'd arrived, along with the orbiting entry station and a handful of communication relay satellites. They probably hadn't done much harm in the short term, but the losses would be quite serious in the long term. Replacing the destroyed installations would be quite expensive.

And Germany might not have the resources to do it, she reminded herself. The Germans had come late to the interstellar party, if she recalled correctly. Germany itself had nearly been destroyed during the Age of Unrest. Even now, the French and Poles were suspicious of their former enemy regaining its power. Abigail freely admitted that groundpounder politics made little sense to her, but she could understand their concern. *Germany is always either the victim or the victimiser.*

She pushed the thought aside as red icons flashed into existence in front of her. Alien ships...five alien ships, already thrusting away from the planet. Her eyes narrowed as she noticed what was missing. There were no fleet carriers...no carriers at all, as far as she could tell. It was impossible to be sure, but it *looked* as though the only alien ships in the system were destroyers. They weren't powerless - she knew from grim experience just how powerful alien weapons could be - yet they weren't enough to take on the task force.

"Long-range probes are picking up three other ships," Poddy said. "They're bugging out."

Abigail frowned, reminding herself - once again - of the damned time delay. The alien ships were heading towards the furthest tramline, already pushing their drives to the limits. Her warbook insisted that the alien ships were freighters, although - again - it was impossible to be sure. But the simple fact they were running certainly suggested they knew they couldn't stand and fight. There was no hint that they were on the verge of reversing course.

"It certainly looks that way," she said, shortly. "But the other five ships are heading towards us."

She frowned, again. The aliens *might* be trying to collect accurate data before the engagement. Admiral Delacroix was using his ECM aggressively, making it harder for the aliens to calculate *precisely* how many ships he was leading into battle. The aliens would certainly want to know what the odds were before it was too late to back off...they might just have classed the five destroyers as expendable. Or the destroyers themselves might intend to reverse course, before they reached the point of no return. It made a certain kind of sense.

"Contact in two hours," Poddy said. "Assuming nothing changes..."

"Yeah," Abigail said.

She watched the in-system display, expecting a flurry of red icons to pop into existence at any moment. And yet, she suspected the aliens were waiting patiently for the task force to get further into the system, further from the tramline leading straight back to Aquitaine - and safety. An illusionary safety, but safety nonetheless. Unless...she wanted to believe there were no alien ships within the system, yet she knew better. Surely, the aliens wouldn't throw away five destroyers for *nothing*.

Admiral Delacroix's face appeared in the display. "Starfighters will deploy in twenty minutes," he ordered, calmly. "Those enemy ships will not be allowed to escape."

Abigail nodded, slowly, as more detailed orders appeared in front of her. The escort carriers would launch first, a wise move given how long it took them to flush their decks. It wasn't ideal - not all of the escort carriers had trained together - but it would have to do. Besides, it would keep the regular pilots fresh and ready to launch at a moment's notice.

"Pass the word to the CAG," she ordered. "And then stand ready to launch."

———

Under other circumstances, Alan thought as his starfighter rocketed into space, *the task force would be impressive.*

It *was* an impressive sight, he admitted privately. Two fleet carriers, seven escort carriers, seventeen destroyers and a couple of makeshift missile ships…it was a formidable force, one that would have been a serious threat only a few short months ago. But now…he had no idea how well the makeshift armour would hold, if the aliens pushed an offensive against the task force. And they would, he knew. Bavaria and even Aquitaine were petty, compared to the chance to take a shot at two fleet carriers. Replacing even *one* of them would take months.

"The CSP is moving into covering position," Savage said. "They'll be ready to cover us if the aliens have a surprise up their sleeves."

"Hey, boss," Greene said. "We don't know if they *wear* sleeves."

"I suppose they probably don't fly their starships naked," Savage said, deadpan. "Unless we're facing the loincloths from Stellar Star."

"If we are, I want to surrender," Greene said.

Alan snorted, rudely. "I don't think we could be that lucky," he said. "And Stellar Star only gets out of trouble because she has a friendly scriptwriter."

"And a smashing set of tits," Greene countered. "And…"

Patsy snickered. "All they'd have to do is dangle a naked whore in front of you," she said, nastily. "And you'd surrender so quickly that everyone else would be left in the lurch."

Savage cleared his throat, loudly. "If we could *kindly* focus on the matter at hand…"

"Just when I had him on the ropes," Patsy said. "I…"

"Quiet," Savage snapped. "We'll be entering engagement range in five minutes."

Alan nodded, feeling old. Hadn't there been a time when he'd enjoyed banter? Hadn't there been a time when jokes about firing at Will had been hilariously funny? Hadn't there been a time…but then, he'd been promoted out of a cockpit. His sense of appropriate humour had clearly gone downhill. Or possibly uphill. Judith had always been trying to convince him to appreciate some of the finer things in life. They just hadn't felt much finer to him.

He gritted his teeth as the alien ships started to go active, their sensors tracking the human starfighters with an intensity that worried him. The Royal Navy had had plenty of time to improve its tactics, but that was true of the aliens too. They'd learnt a few hard lessons of their own. And their destroyers were spreading out…somehow, he doubted it was a good sign. Their weapons made the prospect of friendly fire all the more alarming.

"On my mark, break and attack," Savage ordered. "I say again; on my mark, break and attack."

Here goes nothing, Alan thought.

The alien ships showed up clearly now, instantly recognisable as the starships that had brought so much death and destruction to the Royal Navy. He was no longer inclined to laugh at their melted appearance, or the way they spread out to avoid accidentally hitting each other, not when he knew how dangerous they were. They were already firing, spewing plasma bolt after plasma bolt into space. The odds of actually hitting something were low, but they were already breaking up the human formations. *That* was worth more than a little effort. Besides, it wasn't as if they could run out of ammunition.

"Mark," Savage snapped.

Alan yanked the starfighter into a twisting formation, jerking randomly backwards and forwards as the squadron raced towards its target. The alien starship grew larger and larger on the display, firing madly in all directions. They didn't seem inclined to try and run, even though they had to know they were badly outnumbered. A handful of human starfighters were blown out of space, but the remainder closed to attack range and opened fire. The aliens weren't even prepared for the bomb-pumped lasers. They didn't focus on the torpedoes until it was far too late.

"Twelve direct hits," Savage said. "We *got* the bastard!"

"I think we over-got the bastard," Greene said, as the alien starship disintegrated. "They didn't even hit *half* of our torpedoes!"

"That won't happen again," Alan said. On the display, the remaining alien starships were already updating their fire control protocols. Smart of them, he admitted grudgingly. They'd clearly assumed they were safe, only to discover - the hard way - that a torpedo didn't actually *have* to slam into their hull to do damage. Their hulls weren't tough enough to stand up to a bomb-pumped laser. "They'll be ready for us next time."

And we're lucky they didn't realise what happened during the last engagement, he added, silently. He'd assumed the aliens *would* have noticed during *Haddock's* raiding mission, but word didn't seem to have spread. Perhaps no one - including automated sensor platforms - had survived to make a full report. *That won't last, not when the freighters are already well out of interception range.*

He followed Savage away from the remains of the alien starship and watched, grimly, as the remaining destroyers were obliterated. The aliens forced humanity to pay for the kills - seven human starfighters died during the final attack run - but the loss rate was squarely in humanity's favour. Alan puzzled it over as the starfighters regrouped and started to return to their ships, trying to understand what the aliens might be doing. Had the aliens overestimated their defences? Or had they assumed they could break contact before it was too late?

His blood ran cold. *Or are they trying to lure us deeper into the system?*

———

"There appear to be no more enemy starships within attack range," Admiral Delacroix said, shortly. "Long-range probes and scans have revealed nothing. We will therefore continue our offensive against Bavaria."

I suppose you couldn't declare victory and simply turn around now, Abigail thought. It would be a poor return for all the effort Delacroix had invested in deploying the task force, but it *would* be a victory…of sorts. She had no doubt that groundpounder spin doctors would turn the destruction of five destroyers into the greatest victory since *Ark Royal* had stopped the alien advance towards Earth cold. *No, you have to press onwards into the unknown.*

She watched as new orders popped up in front of her. They were reassuringly simple: rearm the starfighters, then prepare to deploy them as soon as the enemy showed himself. And yet, she couldn't help feeling as though they were flying right into a trap. But where *were* the enemy ships?

Anson glanced at her. "Mum?"

"Stay in formation," Abigail ordered. She was too worried about the situation to rebuke him for calling her *Mum* when they were both on duty. "And keep a very close eye on those sensors."

A handful of new icons flashed into existence as the task force steadily approached Bavaria, alarming her until she realised they were nothing more than alien satellites. It was possible they were automated weapons platforms - or simple mines - but they were nowhere near powerful enough to slow the task force. Admiral Delacroix sent orders through the command network, ordering his destroyers to engage the satellites with railguns. One by one, the satellites vanished from the display. It didn't look as though any of them had tried to offer resistance.

"Orbital space is clear," Poddy said. "The probes are expanding outwards now."

Abigail nodded, curtly. The aliens might have wanted to trap the task force against the planet, but if that was the case they'd missed the shuttle. She knew from bitter experience just how good the alien sensor masks were, yet it was hard to believe they could hide a fleet powerful enough to destroy Admiral Delacroix's task force within attack range. Maybe the alien fleet was on the other side of the system, but...if it was, it wasn't going to be able to impede the task force at all. Admiral Delacroix would have plenty of time to decide if he wanted to fight or withdraw.

Unless they're off stomping Aquitaine instead, she thought grimly. Aquitaine wasn't exactly undefended, but she doubted the fixed defences could stand up to an all-out attack. *That would be a bitter end to the whole adventure.*

Poddy glanced up. "New orders, Captain," she said. "Carriers and escorts are to remain in interplanetary space, destroyers are to secure the high orbitals and demand surrender."

At least we're not gambling everything, Abigail thought. *Just...too much.*

"Do as he says," she ordered. It would give the task force room to manoeuvre, if the aliens really *were* lurking nearby. "Have we picked up any sign of alien installations?"

"I'm not sure," Poddy said. "I've got the unfiltered live feed from the drones, but I'm not sure how to assess it."

"Just point to anything that looks out of place," Anson suggested.

Poddy sneered at him. "You mean like your face?"

Abigail slapped her console. "Concentrate, both of you," she said. She took a long breath, calming herself. As stressed as she was, she shouldn't be taking it out on her children. "Can you see anything out of place?"

"There are a handful of craters in the middle of the colonies," Poddy said, slowly. "My guess is that they bombed anything that might be dangerous from orbit, but..."

She frowned down at her console. "There are a handful of new installations along the coastline, but none of them appear very large," she said. "But they're not shown on the pre-war maps."

Abigail smiled at Poddy's back. "Good thinking," she said. "What *are* they?"

"I don't know," Poddy said. She paused. "Doomed. They're doomed. Admiral Delacroix just sentenced them to death."

So much for trying to take any prisoners, Abigail thought. She checked the live feed herself, trying to determine what had happened to the human colonists. The colonies looked deserted, as far as she could tell. But then, there were plenty of isolated farms where refugees could hide, if they wished. The alien installations seemed deserted too, waves washing against weird half-melted buildings that seemed to blur into the water. *I wonder what happened to the inhabitants.*

She glanced, again, at the display. There was still no sign of anything dangerous. Even the alien freighters had crossed the tramline and vanished. And yet, her sense of foreboding refused to fade. Admiral Delacroix would order a withdrawal soon, wouldn't he? The plan had been to raid the system, not try to liberate it permanently. And yet, what if he refused to leave? Or wanted to take the task force on a long arc towards New Russia? Or...

"They seem to have established contact with the ground," Poddy said. "I don't know what they're talking about, but..."

A red icon flared into life on the display, followed by a dozen more. "New contacts," Poddy snapped. "They just came through Tramline Three! A fleet carrier, four destroyers...seven starships of unknown type. They're heading into the system."

Anson looked up. "Did we take them by surprise?"

Abigail wasn't so sure. It was unlikely the aliens would choose to risk one fleet carrier against two, but...they *might* have different ideas. They certainly had the firepower advantage, even if they didn't have the numerical advantage. And yet, it certainly had the hallmarks of a convoy arriving to discover - too late - that it was in the middle of a battle...

And yet, something was wrong. Something she'd overlooked. But what?

She looked at Poddy. "Time to contact?"

"Seven hours," Poddy reported. "Unless they're a lot faster than we think..."

"Understood," Abigail said. She looked at the display, waiting for orders. Admiral Delacroix's flagship floated in the middle of the formation, looking invincible. She knew, all too well, that that was an illusion. "Plenty of time to withdraw, if necessary."

"Or to fight," Anson said. "We have the advantage, don't we?"

"Maybe," Abigail said. "But it would be unwise to *count* on it."

CHAPTER
THIRTY SEVEN

"Well," Bennett said. "*That's* a turn up for the books, isn't it?"

"It certainly looks that way," Alan agreed.

He shook his head as he sat in the CIC and monitored the live feed from the long-range drones. Two fleet carriers against one...he understood, all too well, why Admiral Delacroix was having problems deciding how to proceed. On one hand, the numerical advantage favoured humanity; on the other, the prospect of losing *both* of his fleet carriers was paralysing. Depending on the outcome, Delacroix would go down in history as a hero - or a bloody fool.

Commodore Jameson's face flashed into existence on the display. "The colonists have requested evacuation," he said. "We're going to pick up a number of refugees before withdrawing from the system."

Alan frowned. *That* suggested that Delacroix wasn't planning to seek engagement, but there were no formal orders from the flag. And that meant...what? Delacroix was playing his cards very close to his chest. Alan resisted the urge to com the admiral personally and demand orders, knowing it would only get him in trouble. Instead, he forwarded the orders to Abigail and started to consider options. The escort carrier was already too cramped to take more than a handful of refugees.

"Seven hours to engagement," Bennett said. He sounded surprisingly thoughtful. "How many colonists can we evacuate before then?"

"I'm not sure," Alan said. Delacroix *had* brought along a number of freighters - he'd considered evacuating the colony, if possible - but the logistics of moving thousands of people to orbit were going to be a nightmare. "I might have to fly a shuttle personally."

"How *terrible*," Bennett said, dryly. "I'm sure you'll hate it."

Alan shrugged as a new set of orders appeared on the display. "I probably will," he said, dryly. "Flying a shuttle is nothing like flying a starfighter."

He checked the roster quickly, then nodded. None of the other starfighter pilots could be spared - and he didn't think Abigail would want to spare any more of her crew than absolutely necessary. There were three shuttles, but crewing them was going to be a pain in the bum. Thankfully, the fleet carriers and destroyers had shuttles of their own.

"Maddy, hold the fort," he ordered. "Bennett, you can accompany me on the shuttle."

"Let me grab my weapons," Bennett said. "Refugees can behave oddly."

Alan nodded. "I'll meet you at the shuttle hatch," he said, as he keyed his wristcom. "Hurry."

He spoke quickly into the wristcom, briefing Abigail. She didn't sound pleased, although she understood the importance of evacuating as many colonists as possible. Seven hours wasn't long enough...not that it mattered, Alan knew. They wouldn't *have* seven hours. Admiral Delacroix wouldn't let them spend more than two hours picking up refugees, not when they had to make a break for the tramline before the aliens closed to engagement range. The orders were all too clear. Commodore Jameson's flotilla was to cover the refugee convoy as it fled Bavaria.

And hope that the fleet carriers can stop the aliens, Alan thought, as he raced to the shuttle hatch. It opened on his command, allowing him into the cockpit. Thankfully, the shuttle had been powered up from the moment they'd jumped into the system. *If they can't, we might be unable to get out of the system before it's too late.*

Bennett joined him, wearing an intimidating set of black armour and carrying a rifle that looked too big to be real. Alan wasn't sure if it was meant for threatening people rather than actual combat, but he supposed it didn't matter. Besides, Bennett was *also* carrying an oversized pistol on his belt and a handful of devices slung over his shoulder. Alan motioned him into the nearest seat, then undocked from *Haddock* and steered the shuttle into the planetary atmosphere. Bennett - damn him - seemed utterly unconcerned by the rough flight as they crashed down towards the surface.

"There's a refugee camp near the river," Alan said, as more data flowed into the communications network. "We're to land there."

"Got it," Bennett said. "Good luck."

Alan nodded, keeping a wary eye on the sensors as they dropped lower. The evacuation hadn't been very well planned, unsurprisingly. There had been no data with which to *plan* an evacuation ahead of time. And there wasn't anything like enough time, either. It was going to be very much first come, first evacuated. He was fairly sure a few thousand colonists wouldn't want to leave, not when the aliens hadn't shown any interest in them. Alan had been envisaging an insurgency, like the one that had dominated the Age of Unrest, but…there hadn't been any direct human-alien contact at all. It was tempting to believe that almost nothing had changed after the aliens had occupied the system.

"Not bad camouflage," Bennett said, grudgingly. "The camp is barely visible from space."

"Good," Alan said. The shuttle touched down in the middle of a clearing. "You go gather the refugees."

Bennett nodded and unstrapped himself, before heading to the hatch. A line of refugees, mostly women and children, were already waiting. Bennett opened the hatch, inviting them to come in and take their seats. A handful of older men were watching from a distance, weapons at the ready. Alan wondered if they were planning to march overland to what remained of the alien bases - their positions clearly marked by plumes of smoke - or simply stay in hiding until the war was over. Either way, he admired their nerve. He wasn't sure he could have stayed behind so calmly.

The hatch shut with a loud *clang*. "Buckle up," Bennett called, sharply. "We'll be taking off in five minutes."

"Do a quick census," Alan ordered, as he powered up the drive. "They'll have to assign them to a slot on one of the freighters."

He winced, inwardly. The freighters hadn't been designed to transport large numbers of people. Their life support was going to be pushed to the limits, just keeping the refugees alive long enough to get them to

Aquitaine. And then…it was hard to imagine what would happen next. Aquitaine wouldn't be able to stand off a full-scale alien offensive, if the aliens decided to throw caution to the winds and attack. Perhaps the refugees would have to flee into the countryside again.

The shuttle shook, violently, as he steered her up and out of the atmosphere. It felt heavier, somehow, even though he knew he was imagining it. And yet…he pushed the thought aside, glancing at the timer. If they were lucky, there would be time for at least two more collection missions before they had to return to *Haddock*. Unless, of course, the aliens decided to show up early…

He looked at the live feed from the sensors. The alien fleet carrier and its escorts were *still* barrelling towards Bavaria, as if they could save their compatriots on the ground. Or, perhaps, catch Admiral Delacroix with his pants down. Or maybe…his lips quirked into a humourless smile. Maybe the aliens wanted to score a cheap victory that would allow them to cover up their embarrassment too. Or was that too cynical? Or too *human*?

"We'll be docking in twenty minutes," he said. Two more shuttles were ahead of them, their crews already encouraging the refugees onto the freighters. Their trip to Aquitaine was going to be an absolute nightmare. "Move off the shuttle as quickly as possible, please. We have to go back for the others."

He did his best to ignore the questions as the shuttle docked with the freighter. There was no way he could answer any of them, even the simplest. How was *he* to know when a particular husband or wife or child would be evacuated? There wasn't even a roster of people to be uplifted! The freighter crews would try to put one together, he was sure, once the convoy was underway, but until then…

The refugees stumbled off the shuttle, looking unsure if they should be relieved or worried that they might have jumped from the frying pan into the fire. Alan didn't really blame them, not when the aliens had largely ignored the refugee camps after smashing anything that looked as though it might be dangerous. Earth was not kind to refugees, even refugees who'd been forced to flee through no fault of their own. It was quite possible that they wouldn't find any safety at all.

There but for the grace of God go I, he thought, as they undocked. *But at least they'll have a chance to survive.*

———

"New orders from the flag," Poddy said. "Commodore Jameson is to assume command of the flotilla - and we're to make our way back to Aquitaine as quickly as possible."

"Good," Abigail said. "Recall the shuttles. If they're carrying refugees, they can unload first, but I want them back onboard as quickly as possible."

She frowned as the command network updated. Admiral Delacroix, it seemed, *was* planning to confront the alien fleet carrier, relying on numbers to offset technological superiority. It was hard to determine if he had a chance or not, but it wasn't a gamble *she* would have taken if she'd had a choice. And yet, she had to admit that it would buy the flotilla time to escort the refugees to Aquitaine. She just hoped they wouldn't get there in time to watch the alien fleet completing the destruction of the fixed defences and occupying the world.

"The last shuttle should be back onboard in ten minutes," Poddy said. "Anson suggests taking his refugees onboard instead of shipping them to the freighter."

Abigail shook her head. "Our life support is already pushed to the limits," she said. The Royal Navy *had* made a number of improvements, but *Haddock's* life support had been designed for a smaller crew. A few dozen newcomers might push them well into the danger zone. "Tell him to expedite unloading as much as possible."

"Aye, Captain."

The task force altered course slowly, the fleet carriers rising up to challenge the incoming aliens while Commodore Jameson's tiny flotilla started to head back towards the original tramline. Abigail resisted the urge to pace her bridge - the bridge really wasn't big enough for pacing - as the last of the shuttles docked and the flotilla picked up speed. The aliens weren't pressing them *that* hard, but she had no illusions. A stern chase wouldn't be a long one for *them*. *Haddock* and her sisters simply couldn't outrun the aliens if they got too close.

"Set a least-time course for the tramline," Commodore Jameson ordered. "And go to full silent running."

He didn't look pleased. Abigail couldn't tell if he was annoyed because he was being ordered to run from the brewing fight or if he thought the fight itself was a bad idea. Probably the latter, she thought. Jameson wasn't above gambling with lives - his included - but he wasn't completely reckless. History would judge Admiral Delacroix harshly if he never came back from the engagement. Hell, it wouldn't take *that* long. She knew plenty of Belters who'd judge her poorly - Belters who were passing judgement from a safe distance - and she doubted the groundpounders were any different.

"Understood," she said, curtly. There was no need to worry about leaving the shuttles behind now. "Let's go."

She leaned back in her command chair and ran through the calculations in her head. A least-time course *should* get them across the tramline before the engagement began, unless something disastrous happened. And yet...Commodore Jameson was already launching a shell of recon probes to make it impossible for the aliens to sneak up on them. The flotilla certainly *should* be able to evade any contacts before it was too late to avoid detection.

Unless we get unlucky, she thought. *And they get lucky.*

Anson stepped onto the bridge, looking haggard. "Reporting for duty, Captain."

Abigail eyed him for a long moment. "Are you alright?"

"I've been better," Anson said. He looked...haunted. "I..."

"We'll talk about it later," Abigail said. She wanted to send him to his cabin, perhaps with a sedative, but he *was* the best helmsman she had. And besides, something that rendered him completely unconscious would be very dangerous if they ran into trouble. "Take your station."

She winced, inwardly. The conditions on the planet had to have been dreadful - she was a firm believer that conditions on planets were always dreadful - but evacuating even a small percentage of the population had to have been difficult. She'd helped to evacuate an asteroid once and *that* had been bad, even though the population had been largely composed of experienced spacers. Thankfully, colonists probably knew how hard life could be even before the aliens revealed their existence. She hoped that meant they'd be able to endure a few days on a converted freighter. Once they reached Aquitaine...

Her console chimed. "Captain," Alan said. "The starfighters are ready for deployment."

"Understood," Abigail said. Hopefully, they wouldn't encounter any alien ships on the far side of the tramline, but it was well to be prepared. "And yourself?"

"I'll be part of the second squadron," Alan said. "We don't have enough pilots to let me stay in the CIC."

Abigail's lips twitched. "I'm sure you hate it," she said, wryly. "I'll see you on the far side."

She closed the channel and returned her attention to the display. The alien fleet carrier was still advancing towards Admiral Delacroix's fleet, although it looked as though the carrier was slowing down. Abigail wondered, idly, if the aliens were rethinking their aggressive posture or - more likely - they were just trying to screw with their enemy's mind. A crew could *not* stay on full alert indefinitely, no matter what appallingly bad entertainment shows claimed. Admiral Delacroix's crews would be stressed and tired by the time the aliens finally deigned to close to engagement range.

One hopes it screws with their minds too, Abigail thought. *We don't know anything about their endurance, either.*

She yawned, covering her mouth guiltily. She'd caught some rest as the task force had crossed Talofa, but it hadn't really been enough. Hopefully, she'd have a chance for some more once they were across the tramline and hidden in the interplanetary void. Besides, Talofa was supposed to be relatively clear. The enemy would have to loop through Aquitaine if they wanted to attack Talofa or reinforce Bavaria. By her assessment, there were easier ways to do it.

"They could have hit the admiral by now," Anson said. "Why are they fucking around with him?"

"Maybe they're stalling," Poddy said. "If they have another fleet carrier on the way, the odds get a lot more even."

Abigail resisted the urge to tell them to shut up. Anson and Poddy were sensible kids - save, perhaps, for Anson's unseemly love for a criminal groundpounder. They wouldn't scare each other too badly. Coming to think of it, Poddy's birthday wasn't *that* far off. She'd be old enough to date in a month or two and then…Abigail winced, inwardly. God knew *she* had made some horrific mistakes before actually getting married. She'd have to sit Poddy down, probably a day before her birthday, and give her a frank description of some of Abigail's mistakes. They weren't ones she wanted her daughter to repeat.

Although telling her not to do half the shit I did will probably make her want to do it, Abigail thought. The Belt had very strict rules on consent - and ways to determine if someone truly thought their partner had consented - but it didn't care much if someone tried something willingly and then discovered, midway through, that they didn't like it after all. Belters were responsible for their own shit. *I'll just have to make that clear to her.*

"Tramline in twenty minutes," Anson said, breaking into her thoughts. "The enemy *still* hasn't engaged the carriers."

"It certainly looks that way," Abigail said. They were far enough from Admiral Delacroix, now, for the time delay to be a very real problem. The battle might already have begun but it would still be some time before they knew it. "Are we clear?"

"Local space appears clear," Poddy reported. "The drones aren't finding anything."

She paused. "Commodore Jameson wants us to jump as soon as we cross the tramline, then head straight for the Aquitaine tramline."

Abigail frowned. She wasn't sure what she made of *that*. A least-time course would ensure they got the refugees to Aquitaine before one or more of the freighters developed problems with their life support, but it had the disadvantage of being very predictable. The aliens would have no trouble keeping tabs on their location, if they detected the flotilla crossing the tramline. And yet, there was no hint the aliens knew where they were.

We shouldn't take it for granted, she reminded herself. The recon drones were good, but they weren't perfect. *They might have shadowed us ever since we left the planet.*

She waited for the last minutes to tick down to zero, then looked at Anson. "Ready to jump?"

"Aye, Captain," Anson said.

"Then jump," Abigail ordered.

Anson nodded, his hand dancing over his console. "Jumping...now!"

Abigail grunted as she felt an invisible fist slam into her chest. It hurt worse every time, these days...she wondered, grimly, just how long she'd be able to keep travelling the tramlines if it kept getting worse. Maybe she was just getting old. Or maybe...

I might be able to buy a modern freighter, she thought, *if I convince the navy to bankroll it or get a loan from...*

Alarms howled. "Incoming starfighters," Poddy snapped. Red icons flashed into existence on the display, far too close for comfort. "We're under attack!"

CHAPTER
THIRTY EIGHT

"Go, go, go!"

Alan gritted his teeth as the starfighter was hurled out of the launch tube and into interplanetary space. They'd been caught flatfooted, somehow. The aliens...the aliens must have tracked them in Bavaria, then plotted an ambush in Talofa. They'd pulled it off too, he told himself. He would have been impressed with their cunning if the ambush hadn't been aimed at the flotilla.

That explains why they dawdled in Bavaria, he thought. *They assumed the remainder of the task force would withdraw too.*

He took stock of the situation as Savage began barking orders, forming the squadron up into some kind of formation. The alien starfighters were closing rapidly, although there was something oddly hesitant about their movements. Alan puzzled over it for a long moment, then decided it didn't matter. Perhaps the aliens had assumed they'd be facing one or both of the human fleet carriers. In that case, the escort carriers and freighters would have been ignored while the fleet carriers were massacred.

And their fleet carrier is actually some distance away. The enemy fleet carrier was making no attempt to hide. Alan didn't blame her commander. *They know we can't attack her without uncovering the refugee ships.*

He wondered, grimly, if the aliens even knew what they were attacking. Did they think they were targeting twelve escort carriers, even though seven of the 'carriers' hadn't launched a single fighter? Or were they just intent on destroying as much tonnage as possible? They'd already shown a frightening lack of concern for civilian casualties, although Alan *did* have to admit that the aliens didn't go in for mass slaughter. They weren't terrorists or insurgents, merely...alien. And there was no way to *tell* them what they were attacking. They might be horrified, later, when they realised what they'd done. But it wouldn't come in time to help the flotilla.

And we can't even recharge the drives and jump back into Bavaria, not before they land on us, Alan told himself. The military ships could withdraw, if they were willing to abandon the civilians. And the escort carriers, for that matter. The hell of it was that cold logic insisted that abandoning the freighters was *precisely* what Commodore Jameson should do. *It'll keep us from losing seven warships as well as the converted freighters.*

He shook his head. The military existed to protect civilians, not to abandon them. He didn't think Commodore Jameson would willingly abandon the remainder of the convoy, no matter what cold logic said. God knew he'd be pilloried by the media when he got home, even though most of his superiors would probably - very quietly - agree with him. *Alan* didn't want to run either. But the aliens were going to tear them to shreds.

"Engage at will," Savage ordered. "Don't let them get into firing range!"

There were no jokes, not this time. The pilots were experienced enough to know that their backs were firmly pressed against the wall, that even jumping back into Bavaria wouldn't be enough to save them. Alan gritted his teeth as the aliens came closer, plasma bolts already flashing through space. He wished, suddenly, that he'd had a chance to record a final message for his daughters. The last message had been almost optimistic. He couldn't help hoping that they never saw it, before or after they heard of his death.

An alien starfighter materialised in front of him, driving straight through the CSP. Alan blew the alien to dust, then evaded a series of plasma bolts as the alien's wingman tried to take revenge. He ducked and dodged until Savage scored a direct hit, wiping the alien out of space. Alan nodded his thanks as he looked for other targets, silently noting that the aliens were more intent on hitting the capital ships than duelling with the starfighters. It was good tactics, he admitted reluctantly, but a little unsporting.

War is not a sport, he reminded himself, as he directed his starfighter to chase the nearest alien fighter. *And there are no rules, save those that can actually be enforced.*

Sweat trickled down his back as the starfighters converged on the freighters. The damned aliens were closing rapidly, evading human point defence as they fired plasma bolts into the warship and freighter hulls. He cursed savagely as his sensors reported a bolt slamming into a freighter, burning through the thin metal hull. The carnage inside would be utterly horrific, a nightmare beyond imagination. He didn't think anyone in one of the outer compartments would survive…God knew the freighters didn't have anything like enough spacesuits for all the refugees. Even if they did, being in close proximity to a plasma bolt would probably set them on fire.

Those blasts can tear through metal, he thought. He'd seen the aliens ripping fleet carriers apart with casual ease. *What can they do to unprotected skin and bone?*

A freighter exploded, pieces of debris spinning out in all directions. Alan shuddered, trying not to be sick. The aliens had killed hundreds, perhaps thousands, of helpless refugees. He hoped they didn't *know* what they'd done, that they hadn't set out to do it intentionally…and yet, he knew it didn't matter. Dead was dead, no matter the intention. Those refugees had left the frying pan and fallen straight into the fire.

He pushed the starfighter forward, heedless of the danger. The aliens seemed to recoil, just long enough for him to snap off a couple of shots. An alien starfighter vanished from the display, but he barely noticed its passing. They were doomed. He *knew* they were doomed. There was no way they could surrender or escape…

At least we can scratch them properly on our way to the gallows, he thought, morbidly. *It might just weaken them enough for Admiral Delacroix to break back through the system, if he wins his engagement.*

He'd known he was expendable, right from the very moment he'd been offered a chance to don the uniform once again. And yet, he was about to die on something that hadn't been *meant* as a suicide mission. The irony made him laugh, despite himself. Perhaps his death would be rather more meaningful than he'd thought.

It wasn't a particularly reassuring thought. But, at the moment, it was all he had.

"They're regrouping," Whitehead said, curtly. His voice was so calm that Alan *knew* it was an act. "Form up on me and prepare to break them up."

Alan blinked. Whitehead? Not Savage? He looked down at the display and swore. Savage was gone. He'd bought it...he'd bought it, back while Alan had been trying to save the freighter. Alan cursed himself for not noticing, even though...he should have noticed, he told himself. Savage hadn't deserved to die. He hadn't done anything that merited death. And yet...it tore at Alan that he hadn't noticed. He hadn't even had time to mark Savage's passing...

Concentrate, he told himself. The aliens were spreading out, angling towards the escort carriers as they resumed the attack. *And get into formation. Now.*

"Shit," Poddy said.

"Focus," Abigail snapped. They'd been caught with their pants down - they'd been caught with their panties down, part of her mind yammered - and they were trapped, but panic wouldn't help. "How long until we can jump?"

"Twenty minutes," Poddy said. "I...I don't think it's going to be enough."

Abigail nodded, curtly. The alien fleet carrier was hogging the tramline, slowly making its way towards the flotilla. She tried to imagine a human starship jumping through the tramline and accidentally interpenetrating with the alien carrier, blowing both ships to atoms, but she had to admit it was vanishingly unlikely. No, they couldn't stay anywhere near the tramline unless they wanted to die. But running away from the tramline wasn't a possibility either.

And staying here will just get us killed, she thought. *They definitely caught us with our pants down.*

She glanced at the communications board, but it remained blank. Commodore Jameson hadn't issued any orders, save for the command to launch starfighters. She wondered, vaguely, if the younger man could pull a miracle out of his arse, then silently laughed at herself for being stupid. No one, groundpounder or belter, could hope to save the flotilla now. Their only edge was the distance between the alien starfighters and their mothership and *that* was closing rapidly. It was starting to look as though all they could do was die bravely.

"Captain," Poddy said. "They're concentrating on us."

Abigail wasn't surprised. The aliens had seen *Haddock* launching starfighters. They knew what she was. The aliens could blow away the war-ships and escort carriers, then concentrate on obliterating the remaining freighters while leaving the starfighter pilots to die when their life support packs ran out. She was surprised they weren't targeting the warships first, but she supposed they saw starfighters as more dangerous. Or, perhaps, they expected Commodore Jameson to abandon the flotilla to save his own skin.

"Stand by point defence," she ordered, shortly. The command datanet was already coming apart, after the aliens had blown one of the destroyers into flaming plasma. It was no consolation to realise that a military forma-tion would have re-established the datanet by now, if they'd lost it in the first place. "Engage the moment they enter firing range."

"Aye, Captain."

Abigail gritted her teeth as the alien craft swooped down on *Haddock*. They'd learnt a few things from the last encounter, she noted; they were targeting the drive section, rather than blasting plasma bolts into her hull at random. It made a certain kind of sense when they were targeting fleet carriers, but *Haddock* didn't have *quite* so many internal systems that could be badly mangled by the blasts. A dull quiver ran through the ship, followed by two more. Red icons flared up on the status display.

"The armour around the rear is holding," Anson said, astonished. "But they're concentrating their fire on the weaker aspects..."

"Keep using point defence to break up their formation," Abigail said. She would have sold her soul for plasma guns of her own. The navy might disagree, but as far as *she* was concerned breaking up the enemy attack was more important than scoring hits. "And recall some of our starfighters, if you can."

"I think they have problems of their own," Poddy said. "They're taking a beating."

Abigail nodded, grimly. Only two of the five escort carriers had managed to get *all* of their starfighters into space before the aliens had descended on the flotilla, their plasma guns picking off a handful of starfighters before their pilots could orient themselves. One of the escort carriers had been hit so badly that the entire flight deck had been smashed, although the remainder of the ship was intact. A dozen pilots had been killed and their starfighters destroyed before they'd had a chance to launch. She silently blessed Alan's insistence on intensive training, even though she knew it had tired her crew. It might have saved a few lives.

Or at least given them a chance to fight back, she thought. They were doomed, but at least they'd make the aliens pay for what they'd done. *Who knows? Perhaps we'll take out enough starfighters to cripple their plans for Aquitaine.*

"They're coming back," Poddy reported. "Captain?"

"Keep firing," Abigail ordered. "Throw everything we have at them, up to and including the kitchen sink."

"Aye, Captain."

Commodore Jameson's face appeared in the display. "All ships, prepare to alter course," he ordered. "We can't stay here."

You should run, Abigail thought, grimly. There was no point in throwing away the entire flotilla, just because Commodore Jameson didn't want to be branded a coward. *Take your ships and go.*

She gritted her teeth as she saw the new course appear in front of her. Commodore Jameson wanted to avoid contact with the alien carrier...it might have been workable, if their enemy hadn't been a *carrier*. There was no way the human flotilla could break contact long enough to slip into silent running, not when the alien starfighters could catch up with the human ships at any time. All the aliens had to do was keep battering away at the human flotilla from a safe distance, trading starfighters for warships and freighters. The loss rate would be firmly in their favour.

"Alter course," she ordered, coldly. "And continue firing."

She considered, briefly, a number of possible options. Commodore Jameson *could* send a destroyer to alert Admiral Delacroix...but what could Admiral Delacroix *do*? His fleet carriers had been two *hours* from the tramline. God alone knew where they were now. Even if the admiral had reversed course at once, there was no way his ships would arrive in time to make a difference. Abigail hoped, grimly, that Admiral Delacroix had succeeded in smashing the alien fleet carrier. It would make the aliens pay, just a little, for what they'd done to the refugees.

Another shudder ran through her ship. "Direct hit, lower flight deck," Poddy snapped, as an alarm started to howl. "We've got a hull breach!"

"Get a repair crew down there now," Abigail ordered. There were *torpedoes* stored down there. If the aliens scored a direct hit, the resulting explosion would reduce her ship to free-floating atoms. "And see if they need to shift the ammunition!"

"Aye, Captain."

"Course set," Anson reported. "I don't think we can get away from them!"

"It might buy us some more time," Abigail said, although she knew it would only be a few more seconds. The warships could outrun the fleet carrier, but not the freighters. "We might as well make them work for their victory."

On the display, the second wave of alien starfighters was already closing. She'd hoped there'd come a time when the aliens needed to return to their carrier to refuel. It was clear, now, that the aliens had more than enough starfighters to maintain a constant pressure. She couldn't understand why they hadn't simply massed their forces for a single, overwhelmingly powerful attack. Hadn't they *known* where the flotilla was going to appear? They must have tracked the flotilla to the tramline...

They might have assumed that they wouldn't get the coordinates right, she told herself. *Or they might have figured the fleet carriers would be coming too.*

She shook her head, dismissing the thought. If *she'd* been planning the ambush, it would have been churlish to complain that it hadn't been a *complete* success. It had come very close to succeeding in the first blow and...and it was still going to succeed. There was no way to evade the enemy, not unless the fleet carriers turned up in the nick of time. And she doubted that would happen. Admiral Delacroix had no reason to assume the flotilla had run into trouble. He would probably have decided, if he'd bothered to think about it, that the aliens would prefer to concentrate their forces against his ships, rather than a handful of harmless freighters and their escorts. And he might well have been right.

Not that it matters, she thought. *They found a target - us - and attacked anyway.*

"They're falling back," Poddy reported. She sounded relieved, even though she had to know that it was just a brief pause in the storm. "Captain?"

"Tell the damage control teams to work as quickly as possible," Abigail said. The aliens hadn't managed to land a knockout punch, but they'd weakened the armour plating badly. She hoped they didn't know just how close they'd come to exposing her drive section. A handful of hits would be enough to cripple or destroy her ship. "We need that armour reinforced."

"Aye, Captain."

Abigail nodded. The first wave of alien starfighters was pulling back, but the second wave was still inbound. They'd messed up the timing a little, part of her mind noted...she cursed herself under her breath. It was wishful thinking, more or less. The aliens had messed up the timing...so what? They were still on the verge of obliterating the entire flotilla.

Commodore Jameson's face appeared in the display. "The warships will cover the freighters as they retreat," he said. "We'll make our stand here."

Abigail swallowed, hard. "Sir...they'll kill your ships."

"It'll buy you time," Jameson said. "Get as far from them as possible..."

Wishful thinking, Abigail thought, grimly. She understood his thinking, but it was fatally flawed. There was no hope of survival. *We're stronger together.*

She was almost disappointed in him, even though she had to admit it was brave. Space was a three-dimensional environment. The aliens would have no trouble evading the warships, if they wanted to press the offensive against the freighters...and if they smashed the warships first, they probably wouldn't have any problem taking out the freighters afterwards.

Jameson was gambling that the aliens would need some time to obliterate his ships, but she knew he was clutching at straws.

"We need to stay together," she told him. "You can't stop them for long."

"We have to try," Commodore Jameson said. His voice was resolved. "Take command of the freighters and…"

He broke off. Abigail blinked in surprise, then turned to stare at the display. A stream of red icons was descending on Commodore Jameson's ship, firing plasma bolts into her hull with savage intensity. Abigail opened her mouth, although she had no idea what she wanted to say, then closed it as Commodore Jameson's face vanished from the display.

"Captain," Poddy said. "Commodore Jameson…"

"I saw," Abigail said, grimly. She wanted to believe that it was a communications malfunction, but she knew better. There was no hope that anyone had survived the ship's final moments. "He's gone."

"And you're in command," Anson said. "What are your orders, *Commodore*?"

CHAPTER
THIRTY NINE

"Commodore Jameson is dead."

Alan barely heard the report. The battle had dissolved into a dogfight, with every one of the original squadrons broken and shattered beyond repair. Starfighter pilots flew with whatever wingmen they could find, trying to stay together long enough to cover the escort carriers so their fellows could rearm. Two of the carriers had even lost the ability to launch and recover fighters, leaving their starfighters dependent on the other starships. There wasn't even time to transfer their supplies from a disabled ship to one that could still use them.

"Stay together," he snapped. His guns were running out of pellets. He'd have to go back to *Haddock* soon, just to rearm. "Don't give them a chance to reform!"

He forced himself to consider the overall situation as he led the charge at the nearest alien formation. Commodore Jameson's death meant that command had devolved on Abigail, unless one of the regular naval officers decided to usurp it for himself. Alan hoped they'd have more sense, although it was unlikely to matter. Lord Nelson himself couldn't bring victory out of near-total defeat. The damage was mounting up rapidly and, when the aliens launched their final push, the flotilla would be annihilated.

An alien pilot snapped off a shot at him, then darted out of his range before he could fire back. Alan cursed, then fired on another alien ship. The alien pilot was sharp enough to evade the pellets before spinning round to fire a hail of plasma bolts in response. Alan cursed again, ducking and dodging as the aliens fell back. It looked as though they were massing for another strike or, perhaps, trying to lure the human starfighters away from their carriers.

Or both, he thought. *We leave them alone, we give them time to mass; we go after them, they can streak past us and attack the carriers.*

Alan thought, fast. He had no idea how long it would take the alien carrier to refuel three or four squadrons of starfighters, but if they were anything like their human counterparts it wouldn't take very long at all. Perhaps *that* was why the aliens were massing…they were waiting for the rest of their starfighters before launching a final assault. Or…his thoughts started to go in circles. Why weren't they just putting an end to it?

He snapped out orders, sending half the starfighters back to be rearmed while grouping the remainder into makeshift squadrons. It wasn't very well organised, but he had a feeling it was unlikely to matter. The enemy ships weren't going to let them live long enough to get home and explain themselves to the Admiralty. Besides, it wasn't as if the Admiralty could do any better. The original formations had been shot to hell. Whitehead, as far as he knew, was the only squadron commander still alive.

His earpiece crackled. "All ships will continue along present course," Abigail ordered. It didn't *sound* as though someone had disputed her authority, thank goodness. The last thing they needed was a dispute over who was in command while the entire formation was on the verge of destruction. "We will attempt to evade contact until the fleet carriers arrive."

Alan shook his head, sadly. Abigail was too experienced a spacer, even if she wasn't a naval officer, to believe that Admiral Delacroix would arrive in time to save them from total destruction. She was probably trying to reassure her subordinates, although Alan doubted there was any point. Her senior officers would know, beyond a shadow of a doubt, that the situation was hopeless. If they'd been fighting the Russians or the Chinese, someone who could actually *talk* to the flotilla, Alan would have advised Abigail to surrender. But the aliens wouldn't accept a surrender…

You'd think they wouldn't want to waste time killing us, Alan thought.

He shook his head. Terrorists and fanatical insurgents on Earth rarely surrendered. They knew they'd be spending the rest of their lives at a work camp in Antarctica, if they lasted that long. It wasn't uncommon for terrorists and insurgents to be put in front of a wall and shot, without any particular oversight. The Great Powers might have a series of treaties to regulate minor conflicts - and prevent big ones - but they saw no reason to pretend that the lesser powers and rogue states were *equals*. And those who chose to wage war by barbaric means could not be allowed to reap the rewards of their actions.

Maybe the aliens don't surrender, so they can't understand why we would want to, he wondered. *Or maybe...*

"You need to rearm, sir," Whitehead said. "I suggest you hurry."

Alan nodded to himself. "Take command of the remaining squadrons," he ordered, as he set course back to *Haddock*. "I'll be back out as soon as possible."

"Yes, sir."

The aliens were still pulling back and waiting, either for the humans to make a move or - more likely - for their reinforcements to arrive. Alan cursed them, again. They *knew* they had the flotilla. Why were they fucking around when they could close in for the kill? But then, Admiral Delacroix was on the other side of the tramline. Perhaps they were being careful about expending too many starfighters. Not having enough firepower to smash two fleet carriers would be embarrassing.

And Admiral Delacroix might be dead, Alan thought. He remembered New Russia and shuddered, helplessly. *The other alien fleet carrier might be mopping up right now.*

He pushed the thought into the back of his mind as he approached *Haddock*. It was easy to pick out the scarring on her hull, places where enemy plasma bolts had slapped against her armour. One of them was far too close to the flight deck for comfort. The last thing he wanted was to be trapped in his starfighter as the starship disintegrated around him, although common sense told him that it wouldn't matter if he was inside or outside the fighter. He'd be killed either way.

"Rearm my ship," he ordered, as soon as he'd landed. "And get me an energy drink."

We can take more drugs, he told himself. *It isn't as if we're going to live long enough to deal with the aftermath...*

His earpiece bleeped. "Report to the CIC at once," Bennett said. "I say again…"

"I heard you," Alan snapped. He unstrapped himself, muttering curses under his breath. "I need to be out there."

"This is more important," Bennett said. "Report to the CIC, immediately."

———

Abigail had never wanted fleet command. It wasn't something she'd had any reason to expect, even though her family controlled a number of freighters. Her uncle had been a firm believer in independent operations and she'd picked it up from him. Now…she was in command of a battered fleet and she didn't have the slightest idea what to do, besides bunching up and hoping they could hold out long enough for Admiral Delacroix to arrive.

A fool's hope, she told herself, grimly.

The reports flashed up in front of her, a liturgy of death and destruction. Half the starfighters were gone, along with their pilots; one of the escort carriers had been destroyed, with another rendered effectively useless. Two more freighters had been blasted out of space, along with their human cargo. Abigail had seen horror - she'd been one of the first responders when Travis Asteroid had suffered a near-complete breakdown - but the slow destruction of the flotilla was beyond her experience. They needed time: time to make repairs, time to transfer weapons and spare parts from the cripples to the fighting ships, time…she shook her head, grimly. She was deluding herself. There was no hope of survival as long as the aliens kept pressing the offensive.

And they will keep pressing the offensive, she thought. *They have a perfect chance to wipe out a number of ships for minimal cost…why would they not take it?*

"Captain," Poddy said. "*Warlock* and *Tolkien* are requesting orders."

"Tell them to stay in formation," Abigail said. She'd expected trouble, but the commanders of the two destroyers had accepted her authority without demur. She wouldn't have minded if they'd unseated her, if they'd had a way to get the flotilla out. But they were as helpless as herself. "Tell them…"

I should tell them to run, she considered. *The rest of the flotilla is doomed, but we might be able to save a couple of ships.*

She tapped her console, bringing up the display. A handful of alien starfighters were massing near the flotilla, but the remainder were nowhere to be seen. She checked the records, concerned that the aliens might be sneaking around under their sensor masks, and confirmed that most of the alien starfighters had gone back to refuel or rearm or whatever the aliens did on their fleet carriers. It wouldn't be long before they resumed the offensive. She couldn't help thinking that the only reason the aliens had given the human ships a breathing space was because they were sure there was nothing the humans could do to take advantage of it.

Unless the remainder of the task force makes a sudden appearance, she thought. *But…*

It was wishful thinking, she reminded herself. They were on their own. Admiral Delacroix was not going to make a sudden appearance. Nor was there any hope of reinforcements arriving from Aquitaine. Admiral Delacroix had practically stripped the base of *every* mobile unit in the system, intent on giving his task force as much firepower as possible. She couldn't fault the impulse, but now…

A thought struck her. *They'll keep attacking us as long as we're here to attack…*

"Poddy," she said, slowly. "Com *Warlock* and *Tolkien*. Ask their commanding officers if they have ECM drones."

"Aye, Captain," Poddy said.

"The aliens won't be fooled if we show them a pair of fleet carriers," Anson said. "And I don't think we can lure them away…"

"We shall see," Abigail said. An idea was slowly forming in her mind. "Give me a moment to reorganise the flotilla."

She started tapping commands into her console, wishing - for the first time - that she had a staff to handle such matters. It wasn't something she should have to handle herself, not when she was expected to command the flotilla. But there was no choice. She talked fast, isolating the ships that were practically cripples. It wasn't many, but it would have to do.

"They've got seven ECM drones between them," Poddy reported. "They want to know what you have in mind."

"Something desperate," Abigail said. "Inform *Tolkien's* commanding officer" - she kicked herself mentally for not having memorised the man's *name* - "that he is now in command of half the flotilla. We'll call it Flotilla Two. I want him to prepare to take his ships into silent running, as soon as I give the order."

Anson glanced at her and frowned. "I think *Warlock's* CO has seniority."

Abigail shrugged. Maybe the navy would put Captain Young ahead of HMS *Tolkien's* commanding officer, but Young had creeped her out. She'd only met him once, but the impression had refused to fade. He hadn't *done* anything to her, yet...her gut told her that Captain Young was dangerous. Besides, he was almost suspiciously handsome. She wouldn't have let Poddy anywhere near him, not without a personal combat suit and an armed bodyguard.

"They can argue it later," she said. "I want to strip Flotilla One of everyone who isn't absolutely essential to keeping the ships running for the next hour or so. That includes the engineers and damage control teams as well as the starfighter pilots and crew."

Anson coughed. "Mum? What are we doing?"

"They want to destroy us," Abigail said. She looked at the display, silently calculating vectors. "Very well. We'll give them a target to destroy."

———

When we start putting together the purpose-built escort carriers, Alan thought as he ran into the cramped CIC, *we'll have to put the flight deck and the CIC a little closer together.*

He controlled his annoyance with an effort. Normally, a CAG wasn't expected to do double duty as a starfighter pilot. He probably wouldn't have been allowed to get away with it if the Royal Navy hadn't been so desperate for trained manpower. And Bennett so understanding, come to think of it. But then, there was literally nowhere for Alan to go. Talofa was practically deserted after the aliens had swept through, blasting a handful of isolated settlements into rubble.

"This ship is being evacuated," Bennett said. He nodded to the display. "The starfighters are being transferred to *Canopus*."

"The rest of the crew is heading for the shuttles," Maddy added. She looked pale. There were dark rings around her eyes. "Sir...the captain asked for volunteers to stay behind. I'm staying."

"No, you're not," Alan said. "You're getting married, remember?"

"Anson won't want to leave," Maddy said. "Sir, I..."

"I think that Abigail won't give him a choice," Alan said, flatly. He studied the display for a moment, trying to follow Abigail's plan. Use the cripples - and a handful of drones - to lure the aliens away from the remaining starships, sacrificing a handful of ships and crews so that the rest could live. It made sense, he supposed. And the crewmen were all volunteers. "Mr. Bennett will escort you to the shuttle."

Maddy looked torn. "Sir..."

"You've done well," Alan said. "And you thoroughly deserve your pardon. Go to the shuttle. That's an order, by the way."

"Yes, sir," Maddy said.

She rose and hurried out of the compartment. Alan hoped she'd have the sense to get on the shuttle before it was too late...she *was* a trained officer, after all. She certainly *should* have the sense to leave, without bothering to grab anything from her cabin. Alan sat down on her vacated chair and brought up the makeshift evacuation rota. Nearly everyone had a slot on one of the two shuttles.

"You should go," he said, without looking up. "I think your duties are at an end."

Bennett coughed, lightly. "You do not intend to evacuate?"

Alan shrugged. "*Someone* is going to have to help Abigail pretend that this is a fully-functional starship for a little bit longer," he said. It was possible the aliens wouldn't be fooled...not for very long, anyway. But if they lost contact with the rest of the flotilla, the ships might *just* have a chance to get across the tramline to Aquitaine before it was too late to make their escape. "And it isn't as if I have anything waiting for me back home."

"You have daughters," Bennett rumbled.

"I believe you said they'd be better off without me," Alan said. "And, in truth, you were probably right."

"Perhaps," Bennett agreed. "But, at the same time, I've come to realise that you're not bad to the bone."

Alan looked up. "Hello? Who are you and what did you do with Bennett?"

Bennett snorted. "I'm not denying what you did," he said, bluntly. "And I have no interest in forgiving you, even if I had the *power* to forgive you. But I've met dozens of people who are utter monsters, Alan. Serial killers, rapists, child molesters...I've watched them die, on the gallows or in front of a firing squad, and felt as though we were doing the world a favour."

"You were," Alan said, quietly.

"You killed once, under extreme provocation," Bennett said. "Don't misunderstand me, *please*. What you did was wrong, but you're not a career criminal. And you have done very well since being assigned to this ship. I think...you probably deserve that pardon."

"They can give me a posthumous medal, after you tell them about me," Alan said. He wasn't sure what to make of Bennett's words. On one hand, he wasn't going to kill again; on the other, he knew he'd have to live with the guilt for the rest of his life. "And if you meet my daughters, tell them that I...that I love them."

"As you wish," Bennett said.

Alan drew in a long breath as Bennett left the compartment. Bennett had changed...they'd all changed. Or maybe *he* had changed and everyone else had stayed the same. Or...it wasn't something he wanted to think about. Redemption wasn't a possibility, not really. The pardon he'd been offered would be meaningless, if he couldn't get a job afterwards. He doubted the navy would be interested in keeping him...

He let out the breath, slowly. Death...if it was fated, it was fated. And at least he had the satisfaction of knowing he would die doing his duty.

The console bleeped. "Alan," Abigail said. She sounded very calm. "I understand you're staying?"

"Yes," Alan said. "How many others are staying?"

"Just you and I," Abigail said. "The automatics should be enough to let us run the ship for thirty minutes or so."

Because the odds of lasting any longer are too small to be calculated, Alan told himself. His training rebelled against trying to run an escort carrier with just two people - he wouldn't care to run anything bigger than a worker bee with just two people - but Abigail knew what she was doing. *By the time we run into something the two of us can't handle, with or without the automated systems, it will be too late.*

"The shuttles are undocking now," Abigail added. "Come to the bridge, please."

"Aye, Captain," Alan said. He paused. "Did you have any trouble getting Anson off the ship?"

"I had to threaten to stun him," Abigail said. "He'll be pissed at me, afterwards."

Alan shrugged. "At least he'll be alive to be pissed," he said. On the display, red icons were flaring into existence. There wasn't a second to lose. "And Maddy will be alive too."

CHAPTER
FORTY

The bridge felt eerie.

Abigail had stood watches alone before, on a dozen different starships. It had never been easy - she'd known she would be in deep shit if she'd been caught sleeping on watch, but she'd had problems keeping her eyes open - yet she'd learnt to cope. Now, though, she felt as though she was truly alone. There were only two living souls on her starship...her *doomed* starship.

The thought tore at her mind. *Haddock* was her ship...no, she was Abigail's *home*. And yet, she was doomed. Abigail loved her ship, despite the crudeness, despite the mechanical problems that had beset her during her first year of ownership. It had been her world, giving her a life so far above the ordinary that she couldn't imagine anything else. Going back to Ceres alone would be different, but going down to Earth would be impossible. She couldn't stand the thought of living on a planet. And if the navy refused to pay the promised compensation...

She felt a pang as she surveyed the display. Flotilla One - the cripples and the drones - was making its way back towards the tramline, while Flotilla Two was sneaking away in the opposite direction. If the aliens were *really* desperate to catch her ships - and she assumed they didn't want to pass up the chance to smash the flotilla - they'd have to pick up the pace before the human ships could cross the tramline. The absence of any starfighters - all tucked away in the escaping ships - would hopefully suggest that the flotilla intended to jump the second it crossed the tramline.

Which will make it harder for them to track Flotilla Two, she told herself. She'd done everything in her power to ensure success, but she knew that a single stealthed enemy picket in a position to spot the manoeuvre could ruin everything. *As long as they're looking at us for a while longer, they should be safe.*

The hatch opened. Abigail jumped, then reminded herself that Alan had stayed with her. It wasn't strictly necessary, now the automatics had been set, but…she supposed it was a good thing. In theory, she could handle everything alone; in practice, there were very definite advantages to having a larger crew. She knew better than to assume she would be able to survive on her own.

She smiled at him, rather wanly. "How are you feeling?"

"I'd like to tell you that I'm ready to die," Alan said. "But…I try not to lie to people."

Abigail snickered. "Don't give up just yet, please," she said, dryly. "We do have a shuttle, remember."

Alan gave her a sharp look. "Are you mad?"

"Perhaps," Abigail said. She took a moment to check her preparations. Everything looked…ready. Maybe not *perfect*, but certainly close enough. "I'm not willing to surrender until the cold equations come for me."

She returned her attention to the display. The aliens had altered course, as she'd predicted, and launched the remainder of their starfighters. They'd be on their targets in less than ten minutes, giving them just enough time to obliterate the flotilla before it could cross the tramline. It wouldn't be *that* long before they realised that half the flotilla was actually nothing more than ECM drones, but…

Hopefully, we can keep them from noticing that for a few more minutes, she thought.

"If you have something you want to recover from your cabin, go now," she said. "I'll meet you at the forward hatch in two minutes."

Alan shook his head. Abigail scowled - the insensitive clod didn't realise she wanted to be alone, if only for a minute - and then looked around the tiny bridge. It was a crude mess, even after the military engineers had done their work, but it was *hers*. Anson and Poddy had learnt how to fly starships under her watchful eyes, along with a string of apprentices who'd served for a few short months and then gone onwards to better things. Perhaps it wasn't the most dramatic command centre in the navy - she had no idea why groundpounders preferred their bridges to look photogenic - but she didn't care. It was *hers*.

She led the way to the hatch and stepped through, leaving it open behind her. It felt odd, as though she was abdicating her responsibilities. Her uncle would have been furious if he'd caught her leaving a hatch open, particularly in the middle of a dangerous situation. But it was pointless. *Haddock* wasn't going to survive the next ten minutes, no matter what happened. Admiral Delacroix might jump into the system in the next sixty seconds and it *still* wouldn't be enough to save *Haddock*.

Her ship felt odd too, as if she was no longer alive. Abigail felt a chill running down her spine, a sensation she hadn't felt since the day she'd boarded a derelict ship as a younger woman. The ship had suffered a fatal accident, one that had been traced back to a programming glitch, but...she shuddered at the memory. She'd had nightmares for months afterwards.

"Take the helm," she ordered, once they were inside the shuttle. "Keep us stealthy. I'll establish a laser link to the ship."

"Aye, Captain," Alan said.

Abigail barely felt the jerk as the shuttle disengaged from the starship and slowly drifted away into space. She was too busy focusing on the live feed. The aliens were rapidly closing in on the flotilla, their sensors already probing for weaknesses. It wouldn't be long before they uncovered the deception. She was already pushing their luck to the limits.

"Detonation in five," she called. "Brace yourself."

I'm sorry, she thought. She tapped an authorisation code into the network, then clicked SEND. *I didn't want it to end like this.*

The nukes detonated as one. Alan cursed as the ships and drones vanished in nuclear fire, each blast large enough to destroy an entire starship. Abigail hoped - prayed - that the aliens would be convinced that they *had* destroyed the flotilla, that the humans had committed suicide rather than fight to the last. Would they notice that there wasn't enough debris to account for the entire flotilla? Or would they assume that the blasts had been powerful enough to ensure that there was very little debris? She hoped so. Rigging the nukes had been difficult, but there had been no choice. If the aliens suspected the truth…

"I'm shutting down everything, bar the basics," Alan said. "We'll be going ballistic in twenty seconds."

"Make sure you send an updated note of our course to the stealthed platform," Abigail ordered. "And then…we wait."

The lights dimmed, just slightly. She kept a wary eye on the passive sensors, but all they could tell her was that the aliens weren't anywhere near the shuttle. Unless, of course, they were stealthed. She doubted the aliens would bother trying to sneak up on the shuttle, unless they suspected it was a weapon. But if that was the case, they'd just blow the shuttle up from a safe distance.

She rubbed her eyes, trying to blink away sudden tears. Her ship. She'd destroyed her own ship. And it felt as though she'd killed a part of herself.

Alan stepped over to sit next to her. "You had no choice," he said. "Really."

"I know that," Abigail snapped. She shook her head, angrily. She hadn't felt so emotional since Miles Barrington had told her his group-wives had rejected her as a potential sister-wife. Damn the man. She hadn't thought about him in years. "It doesn't make it any easier."

"I know," Alan said. "And I'm sorry."

———

Alan had, in all honesty, expected to die on *Haddock*. It would have been quick, he thought, particularly as the starship couldn't have offered any real resistance to the aliens. But instead…he was trapped in a shuttle, watching the life support readings carefully. The systems were doing their level best, but…

He paced the cabin, checking their supplies and recyclers and cursing under his breath. By his most optimistic calculations, they had about a week to live. The shuttle's power cells would eventually run dry, at which point they'd suffocate and die. Or simply go mad eating recycled food. It would be harder to pretend that they weren't eating recycled shit and piss if it was just the two of them, trapped in a small cabin. And while he was sure they could find a way to pass the time pleasurably, even *that* lost its thrill when he remembered that they were on the verge of dying.

"They're not going to come back for us," Abigail said. "I gave them some very specific orders."

Alan frowned. "And so...what?"

Abigail opened a supply kit. "Have you ever used these before?"

"Suspension drugs?" Alan took one of the injectors and read the label, carefully. "Are you mad?"

Abigail shot him a tired look. "Do you want to die here? In this shuttle? Or do you want to take a chance that *might* save our asses?"

Alan swallowed, hard. He'd heard of suspension drugs. They were a routine part of survival kits, particularly when someone was quite some distance from potential help. Used properly, they could keep someone alive - in suspended animation - for quite some time. And yet, there were risks. If the bodies weren't frozen quickly enough, there might be cellular damage to their brains. Revival was always a chancy business. His instructors had discussed the dangers quite bluntly. Medical technology was advancing all the time, but only two-thirds of the people who went into suspension ever came out again.

"They're not going to come looking for us," Abigail said. "We can wait a few days and see if Admiral Delacroix returns, but...I wouldn't care to count on it."

"I know," Alan said. He took a long breath. "I..."

A hundred different options ran through his mind. He wanted to kiss her. He wanted to make love. He wanted to have sex or...he dismissed them, tiredly. Abigail was right. Suspension might be their only hope of survival. It crossed his mind that they might never be rescued, let alone unfrozen, but...a slight chance was better than none.

"I'll set a beacon," Abigail said. "It'll go live in five years. By then..."

The war will be over, one way or the other, Alan thought. *Unless it really does drag on for a hundred years.*

"Do it," he said, softly.

He wanted to hold her hand as he lay down on the deck, but there was no point. Abigail tapped commands into the computers, ordering the shuttle to drop the temperature once they'd taken the drugs, then lay down next to him. Alan almost reached for her before thinking better of it. They'd have a better chance for survival if they weren't touching. Or so his instructors had said.

"I'm sorry," he said, quietly.

He pushed the injector tab against his skin and triggered it. His skin turned cold, although he wasn't sure if it was a real sensation or if he was imagining it. He had no way to know. He closed his eyes quickly, embracing the darkness. His thoughts seemed to be slowing down…or was he imagining that too? He wanted to write a last note to his daughters, but it seemed utterly pointless. They'd be in their late teens when the beacon went active, if it ever did. Who knew what would happen to them?

His thoughts started to wander as his body turned to ice. Someone was standing next to him - no, above him - looking down with cold eyes. Judith…as beautiful as she'd been on the day he'd married her. He'd loved her so much and yet…he wanted to apologise to her, to beg her forgiveness, but he couldn't move. And then she was gone…

Someone was speaking. He could hear them. And yet, the words were beyond his comprehension, as if they were millions of miles away. He was so cold! He could hear the hiss of escaping air. And yet it was so hard to panic. His thoughts were slowing down…

…And then the whole world started to fade away.

I did well, didn't I? He asked, as the darkness claimed him. *I tried…*

But there was no answer waiting for him.

EPILOGUE

The world came back in fits and starts.

Light. Heat. Voices…voices speaking English. And that meant…

Alan opened his eyes. He was lying on a bed, staring up at a white ceiling. A handful of doctors were gathered around him, their faces hidden behind surgical masks. He couldn't move…panic *screamed* through his mind before he realised that they'd strapped him to the bed. He hoped that was a good sign, but he doubted it. Patients who went into Colchester's infirmity were always cuffed to the bed.

"Good morning," a voice said. "What do you remember?"

Alan forced himself to think. "I…Abigail?"

"She's recovering," the voice said. He couldn't tell which of the doctors was speaking. "I need to know what you remember."

"I was on the shuttle," Alan recalled. The memories were sharp, perhaps too sharp. "We took the suspension drugs and…what happened?"

One of the doctors held up a hand. "You're safe now," he said. "The war has been over for five years. And…we need to run some tests before we let you run loose."

Alan sighed and tried to relax. "Fine."

He'd hoped the tests wouldn't take very long, but the doctors seemed intent on making him suffer before letting him leave the hospital. Five days of everything from physical therapy to brain-scans and chats with various psychologists…he couldn't help feeling, by the time he was finally allowed to talk to a naval representative, that he was on the verge of going completely insane. They'd practically wrapped him in cotton wool. Surely, the world couldn't have changed *that* much in five years.

My oldest daughter will be seventeen now, he thought. The thought hurt. *How much of her life have I missed?*

351

The naval representative was oddly familiar. And yet, it took him far too long to recognise Bennett.

"It's been a while," Bennett said, wryly. He looked older, his hair grown out into a long ponytail. "You haven't changed a bit."

Alan looked down at his white hospital tunic. "I feel as though they've poked and prodded every last bit of me," he said. "I…"

The door opened. Abigail stepped into the room. She hadn't changed either.

"Welcome back," Bennett said, as Alan gave her a hug. "It's been some time."

"Longer for you than for us," Abigail said. She sounded steady, thankfully. "I was told I had to speak with you before the wardens let us out."

Bennett's brow furrowed, reprovingly. "They're hospital staff, not prison wardens," he said, dryly. "Believe me, you're lucky to get this sort of treatment."

Alan frowned. "What happened? I mean…with the war?"

"I have a historical packet for you," Bennett said. "You can read it later. Right now…I have a number of issues to discuss."

He paused, meaningfully. "Alan, your formal pardon was granted when it became clear you were still alive," he said. "The navy's original assumption was that neither you nor Abigail had survived the battle, so your pensions and trust funds were paid out to your children. *Both* of your children, I should say. Given the publicity, it was decided to simply give you both substantial sums of money after you were found to be alive after all. The navy takes care of its own.

"That said, there *was* a lot of publicity and some of it was quite unpleasant. My very strong advice would be to take the money and go to the belt."

"Never mind that," Abigail said. "What about our families?"

Bennett grinned. "Anson and Maddy *did* get married, as it happened. They found places on another escort carrier, then went to the commercial world after the end of the war. Right now, they have two kids and a third on the way. Poddy decided to stay in the navy - she's currently XO on an escort carrier. I believe they've both sent letters for you.

"Jeanette and Alice were lucky to survive the war. They…they became refugees after the alien attack on Earth and wound up helping to rebuild

352

parts of Scotland. As the daughters of a war hero, they had no problem winning scholarships to Hanover Towers...which caused some problems when the truth came out. That said, they're both still alive and reasonably well and...we can arrange for them to be shipped here, if you wish."

Alan stared. "And their grandparents?"

"They didn't survive the war," Bennett told him, bluntly. "We don't know precisely what happened. These days...if you don't know what happened to someone, they're probably dead."

Alan felt cold. He'd always assumed, deep inside, that his daughters would be safe. But...they'd come far too close to death. And the in-laws *had* died. He didn't know what to make of it. The world had changed overnight.

For me, it changed overnight, he thought. *But not for them.*

"For what it's worth, we can help you get set up with a new identity," Bennett said. "Or you can just go to the belt."

"The belt sounds good," Alan said. He *had* to see his daughters. But afterwards...? "Do we have enough money to buy a freighter?"

"We can offer you very good terms," Bennett said. He smiled. "You'll still be in the reserve, but...you're both in the reserve already."

"Good," Abigail said. "Has the belt changed?"

Bennett looked at her. "Everything's changed," he said. "But we'll try to help you through it."

Alan swallowed. "We won, didn't we?"

"Yeah," Bennett said. "We won. Barely, but we won."

"Then that's all that matters," Alan said. "I want to see my daughters, then go to the belt."

"As you wish," Bennett said. He bowed his head, very slightly. "And, both of you, welcome home."

The End

AFTERWORD

There are, in my (not so) humble opinion, two kinds of story, at least where military and war fiction is concerned.

The first is an *event* story, focused on a particular event - a war, for example. There's no particular focus on characters, just on a given situation and how they react to it. David Weber's *Crusade, In Death Ground* and *The Shiva Option* are good examples of event stories.

The second is a *character* story, one focused on a relatively small cast of characters rather than the overall war. David Weber's *Honor Harrington* books are good examples: there is, on one hand, a pretty significant war dominating the storyline, but a handful of characters are the real focus of the book.

Very few books (and movies/television series) manage to combine the two kinds of story into a seamless whole. Tom Clancy's *Red Storm Rising*, Peter F. Hamilton's *The Night's Dawn* Trilogy, *Babylon 5, Deep Space Nine*…all balance, somehow, characters and events. It simply isn't easy to do both at once, leading to a colossal expansion of the story's universe and the eventual sidelining of any character development. Indeed, the recent *Honor Harrington* books have - deliberately or otherwise - started to slip from *character* story to *event* story, a shift that has produced decidedly mixed reviews.

When I started work on what would become *Ark Royal*, I was determined to keep the focus squarely on Theodore Smith and his crew. It would, I felt, ensure that the book didn't expand too far, too fast. A number of details about the war, therefore, existed as nothing more than vague planning notes. I considered writing *The Longest Day* before *The Trafalgar Gambit*, simply because the attack on Earth overshadowed events in *The Nelson Touch*. But *The Longest Day* was - it had to be - an *event* book. I made the decision, eventually, to leave it until later. Not all of my readers liked me going back to fill in holes, but I thought it needed to be done.

The Cruel Stars is, of course, a *character* story. It's also something that existed as a vague set of notes while I was writing *Ark Royal*. I mean, the Royal Navy isn't going to sit down and wait for Theodore Smith to produce a victory. *Ark Royal* wasn't going to be the only starship fighting the aliens and buying time for humanity to prepare its defences. But what sort of ships would they be?

I drew inspiration from the escort carriers of WW2, converted freighters crewed by merchantmen as well as military officers. It made sense in the context of the universe I had created, both as a way to slow down the aliens and to showcase another aspect of the universe (the belt communities). But who would crew them? Who would be considered usable, yet expendable? Criminals, of course. Men and women who would have the chance to earn a pardon, if they survived, yet wouldn't be counted as any great loss if they didn't. Cold and harsh, perhaps, but dictated by a universe that had suddenly become very unfriendly to mankind.

I hope you enjoyed reading *The Cruel Stars*. If you liked it, please leave a review...

...And the *next* book in the series will be set after *We Lead*.
Christopher G. Nuttall
Edinburgh, 2017

APPENDIX:
GLOSSARY OF UK TERMS AND SLANG

[Author's Note: I've tried to define every incident of specifically UK slang in this glossary, but I can't promise to have spotted everything. If you spot something I've missed, please let me know and it will be included.]

Aggro - slang term for aggression or trouble, as in 'I don't want any aggro.'

Beasting/Beasted - military slang for anything from a chewing out by one's commander to outright corporal punishment or hazing. The latter two are now officially banned.

Binned - SAS slang for a prospective recruit being kicked from the course, then returned to unit (RTU).

Boffin - Scientist

Bootnecks - slang for Royal Marines. Loosely comparable to 'Jarhead.'

Bottle - slang for nerve, as in 'lost his bottle.'

Borstal - a school/prison for young offenders.

Compo - British army slang for improvised stews and suchlike made from rations and sauces.

Donkey Wallopers - slang for the Royal Horse Artillery.

DORA - Defence of the Realm Act.

Fortnight - two weeks. (Hence the terrible pun, courtesy of the *Goon Show*, that Fort Knight cannot possibly last three weeks.)

'Get stuck into' - 'start fighting.'

'I should coco' - 'you're damned right.'

Kip - sleep.

Levies - native troops. The Ghurkhas are the last remnants of native troops from British India.

Lorries - trucks.

MOD - Ministry of Defence. (The UK's Pentagon.)

Order of the Garter - the highest order of chivalry (knighthood) and the third most prestigious honour (inferior only to the Victoria Cross and George Cross) in the United Kingdom. By law, there can be only twenty-four non-royal members of the order at any single time.

Panda Cola - Coke as supplied by the British Army to the troops.

RFA - Royal Fleet Auxiliary

Rumbled - discovered/spotted.

SAS - Special Air Service.

SBS - Special Boat Service

Spotted Dick - a traditional fruity sponge pudding with suet, citrus zest and currants served in thick slices with hot custard. The name always caused a snigger.

Squaddies - slang for British soldiers.

Stag - guard duty.

STUFT - 'Ships Taken Up From Trade,' civilian ships requisitioned for government use.

TAB (tab/tabbing) - Tactical Advance to Battle.

Tearaway - boisterous/badly behaved child, normally a teenager.

Walt - Poser, i.e. someone who claims to have served in the military and/or a very famous regiment. There's a joke about 22 SAS being the largest regiment in the British Army - it must be, because of all the people who claim to have served in it.

Wanker - Masturbator (jerk-off). Commonly used as an insult.

Wank/Wanking - Masturbating.

Yank/Yankee - Americans

Made in United States
Orlando, FL
01 April 2024

45316110R00202